# Double Room

LUIS MAGRINYÀ

# DOUBLE ROOM

Translated from the Spanish by Allen Young

**DALKEY ARCHIVE PRESS**

Originally published in Spanish by Anagrama as *Habitacion Doble* in 2010.
Translation copyright © 2017 by Allen Young
First Dalkey Archive edition, 2017

Library of Congress Cataloging-in-Publication Data
Identifiers: ISBN 9781628971613
LC Record Available at http://catalog.loc.gov/

This work has been pubilshed with a subsidy from the Ministry of Education,
Culture and Sport of Spain.

Partially funded by a grant by the Illinois Arts Council, a state agency.

www.dalkeyarchive.com
Victoria, TX / McLean, IL / Dublin

Dalkey Archive Press publications are, in part, made possible through the
support of the University of Houston-Victoria and its programs in creative
writing, publishing, and translation.

Printed on permanent/durable acid-free paper

# Ten Minutes Later

## I

IN INTERVIEWS AND other public events where I'm invited to speak, I usually describe myself—when I'm asked to describe myself—as a product of thinking and lucky breaks. That's how I try to modestly explain my role in the success of, among other things, Francis Kuroki, multicultural private eye, and the late Central European novelist Flórián Sidály, who in this country was an undiscovered goldmine. No one seems to pay much attention to the fact that I say "thinking" and not "thought," which is sometimes the word people hear, even though I haven't said it; but of course journalists, like everyone else, are very careless with synonyms. I don't mind: at this point I can't afford to mind if people misunderstand me, and in any case I'm not someone who takes seriously what other people say they say, rather than what they actually do say. I don't make a fuss about being called "thoughtful," though I admit I'm less happy being seen as "intuitive," which is where, in this narrow conceptual universe, a woman who's had one or two lucky breaks in her career winds up.

Let me state here, for whatever it's worth, that I not only lack intuition but don't even know what it is. It's also true, as the competition knows painfully well, that there are certain things I seldom air in public. I can't say, for example, that I settled on

Francis Kuroki because he landed on my desk like a discarded scrap, after being passed over by more seasoned, coveted, and acquisitive—not to say intuitive—hands than mine, and I considered it a bargain. The same is true of Flórián Sidály, although in that case the scrap came wrapped in three short but fulsome lines that his heir, the single-minded and now rich Marina, had managed to dig out of one of the personal diaries of Ferenc Jámbor, an author my mother used to read. In other words, on that occasion, too, not only did I sense a bargain, but I was guided by a remote and fairly personal sentimentality, rather than intuition. I figured that if my mother liked Jámbor in the sixties, maybe the mothers of today would like Sidály. And even that I was wrong about, because it's really single women who like Sidály.

A word about bargains, which I've mentioned twice already: they're a part of thinking. But perhaps I should explain what I mean.

When I say "thinking," what I mean is that I hear voices and I'm not crazy. Voices that counsel, dissuade, contradict, command, or silence me, or simply comment, or sometimes—these are the tricky ones—speak nonsense, or at least apparent nonsense. I have the feeling that I'm not just inhabited by others, but loudly and sometimes belligerently so. What keeps me on this side of sanity is that I'm fully aware of who the voices belong to, where they come from, where they speak from: I can usually identify each one pretty well, and recognize whether it comes from a family member, a friend, a childhood teacher, or an annoying passenger I happened to sit next to on a plane. I also know, more or less, when I first heard each one say what it says or, if it's something no one ever actually said, who would have or could have said what that voice is now saying—who inspired it, in other words. These last kinds of voices, the speculative ones, tend to take on a tiresome leading role, but only because past experiences aren't content with merely having occurred (and sometimes recurred), but are propelled by the idea that they can influence what has yet to occur. That's why they express such vigorous, self-interested opinions. I don't know whether I'm making sense. You have experiences, you live through them, and from the past they return. They hound you. They say things like: "Don't do the same thing you did last time," as if last time were anything like this time.

I should clarify that my awareness of these voices, the speculative ones as well as the others, is occasionally murky and vague, probably because my memory, which was never great, is getting more and more disastrous by the day. And also because—I don't want to give the impression I'm skirting around this curious fact—the unconscious does indeed exist, as does the superego. For both of these reasons, the vagueness or murkiness makes it hard to recognize the source of certain voices, and ultimately the reason they're there. But I've reached the conclusion that these voices aren't so important. Precise identification is still the ideal, because it lets you put things in the right place and determine what kind of pressures or persuasion you're up against—that is, whether you're obeying your father, a character from a novel, or an ad from *Publisher's Weekly*. But I'm no Kuroki, private eye, and I can't always piece together who's to blame in some dazzling final scene. A clear sign that there's a voice, another person there, expressing themselves openly, can be enough. It's usually enough for practical purposes, at any rate. The voices almost always, if not always, behave like an especially tedious pressure group, so knowing that they're the ones applying the pressure is enough to avoid falling into the trap—the trap they're leading us to—of mistaking their view for the view of someone we could rather cautiously, amid that confusion, call ourselves. At this point, depending on your character or circumstances, you can decide whether to talk to, bargain with, succumb to, or ignore the voices. The main thing is to realize that even when you think you're most alone, you're in company, and not necessarily good company.

That, in short, is what I mean by thinking.

I'm explaining all this for two reasons: first, because I've always been worried about going insane. I have a family history, though luckily nothing too direct (one of my uncles, my father's brother, who died in a park in Valencia), and I personally set foot on the threshold of insanity ten years ago, as the result of an accident. I'm inclined to think that's what it was. So I have my reasons for taking an interest in the voices and tracking them closely. The second reason is of a very different nature, and perhaps more abstract, though entirely subordinate to a specific purpose and practice.

It's worth expanding a bit on this point, which has to do with the shape that I initially wanted to give this little exposition of what happened over the course of one particular morning. It occurred to me that I should adopt the technique called, when a text is written in the third person, the historical present, and called I don't know what when written in the first person. The idea is to give the impression that you're recounting the events at the same time as they occur, as if you had some sort of recording device—a camera, a tape recorder, even a rudimentary notebook and a quick hand—that could let you take down what happens at the exact time it happens. Because I started writing like this, I have an example handy of what such an account could look like. Consider:

The alarm clock sounds and I shut it right off. I don't want to open my eyes but finally I do. I strike my first compromise of the day: fighting laziness and sleepiness by lounging for a minute in bed with my eyes open. Then I do the first thing people with bad eyesight do: I reach for my glasses on the nightstand (well, not everyone with bad eyesight has nightstands; more dramatically, some don't even have glasses). I put them on. My next action is to sit up (no exceptions here) and join the world. I get up to go pee. The toilet lid is up. I lower it. I'm about to sit down on it, but happily I stop in time. My first slipup of the day. I don't always stop myself in time, but this time I win. I lift the lid again and sit down.

That's enough of an illustration, I think. I'd actually already written several pages using this method, which I found so fitting, when I gradually stopped thinking it was. The problem, I discovered, lay in the fact that, if you have no recording device, you have to rely on your memory and sit down to write *after* things have happened, as I'm doing now. Memory is important in the reconstruction work, with its imperious but revocable provisions, but equally important—more so—are the new things happening as you write, which probably weren't happening when the things you're describing were. Let me explain: it's likely that the first thing I did this morning was grope for my glasses on the nightstand and put them on; it's very unlikely, on the other hand, that as I did so I thought about how not everyone with bad vision has a nightstand or glasses. No: I had this thought as I was writing, not as it occurred. Nor did I think then, probably, that lounging in bed and forcing my eyes to stay open was "my first compromise of the day." I'm not denying it, I'm not saying this wasn't my first compromise of the day, nor that I'm unaware of this fact (otherwise I wouldn't have written about it), just that my awareness wasn't active—how could it be?—in those groggy moments. It was activated later: awareness belongs to a waking state, and specifically to that unique waking state you enter, unless you're a surrealist—and even if you are—when talking or writing. The time things occur and the time you talk about them are necessarily different; so are the voices you hear, the thoughts you have. Usually in the second time you hear more voices and more things happen.

In the example I've given, then, it won't be hard to perceive now that the two times mingle, and that this mingling, despite the use of parentheses, can be deceptive. It creates an attractive persona, certainly, one with integrity and a quick wit, able to unite event and awareness with heroic ease, transcending the prosaic division between thought and action that defines most mortals. On the other hand, it raises a certain dilemma which may not be irrelevant: what should you tell—what you know when something is happening, or what you know when you're telling it? I think the latter. And more so if you hear voices. Of course you can always try to make an effort to eliminate everything that didn't happen, all the voices that you didn't hear, when the story you want to tell was taking place. But that would require a gift of discernment, not to mention honesty, which my skepticism has no room for. It also takes a willingness to deactivate your awareness at the very moment it's most operative, which seems almost dishonest. I don't want to suggest that my awareness is a friend, someone I could betray; but it's here now, awake, just as this morning it was half-asleep, relying on reflex actions, grumbling about the consciously chosen ones, and distinctly annoyed at having to point out such unforgivable, obvious things like the fact that you have to raise, not lower, the toilet lid to pee. It's here with me, now, as I write, adding, recomposing, chattering—and *now* is when I'm writing.

That's all I'll say about thinking. On to lucky breaks.

This way I can get into the matter at hand, because who this is all really about is Benjamín, which is the name of my latest lucky break. As an example of my good fortune—which Benjamín would say I shouldn't read too much into—I cited the success of two series of novels, the Kuroki series and the books by Sidály, the Central European, which I ended up getting after just about every important publisher and even some unimportant ones turned them down. I've also said that what others call intuition—or a "good eye," as Markus puts it—I call getting lucky. That's why when that other lucky break fell into my lap, even more unexpectedly—and, I might add, not at all sought out—I received it with some caution. For a moment I almost missed it. One obvious reason for this momentary blindness was the fact that Benjamín hadn't had the chance to pass through many other hands before mine, since he physically hadn't had the time. And while he had suffered rejection, he was at an age when you can compensate for such setbacks by having a calling, or even—though this isn't the case for him—by not having one. In what we might call "life," tearing off its tragic mask, such experiences still belong to the early scenes. Benjamín was twenty-seven when I met him, and I was getting dangerously close—and still am—to fifty. I know what everyone says, of course. And yes, let's get this out of the way right now: I could be his mother.

Neither he nor I agree with everyone else, nor do we share the belief that the only way to explain an age difference of just over twenty years between a woman and a man is through the antiquated, loathsome myth of maternity. But I do admit that the two of us heard what everyone would say before they began to shout. When things between us were still a secret, we used to enjoy imagining the scandal, or maybe instead—definitely in my case—preparing for it. We calculated how we'd feel being singled out, with him being called "the child I never had" and

me being called either a "surrogate mother" or that delirious and
embarrassing emblem of frustration, "the mother I never was."
(I'm apparently such a prude that not even the cattiest voices,
quite capable of imagining a "kept boy," can even conceive of a
"dirty old woman.") Then we took the step from living in secret
to living in public, and even announced that we planned to get
married—long before I, but not he, would have liked. Suddenly
our ears, which we vainly hoped to make immune, were assaulted
by a cacophony of armchair psychologists, sexuality specialists,
keepers of the socioeconomic order, and—worst of all—loyal
friends. As in any inquisition worthy of the name, we were bad-
gered with questions that weren't questions at all, but rhetorical
answers; and since hardly anyone was willing to accept an answer
they didn't expect, we found it pleasantly easy to provide one. So
everyone ended up the same as they were before, which is usually
what people want: in other words, they still don't understand a
thing. We emerged a bit more exhausted, but impressed that
no one had unearthed any damning files that could shake the
foundations of our defense. The case remained obscure in spite of
the inquisitorial prying. I know some people are confident that
time, that ruthless record keeper, will end up proving them right.

All this was more or less predictable, and it happened more
or less just as we predicted. Yet there was another kind of myth
I found it difficult to make predictions about, and still do. I
couldn't quite put to rest my worries about the issue of the
flesh—or, to put it more broadly, inexperience. Ever since I
almost went crazy around ten years ago, experience has defined
my fears and guided my decisions. I know that experience doesn't
prepare you for anything, much less teach you anything, even
though it's a powerful force that tends to think it does both. At
most it rattles you. But I know this now, and I didn't when I
was twenty-six. So I worry that a kid with so little experience of

the flesh, who couldn't be expected to be so enlightened, might one day regret throwing away his chance for more carnal variety. Benjamín hates it when I say "flesh" and would rather think that, if at his age he hasn't been "around the block" the way some others have—and some have been around a few too many times—then there must be some reason. Perhaps it's some "tendency" (a word he does like) in his own "nature" (a word he almost likes even more). Besides, he adds, with certain indignation, why do I cling to the conservative belief that the couple is the pinnacle of maturity? Do I really think there's nothing else? I reply that the temptation to do things, or simply the compulsion to do them, can be irresistible: for proof all you need to do is look at the number of self-help books people buy. He counters that the people who read those books do so precisely to avoid having to change. That doesn't invalidate my argument: it only confirms there are temptations that have to be managed. But then, with a disarming grin, he asks me whether I really think I'm not allowed to go along with a "poor kid with goofy bangs," who's convinced that he hasn't made a mistake and won't feel a desire to make one. He flatters me, of course: he elevates me to the exalted realm of good choices. But how about some flattery that doesn't induce so much vertigo?

So no matter how I try, I can't get it out of his head that I'm a good choice. If I accuse him of burdening me with responsibility, he points to Markus as proof that he's right, as if two people couldn't be just as mistaken as one. In fact it was with Markus, a proponent of the good choice theory, that my morning began: he rang me on my mobile and said he needed to see me. Once again I was reminded how clearly he belongs with all those voices that see lucky breaks as a product of a mysterious feminine intuition or "a good eye." That morning he was calling about an album cover, but it's always about Benjamín. Markus is convinced that, if he keeps sticking to him, the Midas touch will turn everything that he does and that I bless into gold.

"I didn't tell Benjamín I was coming. He doesn't even know I stopped by the studio to pick up the photosetting proofs. They didn't want to give them to me, and I have to bring them back this morning." Pause. "But you have to see them. It's not the same as seeing it on a screen."

It was just after ten. I'd just come out of the shower and had a bathrobe on. Between when he called and when the doorman let me know that "one of those young men" was on his way up—the doorman has a financial incentive for telling me when I have visitors—not more than twenty minutes had gone by. I barely had time to make myself presentable. At that time of the morning I don't deal well with impatience or overfamiliarity, and now I had to handle secrecy, too: Markus knew Benjamín was in Málaga, on one of those lightning gigs he's got such a knack for (and thanks to which, by the way, I met him). This time he's at an Asian film festival, and when Markus called he said he was coming in secret. And worked up.

"I only need a minute."

I had on a skirt and a minimalist two-tone gray blouse, a choice I'd only half made the night before, thinking about my appointment with the Ringuelet sisters that morning. But I also had to consider my lunch date, a somewhat more delicate matter, because I never know what I want Benjamín's mother to think of me. Probably not the same thing I want the Ringuelet sisters to think, though. With Benjamín's friends, and the rest of Las Preocupaciones especially, I always try to project an image of desirability, since what I have with them, or what I ought to have, is an erotic sort of relationship, like an Arabian princess—a middle-aged princess—who sneaks into her musicians' chambers. I don't want them thinking Benjamín is crazy. I'm afraid I don't pull it off, or do so only partly. I could say they look at me and wonder, and of course none of them has called me "grandma" to my face, but in any case I clearly wouldn't get very far with these young musicians in my gray blouse. So Markus found me dressed as an asexual publisher, in a hurry and off guard. I had several reasons to find his visit inconvenient.

But he was driven by anxiety and a conspiratorial urge, two very potent forces.

"You have to see the proofs. Printed and glossy they look totally different. I really think the best one is the one you and I liked."

"But hasn't that already been decided?"

Doubt, irritation, and above all flattery. I hear the voice: *You judge them like children.*

"Right, it was. It is. But I got them to make a proof of the other one, too, and I think we can still change our minds."

"And you think they'll agree, this late in the game?" By *them* I was referring not only to the rest of Las Preocupaciones but to the people at the record label. "And all by noon? With Benjamín in Málaga?"

"He's seen them a thousand times on screen and said he doesn't need to see the proofs. We can call him. If you're on board, he won't put up any resistance."

Incredulous but resigned, I watched as he opened the folder on the dining room table. I have to admit, proofs always have a realness that you don't get on a computer screen: that intense anticipation, that last-minute hesitation, that feeling that the fear of being wrong was justified. I thought of Benjamín—or am I thinking of him now?—so far removed from this kind of fear, which isn't in his "nature," nor in his bangs, nor in his always bare shoulders. I sunk helplessly into a wave of solidarity with Markus. I suppose I thought I shouldn't let it carry me away, and maybe also that the fear of how things will turn out can always be exposed as ridiculous by a lucky break.

"Tell them to tone down the blue a bit," I said, as if I could be neutral. "They both look really good," I added quickly.

The image that had ultimately been chosen for the cover of Las Preocupaciones' first album, after long deliberations—to use a flattering name for a repetitive series of late-night arguments, enthusiasms, delays, beer and marijuana—was a partly blurry close-up taken from a video that showed the feet of all four members coming down a staircase. One pair of feet, Benjamín's, had no shoes. It's a sort of perverse synecdoche—feet instead of a face—a literally inverted way of singling out the front man, who is usually responsible for being the voice and face of the group, even if he's not the leader, as is the case here. The leader of Las Preocupaciones, their musician and brain, is Markus, the bassist. He's very much aware that, inspired and competent as he is, he lacks a pretty voice, much less the range for all the high notes he comes up with. His brown curls, his thin lizard lips and his general air of a decent, even pedantic college kid, also push him to the shadows, where certain people who believe more in their creations than in themselves often nervously hide. In fact, one might suspect that Benjamín is entirely his creation, from his spine-tingling falsetto down to his beautiful bare feet, were it not for the fact that a lucky break delivered Benjamín to him fully formed. Benjamín was like that before Markus stumbled upon him. Of course, artists aren't just artists because of what they create, but also what they find, and Benjamín provides all the satisfactions of an *objet trouvé*. Markus has been delighted ever since he saw he could fill a need without making a compromise: he still held the strings, and now had the perfect puppet to boot.

The close-up on the shoes, with Benjamín's bare feet, is an eloquent commentary on the group's organization and the issue of its unusual leadership. Other images they considered side-stepped the issue by leaving out Benjamín and the band members altogether. Dense fogs, views of planets, a collage of squid eyes and tentacles, or any kind of "earthly penetration"—that's the title of one of their worst songs—would ensure that Benjamín and the band members, not to mention the real world they lived in, would be absent. One evening, however, from behind the drum set Javi was apparently heard to philosophize: "But what are we? A group or an idea?" And Markus himself, thoroughly classical and sometimes ridiculously so, grasped that their ideas about the "earth" were a sacrifice to a foreign god. His real god, the god of the traditional four-man band, demanded a human element—or, to be precise, a charismatic element. That's how they came up with the idea of the feet, and everyone eagerly signed on.

But it so happened that there was another shot that some-one thought to set aside. In the foreground a still-barefoot Benjamín is sitting sideways on one of the steps, back against the wall, looking at the camera with his perpetually perfect bangs. Above him, at an arbitrary distance from each other, the other Preocupaciones are descending the stairs, and you can hardly tell one from the other: Javi and Edu have their heads down, while Markus is only a blur. Benjamín is sitting still, mostly in focus and, as I said, looking at the camera. The shot reminded me, in a MySpace sort of way, of the accidental choreography of classic street photographers, though obviously this picture came from a carefully staged shoot. Even so, among the other pictures this one seemed like an afterthought. It was really good. But I doubt it was that spontaneous beauty that roused Markus's sleepy clas-sicism, since he reacted as though he'd been drugged and taken advantage of.

"Isn't this the true image," he kept saying that morning, "of the group and its front man?"

"What makes you think the other one's not true?"

Probably truth has never been the issue. The issue is the "front man."

"Would you make do with a photo of your boyfriend's feet? When you could have the whole body?"

Here I could have replied: "But Benjamín isn't your boy-friend," something he knows as well as I. Better, actually. He's conceived of Benjamín as "the boyfriend" every girl wishes she had—some only privately, others blatantly—and he simply thinks that, for anyone who still isn't familiar with him, he'll have a harder time winning their hearts if he shows them only his feet. One sign of Markus's increasingly unabashed mainstream aspi-rations is that he believes in great upheavals of desire, whereas I only hope—I hoped so before and I hope so now—that they can be avoided. Or if that's too much to ask, that when they happen they don't go overboard. When they asked my opinion on the choice of a cover image, I sided with the majority—that is, Javi and Edu, because Benjamín said he didn't care—and voted for the foot picture, although the truth is that I'm a living, breath-ing example of the power of upheavals of desire, and I privately preferred the other one, since it showed Benjamín's face. Markus saw that I liked it, that I was seduced by it—and in his promot-er's zeal, he insisted on finding out whether I'd simply already been seduced or had actually seen something more. Specifically, something like the possibility that they'd make it big. Ever since he found out I was Flórián Sidály's publisher, an author he reads, probably to the detriment of his good taste, Markus consults me like a sort of carnival fortune-teller. He thinks that if Benjamín caught my "eye," it's because I had a "premonition," which is apparently what I usually have. It never occurred to him that I was the one who caught Benjamín's eye. Because of this Markus imagines that we share the same talent for locating buried treasures, or at least that my "eye" corroborates his. And that's what he was looking for that morning: corroboration.

The people from the record label, who had also been consulted, initially leaned toward the other image showing the whole group, just as Javi and Edu had predicted. They were dead set against letting the record label intervene, assuming it would always choose something "easy." But then a genius from marketing came along and decided that the photo of the feet "connected better," and that the album artwork for a "demanding" group like theirs should give the impression that they're "going for" something, though he neglected to specify what. Markus, a fan of the "easy" option, had been counting on his support, so when he heard the news he was irritated, but also confused, since, as I've said, he tends to value the opinion of professionals very highly. Unconvinced but resigned, he said: "Ultimately, it's just the album cover," and he agreed to delay the ravages of desire until buyers opened up the liner notes and found the more direct photos inside.

"Don't keep second-guessing yourself," I said. "It's normal to have doubts, but a last-minute choice isn't always the best one."

This was practically moralizing on my part, a sentence of my father's. Now I regret saying it. Yet for these kids, the idea of rock as a way of life is something like their grandfathers' war stories. Markus is really the only one of Las Preocupaciones who thinks this is all a matter of life and death; the others are just happy not to be flat broke. I don't just mean that they live in a tolerant and very much non-tragic environment, and that no matter what happens, they can pick up the pieces and put them back together. Rather, I mean that most of them see this first album as the achievement of a goal, not an uncertain, transitory state.

Markus, on the other hand, doesn't live in celebration but in suspense. I think he hears too many voices, which are naturally unable, at his age, to extend into the past, and therefore make urgent statements about the future. I suppose that's what being an ambitious young man means.

"Come on," he answered, "this isn't a last-minute choice. I've always said this one would work better. What if we're making a mistake?"

"All I do is make mistakes, and I'm still here."

Maybe he wondered then just what he was looking at, an older woman who had fallen head over heels for a kid, or living proof that fate sometimes lets people turn back the clock. I didn't identify with either of the two hypotheses, but the second could relieve his uncertainty. Standing there, both of us hunched over the table, looking at the photos spread in front of us, must have made a strange pair: he like an anxious Kuroki, P.I., in the midst of poring over documents, and me—well, I hope *not* like one of Sidály's trembling widows, looking at photos of another time. Determined to give my character an air of comedy, I added:

"Why don't we call Benjamín and see what he says?"

This didn't exactly provoke a reaction, but it did make him stop.

"You're right. Sorry, I just wanted to make sure." He began putting the photos back into the folder. "The one with the feet is good."

"It's a great image."

I left him alone for a minute as I went to my room to get a jacket. It was getting late and we'd have to leave together. When I came back I found him in the entryway, looking at Cy Twombly's flowers. The terrible ordeal of the feet seemed to be over.

"I don't understand why Benjamín says he doesn't like this place," he said, smiling. "I'd be thrilled to live here."

"Want to buy it?"

In the elevator he persisted with the complements and asked if I had other Sidálys on the horizon. He was very happy to hear I'd have a new one in the fall, but I insisted he shouldn't waste his time reading those things. He thinks Sidály is a wonderful exponent of "Central European miserablism," which is how some people interpret a certain excess of bourgeois melancholy. We disagree: for me "Central European miserablism" is about vengeance and resentment, not sentimentalism, and he's surprised I think so. He doesn't yet realize—it's painfully clear—that having a job is one thing and believing in it is another; he doesn't understand how you could be Sidály's publisher without being an admirer. But I don't think I should drag him down that path, because he'll start thinking cynicism is a professional virtue. In any case, when we stepped out of the elevator, we found the doorman waiting with more compliments.

"When's the new Kuroki case coming out?"

No doubt this was an attempt to get us to stop so he could inspect the "young man" and see if he was as nice as Benjamín, who's always ready with a comment about motorcycles or football. But I kept walking and didn't turn around.

"Soon," I said.

Once outside, Markus called Benjamín to tell him about his latest "panic attack," which he had overcome, he said, thanks to me. I asked him to pass me the phone and hastened to clarify that I had nothing to do with it. Benjamín laughed as if he had expected both of our reactions; but he said he was doing well and the work was "entertaining," and he told me not to forget I had a lunch date. I hadn't forgotten, and it kept circling my head after I hung up. So much that when I thought I saw a place to buy cigarettes I told Markus:

"See you later. I'm stopping here to buy a pack of cigarettes."

"Here? But this is a pharmacy …"

So it was. A moment later I found the real tobacco shop and said goodbye.

I took a taxi to the Ringuelet sisters' agency, which is on a nicely appointed second-floor office in a modest building on Calle del Pez. They haven't been operating in Spain for very long, but they seem to be doing well. They've made it so that practically every Argentine author has to go through them to publish here, and apparently they're trying to apply the toll to the rest of Latin America, too. They're also subagents for a few relatively new but flourishing European and U.S. agencies. I bought *Curry and a Toy Piano* from them, one of those promising debuts that apparently in the U.S., with no other guarantee than the agencies' well-rehearsed enthusiasm, sell for between six or seven figures, and which I grabbed for four—and the figure on the left was pretty reasonable. But the novel has more or less taken off, and we've sold twenty thousand copies in three months. So it's in my interest to tie down the second—the author has already written another one—before everyone else finds out and the prices skyrocket. For now, everyone knows we're in our fourth printing, but not how many copies we've sold, and I intended to make the Ringuelet sisters believe, if pressed, that we'd only sold about half as many. They wouldn't see the royalty figures for six months, so now was the time to act.

Clearly, I'm very fluent in what we might call the middle voice, and this doesn't surprise me. In the middle is where I learned to say things like "the novel is taking off" or "it's time to act." Maybe I could have had better training, but I doubt it. I started the press because I liked novels and got a loan that my father countersigned; and also, I suppose, because I met Ramón. Back then I divided novels into three categories: "good," "interesting," and "bad," and I only published the first two; if the media reviewed them and people bought them, I figured I'd gotten lucky, and if not, I figured I hadn't. I didn't blame the books. Eventually I learned I had terrible taste, but this wasn't a tragedy. I realized, with my first big hit, that "good" and "interesting" weren't valid concepts, because they could be thrown around and they grouped together things that were too different. Besides, no one called that novel "good" until it became a success, as if they needed to justify something. Determined to figure out what, I re-read the book right at the height of its redemptive popularity. I didn't figure it out, but I realized that, even though I still liked it, it was dreadfully bad. Success provided me that distance, and somewhat alarmed, I started sifting through the novels I'd dismissed as "bad" in case I'd missed one that was actually "good." Fortunately, I hadn't been wrong about those: they were even worse. They were very focused on being likable, in a very obvious way, and to be considered "good," a novel has to bluff a bit, to convince readers it didn't just satisfy their appetite, but actually taught them something, usually some nonsense about the human race.

Until then I'd assumed taste was a prodigious, subjective power, something in nature itself that more or less distinguished you from others. Seeing it bound up in the vulgar confines of objectivity—learning that taste is manufactured—was an unpleasant surprise. An uncomfortable surprise, too—or a secret, more than a surprise. Many publishers can't handle the disassociation, and in order to keep going they need to believe everything they publish is "good," jeopardizing their mental health in the process. I'm not cursed with a tragic personality, and at least in this area I can keep things separate. I can obey two laws. I knew I couldn't go around offending readers by talking about appetites and saying they liked something only because it was designed to please, but I did eliminate "good" and "interesting" from my vocabulary when I had to talk about these things that quench the thirst for subjectivity and curiosities. I knew I needed this split consciousness to work. I could just as easily have shuttered the publishing house, but I already said I don't have a tragic personality. Or I could have devoted myself to publishing "good" novels, but these would never have tried to suit my tastes, and taste, even terrible taste, is the only thing I have. Other than my lucky breaks.

So it's hardly surprising that once I understood what I was getting into, I quickly brushed up on the language of the trade and learned to talk about what "takes off" or "doesn't take off," what "sells" or "doesn't sell," and to say, "let's see if there's a nibble" when things got a little dicey. I don't know if any of this spread to other areas of my life, because frankly I'm scared to think so. For ten years I barely had a life—instead, I had a bubble of despondency and books—and now I don't want to put Benjamín in the same thought as taste or likability. I know others do: Markus, for instance, has him in his group so that both his group and his music, which after all are a little demanding, seem likable. Is Benjamín, as Markus thinks, destined to be liked? Was he destined to be liked by me? I don't think so. Benjamín is persuasive, not a product of persuasion. He really had to persuade me that I liked him. And even so I don't think he managed to get in through the door of likability.

The older Ringuelet kept me waiting, while the younger one, the good cop, always the less busy of the two, came to the lobby to say hello. Apparently her boyfriend, who knows the music industry, is something of a fan of Las Preocupaciones and swears they're the best of "the city's indie scene." I asked whether her boyfriend was a journalist, but at first she replied that she knew the album was about to "drop," that it was highly anticipated, and that they already had imitators. I'm starting to get used to these displays of solidarity I get from some people now that the relationship is public. Such people assume that avoiding the topic would look suspicious, or at least more suspicious than being "natural." They assume discretion would be hypocritical, and that by openly acknowledging that I'm the talk of the industry, I'll conclude that they at least aren't saying anything bad. The occasion lets them show they're liberal or worldly, but sometimes I also detect a glimmer of real curiosity—about me, I mean, not about themselves—and occasionally even, as with the younger Ringuelet sister, a certain desire to be at the same level.

"What's it like?" she finally decided to ask.

"What's what like?"

"You know ... what does it feel like?"

"Well ..." I hesitated, "like something new, I guess. What's yours like?"

"Mine?" she asked, with a little disappointment. "There's no comparison: he's in his forties, he worked for years for the music press in Argentina, and now he's trying to make a name for himself here. In practice, he's a *mileurista*, he makes a thousand a month."

"That's something."

"Yes, sorry—that's a lot!" We both laughed. "Seriously, you have no idea how jealous I am."

My cellphone's ringer interrupted the giddiness. It was Lucas, who makes less than a thousand per month, and who will barely survive the end of his temporary contract. His go-getting energy has worn the whole office out. And no, even if the eighties were back, we were not going to publish the memoirs of a Chippendale's stripper.

"Benjamín is really great," I agreed, once I'd gotten rid of Lucas. Suddenly I was thrilled to be a source of envy.

"I know, I've seen him. I've seen him!" she repeated. "My boyfriend pointed him out to me."

"Oh, really? Where?"

"On one of those nights when I have no choice but to follow him to a concert, if I want to see him at all. He was in the audience, and my boyfriend pointed him out. He seems great, but … I didn't hear him sing. How's the group?"

"I've come around."

"Of course," she smiled. "That's part of the bargain, isn't it?"

When her sister came out and saw her previous appointment to the door—a pair of clean-cut boys from a business and management publishing house—we were both very much making jokes, and in fact dangerously mixing business with pleasure. The older Ringuelet's permanently severe smile and senatorial hair provided a timely, emphatic reminder of our obligations. Another reminder, more unexpected, awaited in her attractive office with views of the street. Inside the office stood a man, backlit, turned away from the window, whom I hadn't seen in possibly ten years.

"I think you two already know each other," said the older Ringuelet, and turning to me, added: "Carlos is working for us now. We're delighted to have him."

"Nice to see you." Carlos gave me his hand. "It's been a while!"

"Where have you been hiding all these years?"

He made a complicated gesture with his arms and mouth before answering:

"Now I'm back."

This wasn't an answer—or no doubt it was. Carlos worked for a time at my press. He was a friend of Ramón's, I think from the university, who helped him out with accounting. One day he showed up out of the blue and Ramón said we had to help him; he worked for us for a few years, then, ten years ago, he vanished. Now I see he's got a knack for reappearing. He was disheveled, clumsy, obscure, unsociable; Ramón said Carlos had helped him out, so I shouldn't be too hard on him. Today he had the same long, dirty fingernails. Suddenly I had an extremely strong desire to leave.

The older Ringuelet didn't skip the preliminaries, which I tried to use to recover from that sudden intrusion from the past. I hadn't expected it, as I've said, and at such times of adjustment not expecting something is very similar to not desiring it. Also right then—and I mean what I say, because it happened there, in the office of the Ringuelet sisters, around noon—a memory emerged from who knows where, awakened by an almost diabolical force, demanding my attention. I saw Carlos taking off his shoes, shaking them forcefully against the gray carpeting in the old office, leaving a residue of gravel and dirt. I saw the soles of his feet, the dusty, faded mesh of his executive socks. I saw this, I insist, that very morning: this isn't a deceptive blending of times to make myself seem visionary. But the thing is, as I write this, I can see it again. It's a very unpleasant image taken from one single moment on one single day … or at least I don't remember him doing those things often at the office. The image lay submerged for over ten years, and now something had unearthed it.

As I was still struggling against that chaos, the older Ringuelet turned to the matter at hand, and began to rattle off, as though she weren't reading it off a sheet of paper she held in front of her, the virtues of the new novel by the author of *Curry and a Toy Piano*. This one also took place in the Second World War, though now the Holocaust receded to the background, specifically to the background of the British Isles, where a Jewish refugee and a Scottish lieutenant with shell shock find themselves staying at the country manor of some Lord—something-or-other Hall—that was being bombarded by the Luftwaffe. Their troubled relationship is witnessed and described by the son of the cook. A tale of love and war seen through innocent eyes, it also has a side plot involving family secrets—the family of the Lord, I imagine—and a surprise ending. It's "mysterious, intense, poetic," and "solidifies the author's reputation as a bold, imaginative writer."

"I'm especially eager to read it," she said. "Soon we'll have galley proofs."

This was a way of saying that she wanted more time, and that if I wanted her to sacrifice that time, I'd have to pay for it.

"I think I get the idea. I'd like to make an offer now."

"You see? I told you this author was reliable. *Curry* is already a hit in twelve languages."

"It's not doing bad."

"You've always had a good eye," Carlos broke in, with his forgotten voice. "Even back in the early days. Neither of you knew her back then," he said, turning to the Ringuelet sisters, "but she's always had an eagle eye."

Having an eagle eye considerably compromised me in the present circumstances. It raised the price on something I wanted to get for cheap.

"I also buy things that don't pan out." This was a not very oblique reference to a few things I bought from the Ringuelets. "That's how this job goes: the real best-sellers are unexpected."

"Some people know the recipe," Carlos remarked, clearly on the other side.

"*Curry* is already in its fourth printing," added the older Ringuelet in support, as though providing evidence.

"You know what publishers are like. We put out a small run and fill the jacket with hype."

"How many copies have you sold?"

"About nine thousand," I lied, and then lied again: "But I think this book has already found its readers. *Curry* is your typical ten-thousand-copy title. I'd be surprised if it sold any more."

"When someone with an eagle eye makes predictions, we should take note," said Carlos, with an irritating double meaning.

"Let's just stick to the predictions of a realist."

Just then the younger Ringuelet looked at me strangely, and now I think perhaps she was wondering if I was a realist in my life decisions. Either because of this question, or because it was the order of the day—I'm not sure—she said:

"But wouldn't you rather wait until you've read it? We'll have galley proofs in two weeks."

I had no interest in reading anything, much less in waiting for galley proofs that others could read.

"Why wait? I decided on the first book and now I want the second. Isn't there a bit of deference," I added, almost comically, "for the publisher who bet on a first novel by an unknown writer?"

"*Curry* came very highly recommended," the older Ringuelet reminded me, immune to these tricks. "You know what an impact it had in the U.S."

"Ah, the U.S.! How many novels purchased on that recommendation are sleeping in storerooms, awaiting their turn at the shredder? Didn't I buy *The White Gang Train* on that recommendation?"

I wasn't as angry as I sound, now that I'm writing. The key is to take a position, never to argue, not even to persuade. We all try to seem persuasive, but only because a minimum of social decency keeps us from showing ourselves as ruthless invaders bent on seizing territory. The decisions—to invade and to defend—have already been made: they follow from force and are moved only by force. Motivation, seduction, even negotiation are merely the rhetorical form of force. They let us feel civilized. But there comes a time when the iron—how ridiculous this sounds—has to be flashed.

"The offer is €20,000. A realistic calculation based on an expectation of ten thousand copies."

The younger Ringuelet looked at her sister, who took pleasure in drawing this out, as she'd planned.

"Send us an email with the offer and we'll pass it along to the U.S. I don't know what they'll say."

"Try not to let them say much."

Then we relaxed and could move on to general matters. That's it: the process is organized so that the blade is flashed only very briefly, almost inconclusively, and then it's all over. Afterward there's time for pleasantries and chitchat. In fact, it's all rigorously, cleverly divided so that this last part seems like the most important, and the rest just a game. I showed curiosity about the new catalogue, they tried to interest me in some young Argentine authors with a "literary profile," they told me stories about their "body pump" workout, we compared brands of sleeping aids, though I no longer take them. They told me that they often run into Esperanza Aguirre, the head of the Madrid regional government, with her showy entourage, who everyone's been talking about since the fiasco of the general elections, because of her struggles within her party and her air of moral superiority. The image of Carlos's socks faded, as Carlos, like a character only needed in battle scenes, stopped participating in the conversation, and I got the impression that, just as he'd been roused, he could fall back to sleep. The Ringuelet sisters didn't seem to notice his sudden withdrawal, which may well be included in his job description and even stated on his resume. I wonder how he ended up in their hands, and how exactly they thought he could be useful to them. Nevertheless, there he was, probably more for me than for them, nodding, clearing his throat, smiling, resting his elbow on the table and his head on his hand, with a familiar bored look on his face, and, I could have sworn, a stain on the tip of his tie.

"I don't get how you people can vote for that woman."

The older Ringuelet's second allusion to the notorious politician forced Carlos and me into a shared communion of guilt. Some people you'd rather not have any connection to, but there's always one that can be found. The look of protest we both adopted was the same, and it didn't help that our accuser, who might have a revolutionary past, added that even those who don't vote for her give her their consent.

I called this kind banter "pleasantries." Sometimes it's hard for me to grasp what they are.

When it came time to leave, Carlos walked me to the stairs, and the Ringuelets, out of an inopportune sense of discretion, left us alone.

"You don't know how happy I am to see you, and to know I'll have a chance to see more of you. You're still at the top of your game," he said.

I couldn't say the same of him. He has never, so far as I know, been "at the top of his game."

"Well, I really haven't moved from where I was. Where have you been?"

"Lost!" he said with a histrionic smile, but not as though he had been anywhere particularly pleasant. "I imagine one of these days we'll have a chance to talk."

"Sure," I said without conviction. Why would we talk now, if we never talked before?

"I heard you've got wedding plans. Is that right?"

"More or less." This answer was much more accurate than I'd have liked, but no doubt it required some clarification. Luckily he didn't ask for any.

"I'm really glad. I wish you all the best."

I seized on these good wishes to start down the stairs. I thanked him and left with a "See you soon," which I fear is a sign of more resigned encounters with his joy.

When I got outside, the first thing I did was call Benjamín. He was busy just then and I had to hang up. I didn't quite know which way to go. I didn't feel like going back to the office, and as I lingered in front of a trekking and adventure travel agency, I saw, not the head of the Madrid government and her entourage, but her lapdog Sánchez Dragó. Really, the Ringuelet sisters have landed in one of the lower circles of hell—no wonder they're spooked. I considered calling Estrella to have her send them an email with the offer, but then I thought better of it and told myself that getting impatient wouldn't help. But I wasn't really impatient, just scared I'd forget. Maybe when I got to the office that afternoon I'd forget to tell Estrella to send the offer. These days I forget both the important things and the unimportant ones. At the corner of the convent of San Plácido my mobile rang. It was Benjamín. A minute earlier he had been with some "very annoying" and "hard-to-understand" Koreans, but eventually managed to figure out what they wanted and now needed to take them to the Picasso Museum; he loved me, he missed me, he hoped I wouldn't forget who I was supposed to meet for lunch. That reminded me of the gray blouse, and how I definitely needed to go home and change. While firm, however, this thought was secondary: there were others above it. I heard several voices at the same time and the most recent—the voice that had said "I hope you're very happy"—seemed to be raving.

By then I was on Calle Silva, and almost without meaning to, I stopped for a moment in front of that church whose name I don't know, a little one built out of brick and white stone, wedged in between buildings, which stands out because of its strange Neo-Moorish decorations. I've never seen anyone going in or coming out, and a precarious sign on the front—"Mass celebrated on Sunday the 20th"—seemed to confirm it offered irregular services. As in other churches in the city center, an altar with an image can be seen through the dirty glass on a black iron door. Unmaintained and unilluminated, it reminds the passerby that, beyond the demands of schedules, there's always a moment for devotion. The image is of Our Lady of Mercy: her arms are open in a cross and under her mantle are two groups huddled in prayer. And as I looked at the scene, I began to feel ill.

I should now pause for a brief parenthesis to cite a passage by Flórián Sidály. The idea struck me and I'm going to do it. I'm interested in comparing "experiences" and I didn't have to look very far.

The gunmetal sky was threatening to storm, and the crowd had dispersed when at last I walked down to the beach. Weary, I sat down on the sand, heedless of the first drops of rain mingling with sweat and humidity. A seagull had touched down on the deserted beach and now suddenly took flight, as if attempting to pierce the clouds, and the sight made me think of those fugitives who, like me, flee the sun and calm and find refuge in the gale.

Liar. The seagull's flight didn't make you think of anything as you sat on the sand. That's what you're thinking now, as you write. Because you feel it fits your character, makes him earthier. A man of action *in* thought! But no: the person sitting on the sand isn't the same as the person writing about sitting on the sand. Besides, I bet there was no seagull.

I needed to say this because I want things to be as they are. Yesterday morning I stopped in front of a statue of the Virgin on Calle de Silva, and all I can say is that, when I did I felt ill. I could have pretended I had a sudden inspiration, as I think I do now, and somehow commended my soul to God and prayed; but I didn't. I just felt ill. I felt dizzy, I felt a cold sweat, I took a deep breath. Now, after listening to the voices, I can give an explanation for what happened, and with a bit of luck fix it. Now I can do what I didn't do then. What's more, I want to do so, I need to, because I feel I owe it to you.

Despite his obscure musical influences and his fondness for indie rock, Markus's lyrics for Las Preocupaciones draw casually on the comfortable classics of the pop repertoire. Yes, they cultivate a sort of anti-city romanticism, with no lack of scorpions and undiscovered suns, and yes, the speaker in his songs tends to dwell on the bleak and forlorn, but there's also the occasional "I'll never leave you" or "It's too late" or "I can't live without you." The first time I heard Benjamín sing "I can't live without you" it was in a concert in one of those tiny venues designed so that forty or fifty people make a crowd; he wasn't next to me, of course, but on stage, and I felt a little trapped. I heard all my voices, much less restrained than they are now, demanding to know what the hell I was doing there, or thought I was doing. At that time the only thing capable of silencing them, submerging them in a respectful confusion, the only thing that switched on inside me to stop them was the sudden awareness of how terribly literal that refrain is—"I can't live without you"—when applied to someone who's dead. In other words, I thought of you. Through Benjamín I think of you. It's not an activity I want to fuel, I assure you, and gradually the association is weakening, and I'm convinced it will eventually disappear, but the fact is, it's taken a new love to bring me this kind of vivid contact—the most palpable, most precise that I can recreate—with a love I lost long ago. That's how you've been resurrected before me, old friend. I thought that over these ten long years, not counting perhaps the first two years of madness, nightmares, and silence, I'd managed to endure my solitude with novels and the mourning of your memory. I thought I'd built a lovely bell jar, where the noblest devotions would console me, and the least noble would renew, through a window that let me out but no one else in, my credentials as a member of society. My strength of mind was admired, and I don't know of anyone who, after the initial shock, could have pitied the poor widow. Now, though, I see that all the activities of my solitude were intended above all to keep you out. I didn't remember you, I didn't cry over you: the bell jar was a barrier against you. Remembering you entailed too many other things. It was a tainted process that didn't involve only you: through no fault of your own, with you came the idea—the voice—that I hadn't been able to save you, a thought I still can't bear. I couldn't pretend you didn't exist, or even that you never existed; but since I fashioned a bell jar for myself, I could leave you outside—let you exist, but not be present. Everything we shared, everything we had together, became mine alone. You'll say it was an extravagant way to mourn, this purging of your remains, but don't forget the pain was mine alone. You, wherever you are, and I hope you're in the Heaven of a merciful God, don't know what it's like, you can't, you can't fathom what pain is. You were truly outside, that's where I left you.

But you weren't alone, out there. Where else was that kid with the bangs hanging around when he showed up, scratching, even kicking at the bell jar? Letting him in would be dangerous—not, as I was afraid, because he would upset my delicately arranged little refuge, but because of all the things that might slip in with him. Once I stopped resisting, I was surprised to see that one of the things that slipped in was you, but in its strange way this too made sense. Both of you had been barred, you appealed to ideas and feelings that I'd locked away, you barely had a voice: you two shared a lot, and none of it was "mine." And so, by opening up my world, he brought you to me like a being of flesh and blood, like what you used to be—and at twenty-six, no less—and not like a memory. Benjamín let me see you anew; I could touch you, breathe you, listen to you, kiss you … and don't make me be any more graphic. I had the feeling, always a bit false but inevitable, that I was giving myself to you. This won't last, as I said—it can't. But I needed it so I could do what I never did before: say good-bye to you, and to finally have, after all these years, something that belongs to "us," a secret. I buried you without letting you take anything of mine: take this now. The earth you lie in has been purified by the most vivid memories, and you can now be one of the dead who rests in peace. Take, with this last encounter, my gratitude. I'll take comfort, knowing nothing of divine plans, trusting in what is surely proof of Divine wisdom.

So. After not doing what I didn't do in front of the image of Our Lady of Mercy, I walked to the Gran Vía, a bit anxious and dizzy. I lit a cigarette to calm myself down and stood patiently next to the crossing signal, looking down. But as luck would have it, when I tapped the cigarette, a sizable ember landed on the head of a baby in a stroller coming in the opposite direction. The mother swatted it off and raised hell, of course; but the child was fine—tickled, even, watching how I endured her rage.

# II

Ten minutes later I was getting out of a cab in front of my building.

"You've got company upstairs," said the doorman when he saw me, and frankly I was in no mood for jokes.

"Who?"

"Some friends of yours. They had a key."

No one had a key except Benjamín, and Benjamín was in Málaga. I gave him an irritated look, but he pretended not to notice: instead, he looked back at me as if to say it was about time I accepted the consequences of the life I'd chosen. I got in the elevator convinced I couldn't postpone having a word with the doorman much longer. But when the doors opened I suddenly remembered why I kept on putting it off.

That wasn't all I remembered. I heard talking and footsteps, but before I had time to be alarmed, I recognized Cecilia's voice: then I was alarmed for another reason. I forgot she also had keys, and was planning to show the apartment to a couple that morning. It's the fourth time she's shown it, and each time I've made a point of arranging not to be there.

She heard me, too.

"Is that you? What are you doing here?" She appeared in the entryway, alone.

"Sorry, sorry. I forgot! I stopped by to change clothes, but I'll just be on my way."

"Don't be silly ... but now that you're here I'll have to introduce you."

"No, really." I held back, I had my hand on the door. She lowered her voice.

"It's the second time they've come ... and they're taking measurements. I think it's in the bag, so you have to help me out. They're going to love meeting you. They're very curious."

"I feel awkward. You know I haven't made up my mind ..." Now my back was against the door.

"Sure you have. Come on."

True, I'd been mostly free from Cecilia's voice for a few days—so free I forgot she was coming. Probably nothing I had to do that morning was more important than this, and as much as I'd like to think otherwise, my forgetfulness was clearly not innocent. In fact the blame was complex. On the one hand, forgetting the appointment played into my inhibition, an art I'm lately becoming very adept at; on the other, had I not forgotten, I probably wouldn't have come home, and the fact that I did come home under such circumstances is almost certainly due to a desire to prevent it. Prevent the sale, I mean. Since the voices against this dubious proposition were strangely silent, they'd clearly decided to manifest themselves in other ways—through tricks, for example, like the one they played on me this morning, no doubt to counter the din of the voices in favor. That's probably why for the last two or three days, ever since I arranged to have Cecilia come—and arranged to not be here—they'd been so quiet, occupied as they were keeping the opposition in check. The opposition, the voices in favor of selling, admittedly show more perseverance: they have a higher, steadier pitch and usually a flattering tone, and they express needs and intentions, often saying "please." Cecilia's voice in particular is more imperious: I have no idea how much she needs the commission, she says. Benjamín's voice is calm, cajoling, pretty: he says that we need "something new," and that I won't regret it.

I don't know which voice came out on top just then. My forgetfulness put me on the defensive, of course, but Cecilia made sure to turn the opportunity to her favor. She pushed me into the bedroom—of all places—and introduced me to the potential buyers.

"Perhaps you expect us," said the male component of the couple, holding a tape measure, "to haggle over every defect and flaw we find. We could say there's one wall too many here, and another one missing over there, that the layout isn't quite right, that we want to add another room, that the bathrooms are too small. We could try to make you see that with all the remodeling we plan to do, we'd incur substantial, troublesome costs. But we're not going to do that. We like it just the way it is. It's simply"—pause and hand gesture—"perfect. So we won't try to haggle using those kinds of arguments. Our only argument is the amount we have at our disposal, making, if I may, no mean effort. And we can only trust in your sympathy and your understanding."

The voice of Judge Beltrán—as he was later identified—threatened from the start to join the chorus of voices in favor of selling, one of the very things I wanted to avoid by staying away. The honorable judge was a relatively young man—younger than me, in any case—with a sharp, attractive face, baroque hands and silvery hair, and apparently very well versed in flattery. "How else do you think he managed to marry such a fabulously wealthy woman?" asked Cecilia later. That fabulously wealthy woman had a look and attitude that stood out less: next to her powerhouse of a husband, she could have been—and probably is—at the head of some company's ineffectual senior management. By herself, probably what stood out most was her inelegant slimness—I'd swear she eats nothing but yogurt—and her dated highlights. But no doubt she has her own talents:

"I love Kuroki, P.I.—he's so quirky!"

I would have said that she looked more like a Flórián Sidály type, but tastes change! She praised mine, anyway, in other topics she found for conversation.

"That vintage desk is Danish, isn't it?"

Cecilia felt obliged to intervene.

"The furniture isn't for sale."

She said so before I could, clearly aware that my tone would have been different, and that I might have added that the apartment wasn't for sale, either. Ultimately I didn't help Cecilia very much: I told her I wanted to leave, but she forced me to stay, and that's how I reacted: sullen, uncooperative, mentally absent. The judge understood everything.

"Of course, dear," he said to his wife, with the weight of good sense, "this isn't *just* a desk. It must be difficult. I don't know your reasons," he said, turning to me, "for wanting to let go of such a personal, lived-in home, but it must be difficult to give it up to others who will wipe away your traces and maybe even leave some of their own. On top of that you've arranged it so that no one could feel out of place here. I could spend my whole life here, just as it is now, among these traces of your life."

"I feel like I'm already living here," his wife chimed in.

"It's clearly the work of a whole lifetime. It must be hard to let go of."

In the end the judge thinks like Benjamín; I've already mentioned that the chorus of voices in favor of selling would happily make room for him, not that there's any need—why would I want that chorus to grow?—and I can already hear his voice, adding a very dangerous note of benevolence to Benjamín's solos, which thankfully lack that element of softness. Benjamín also sees the traces of my life throughout the flat, but he still doesn't see any of his, and that bothers him. He says we need something new, something that "starts with the two of us," not because he's jealous but because he wants to take preventive measures: he doesn't want me to one day have the excuse that I see him as an intruder. He's very aware he's entered a bell jar, and he's a little amazed that it hasn't broken now that he's inside. He thinks we have to build another one "somewhere else," but I'm not so sure. That memorable day when we decided to give up secrecy and show ourselves in public, he not only said, "Let's tell everyone," but also, "We'll find a place to live together." It was almost as if the publicity slightly compromised, in this regard, his honor. The issue of Benjamín's honor is a little out of place here, but not to consider it, once it's been exposed in all its instability, could lead to something dramatic. So everyone found out we were "going out" at the same time they found out we were "looking for a place," which was predictably a much more diffuse wish than just "getting rid" of mine. He never tells me to "sell" it: in avoiding one rude misstep he makes another, worse one, which he naturally knows hurts me. But ever since it became clear—especially to him—that what we had would last longer than "just one night," he's trying to cast out the specter of a fling with the zeal of a psychic, not seeing the secondary ghosts he's conjuring up. "Get rid" of my house! As if it were a burden, a body bag, a collection of damning evidence.

He also says that there are "too many memories" here. If he only knew! On Ramón, Benjamín's line is "not to dwell." We talked about it one day, and then another, and when we saw we disagreed, he felt we should set it aside, not realizing he was the one who had resurrected, and embodied, a memory I had until then kept under control with a restraining order. His understanding of symbols is limited: his distaste for the flat, for the furniture, for the paintings prevents him from seeing that he's the most potent image around of that lingering ghost. Sometimes he seems aware that he's asking too much, and he sinks into an unhappy silence, as though he didn't have authority or merit for his demands. Then he turns to self-pity, flights of fancy, class struggle, and lyric antitheses on what "having it all" and—very imaginatively—"having nothing" would mean. And when the world is about to collapse, as in a momentous passage in Sidály, suddenly, to my relief, a look of hope appears, and he's sure we can overcome any obstacle and raise a flag somewhere remote and undiscovered. It's not just a pioneer fantasy: after raising the flag, he'll still have to delimit the terrain, get to work and build another bell jar. But do I really want another bell jar? Have I ventured out of one just to enter into another? Benjamín sees our life together as a whole world; I don't want to have any fences between our togetherness and the world, now that I've gotten reacquainted with it.

Cecilia's view is somewhat simpler. After seeing the illustrious couple to the door, she laid it out:

"They're offering €1,400,000, and they won't budge."

"Is that the asking price? €8,000 per square meter?"

"It's a bit less, but it's a sure thing."

"How much less?"

She didn't have to think about it.

"A little over €6,300 per square meter."

My father's voice, in a tone very much my own:

"That's less than it's worth."

"What world are you living in? Have you heard of the real estate bubble? Do you know that sales have fallen 73.5% in the first quarter of this year alone? No one has any money, the banks won't issue loans, and home prices are sinking for the first time in ten years."

"In that case it would be better to wait."

"If you can." And with an ungrateful scowl: "I can't. I'm one of those people who doesn't have any money. I'm living month to month, I swear." This overblown maneuver was unworthy of an intelligent person. But Cecilia, I'd forgotten, isn't one. "With the market like it is, when a buyer is willing to put €1,400,000 on the table, it's a done deal. It could take years for another one to show up."

"Well, they're only the third couple to come."

"But they've come twice. Look, make up your mind." She spoke clearly and with spite. "If you don't want to sell the flat, don't put it on the market. Be realistic and don't waste my time."

Later she calmed down a bit when I promised I'd think about it. I wasn't lying, and she must have seen signs in my face of the overwhelming pressures she assumed would work in her favor. She also apologized for her last comment, adding that her own financial well-being depended on the market, which I, lucky me, didn't have to worry about.

When she left, the market noise vanished with her. Instead I heard, and still hear, other arguments. Sell low, for love? The voice of everyone (including loyal friends): "Not on your life." The voice of Benjamín: "Isn't what unites us the fact that we disagree with everyone else?" Yes, but with €1,400,000 I can't buy anything like what I have now; what I have is worth more. Benjamín: "Yes, yes, you'll be ruined, you won't have a penny to your name." Good God, such a moral cleansing! What do you think, Ramón? But I know, I'm liable to do it.

Proof of how liable I am to sell is that once Cecilia left, the feeling of having just gotten out of a bind automatically made it easier to concentrate on the conscious tasks I brought home. I took off my blouse and put on some black Montana jeans that you have to look at twice before you notice they're jeans. I looked through the closet before settling on a white shirt with fraying pockets that I bought at a street market at the last London Book Fair, which elongates my neck and shows off my near-perfect cleavage. I also put on some black boots and three ethnic neck-laces of different lengths, and removed all the precious metal from my ears and hands.

I said before that around Benjamín I try to look plausibly erotic, and I suppose sometimes I go a little too far, I don't know. I don't care. (I was wearing gray when I met Benjamín, and was wearing gray when he pursued me and I fell for him.) But with his mother the issue is more complicated, because as much as I want to prove to her that her son hasn't, after all, lost his mind, she's still my boyfriend's mother, and in front of your boyfriend's mother you can't go around showing off how much testosterone you're able to generate. Besides, she's only two years older than I am, and like me, "lost" her husband, in her case in a tempestuous divorce ten years ago. This apparently puts us on the same plane, and Benjamín would like us to make some ben-eficial connections. Some of these connections would come from what he calls my "bearing": it would be good for his mom to see that "she still has potential," even though she's withdrawn from such calculations. And, I might add, it would take a weight off his shoulders. Benjamín says that he'd pay to "set his mother up" with someone, and he thinks my experience will give her a little nudge, though apparently she first has to kill her ex-husband, something that I, for all my bearing, can't help her with. He's been encouraging her for years, setting her up on dates, keep-ing a lookout for opportunities. Most recently, he sent her to an ayahuasca session last weekend.

For me, all this just makes me aware of my own age, because sometimes Benjamín's objectivity, as I have to remind him, bor-ders on rudeness. Then he accuses me of having prejudices, and I tell him to hold on tight, because if I have prejudices now, he should wait until ten years from now, when I'm around sixty and he's still a presentable thirty-something. I didn't know quite what his mother's prejudices were, but I very much doubted that she was the kind of woman who listens to the voices around us and thinks she needs a man to be happy. From what I've heard, her own experience has led her to the opposite conclusion, though "it would be nice," says her son, if she let go of some of her terrible certainties. For her, age isn't a fatal current with pleasant eddies, but a growing store of grudges with no room, it seems, for surprises. After the divorce she had to get a job, and her first foray into the working world, which she hadn't been educated for, only heightened her passion for revenge: not only had her husband left her for someone else, with two unruly teenagers who never even considered following him out of the nest, but he had also thrust her into the rough and tumble world of people who work for a living. At any rate, she's a competent, capable woman, and the trouble she had finding an unlikely but respectable position in a minor local museum awakened her talents and revealed a strength she didn't know she had. Maybe she still bears a grudge, but more than anything else, perhaps, she's a proud woman.

I deduce all this from my conversations with Benjamín and my own obviously limited knowledge of her. We've only seen each other alone twice—this time was the third, and after this third time, there's very little chance there will be a fourth. The plan for us to become "friends" won't work out. I didn't arrive late, but she was already waiting at the restaurant, sitting at a table. She was dressed almost identically to me—black jeans, white blouse, ethnic collar, though with fewer designer names, and an enormous belt over the blouse—and this fact might have occasioned some remark. Neither of us made any, perhaps in a sign that we were both disappointed by the coincidence. But as always, her reaction was cordial, curious, with a touch of nervousness she kept admirably under control. Presumably she had rich experience in the field of awkwardness. She has her son's pale

skin and gray eyes, and a similar way of putting her index finger
to her lips; her eyes show resolution but she holds her chin up
unnecessarily; she's shy and therefore generous with confidences;
maybe we have other traits in common, but so far I haven't been
able to detect them.

"Benjamín must have told you that I finally vomited out his
father, I assume?"

So could this be our reason for meeting? But no, he hadn't
told me.

"Maybe it's just the drugs, but the truth is I still feel the
effects. And I can't say I'm not glad … I hope I'm not the first
mother whose children get her to take drugs! I thought that only
happened in movies."

Her children, it turns out—mostly Benjamín, because the
other one is living as a squatter and barely shows his face at
home—persuaded her to sign up for an "Amazonian medicine
session" led by an alternative psychotherapist, since years of
attempts to get her to see a conventional therapist had failed. It
seems traditional therapy posed a threat to the good lady's honor
and patience; going to a delightful country house and for just one
weekend of therapy involving modified states of consciousness,
by contrast, compromised only her morals: she had read that
drugs, even the most Amazonian ones, can have ruinous health
effects and lead to a weakening of the will. Fears of addiction,
cardiac arrest, and holes in the brain weren't hard to overcome,
though her children had to do more than just ask if they looked
like they had holes in their brains: they had to amass an arsenal
of somewhat more persuasive scientific literature. But she was
opposed to anything that smacked of letting go. After a life of
never letting go, she felt she had a duty to stay locked up, and
she had so steadfastly rebuffed every one of Benjamín's attempts
that at one point he was on the verge of giving up. Eventually he

managed to convince her she wouldn't get "hooked," but even then he couldn't make her see the profound side of what she still considered sinfully recreational. Then another solution put an end to the crisis, and she agreed. Partly she did so out of resignation, no doubt, and an irrational desire to please her children, no matter what they dragged her into; but what really clinched it was the idea that she could take along a friend. Benjamín had one in particular in mind—a bad influence, he said, also messily divorced, but flightier. She and his mother often get together to vent bitterly about their exes. This friend liked the idea of doing something out of the ordinary, and if it involved some ancestral rite, so much the better. She did worry about the "kind of people" who would go, but she was ultimately persuaded by the chance to gain a little "inner peace" that was different from the methods she already knew—different, for example, from rum and coke.

"We were convinced," his mother explained, "and I even went willingly. I'd been thinking, you know? Besides, my kids wanted me to go. I was scared, because it's a drug, but really, if they don't take it, if it's not something they do while out partying, it must be a special drug. On the retreat they don't call it a drug, they call it the *abuelita*, the grandma, did you know that? Now I see why my kids don't take it: who could get them on a retreat like that, with all that peacefulness and music, where they'd have to talk about themselves? They're probably afraid of what they'd learn."

"So you're supposed to learn something?"

"Well," she said, making a hand gesture to suggest something very broad, "it's hard to explain. The first surprise is the people: one or two do look crazy, but mostly they're just like you or me, normal people"—I smile as I transcribe this—"not like my kids. By the way, do you know why Benjamín doesn't take it? Because once he went to a session and the *abuelita* told him he had to give up marijuana and all other drugs. He didn't go back, of course."

"Funny, he never told me that."

"He didn't tell you he went to a session?"

"Yes, that part he told me. He didn't tell me about the drugs."

"Well, well, well … he's hiding things from you!" She couldn't conceal a certain satisfaction. "He didn't tell you about what the *abuelita* said?"

I avoided the question, defending him, and defending myself.

"Sounds like the *abuelita* exaggerates. Benjamín doesn't need to 'give up' anything."

"Ah yes, the master of self-control," she laughed. "Just like his father. Well," she said, relishing the moment, "sooner or later you'll see. Anyhow, as I was saying, the people are all very normal. Susana, my friend, was thrilled. The next day, during the group reflection, she said she felt like she'd known them her whole life, even though what she was most afraid of before she got there was that she'd be stuck with a bunch of druggies. She made everybody laugh. Before, during, and after, poor thing: she's quite a case. So before the session, the guide, that is, the therapist, gives an introduction explaining all sorts of things about botany: what entheogens are, what they're good for, where they come from, and so on. He talked about plants and Amazonian rituals, their applications in psychotherapy and for personal growth, and all of us, sitting in a circle, listened to him silently. But Susana wanted to know how they brewed the ayahuasca, and when they told us they were going to give us something that had already been prepared by real Amazonian shamans, she didn't trust them and asked for the recipe, to make sure they wouldn't just give us "some sort of old dishwater." The guide laughed and said that the recipe for the brew didn't include dishwater, but he was very friendly and spoke about bark and vines, giving the scientific names for the plants, and about how the shamans mashed them, mixed them, cooked them for ten hours or more and then strained them. He was very patient, because this information wasn't new to anyone, but all the same it was important for all of us, including Susana, to be prepared. Susana eventually quieted down, but she had a laughing fit when we were doing relaxation exercises, and when she wasn't laughing, she said she was hungry. We basically had to fast for two days, but we weren't really very strict: at lunchtime we stopped in a town and polished off some lamb. We both have big appetites. That explains the vomiting. They warned us, mind you, and the day before we were good and hardly had anything to eat, just some lettuce, and that day all we had for breakfast was an herbal tea and a piece of toast, but when we stopped by the town we couldn't help ourselves. I threw up discreetly, but she made a scene.

Susana's experience had apparently monopolized the trip, so much so that she considered her own irrelevant for now.

"And then what happened?"

"For about an hour before we threw up we felt horribly nauseated, and really anxious. Especially her, she wouldn't stop muttering, which made me even more anxious. I understood right away that the experience required silence; she didn't. The guide had to escort her out, and as he did, she began throwing up everywhere; they took her outside, but we could still hear her. And that was the signal. Three or four people with green faces began to line up at the bathroom; others went up to their rooms, but the rooms didn't have individual bathrooms, so I imagine they must have done it into a bag or something. I waited patiently in line for the upstairs bathroom, the only other one, which was next to the bedrooms, and I only had to wait for one person."

"And then what?"

"I literally threw him up," she said, triumphantly. "I saw my ex-husband's face in the vomit, in the toilet bowl. I laugh about it now, maybe it sounds funny, but at the time it was very dramatic. Well, no—dramatic's not the word." Now we were getting into her experience. "I told you, it's hard to explain. But that was the only point at which I felt really unnerved: I had this vision of my ex's face, basically, if you'll pardon the expression, right where he belonged. With the waste. And it really wasn't gross: it was like I found a place to put him. I think I spent at least a half hour in the bathroom, looking at him. Good thing there was no one else in line."

"But was it really a face made out of vomit?"

"No," she replied, meditatively, "not really. But he was there, and it really was his face. I looked at it with a strange sensation of peace. I thought about the experience a lot."

"While you were looking at it?"

"Yes, and then later, when I went back downstairs. The guide asked me if I felt all right and invited me to lie down on a mat. I didn't see Susana, and I didn't ask about her, either. Later I found out one of the guide's assistants, a very nice young man, had taken her up to her room. When she came back down she was calmer, too. Now she says that terrified is what she was, because she couldn't stop seeing bursts of colors. But when I saw her she looked calmer."

We'd gotten off track again. I said nothing.

"It's true that the *abuelita* talks to you," she went on. "Still, after I threw up, I never felt like I was drugged. I know it's a drug, and I won't try it again, because it can't be good for you, it's probably terrible for your brain … I don't have much experience, but I didn't feel drugged."

"But is it like a special state?"

She looked at me as though there were something suspicious about my curiosity. "I don't get why Benjamín doesn't get you to do these things instead of me." I don't know if she expected a response, but since she didn't get one, she went on. "I felt relaxed, calm, very clearheaded ... except that I was hearing a sort of voice. I don't know, a voice that was mine, but from higher up. It convinced you that you had to listen to it."

I could have told her about my own wide-ranging experience with voices, and about how carefully you have to listen to the very ones that sound most reasonable. But I didn't want—I've never wanted, with her—to draw attention to myself.

Now I have to briefly do so, however. I had to stop writing for a few minutes because for a while now, I think ever since I wrote my "farewell," I've been hearing a voice that can only be Ramón's. I disengaged, I focused, and I listened. He's not saying anything yet, though I'm starting to feel certain he will; for now he sounds like he's warming up, like he's gauging and testing his powers, the sounds he can make, after staying silent for so long. He's out of practice, and I'm afraid he'll blame me. I can't help it. The feeling isn't pleasant or even neutral: it's ominous. After the confinement I put him in, impressed by my own authority—so precarious in that first year of mourning, so threatened by madness—I suspect he's not going be happy that I've summoned him now, only to ask him to leave again so soon. Ramón may not be happy with such a quick transition from banishment to burial. He may not like being revived through Benjamín; that may simply not be enough for him. Or he may just feel like talking. Can't he see I only survived because I stopped listening to him? Maybe not. In any case, now I'm not alone. Nor will he be alone inside my head. I have help.

Back to Benjamín's mother. By now we must have been on
the second course. I'd chosen a restaurant near my place, a neighborhood institution that had recently been remodeled: now it's
in the guidebooks, and people come from all over to eat there,
especially at night. They know me, and I take a lot of people
there, because it's virtually impossible for anyone not to like
it. Still, I'm very much aware that in this restaurant I'm in my
home territory, which is where I like to be for business—and
oddly, with my boyfriend's mother. She knows this, but doesn't
seem to mind. She's not sure she has anything similar in her
own territory, though once she tried to take me to a pub near
her museum; in the end I couldn't go, and she hasn't tried again.
She indulges my familiarity with the menu, with the waiters,
with Antonio, the owner, and perhaps she thinks a woman in an
awkward position deserves these small securities.

On the other hand, there she was to remind me what I lacked.
"Ever thought about trying it?"
Maybe so we'd have more in common?
"Those things scare me."
"Me too!" She made a gesture to underscore how obvious this
was, as though my reasoning were not only insufficient, but also
unclear. "You must have something to let go of!"
"Every day there's something." It was an evasive maneuver,
and maybe I sounded like what I wanted to let go of just then
was her. I hastened to clarify. "Is that what the *abuelita* asks you
to do?"
"She didn't have to ask me to let go of everything that hap-
pened with the father of my children, that's for sure." She smiled.
"I went in very willing to let go of *that*. Benjamín says I can't
stop thinking about it because wallowing makes me feel strong.
The *abuelita* agreed. You've got to find strength somewhere else."
A little reluctantly, she added: "We'll have to be constructive."

Then I smiled.

"But let's leave a little room for wallowing."

"Does Benjamín say that you wallow, too?"

"He says pretty much the opposite. In his view I'm too practical."

"To each her own." But then, since this sounded like the motto of a fair man, she corrected herself, adding sarcastically: "Why does he always know everything?"

What could I say? That he didn't know anything? Luckily she continued on her own.

"Even the *abuelita* seemed to be working for him! All she did was repeat what he says!"

"Well, maybe it wasn't the *abuelita* ...

"Frankly, I have my doubts." Pause. "But it was her, I know. Because of what happened next."

"What happened next?"

I think at this moment the waiter arrived with a white chocolate mousse. She seemed to think the dessert course was the appropriate time for what she had to say, not—I like to think—as a grand finale, but because she now had less time to finish.

"What happened next was that my children's wisdom, Benjamín's in particular, was sort of discredited. His father was easy to extirpate, and maybe the *abuelita* wanted more of a challenge. I suppose she wanted to show her power, so she moved on to my kids."

Very cautiously I asked:

"Did she say anything interesting?" I was paving the way for her to backpedal, but either she didn't notice or I didn't succeed.

"She said they were next." I almost prayed for her pause to be a sign of indecision, and for her to stop there. But since she said nothing, I had to ask:

"Next in what?"

"Next in line for the operation. You know"—she made a rather brutal surgical gesture—"two more lumps to extirpate. That's why I think that it really was the *abuelita* speaking to me, and not Benjamín through her. Benjamín would be the last one to suggest he should be extirpated."

"You don't think he's doing anything to cut ties?" I answered imprudently, almost offended. And I misspoke.

"Well, to be honest with you," she said, seeing I felt slighted, "the one who's cut ties is his brother. Ever since he moved into that squatter's flat he doesn't need me at all. In fact, he doesn't even confide in me, which I admit bothers me a great deal. For him, the only thing I have to let go of is my own irritation. With Benjamín it's different: he's always managed to make it seem like he doesn't need anyone. But in my opinion, ever since he finished school he's led an extremely unreal life … Think of his long string of odd jobs. Think of all the things he gets bored of. Look at that group he's in. Look at the songs he sings. Scorpions and planets! 'What do you know about scorpions?' I asked him one day. 'You've never seen one in your life!'"

"He doesn't write the songs," I said, falling into the trap all by myself.

"Exactly. He doesn't even write the songs. If he had to, what would he write about? How would he come up with a respectable persona? He'd rather keep hiding behind others, with that pretty face, convinced, he says, that that's how he'll make it big. And he's not going to make it big—you know that, right?"

"I don't really care if he makes it big."

"Don't get me wrong," she said gently. "I'm not one of those people who's impressed by the success of others. A person with no profession, no career, only a lifestyle, has to lower their aspirations and find an ordinary role to play. They can still aspire to stand out in that. I came to have career ambitions only very late, and only because I was forced to. Since my education leaves a lot to be desired, my aspiration in life was first of all to be a good wife, and when that didn't work out, to be a good mother. That's what you devote your time and your talent to, if you have any, when you can't make it big. To doing your best to be like your mother. I'm very aware of this, I didn't need any *abuelita* to tell me. But I'm also a practical woman, so I don't see any reason to resent having become, if nothing else, so much like her. It was no easy task, and don't think I don't take a certain satisfaction in it. Part of that satisfaction comes from seeing your children get on their feet ... and that's why, until I see that they really are on their feet, I don't think it's appropriate for anyone to ask me to let go of them. Not even, as the *abuelita* implied, for my own good."

I tried to keep my distance from this extreme vigilance, and to regard her, as I'd intended, as another concession to Benjamín's wishes, or rather as one of the compromises that publicly becoming a couple entails. Getting to know his mother and meeting her for lunch once in a while might not be, from this point of view, any more of a burden than letting him put on psychedelic trance during foreplay. The voice of love, which is oddly quiet and heard only in murmurs and hums, causes a strange state of abstraction. Under its drone, it's often amazingly easy to ignore things you don't like. I'd been revolving around that voice almost all morning, muted though it was. But a conversation like the one I was now subjected to in that restaurant required a degree of abstraction so great that it practically amounted to an act of faith. Yes, I'd declined to defend myself, and yes, I'd chosen to suffer fools, and yes, I was convinced that this woman, who had lived with Benjamín for twenty-seven years, was confusing him with someone else—probably someone of her own invention. But I still had to restrain myself from getting up and walking out. Benjamín, I won't forgive you for this.

At last, it's happening. The voice of Ramón is taking shape; it's already taken shape. He sounds a little hoarse, a little weak, but he speaks clearly. He says: "You'll forgive him." What does he mean? More importantly, what will he say next?

Let's see what came of his mother's rebellion against the *abuelita* and my efforts to practice restraint. It went more or less like this:

"And I'd like, I'd love to see my children succeed. To see them not wind up just like their father, the way I've become just like my mother. That's what would be most 'for my own good!' I'm fine the way I am, no one can ask me to be anything else. But they should go further."

"What would it mean for them to wind up just like their father?" I asked.

"Leading an easy life, like he did: shallow, artificial. Comfortable."

"Like the life of a squatter, for example?"

"He's not exactly the one who has it easiest. And at least he follows through."

"Does Benjamín not?"

"Benjamín?" she laughed. "To follow through you have to have something to follow through on. You have to have something to start with."

"Sometimes," I said deliberately, "it's better to start with nothing."

"If you start with nothing, you never build anything!" Suddenly she changed her tone. "Maybe I'm not making myself clear. I worry about him, I worry about his future, his happiness. I understand that at a certain age it's fine to just fool around. I suppose it's fun and it's satisfying, and once it's over, since it didn't mean anything, you move on to something else. But Benjamín is at a different age, an age when fooling around can get serious, and something inconsequential can turn into something important. He might get comfortable, get used to it … because you don't need me to tell you he's lazy. He may think it's just a game, but the truth is, he's not playing around anymore."

"That's a dramatic way of looking at his age—and mine— which I doubt he'd share. I certainly don't share it. I'd rather be playing around, as you put it."

"And once you've gotten over all this, and you see that he's not at your level, what will you do?"

"Can you tell me what 'all this' is?"

"Me? I don't know. Can you tell me?"

I hesitated for a moment. I could have told her perfectly well, but I've learned how little a pointless gesture is worth. Still, I didn't keep silent.

"Sometimes I wish we'd never made 'all this' public. We thought we needed to take that step, to show we could hold our heads high, but now it feels more and more like we gave in, like we made a concession to the demands of others. If people aren't interested in what's actually going on between two individuals, why give them a show?"

"But is there really something going on?"

"You bet there is."

"I'm not going to have coffee. Are you?"

A wonderful opportunity to ask for the check. She didn't let me pay. Her final satisfaction lay in dividing the total perfectly and providing the exact amount in bills and coins. I had to wait for my change. I left a twenty-euro tip.

When we left we exchanged a few words out of courtesy, well aware that leaving in silence would be harder to explain. I still haven't told Benjamín anything, and yesterday, when I spoke to him, and even today, I got the impression that she hadn't, either. I only said that his mother had plans for him, and he answered with a laugh: "She always does!" At any rate, his view of her, as a woman of familiar but inconsequential quirks, wasn't the view I came away with when we said goodbye outside the restaurant. Personally I think this is another one of the things that "came in" with Benjamín and that I'd have been happy to leave outside. Every entry is subject to conditions, I know, but now I wonder if I'm the same person who, fifteen pages back, said she wanted there to be no fences between our togetherness and the world.

I was in no mood to go to the office and decided to return home. I got a cab. When I gave the driver my address, he looked at me in indignation.

"But ma'am, that's only two blocks away!"

Surprised, I could hardly reply.

"Who cares? Take me anyway."

But the man very rudely made me get out, and I had to go on foot.

# Luxor

## I

THE SUN'S NOT blazing anymore, now the light's just warm, and there's finally something harmonious in the row of people crowding over the railing on the prow. Another equally crowded row, their faces visible, showing no sign of losing their good mood, is watching the same spectacle from the shore: the slow procession of tourist boats waiting in line to go through the locks. For those on the shore this must be, at this hour of the afternoon, a bit of harmless entertainment; for us, even though spirits haven't started to flag, it's clear that the entertainment will last less than the delay, so rather than wait I've decided to seize the opportunity—especially since Sebastián hasn't given up yet, either—to go down to the cabin to write you both. Still, when viewed from behind, at a panoramic distance through the camera's viewfinder, these people leaning over the railing, animated and unruly, make up an almost endearing line of humanity. For once they all seemed to be thinking about the same thing, perhaps even having the same thoughts, unencumbered by the individual they carry within them, which—I've discovered—can be quite demanding. And on the other hand, here they seem to be brought together by pleasure, or logic, free from that thick veneer of docility that keeps them from breaking off from the group when they fearfully step off the boat. This row of people, the straight line, could well be something of an achievement: it's economical—the shortest distance between two points—and it's democratic—every point, every set of shoulders, is perfectly distinct, doing its job non-hierarchically. It ordains them in the calm of the spirit. The spirit! I imagine a great horizontal composition. Nothing could be further from those self-defense squads organized to guard against all kinds of imaginary threats—"They're liable to leave us stranded here," "Careful or we'll get lost," "Keep an eye on your purses and wallets"—nor from that anxious herd, really vicious, that fights over the ample dishes on the buffet line. In three days these are the only configurations I've observed in this group's choreography. That's why seeing them all lined up now, faces hidden, voices muffled, with a common purpose that wasn't petty, gives me some hope. You two know what I'm like, always on the lookout for hope … because I know it's one of those things that you eventually end up finding if you look for it long enough. It will probably be my best photo yet.

I have moments like this, when I imagine victories, and today is turning out to be fertile for the imagination. I never thought I'd find harmony in a group like the one up on deck. As for me, I should say that I'm not really looking for "my best photo." I have larger, more satisfying concerns. For example, I feel much prouder for having already obtained, thanks to the distraction of some passengers, absorbed by the spectacle of the locks, a large piece of grass-green carpeting, from a corner I discovered was coming loose by the pool yesterday, and which I just cut off with my large scissors. I hope it's not too noticeable! Well, yes, it's noticeable, but no one saw. It's a respectable size, and I can use it whole or cut up into smaller bits, however I like. For the moment I still don't know what I'll do with it, nor with any of the other items filling up my box. So far it contains several treasures that I take a certain pleasure in enumerating:

1) a thick section of rope from the felucca at Aswan, where we had a wonderful ride and Mom smiled for the first time;

2) a photo of the sullen helmsman who steered it and another of his amiable assistant, which have already been developed, thanks to the good offices of our guide Yusef—"Call me Pepe"—and his susceptibility to tips;

3) fifteen rare porous stones from the island of Elephantine, which I like to think of as being the same "reddish ochre" color used to dye the beer that the perfidious lioness Sekhmet confused with blood;

4) two sugar cubes in their paper wrappers and one silver-plated coffee spoon—I'll have to ask Mom whether it might not be sterling—with hieroglyphic inscriptions from the luxurious Hotel Oberoi, where we stopped for coffee;

5) one single-serving box of cereal and two plastic packets of plum preserves with Arabic writing, nabbed without effort from the breakfast table;

6) a plastic wrapper from a pack of Marlboros filled with sand from Kom Ombo;

7) a large piece of sandpaper I rubbed against one of the imposing outer walls of the temple of Edfu—such obstinacy, such haughty awareness of another world— which I hope retains, perhaps spitefully, some of the dust of its lost power;

8) a turquoise industrial robe that I bought without haggling from a stall this morning and plan to rip up by hand, not cut;

9) a stained white cotton tablecloth that over breakfast was the scene of an interesting confession I'll tell you about below; and

10) practically the most important thing, since we can't forget where we are and why we are where we are, some forty centimeters of what is no doubt dry insulation cable, which I also found this morning on the dock.

I also have other photos from the roll I had developed: I think I'll be able to use a few sections of sky, and perhaps, blown up until the grains are visible, a fragment of the rippled blue Nile at the foot of a structure of gold-colored stone; none of Dad; the photo of Mom smiling on the felucca—I captured it!—I'm afraid will be useless until I get another one, for example, of the guilty face she made a few hours ago when I showed it to her.

A few hours ago, in fact, things were headed back that way, gloomy and upsetting. Just now, when I recklessly left her under Dad's care, by the railing, she was having one of her episodes of abstraction, which aren't, as we well know, the most worrying kind. I suppose you're wondering what effect the new green and white capsules are having on her, after all the psychiatrist's enthusiastic hype. Whether they really are the "cure from America," as he said, won't be proved here, and whether they're "a true revolution," as he also said, remains to be seen, though by now, three weeks later, one would think they ought to have shown some effect. In any event I'm not skeptical, nor do I blame the medicine: we know very well that it has to make its way through a recalcitrant brain, long adjusted to a strange working order. You both know I believe in the spirit, just as I believe in harmony and victories, in spite of the fact that I spend all day cutting off pieces of matter, and in spite of our family's fate, which has made me a slave to electricity, at least for now. But I also believe that the spirit doesn't miraculously take hold of the mind and the body: it has to find the right conductors to manifest itself, and if it can't find them, or finds them obstructed or frayed, or finds only insulators, it's unable to reach the darkened zones, and it floats impotently through a hostile medium, looking for entryways, openings where it can find a way in. Here perhaps the capsules can help her, acting as a sort of plunger, and her spirit will no doubt make use of the help. Because even if the spirit is sometimes powerless, it's tenacious. The day before yesterday, on the felucca, we saw a display of its tenacity. Mom's expression changed, she looked up at the sky, took off her jacket without anyone asking her to, smiled. And in a sort of ecstasy she said: "This sun, this breeze ... it's like when I was eighteen." Dad and I looked at each other, shocked, and then almost happier than she was, and didn't say anything. Today at midday neither one of us could suppress a look of annoyance when, at Edfu, in the middle of the columns of the hypostyle, she had an attack of dizziness, "from the heat." True, it was very hot, it might have even been forty degrees, but as far as I know the heat doesn't cause dizziness. We had to lead her quickly to the shade and sit her down on the ground, where her spirit no doubt got lost again in some damn circuit. "I'm dying, I'm dying," she started to say, looking pale as a sheet, "everything is spinning." And when it had passed, and she found herself surrounded by a macabre chorus, more interested in demanding an explanation than lending a hand, she hid her head between her knees, and we heard her murmur, whisper really, that she was sorry. Dad crouched down and hugged her, trying to calm her down, but she kept her head down with that pitiful refrain: "I'm sorry ... I'm sorry." Later, of course, trying to keep her from hearing us—she heard us—Dad and I fought. The question of whether or not we ought to have declined this invitation to a voyage, a voyage she felt pushed into, to put it mildly, looks like it's still not settled—not even now, when the two of us most need to cling, like predators to their prey, to the initial idea that it would be for her own good.

I'm ultimately not sure what effect the dizziness and the compulsive, recurrent need for redemption had on an opportunity which presented itself this morning and which I, improvising but *tenacious* (like the spirit), tried to guide back to the path of *her own good.* I'm afraid I have to start from the beginning. There's a very curious man I hadn't met who stands out from this crew of galvanic but lackluster guests, among other things because he's the only one who speaks English, the only one traveling without his wife, and the only one, most significantly, who wears a tuxedo to dinner, as if he were on a cruise in an Agatha Christie novel. He's a man of considerable height, burly but a bit flabby, and he reminds me of an older version—he must be well past forty—of Dan Aykroyd in *Trading Places*, that marvelous John Landis romp from … how many years ago? Six or seven. Anyway, he takes pains to cultivate a comic romantic air, and every night he saunters down the jostling buffet line in formal attire, then joins a table of eight where most of the jackets are plaid and none of the jewels are heirlooms. And afterward he paces the deck alone—this is his crowning moment—smoking a cigarette whose ember flickers like a little beacon over the darkened blue of the river. Meanwhile, all I can think about is, first, getting the chance to cut off a piece, if only a small one, of his tuxedo, or at least stealing his bowtie; and second, the grotesque but fabulous image of Dan Aykroyd disguised as Santa Claus devouring a whole salmon through his fake beard. Or at least that's what I thought of last night, when the man sat down at our table with a tabbouleh salad and, after graciously accepting Mom's praise for his "elegant attire," got entangled in a long conversation with Dad about the delay in Señor Ribot's deliveries … There they were, both of them, criticizing their host! How can I express this? How to express, rather, how much chatty professional complaining took place between two people who were otherwise in competition, one of them in a tuxedo and the other in an ancient but only newly worn navy jacket? That was when I thought about pretending to drop something so I could slip under the table and give his cuffs a little snip, but unfortunately I didn't have my scissors on me. I'll do it tonight.

I suppose a true artist would have no need to stoop to such vile acts, but would instead introduce himself, explain his aims and ask for what he wanted. By all accounts the hasty, vandalizing snip, secret but exposed—robbery, in short—is for amateurs. I must admit, though, that since this morning my impressions of the man in the tuxedo have changed somewhat, and I think I'll even feel guilty when I see that irregular, frayed bit of black fabric catching the light in my box. He sat down at our table again, now with some toast and a pair of croissants; only this time we weren't alone, as we were last night. Sebastián was with us, the nihilist kid I'm sharing a cabin with: our cohabitation was decided in view of the fact that we were the only "children" to venture along on this expedition where everyone else is a parent. Señor and Señora Ramírez were there, too, the tedious beings who gave the kid such an abominable life. The fact that Sebastián and I were present played I think a decisive role in what happened, since we served as a source of desperate inspiration for the poor man. Desperate indeed! you'll say, if the inspiration comes from someone like me in my state, accompanied by Mom and Dad in theirs. And if you two had seen Sebastián and his parents—a core of militant disappointment circled by varying states of resistance and resignation—you'd understand what a sad scene we all made. I should clarify, though, that to judge by what we were about to hear, the desperation was amply justified: there was a previous son, a son who belonged to the man in the tuxedo, in whose shadow, it seemed, we all paled.

"You must be proud of your sons. Yours"—he looked at Dad—"has been working with you for years, he's your right-hand man." Dad was about to protest, but in a sign of his recent state of uncertainty, he refrained. "While yours"—he turned to

Señor Ramírez, and here he couldn't help smiling—"may not work with you yet: he's still young. But give him time, he will. Or he'll do something else. But for now it's clear that he dotes on you and follows you around."

This description would apply more to a labrador, an animal I very much doubt is a nihilist, and in any case it didn't satisfy Sebastián's father, who unlike ours wanted to make his disagreement clear.

"Actually I'd say I'm the one following him around," he said rather curtly. "Don't let him fool you, if he's here it's because he couldn't get out of it. We didn't dare leave him home alone." And looking at his wife: "And that's how things are going to be until he finds something to do."

Such a prospect seemed as unlikely as a rich man entering the kingdom of heaven, but our man didn't back down.

"That's the saddest part. My son …" He hesitated, as though he really were missing something. "Our son, that is, we're forced to leave him alone. Psychologist's orders. That's why I'm here, to get away from him. His mother …" Again he hesitated. "His mother couldn't bring herself to leave him, and I now know she's making a terrible mistake."

He had become very serious, and it was hard to see in him the anachronistic hero of nighttime cruises up the Nile. Suddenly the tuxedo struck me as a melancholy disguise and became even more valuable.

"If only we could get rid of ours," intervened Señor Ramírez, with equal frankness, gesturing to his son. "But he needs us like a leech." He looked like he was about to slap him across the face, when our tablemate interrupted him with a smile that revealed, at this point, greater moral experience.

"Don't complain," he said. "At least you're here, and you can hold onto the illusion of family togetherness … even if it's just an illusion. We don't even have that."

Then Mom, overcome by empathy, or guilt, or whatever it is, because at this point I don't dare assume anything about her mental states, opened her mouth and started in:

"We can't hold ourselves responsible for our children's happiness."

"That's something we let go of long ago," replied the man. "We don't worry much about his happiness anymore. We just worry about whether he'll still be alive."

"Is he ill?" asked Señora Ramírez.

"I suppose that's one way of looking at it. He's an alcoholic."

No one knew what to say. Expectations had no doubt been raised, but probably not sufficiently intense ones. A mix of respect and discomfort around revelations that are too personal or, in any case, unasked for, settled in among the toast and café au lait. Of course I had no desire to hear the story, but it occurred to me, almost against my will, that the exposition of a severe family disaster could help us put our own situation into perspective, if nothing else. Therefore I took the first step toward harmony:

"Is he in treatment?"

"He's an alcoholic," he said again. "And it's funny how, when you say that, it sounds like you are, too. 'I'm So-and-So and I'm an alcoholic.' 'I'm So-and-So and my son is an alcoholic.' Is there any difference? We're both confessing! Confession puts us both on the same plane. Some things are so hard to state simply … The prompt, direct words, the unconditional admissions they demand in those therapeutic sessions, the clear assumption of guilt, that incredible stigma! There's nothing simple in any of that, nor is there a worse trap than trying to reduce something

so hard to an easy-to-memorize line. Sure, it's easy . . . so easy
that you end up not believing it. Do you drink?"

"Well," I said lamely, "when the opportunity presents itself . . ."

"I find alcohol revolting," added Sebastián scornfully.

"Then confessing isn't something you do. No doubt you
have other sins. And they say"—he turned to look toward Dad
and Señor Ramírez—"that the sons must pay for the sins of the
fathers! That's a legend like the ones Yusef tells us. In my case,
my son's the one who made me guilty. He's been drinking since
he was fifteen, without interruption, indiscriminately. Alone and
in company. When he's having fun and when he's bored. He's
as addicted to *calimocho* as he is to Dad's single-malt scotch . . .
when we still kept scotch in the house. He's made teetotalers out
of us—or worse yet: we're closet drinkers! When he was sixteen
we had to put him in a special center; back then they counseled
discipline. You should have seen the result: a troupe of lifeless,
listless kids, heads crammed with slogans, incapable of doing
a single thing they weren't ordered to do. True, at that center
he made it through the whole program without drinking, but
his mother and I couldn't bear it. We began to think we'd gone
too far, that we mistook a simple teenage episode for a catastrophe that would turn into a life sentence. Treating him like an
alcoholic began to seem crazy. More than crazy—a dangerous
provocation! We'd given them our son, who was still a child, a
child who had been happy and lively and smart . . . and *this* is
what they sent back! We'd marked him as a pariah, what did we
expect? And when a marked pariah is cured, they suddenly find
they've been assigned a personality profile, they're confused and
terrified of the possibility of a relapse; they watch what they say
and they're monstrously self-conscious about their past. Past! Do
you know what that is? We'd given a sixteen-year-old boy a past!
A past made up of just one year of benders, hangovers, rowdiness,

apathy. Anyway ... Convinced we'd been unfair, we decided not to send him back to the center, and next term we enrolled him in his old school. We still thought he was only a child, that what he did one year he could undo the next. We talked to the principal, the teachers, they promised to help boost his self-esteem, which was, they said, usually an issue in such cases, and they suggested therapy with less of an emphasis on discipline. We got a new psychologist, one who looked like he had common sense, at first, and who we all—all of us!—had to see, separately and together. We had to start over with our family, he said. The boy didn't feel certain he was a part of it anymore; he didn't feel certain when he 'left' and didn't feel certain now that he was 'back.' He was 'caught in the middle,' he had no grounding, he was doing a balancing act, something very dangerous at his age. When is it not dangerous? And whose life doesn't involve a balancing act? Fortunately, according to this psychologist, at least, our son wasn't an alcoholic—but the job of finding out what he was lay in his own hands, and in ours. Ultimately we were doing more of the same, demanding the poor kid get a personality. It was too much for him. Halfway through the semester the school called to ask why he wasn't going to class. And even he couldn't give us a good answer. That day he cried. We were asking too much, he wasn't cut out for school, he understood what we were doing for him, he didn't blame us. It wasn't our fault he turned out like he did! But it wasn't his, either! The psychologist changed tactics and began accusing him of running away from himself. What a mistake. He didn't go back to school or to the psychologist. He locked himself in his room, or that's what we thought. Sometimes he wasn't there, he'd sneak out. We thought he was in his room at six in the morning one day when we got a call from the hospital. He'd been in a motorbike accident with another kid he barely even knew: they were both drunk. He

broke some ribs, had serious burns on his legs and arms. He lost
an eye. The psychologist beat an undignified retreat: after two
sessions in the hospital, he concluded that our son's case required
specialized therapy, and he referred us to an association of former
alcoholics. 'I'm leaving you in good hands,' he said ... while he
washed his of us! 'But didn't you say,' I asked, 'that our son wasn't
an alcoholic? That it was very important that none of us accept
the diagnosis?' 'Seeing how things stand,' he said, 'everything
will be easier if he receives a diagnosis. I'm afraid he's become a
medical case.'"

"I imagine you'll be pleased to know that Saddam Hussein
freed all the Western hostages yesterday. Weren't there some
Spaniards among them?"

This interruption by Rachid, the guide for the other group—
there's another group in addition to the guests of Ripalux, S.A.—
was met with partly masked relief, and in a few cases with partly
masked annoyance. Rachid had come to remind us we were
dallying over breakfast—the other tables were by now empty—
and had to hurry to fulfill our duties as tourists. Señor Ramírez
was especially happy to be able to tell Rachid that the Spanish
hostages had been freed in October, "thanks to our diplomatic
efforts," and the inconsolable father seems to have recalled, after
a moment of sad irritation, that the audience for his venting
may after all have been more captive than captivated. Señora
Ramírez seemed dismayed that her son still had both eyes, and
she got up from the table as though a nurse had called her name
in an emergency room. In fact, only Sebastián and Mom looked
disappointed, but one of them I don't know well enough, and
the other I know too well, to understand why they wanted to
keep listening to that confession of the calamities of others. As
for Dad, well, Dad went along with the dominant mood, after
taking a few minutes to figure out what it was: seeing it was

somewhat divided, he opted to join Señor Ramírez and state that he didn't trust Saddam even so. I waited for the place to clear out a bit, and as soon as I was alone I took the tablecloth, stained with coffee and jam, less as proof than as the very scene of events. Sebastián, on the other hand, will get to hear, if not the end of the story, its continuation. No sooner had we stepped off the boat than he peeled off from his parents, perhaps only to make a point of doing so, and followed the man in the tuxedo—now wearing a stylish safari jacket—like an unconvincing but not unappealing double for his absent son. I don't know what the absent son is like, but Sebastián is a lanky, angular nineteen-year-old, with dark rings under his eyes that almost look like makeup and an expression that's on the whole more tender than his rough and rather withdrawn spirit would like. He wears unpolished police boots. I like him, although when they told me I'd have to share a cabin with him all the way to Luxor I felt that Ripalux's generosity was waning. I wanted solitude, for as long as possible, like the solitude I'm enjoying right now; but wishes aren't really my thing, so I got stuck with Sebastián, who I don't think has showered even once on this trip. I probably won't have to steal from him because he'll give me anything I ask for. He expressed curiosity about the box, but I was mysterious about it, and that strategy will bear fruit: I'm planning on showing it to him before we say goodbye, perhaps on board, perhaps in Cairo, though I don't know if our forced cohabitation will continue in the hotel. If he persists in his refusal to take a shower—"I don't like the water"—I'll ask for that green t-shirt of his and a lock of his hair.

I have before me a list of the boat's services, in three languages, in an outrageous cursive on good cream-colored card stock. The emergency instructions are framed and hanging on the wall of the little hallway, facing the closet. I'll have to take all of this, it will be a good background.

Sebastián, as I said, trailed the poor father with his strange dignity. I saw them together during the whole tour of the temple of Edfu, unmoved by the terrifying Ptolemaic monumentalism or Yusef's lurid legends. These legends, in an attempt to smooth over the rigors of history, end up being almost equally bloody. Sebastián says they're a "cleansing" of the blood spilt by "the powerful" so that "the people" can take heart thinking that their deaths contribute to their country's glorious history; underneath them, he says, all you can see is a primordial world of poverty and violence. I don't think it's so primordial, nor that it's only visible underneath. The temple of Edfu commemorates the last battle between two deities, the benevolent Horus and his uncle, the evil Seth, him of the "pestilent head." Seth took the shape of a great red hippopotamus to try, for the umpteenth time, to finish off his nephew and secure for himself the accession to the throne of his father, the god Ra. The strange thing is that both of them, uncle and nephew, had already died on at least one occasion: Seth, who had transformed himself into a scorpion, stung Horus when he was a child; Horus, when older, cut off Seth's head and hacked his body into fourteen pieces. In both cases, their souls managed to get away.

Dismemberment seems to be an Egyptian specialty: the fourteen pieces of Seth, the fourteen pieces of his brother Osiris (also Seth's doing), the unspecified number that the great red hippopotamus was cut into to serve as food for the fauna of the Nile. It should be noted that a dismembered body prevented the soul from reaching Duat, the kingdom of the dead and eternal life; it also frustrated any possibility of spiritual life, and therefore was the greatest sacrilege. It seems that in the end the ancient Egyptians, flying souls notwithstanding, believed that the soul was inseparable from the body, or at least from a well-preserved body. Obviously they saw the body as a unity, for unity is essential for the concept of the soul, which requires an undivided seat. Maybe that's why I'm so obsessed with thinking up ways to imbue loose, torn off bits, the ones I keep in my box, with a soul; maybe it's impossible, maybe that's the point. In any case, for the Egyptian mind, from a time before psychology, the other possibility—a dismembered soul—seems not to have been conceivable. And I get the impression that today the soul can't flee the body, can't fly away: now the body isn't just its seat, but its instrument, its noose, its trap. Look at Mom fainting from "the heat." The ancient Egyptians could never have imagined that the course of centuries would produce such a paragon of unity.

Yusef provides these amenities—the stories, that is, the speculations are mine—with the voice and air of his best Oriental storyteller, astutely aware that the Ptolemaic period, Cleopatra VII, and the illustrious archeologist Auguste Mariette capture tourists' attention less than the blood and incest of the gods. Apparently the other group, under Rachid's tutelage, is more often bored, though today, with the news about Saddam, they got to indulge in a discussion of modern warfare. They did so with a certain relish that, to Yusef's dismay, soon spread to our group, though it was tinged with the usual note of fear. The group of electricians, led by Señor Ribot, CEO of Ripalux, S.A., found the prospect of an international war over "sovereignty" very likely, and thought that Saddam Hussein's decision to free the three thousand "human shields" he had kept in buildings likely to be bombed should be interpreted as a sign not that he was backing down but that he was "plotting something." That plot suddenly seemed to involve all of us when Señor Nicolau wondered aloud whether we were "safe here," and then added, very rudely for our host, who tried to calm him down, that he questioned whether this was a good time for "tours." Yusef, annoyed at having to set aside his legend, reminded him that Egypt and Spain were allies, that "our men" were all taking part in the embargo, and that President Mubarak's efforts at mediation had already been and would continue to be decisive for peace. When Rachid joined us, shortly thereafter, he very inconveniently recalled that the only terrorist attacks in Egypt that year had targeted Israelis—two of them, one very recent, just a week ago—and an Egyptian, Dr. Rifaat el-Mahgoub, speaker of the People's Assembly, and that therefore, as a "friendly nation," we had nothing to fear. "Egypt is a safe country," he declared. But now the threat of terrorism, which hadn't crossed any of the electricians' minds, distinctly joined the threat of war, which everyone had already acknowledged, and every other threat—robbery, losses, swindles, tips, supposedly incompetent management, as well as, one might add, the egregious numbers of "*moros*"—that could conceivably hang over the heads of these defenseless travelers. To make matters worse, Rachid's tactlessness—intentional, I sometimes think—led him to add that, as far as terrorism was concerned, we were safer here than in Spain. He thus set off a wave of patriotic indignation. Yusef could barely contain it in an epic effort to return to neutral territory, which for him meant the floating island of Jemmis, drifting in and out of his stories just as in bygone years it drifted up and down the Nile. I think it was then that Mom had her dizzy spell.

Among its effects, this remark by Señor Simó is worthy of note:

"Yusef …"

"Call me Pepe."

"Pepe, you guys always take us to see the temples during the day, with this sun and this heat, when what we really want to see is a show with light and sound."

And joined by Señor Andreu, he began to gauge the potential of some posts that could be seen over the walls.

When Mom recovered and stopped apologizing, Sebastián, perhaps guessing at some obscure connection with the incident, came over and told me the rest of the story of the man in the tuxedo, since all morning he had been his privileged confidant. At the time I thought he was right to tell me, for no doubt I could trace more obscure connections than he could, as I'd already sensed over breakfast, and I likewise thought I'd be able to use them. "The weird thing is," he said, "the guy really did sign up for the trip to get away from his son." We had left the son at a critical juncture, when he'd just lost an eye and professional psychology had given up on him. Though not entirely, it seems, for the alcoholics' association that the boy was passed along to had a wealth of therapies: in addition to medication—nothing as advanced as Mom's capsules, I suspect—he received new diagnoses like "alcohol use disorder" and "dissocial personality disorder," group support, chores like gardening and painting, preventive confinement in a rehabilitation center, and finally, after a year, once he was no longer a minor, voluntary residence in a "halfway house." A diagnosis was awarded to the parents, too, which convinced her to embrace pharmacology and him, harder of spirit, to sell off a plot of land where he hoped to build a country house. The father still believed, with an impotence that hadn't waned, that all those diagnoses did less to solve the case than they did to compound it, since all they amounted to, he apparently said, was just "one stone on top of another." Sebastián agreed entirely on this point: "For me, for example," he said, "the more they tell me I have no future, the less I feel like having one." At any rate, after his confinement ended and he dutifully entered the halfway house, the kid apparently made a point of living up to his diagnosis, even developing certain symptoms—such as "secondary cognitive deterioration" ("Mine is primary, I bet," added Sebastián)—he hadn't previously displayed. Soon

enough he was able to dispense with the nuisance of listening to
rehabilitation speeches in person: he turned eighteen, an event
he wanted to celebrate in a less parental environment, one less
steeped in moral or scientific authority. Legally, he was through
with health professionals, and perhaps even with "health itself,"
in his father's opinion, but he seemed to care less about health
now that he'd found a little freedom in law. "You'll wind up
in prison," said his father a few months later—though he now
regretted it—after the boy left the halfway house and moved
back home. He had nothing to keep him busy and soon he
began disappearing again, making a string of mysterious friends
that didn't last, borrowing money he'd later lose, and showing
up again, unannounced, at any hour, dirty, exhausted, shivering
and reeking. Eventually he stopped bothering to hide his drunk-
enness or his means to achieve it: he'd come home with bottles,
lock himself in his room with the music turned all the way up,
sometimes shouting and cursing; he stole from their purses and
wallets, and when he got his hands on the key to the safe, jewels
and watches disappeared. One morning they found that "all the
silver" had disappeared from the dining room hutch. After this
came a long absence that required police intervention, though
ultimately the police determined that a "boozer" didn't need to
be put on a missing persons list. One time he returned home
apologetic; another time, shouting threats and breaking things;
a third time, their fur coats and table linens disappeared. Those
were the most valuable things they had left in the house. The
mom called him a "filthy drunk," and for that she was beaten;
then the father beat him.

Unapologetically, meanwhile, the health professionals continued to offer diagnoses, though now just for the long-suffer-
ing ears of two parents who had lost hope. "That's impossible,
though," said Sebastián. "Parents never lose hope. How else

would I be here?" I don't know about here, but there, in those labeled depths, a sort of light went on. A change in strategy was suggested: maybe the child couldn't be saved, but it was well worth trying to save the parents. A new psychologist told them about "assertiveness training": they had to "learn to say no," and that meant, first of all, changing the locks. The outcast son needed to be cast out by someone other than himself. Then came the invitation from Ripalux: what a perfect opportunity, they were told, to close the door! To let the son who thought he was alone feel true solitude! The abuse of charity had to stop. "But how can I, how could I refuse to help my son if he asked?" asked the mother. "There's nothing more you can do," replied the expert. And so, half-convinced, she began to pack her bags for the Nile. Except that three days before leaving, her conviction was put to the test and only half-succeeded. The son came home one night, and finding the locks changed, furiously rang the doorbell; and then he began to beat and kick the door; he did that for "hours," and his restlessness "roused the neighbors." But his parents didn't open the door. They'd made a promise—to themselves, they wanted to think—and they clung to it desperately. Tears and hesitation didn't stand in the way of victory. They didn't open the door. Exhausted, the son left. Some victory! But they hadn't had any success in "such a long, long time" that the father, at least, had the medicinal feeling he had finally accomplished something. The mother did not. The appeal of assertiveness escaped her. She wanted to postpone the trip: what if their son came back? Her husband refused. And they couldn't reach an agreement. He left, she stayed.

I realize, as I write this, that this story I'm telling you with detachment still casts a shadow over me, and I'd like to think over all of us. Sebastián no doubt sensed this shadow, and with surprising thoughtfulness for someone who's supposed to be vegetating in a state of inertia, he immediately opened himself up to receive it; I'd like for us to do the same. Of course, in Sebastián's case, a perverse motivation, tied to the contempt he feels for his own immobile parents, must have played a role in why he felt drawn to the father in flight. I don't think I'm moved by contempt. But ultimately, in this sordid struggle between spirit and science, both of our conclusions have been more abstract than concrete; and one way or another we've taken control, each for our own ends, of what we might call the story's dramatic circumstances.

Above all, it was the thought of that poor kid in the hallway, practically destitute, pounding on the front door of his heroically cruel parents' home, "rousing the neighbors," which made me see—and maybe made Sebastián see, too—the calm hallway outside our own flat, where such scandals have never occurred. Our dramas are secret and rare, our suffering barely reaches the surface: perhaps others can sense it, but we certainly never talk about it. Even so, what is it we're not talking about? We're not victims of fate, because we're not religious and don't believe in such things; we're not prisoners of history, only its guests, and as guests we follow along; we're not persecuted, we're not martyrs. Some remote country might invade another remote country, and those who keep watch over the world order might demand our support, with all it entails for our speech and our economy, but none of us is called up for duty. The great scourges of mortality— disease, hunger, death, even insanity, I'd say—hang over other heads, and our empathy is fickle and hypocritical. Our diagnoses, which we numbly accept, don't torment us, they don't lead to or follow from extreme behavior, and not even the physical manifestation of a symbolic force—in alcohol, for example—can bring out the worst, or the best, in us. I don't at all mean that our share of suffering is trivial or pointless: that would imply there's some kind of suffering that isn't pointless, which is absurd. I'm well aware that everyone suffers as best they can, and that perhaps part of what's most unsettling about suffering is how it occurs outside the bounds of morality. Suffering, it seems to me, is a cruel subjective privilege, and subjectively, Mom doesn't suffer any less from her harmless spells than a convict who's condemned to die. You'll say I'm being outrageous, but don't blame her! You moralize about the causes, not about the suffering itself. Don't you think she's got reason enough, having to put up with everyone, with Dad, Aunt Isabel and Uncle Rolf, Granddad when he was alive, as well as me, and you two, the king and queen of avoidance? Who else was going to come along on this trip if not me? Was there any other option? Of course there was! But one of you had "a girlfriend at the moment," and the other had "finals" (what finals, if you don't even show up to take the tests?) ... Best not to talk about causes. Can you imagine what your life would be like if I weren't around?

Anyway, I didn't mean to get into all this ... though you have to admit it's not unrelated to everything that's going on. But don't worry, at lunch today, after the incident at Edfu, I didn't talk about you. I tried to find a secluded table, I asked Sebastián to find another place for himself and his parents to sit, and in fact I didn't need to convince anyone else that a woman dizzy from "the heat" and desperate for forgiveness deserved a little time alone with her family. My intention was to relay Sebastián's report, which I felt authorized to do, since I'd already gotten it secondhand, and it consisted of the confidences of an undeniably frank man. And that's what I did, not as I have here, but trying at all times—I'd almost say artistically, though you don't give a hoot about that—to bring this story, seemingly unrelated to our own experience, to a common ground, or at least an eloquent one. That ground, as you can imagine, was hope.

You'll say I'm petty and naive to try to use such a tired argument as "others have it worse"—an argument that has, in any event, been brandished before, to no visible effect. Perhaps. But we've never been so close to a living example, a case that spoke so expressively under our noses, as we are with the man in the tuxedo, able to shoulder his burden with undeniable integrity and a rare insight. Until now, for Mom and Dad, "others" were ethereal characters in an edifying but abstract drama, and could just as easily have been a clever figment of their sense of compassion. Indeed, in their circle there's really no one who's "worse off." Is Uncle Rolf, so happy with his hotels, "worse off"? Could Aunt Isabel be "worse off," when her most worrying symptom is compulsive shopping, which, admittedly, adds drama to her home by making it harder to get around, but which hasn't, so far as we know, ruined her? Is Mom's good friend Blanca worse off, with her happy new life as a widow, free from the tyranny of her marriage and now in an affair with another good friend's husband? What about Rosa, so beside herself because one of her children, both of whom are conservative lawyers, recently married "a penniless climber"—is she "worse off"? I know of no more profound drama, in short, that Mom could have witnessed, much less taken part in, unless we go way back in time. As I saw it, fate happened to place one before us, so we shouldn't waste the opportunity. A great artist once said: "Artists don't take risks. Window washers do." And even though Mom's not an artist, it will do her good to meet a window washer for once in her life, in the man in the tuxedo.

(A window washer! Or an electrician? Though it's been a while since I've done any of the "dangerous" work, the manual work, and I spend my time now almost exclusively on customer relations, it would be funny if being an electrician were the most genuine life I could imagine.)

Anyway, Mom, though clearly in a post-crisis state, and perhaps vaguely aware she demanded too much attention over the
course of the morning, followed the rest of the story with interest; and while disappointed by its woeful lack of conclusion, she
not only made some pertinent observations but was even able,
in a way, to relate. She said she "understood" the father and his
submission to discipline, but she couldn't help putting herself
"in the mother's place," because "a mother," she declared with a
dangerously universal certainty, "can never abandon a son to his
fate." When she realized that this judgment, in her case, lacked
any empirical foundation, and not finding another foundation to
compensate, she experienced a moment of confusion. It looked
like nothing good would come of it. She overcame the confusion
with these words:

"You have to give me some time. I know I've lost my way and
have to find it again. I have to take back the helm of this family,
and eventually I will, you'll see. But I need some time, and you
have to help me."

"Thank God none of you kids have given us trouble like that,"
added Dad, quite moved.

Given the circumstances, I suppose these spirited visions of
Mom's should be taken as a sign that things are going well. If the
circumstances were different—and I really wish they were—I'd
very much have liked to tell her how wrong she was, and how
much time I'd love to give her to do anything else but take back
"the helm of this family." Dad, on the other hand, was more on
point, refusing to lend even hypocritical support to her captain's
dreams, and tactfully returned to the topic at hand. He said he
couldn't even imagine what "that sort of thing" must be like, and
wouldn't want to be "in that man's shoes" because he wouldn't
know what to do.

"You never know what to do," interrupted Mom, in a tremendous effort to make the most of her helmlessness.

In view of the fact that neither of us had shown support for her ambitions—and hadn't dared to oppose them, either—for a moment she seemed to enjoy a morbid advantage. But luckily she's not at her best: she seemed to lose power suddenly, as though a circuit had blown, and she couldn't keep herself there. Dad, making an effort to pretend he hadn't heard her, repeated that "thank God" we'd never put him in such a "predicament" because "there's nothing worse than feeling cornered"; both the mother's "concessions" and the father's "principles" seemed understandable, though above all "hard."

"It's always hard to have to decide."

Before Mom thought to open her mouth, I said:

"The main thing is not to lose hope. That man, with everything that's happened to him, hasn't lost hope."

I left it there, hanging in the air, trusting that one of them could fill in the blanks, since I thought I shouldn't allude directly to everything that's happened to us. I think they caught it, but they didn't say anything. Then I, too, started to have my doubts. I felt a certain sense of failure, frankly, and the best proof is that, when we got up from the table, I stopped to think what I could take for my box and couldn't think of anything. And I left with a bad feeling, as though nothing had left a trace.

I now remember another failure, quite different from mine. In 1952 or 1953 an unknown artist who would go on to be one of the major figures of the twentieth century, held an exhibition in Florence of a collection of "contemplative boxes and personal fetishes." The boxes, made of wood, contained rocks, rusty nails, shards of mirror; some of them made a noise when shaken, like primitive musical instruments; others were open, inviting the spectator to touch them, perhaps empty them out or alter them by adding new items. The "fetishes" were disparate objects joined—tied—by laces or ropes: feathers, bones, hair, seashells, snail shells, and other bits of natural life, mixed with bits of industrial life, like pieces of pipe, wood, or fabric. The exhibit was a disaster: since the artworks were cheap and the artist a nobody, a few people bought them just to laugh at them. One critic, after a detour through the long and extraordinary history of Florentine art, wrote that all those vile objects deserved to be tossed into the Arno. Reading this, the artist decided this would be a wonderful way to complete his work, an inspired sign of what its natural fate should be. So he grabbed his boxes and his "fetishes," found an out of the way place—this was supposed to be the culmination of an artistic process, not a *happening*—and tossed them into the river. I can't help imagining the host of feelings that must have overcome him—humiliation, rage, but also serenity, courage, discipline: submission to the demands of art, even when they've been revealed by an enemy—as he saw how, one by one, his delicate creations sunk beneath the surface, where they'd end up, with other detritus, in the riverbed. Then he wrote a note to the critic saying he'd taken his advice.

Indeed, as Dad would say, the hard part is deciding. In any case I don't plan to toss anything into the Nile. I won't take your advice, which I can guess at every time you see my "garbage" or hear about it. I'm starting to grow tired of your silent reproaches. For once I wish you'd stop and think that it's me, and not you, here trapped in the locks at Esna, just outside of Luxor, in the middle of this crazy situation. Besides, do you realize how much time, thought, and effort I put into trying to fix it? I wish for once you'd think about everything you don't have to do because I take care of it. About all the things you can do simply because I do the others. Maybe then you'd stop laughing and making snide remarks each time I … Do you want to know where you'd be if I weren't around? I could tell you, I can imagine it perfectly clearly. You don't want to know? I'm not surprised. But I'm afraid I'm going to tell you, so you'll have to listen. Imagine it in the style of one of Yusef's legends. You belong to the era of psychology, but I want you both to go back to the era of elements—that way you'll understand better. Forget any technical refinements, too: imagine the world when electricity wasn't called electricity, but was only a secret force in amber. Imagine the day when Horus, with the help of Thoth, the god of magic and wisdom, created the first thermal power station on the shores of the Green Sea; imagine, too, the day when, advised by some thieving deity, he created the first hotel. Thoth, who in his wisdom had revealed the properties of amber to his friend, had shown himself to be prudent with the sharing of his secrets, but Horus saw in amber a source of riches for human-kind, whom he liked to favor, and he decided to entrust to them its use. A woman drawing water from a well saw lightning strike that day, and sensing some disturbance in the sky, prophesied great misfortune.

And indeed, at that time Khonsu, god of the Moon, who bore a certain grudge against Thoth from the day he lost some of his light to him in a game of checkers, and was thereafter reduced to appearing every so often in humiliating waxing quar-ters, happened to be in the company of some of the gods of dark-ness, among them the everlasting Seth. None of these individu-als approved of giving amber to humans: they saw it as part of Horus's perpetual endeavor to extend his light and deprive them of the dominion of darkness and the night, where they were still strong. Therefore they devised a terrible plan. Seth would take it upon himself to spread a covetous and slipshod spirit in Horus's hotels, seizing on the weak points in Horus's generos-ity. As for Khonsu, he would use humans' complicated spiritual endowment to his favor, leading them to weakness and obfuscation, just when amber seemed to bring men greater independence from their nature and greater abundance to their society. Ignorant of all these machinations, the good Horus had taken note of a chaste and rather indolent man, none of whose spiritual faculties seemed especially active, or (therefore) very vicious. This man's name was Huti, and his father had destined him for the ancient profession of agriculture, at which the family had excelled for many generations. Nevertheless, Horus decided to change his fate and sent Thoth to instruct him in the wonders of amber. A new Huti was thus born, who left all his relatives dumbfounded with his magical illuminations. But Horus still had another surprise in store for them: he placed in his path an enterprising man, who offered to buy a large portion of his lands to build a hotel. Horus had instilled in the souls of the people from the north a desire for sun and warm water that very few could resist, given the Eye of Day's miserly appearances in those parts; and the enterprising man, knowing of this Nordic fervor, had spotted a good place to satisfy it in the good farmer's lands nearest to the coast, filled at that time with lovely pear trees. The farmer, naturally, was sad to lose them; but he also wanted the best for his son, and when the enterprising man, in his guile, promised he'd put Huti in charge of the supply and installation of amber in the new hotel, and in other ambitious construction projects he had in mind, Huti had no doubt he should accept the deal.

That day Horus smiled in the heavens, pleased by the unremitting evolution of human affairs. But alas, he was not the only one to smile. Evil Seth, in the form of a rat terrier, had also witnessed the negotiations and sought to muddy them with unexpected complications. He consulted Khonsu and the lioness Sekhmet, goddess of love and its despair, and while he, in his primordial fury, favored destroying it all with fires and floods, her advisers persuaded her to aim for the human heart, source of the perhaps subtler but equally unerring misfortunes; and between the three of them they hatched a laborious plot. They noticed the enterprising man had two daughters, both graced with remarkable features: the older one, Ahura, had inherited her father's wit and will; the younger, Tewosret, exceeded her in grace and beauty. Huti, when he met them, at once fell in love with the younger sister, freed for once from his indolence: the first time his soul awakened from its comfortable lethargy and ceased to be a pliant instrument in the hands of others. He felt an unfamiliar passion. The beautiful Tewosret wasn't indifferent to his wooing, and the enterprising man, eager to keep them happy, did not stand in the way. Thus the happiness of Huti was complete, and he convinced himself that harmony had aligned his desires with his destiny.

Then the powers of darkness decided to intervene. Khonsu cast a powerful spell on Tewosret, so that each night after she bid farewell to Huti, while she believed herself peacefully asleep, her *ka*, or spiritual double, would fly to remote regions, specifically to a dark Nordic forest. There the girl's *ka* would bathe in the moonlight in an icy pool where wolves and wild boars went to slake their thirst. Another visitor frequented this frightful place: a tribal prince, valiant and melancholy, who night after night would watch the spectacle in rapture. The apparition's dark skin, brown eyes, ringed tresses, and slender form called to mind, thought the prince, the legendary Green Sea, which intrepid travelers had spoken of with wonder. Timidly at first, and later with passion, he began to reveal himself to the stranger and make known to her his love; and since Khonsu had erased the memory of Huti from her *ka*, she welcomed his attentions with unfeigned gratitude, for the enormous forest and its creatures filled her with fear. The prince would watch her sadly vanish each dawn, when the girl awakened in her bed with vague recollections of a strange dream. Khonsu decided then to put the prince to a test: he interrupted the flights of Tewosret's *ka*, and waited for the prince's grief to move him to great feats that resigned spirits would not attempt.

Indeed, far from giving up, the grief-stricken lover led an expedition of fifty-two fierce men through the thickest of forests, over the deepest of rivers, up the steepest of mountains, until they reached the shores of the Green Sea, on whose islands the graceful bather said she made her home. With a bag of gold he paid some fishermen to take him … Hold on, there's a knock at the door.

I've had a bit to drink, though I'm not drunk, I'm wide awake. All kinds of impulses and frustrations are sorting themselves out in my head, contradictory forces that won't let me sleep. Sebastián, however, is sleeping like a log, breathing easily, unbothered by the lamplight or my activity. If that's nihilism, sign me up.

I have the life buoy here—I managed to get ahold of it. It's still wet, though that's not why I still haven't put it in my box: it just doesn't fit. It's too big, too orange, too rubbery. And at the same time I can see with perfect clarity that it's going to be the key piece, my greatest find. Now I won't need that snip of tuxedo I longed for this afternoon, which now almost seems ridiculous. My imagination, just a few hours ago floating in amber and, to judge by what I was writing, devising vast experiments in symbolism and color, seems to have descended to the most prosaic level. It's a mistake to try to spiritualize everything: it was a mistake to try to tell you the story of our family—the story of my life—"in the style of Yusef," with gods and *ka*s and times immemorial, and while I could continue now, I wouldn't want to. I'm sorry to leave it like that, before Tewosret married Uncle Rolf and Dad had to make do with Ahura, and especially before the arrival of you two, for whom this whole story was intended: another mistake. Why was it intended for you, if ultimately, as I've done so often and in so many ways, I was telling it all to myself?

No, the hard part isn't deciding. The hard part is seeing. What a delusion, to think we decide anything. We're always dragged along, and all we know is the current. There's nothing we've chosen here, only what we've gotten by chance. Not the bit of tuxedo from the man who caught our attention, but this life buoy which truly did play a role in our life, maybe even encapsulates it. That's why it doesn't fit in the box. That's why it makes everything the box does contain—except perhaps the dry insulation cable—seem like a lie. All art bears the curse of autobiography, not because it has to detach itself to reach a more elevated or impersonal order, but because that very autobiography breaks off from itself. Real autobiography from the autobiography of desire. One wishes one's world could be encased in amber, and not in some damn fuse box on the wall; that one's fortune could change with a mysterious dream, and not because a fuse has blown; that one's dance partner could be the pharaoh's daughter, not Señora Ramírez; that the voyages one takes were to see the world, not the people one sees every day. But one has to work with what one has, whatever that may be; no one can really invent themselves. This afternoon I spoke of the undramatic void of our lives and our lack of objective reasons for "true" suffering; I almost implied that Mom's whole crisis, which tonight showed signs of having been cured all at once, was an invention to create an interesting personality, an interesting persona. I don't know if that's true, because the undramatic void itself has dramatic components, but it could be: such is the need of empty beings for pathos. In any case what's valid for each individual's life isn't necessarily valid for art. An artist can't fabricate suffering, just as they can't fabricate gratification. There's nothing more stupid than an interesting artist.

I have, after everything that's happened, a certain feeling of lucidity, but I'm not calm, much less at ease. How can I be at ease with my unavoidable autobiography, and especially with my unavoidable *real* autobiography? Knowing that if I want to be good, I have to refrain from mythologizing it? No, art isn't self-sufficient, even if it does obey a higher law: it has to incorporate the world ... but *this* world? This world of *mine*? This ugly, unshapely world? I've always been aware that I have nothing more than what I've got, and here are those snips of green carpeting, those rocks and cereal boxes as proof. And I've always been aware that I know no more than I know, and that my knowledge is probably limited to how electrical circuits work, and perhaps how to deal with the capriciousness of certain suppliers and clients. If I want to be honest, do I then have to build one of those horrible circuits—try as I might, I can't find beauty in them—and cover it, for example, with the tablecloth on which a man of more mortifying experiences spilled some confessions? I'm afraid so. That would be my only possible artwork, my only true one, at any rate. I have no choice but to make peace with such a scarcity of choices. And on top of the tablecloth, continually sprinkled with water by some hidden mechanism, would be this orange life buoy.

Dad was still clinging to it when I went up to one of the corridors on deck, a few hours ago, following poor Sebastián, suddenly transformed into a nervous wreck. There was Dad, lying on the deck, totally soaked, staring blankly and incapable of uttering a word, while a crew member was helping him sit up. A man from the other group, who someone quickly identified as a doctor, was taking his pulse. I don't know if there was mouth-to-mouth, but if so it was over. Next to the doctor was Mom, pale as a sheet, with one stiff hand on Señor Ribot's shoulder. When Señor Ribot saw me, he pointed a finger at me and motioned impatiently for me to take over. But I knelt down next to Dad, not questioning even for a second that this was my place.

"What happened?"

Right now this question seems almost rhetorical, but at the time it expressed urgency and distress. Dad, unable to make sense of anything—least of all his own situation—barely looked at me, but took my hand and held it with a strength that, since it couldn't transmit calm, at least tried to show gratitude. Otherwise he was dazed and not speaking. The doctor told me not to worry, it had only been a "scare," and in a few moments he'd get over it. He suggested I take him back to his cabin and get him out of those wet clothes. Yusef appeared with some towels and a bottle of cognac. I wasn't scared. I mean, I wasn't afraid anything would happen to Dad; but I was obviously worried about what could have happened. The crowd around us was growing larger and more menacing.

"I saw him. He had his hands on that railing, looking out at the river. Suddenly he tipped forward and fell."

"He fainted, I saw him."

"I told you those railings were too low. This boat doesn't even meet minimum safety standards."

"It was the heat. It was the heat!"

Then I turned to Mom:

"Where were you? Did you see him?"

But she still clung to Señor Ribot, as though any other action would throw her into much more ominous depths than the ones

Dad had just been rescued from. She was the only one at this point still keeping the feeling of terror and danger alive. Among everyone else the "scare" explanation had won out. "Quite a scare," said Yusef as he forced Dad to drink several swigs of cognac straight from the bottle, which did in fact have a certain effect. After a few minutes the color returned to his face, he regained a rational look in his eyes, and he moved to get up. Rather overwhelmed by everyone's expectant stares, he whispered his first words.

"I'm all right, I'm all right."

Wrapped in a large blue towel with a compass rose pattern, still hunched over and dripping, clinging to the life buoy unconsciously with his hand, as though he still needed some sign of security, Dad let the doctor and me help him up, each of us taking a hand. Once he was up, we started to push through the crowd. His wet shoes made a terrible noise as he began to walk.

"Wouldn't you rather take them off?" asked the doctor.

"Give him a good shower," we heard. "That water is probably contaminated."

Thus we began our descent to the cabin, followed close behind by Mom, holding tight to Señor Ribot. Now that he had regained the power of speech, Dad wouldn't stop saying he was all right, and when we reached the cabin, the doctor thought it prudent to endorse this diagnosis. With a somewhat crude perspicacity he turned to Mom and asked whether she had any sedatives; she gestured vaguely at the bathroom.

"They'll do both of you some good."

With this he decided the case was closed and took his leave. Señor Ribot left even more quickly. Mom sat down on the bed, still completely out of it, while I took Dad to the bathroom, took off the towel and helped him get undressed. When we got to his trousers, modesty overcame him and he repeated that he was all right and could manage by himself.

"What happened, Dad?"

"Nothing. I fell over the railing like an idiot. What a scare."

"He didn't fall!" Mom's voice rang out suddenly, clear and powerful. "I saw the whole thing! The fool threw himself over."

"Is that true?" I asked him in a hushed voice.

"I fell."

I didn't leave the bathroom until I found Mom's supply of Lexatins in her toiletries and made sure Dad took one. Carrying another one and a glass of water, wondering whether there was really any difference between falling like an idiot and throwing oneself overboard like a fool, I walked back into the bedroom. Mom turned her nose up at the pill, saying she had taken one just three hours earlier, but I didn't have to insist to get her to take another. Then came the explanations, haltingly ambiguous. She had stepped away from the group by the railing on the prow, she got tired of waiting in front of the locks. She sat down under an umbrella, next to the pool, and asked a waiter to bring her some tea. No one was nearby, she was alone. She thinks she dozed off. When she came to, her tea, now cold, sat on the table next to her, and almost no one remained at the railing. She didn't see Dad. She was surprised she couldn't find him: these days he hadn't let her "out of his sights." She nonetheless drank her tea calmly. She felt good. She thought about going down to the cabin to get her book, she felt like reading. She got up, and as she turned down the corridor, she saw him at the other end. He was leaning over the railing, with his body—she noticed— "very far over." He looked at her. And then ... headfirst ... "it was horrible."

And then ... When Dad came out of the bathroom in a robe, after showering, he looked and sounded better. He apologized for being "so clumsy" and causing "such a fuss," but he was almost laughing. He looked at me especially. He got in bed and asked us to let him rest. Mom said that we all deserved to rest and wanted to leave it at that. Her expression was no longer dismissive nor angry: it only revealed the precise state of mind needed to reach a new pact. I should have taken a photo of them just then. Dad's life as a tragic subject had ended, and at dinner, while he was still asleep in the cabin, convalescent, Mom became the chief proponent of the "accident" hypothesis, which had now, with welcome swiftness, begun to replace the "scare" hypothesis, more grounded in fear. She had no shortage of allies. Everyone was eager to cheer up the glum family members, and even the man in the tuxedo seemed hounded by a lesser trouble. Señor Ribot again considered us worthy of his invitation as "high-value clients," perhaps because no one blamed him, or because no one else treated us like killjoys. Señor Ramírez and Señor Vidal were glad it was the last night we'd be spending on the boat, though they hastened to add that the boat wasn't Señor Ribot's, and he wasn't responsible for such accidents, which were probably commonplace in a country so ill-equipped for tourists, which still had a lot to learn from "us," and where you saw—Señor Ramírez had seen them—children running barefoot around exposed high-voltage power lines. In fact, Señora Ramírez hatched a charitable plan for such children, using the ship's booty: she planned to take the bath gel, the soap, the combs, and all the toiletries from her cabin and give them to those kids running around so dangerously. She advised Mom to do the same. When Sebastián asked, shortly thereafter, "Can you believe this nonsense about your father?" I made him laugh by replying I preferred the keen analysis of his own father.

Fortunately, all these appraisals took place in Yusef and Rachid's absence. Later they came over to ask how Dad was doing and remind us that after dinner we were having the "farewell party" for the cruise. But it would have been interesting—more interesting, in any case—to hear Rachid's reaction to the recommendations offered by the clients of Ripalux for the management of his country's tourist industry. This morning I heard him say he felt sorry for Iraq under the embargo, because Iraq, like Egypt, imported fifty percent of its food products, and he wouldn't want any country that depended on others as much as his did to be condemned to hunger. Tonight he remarked to Señor Nicolau, perhaps the nicest of the bunch, that last August, when Kuwait was invaded, there were some two million Egyptians working in Iraq and sending money home to their families, but now they were high-tailing it back.

After dinner, since we'd finally reached port in Luxor, I had the idea of slipping off for a bit and asked Sebastián if he wanted to join me. He was game, but Mom, whose energy hadn't flagged for even a moment all evening, was dead set against it:

"You're going to leave your father all alone?"

Isn't my father already all alone? An old and powerful fear compelled me to stay. Not even I could escape the party, which was full of games and entertainment. Mom held a magician's handkerchief. Señora Ramírez and I danced the potato dance, balancing a potato between our foreheads without dropping it. Meanwhile Sebastián laughed.

I've got the potato here, of course. It sums up my life, like the life buoy sums up Dad's. I suppose it will look a little cryptic in the installation. Pieces of an autobiography. Not that it means anything: perhaps it symbolizes my life up till tonight, and especially tonight, but at some point the autobiography might be different. Maybe I'm wrong and there will be other potatoes, other life buoys. There will be. Maybe, as a person of limited experiences, I'll set one in motion myself, or several—experiences that aren't very dignified, even for me. Maybe I'll wind up, God forbid, inventing myself. Right now I view that as a lesser evil. I'm not yet thirty. I have time to invent and uninvent myself many times over. I've come home drunk before and found the elevator out of service. I've had to walk up all six floors on foot. To keep my balance, I don't lift my eyes from the ground and I count the steps. One, eight, twenty, seventy-five. No, the hard part isn't deciding. I'll let it go. I'll let you go. I'll let go.

## II

The middle class doesn't have the simplest relationship to luxury. Right now all my caveats and hesitations are mixed with a positive, if unsettling, enthusiasm: the fact that it's unsettling, more than mixed, is what really complicates matters. I wouldn't be lying if I told you that at the front desk I stood in line behind Juliette Binoche, wearing black plastic glasses but looking as disheveled as ever, especially as she does in that Haneke film we just saw, *Caché*. The same bald attendant who checked her in, with three rows of gold piping on his cuffs—just one on his lapel—welcomed me in flawless Spanish, not only just as diligently but also just as warmly, something you don't associate with luxury. I was the only one, in short, who hesitated when I heard him ask for that specious proof of social existence, my ID, after confirming the reservation that Mercedes made in my name for Story Press. Professional credentials usually prevent closer inspection, though in this case that wouldn't have even been an issue, since, if we are what we do, then three awkward years drifting through the magazines published by the Story Press Group don't seem to have made it easier for anyone other than hotel clerks to identify me. It's certainly not easier for me. The fact that I still don't know what position I hold is no doubt less interesting than the fact that Story Press doesn't; and even so I must admit that when I stepped out of the taxi and saw this monumental hotel, and not the dependable modesty of my usual accommodations, I almost felt that for once someone was looking out for me. Standing behind Juliette Binoche, in a sumptuous wedding-cake lobby—a grand piece of stupefyingly white plasterwork, with a carpeted wooden imperial staircase opening onto an arcade gallery—one might wonder whether everyone sent abroad by Story Press enjoys these perks, or only those who, for reasons of professional prestige, have to somehow be at the same level of dignity as the person they're about to interview. True, until now the farthest I've been sent is Barcelona, and they've never before given me a break like this—an expression that's been ringing in my ears lately—to "work" someone of the stature of Dr. Van Booven, a man about whom I knew nothing five days ago and who I'm now convinced has changed and will continue to change the history of the world.

Can it be that *Enigma* wants me to meet the doctor in the hotel—tomorrow morning—so he won't think his statements will end up in some pulp rag? And if so, will the hotel provide sufficient cover, not just for the magazine, but for me, too? The attendant, at least, didn't raise an eyebrow, and without hesitation he handed me the magnetic key card, wished me a pleasant stay, and reminded me that "the butler on the executive club level" would see to my needs twenty-four hours a day. Just now, as if to offset the high, I bitterly recalled that the interview so insistently sold to me as a "big break" was originally intended for Víctor Comas, one of the stars of the group, and not for *Enigma* but for *Class*. If it wound up with me, an employee no one had taken much notice of for anything other than editorial tasks, it was thanks to a bit of serendipity whose causes, to say nothing of its effects, can't easily be determined. The effects I'll have to determine myself, I suppose, which means it's not my recollections that are bitter but my outlook.

Bitter, but also, I can't help it, thrilling: like a fool I've fallen into the electrifying trap of the "big break." I'm thoroughly prepared for the interview, I've read the doctor's three books and another by one of his detractors, I know more about him than Víctor Comas likely ever will, my English is excellent, and I'm confident enough in my editorial abilities to fill in any gaps and iron out any wrinkles. The columns, the archways, the coffered

ceiling, the triglyphs and metopes, the opulent molding—the
whole wedding cake, in short—and then the gilded elevator, the
wall lamps shaped like torches, lending a warm light to the long
hallway on the executive club level, the pre-announced arrival of
the butler, in his gray pinstripe suit, offering me a copy of today's
*El País* that I'd say had been ironed, or at least artistically folded,
this room with a view of the Amstel River, and far more furniture
than strictly necessary … all this is no doubt having its effect.
This room looks like something dreamed up by my aunt Isabel!
Though, to be fair to her—she deserves that much—I should
say it seems like something she created … and it would be, if
her hotels ranked above three stars. My aunt Isabel has always
subscribed to the fragile belief that having money isn't the same
as having "class," and even if repeating the line makes her seem
a bit anxious and sometimes very misguided—after all, you've
seen her Victorian dining room—we should acknowledge how
valiantly she strives for balance. I'm especially grateful to her for
being the only one in the family who dares to openly utter the
words "money" and "class," since my family has always, as you
know, shunned them both in favor of "work," out of an obsessive,
almost Protestant guilt and a pathetic fondness for false poverty.
My parents have always slummed it, and for them "class," which
they never mention, is an affectation if not a sin; and ever since
my siblings had to start working, I've noticed—with a certain
vindictive satisfaction, I admit—that they're begrudgingly starting to lay their former pretensions to rest. Meanwhile, I still talk
about "money" and "class" as much as I like, even though I know
it's poor form in this world where everyone pretends they live in
a social utopia, and only feels comfortable with their supposed
talent for discussing love affairs and real estate, because in this
crass meritocracy we've set up, privilege and bad luck are ban-
ished, and any blustering product of vulgarity or incompetence

is deemed worthy of merit … All right, all right, I'll stop. Don't get angry.

But back to Aunt Isabel. I know we have some friends who are architects, others who are interior designers, and they'd probably find this place terribly eclectic and kitsch—though once inside, they wouldn't turn up their noses or indignantly demand to be moved to another, more restrained hotel. But as my aunt says, luxury is not a style but a feeling, which means it's absurd to try to avoid eclecticism or kitsch. Hence, after the Italian-inspired lobby, the English mahogany staircase and, from what I see here in the brochure, the Turkish pool, with a whole ceiling covered in painted clouds, we have this French room. There's pastel pink carpeting with a miniature fleur-de-lis pattern and a veritable feast of maroon *toile de Jouy*, starting with the curtained back wall, where the bed is, and continuing over the headboard, the coverlet, the four large pillows, and even extending to a bench at the foot of the bed, perhaps intended for someone to sit down on as they take off their shoes. I lay down for a moment and didn't feel out of place among the luxuriance of landscape scenery; I could almost have been a fountain or a tree. From the window, under a dreary, overcast sky, the river perhaps offers a contrast in its wintry colorlessness. There are two potbelly nightstands that match a side table with a nickel silver wine chiller and three decanters of cut crystal, one for whisky, one for port, and one for cognac: the minibar of a gentleman. I don't feel like unpacking, but I have a walk-in closet room with a large mirror and a wardrobe with a light that goes on when the door is opened. In the bathtub I won't have to stoop, the showerhead is enormous. My mobile is lying on a desk under which both of my legs fit, even when crossed, something very unusual in a hotel room. I can relax or read on a lovely armchair with a footrest. Who said that Story Press doesn't treat its employees well?

I don't mind, not anymore, that all this was supposed to be for Víctor Comas; I think someone wanted me to see how the big names in the group travel. Nor do I mind these childish emotions sparked by my lavish, though not exactly tasteful, surroundings. In fact, I'm enjoying them. I feel good being worlds away from minimalism. I have a reassuring *feeling* of being provided with more than I need. The interview will go swimmingly.

I'm going to call Hendrick now. I feel like showing off—I was going to say sharing—all of this. I'll tell him to come over. I spoke with him earlier at the airport; he seemed eager to see me. When was the last time? Seven years ago? Well, you wouldn't remember, you and I hadn't met yet. I hope he hasn't changed much, because I like holding on to the few idealized memories I allow myself. Of course you know I won't force anything, but I will let things run their course. What if we messed around on this *toile de Jouy*? Doesn't he deserve that? I'm going to call him.

I'm writing now, nearly twenty-four hours later, from another hotel, on a table barely large enough to hold my laptop, sitting on a white plastic folding chair. My legs don't fit, either, in case you're wondering. And no, I'm not in a courtyard: they do have one out back, a tiny one, and as alluring as it must be in the summer, it's closed now. Outside everything's so cold and gray that it looks as though it might snow. So streamlined is this hotel that the same room serves as reception and breakfast buffet—two kinds of bread, two kinds of cheese, two kinds of cold cuts—with a long wooden table running from end to end with benches on either side, like in a student dining hall or a backpackers hostel. Conclusion: we had breakfast out. Don't think I'm in a bad mood, though. Perhaps still a bit embarrassed. And with new responsibilities I didn't ask for: I seem to have been, in Story Press, the pawn in a conspiracy that will turn out badly for someone. But I'm still laughing. In fact I've been laughing ever since last night. Mercedes just called to apologize again, and to tell me she got a good dressing down. In her last call—it must have been eight thirty—she hadn't gotten it yet, and was dreading it; she also had to tell me that Dr. Van Booven's agent postponed the interview until tomorrow. Is this the relief a convict feels at a reprieve? I'd like to think not! Even though you sometimes say I'm a "negative subject," that's true only in a very philosophical sense: because of what I flee and what I lack, but not because of what I refuse to do. Didn't I say I was in a good mood? Maybe my laughter is foolish, but it's not cynical.

I've got all day to think and write, in this room which isn't quite cozy, but isn't quite uninviting, either. I've got a magnificent view over the canal, the Insel, with its silent boats and still waters just a shade darker than the buildings, whose brightly lit windows I could even peer into, if anyone ever drew their curtains. No city invites voyeurism like this one, with its phony assurance that it holds no secrets. I also see bare trees, beautiful skeletons that the snow, if it falls, could blanket. I don't miss the Amstel's size, its arrogant breadth, its chromatic harmony with the *toile de Jouy*. In short, I have plenty to distract me if I get bored. I know you'd tell me to go out; I also know what you'd say if I replied that I'm not here on vacation and what I really want is to go home. Let me imagine I'm at home, and not writing for you.

It would be so easy to select everything I wrote yesterday and hit the delete key ... after all, if I'm not writing for you, why not get rid of anything that's compromising? Probably because, out of all that's happened since yesterday morning, my ridiculous enthusiasm isn't the most compromising part. Later there came other, more significant compromises, next to which my naive excitement shrinks to a mere anecdote. I suppose I'm still a little confused, but confusion, which provides so many people with a comfortable outlook, isn't a good vantage point for me. In this world it seems difficult not to get used to adopting a look of astonishment and supine incomprehension, not to let oneself get carried away by the current of mystery. But what I long for above all—perhaps because I work for *Enigma?*—is a little clarity. The fact is, of all the mysteries that have piled on top of me, I think I've solved most of them. But one, I admit, eludes me.

I'll start with that one, since it's the hardest and perhaps—I can't quite tell—the one that affects me the least. It's Hendrick's flat on the Prinsengracht, the Prince's Canal. The question of housing is I think going to be the leitmotiv of this trip: the transience—literal and symbolic—of hotels, which you can run away from, one way or another; the necessity, on the other hand, of taking possession of the place you stay, however transiently; the permanence—literal and symbolic—of the place you live, its hold on you, its power to make you identify with it; the places that make you want to take to your heels, and the places you wouldn't mind being trapped in; the rooms where you sleep. In the end I didn't manage to entice Hendrick to come to the hotel, as much as I would have liked for him to see me, after seven years, pampered in such luxury, and in spite of all my attempts to see that, between the two of us, we gave that luxury its due. When I called he said he couldn't meet right away: in fact he wasn't even in the city, but in an industrial park on the outskirts of town buying lumber. He suggested I go on a walk to his place, where he'd meet me within an hour at most. He took longer. I went on the walk, under the clouds and the cold, and I observed the lively darkness of this city I'd only known, radiant and calm, in summer or spring. I spent fifteen minutes lurking in front of an attractive building wider than most, but which somehow managed to stay true to the national tradition of narrowness. With its clean, schematic symmetry, punctuated by two mansard roofs topped with a rounded pediment, and linked at the base by a strange curving decoration, it gave the impression of being two buildings instead of one. Two lateral doors, which must have led to the apartments on either side, and one door in the middle, which must have led to the basement units, heightened this effect. With the characteristic air of elegant restraint and ingenious remedies—some strips of iron attached to the façade, like braces, seemed to prevent it from cracking—it had only three stories, plus the mansard attic, which stopped at exactly the same height, not an inch more, as the neighboring buildings. I surmised that the six windows on each floor corresponded to two apartments, and that, since the three on the left-hand side of the third floor lacked curtains—one more feature of the economy of privacy—they belonged to Hendrick's apartment. I was right. Only it wasn't three windows, as I'd soon discover, but four.

We started off in a very gentlemanly manner, embracing and telling each other that neither one had changed. "What do you mean?" I said in my defense. "I'm practically married." So you, it turns out, were our first topic of conversation, the impetus of my change, the driving force behind my new life. Don't worry, we quickly left you behind. Hendrick looks different and, not coincidentally, a bit like you. He isn't the unpresentable bohemian he was seven years ago, stuck as I was in a transitory state that had taken on a metaphysical dimension. Like me, he's become solid and fleshy, right at that age when bodies go from being an attribute of the soul to one of their most imperfect accidents. I don't mean that he's any less attractive, just that he used to not weigh anything and now he does—something which, at our age, when we're men and not boys, should be considered attractive.

He no doubt dyes his hair, but at a good salon; he takes care of himself, at a gym with guys who likely remind him of himself; and his clothes are in an intermediary stage between the age of black polos and the age of ripped jeans: let's not forget that his business is bars.

Where he's become most visibly solid isn't in his body but in his home, which is something that's never hard to relate back to the soul. Hendrick and I met each other at a stage we both knew was drawing to a close: we couldn't revive it, and had we tried to prolong it, we would have just slipped, surreptitiously and with pointless bitterness, into another very different age, an appallingly objective age that others would soon assign to us. Perhaps we could throw time—that spreader of false rumors, as a Wilkie Collins character says—off our track, but we weren't going to fool those scathing commentators known as everyone else. We were thirty-six years old, good-looking, artistic, and unique. We were always skittish, but we had to accept our social existence—that is, the fact that soon no one would let us get away with only being judged by ourselves. Our romance was wonderful because it grew out of the stirrings of this awareness, which united and secretly privileged us, and out of the final throes of that asocial energy, which became all the more furious and acrobatic for being nearly spent. On the other hand, the transitory nature of the relationship sustained us: I liked him because he was going to leave; he liked me because I was going to stay. And the knowledge that neither of us was going to take any steps in that romantic comedy of vagabonds made us—careful with what I'm about to say—feel real. We were furious that we were living out our last dream, but we enjoyed it like none other because it was the last. No doubt that made for another romantic comedy, but ultimately it, too, was the last one. The grand finale assured us a sort of future, something that until then neither of us had

had or, to be precise, something that each of us, at one point, had relinquished: it assured us that after "us" a new life awaited. But that's why it was so important for "us" to be a reality.

"Both of us were pretty fucked up," said Hendrick entertainingly yesterday, over lunch, "but instead of doing what two fuck-ups normally do when they meet, we opened our eyes and started laughing. Have you ever noticed how when two fuck-ups meet, they usually fuck each other over, so they can each think the other one's more fucked up?"

That's one way to look at it, a pretty good way. In any case, the "us" doesn't seem to have turned out too bad, appearing as it did right at a turning point: on the other side was a future, a new life, which led me to you and, for that matter, to your flat, which now feels—you're so damn generous—like mine. It led Hendrick to his two.

Because he actually has two flats. After hearing the story it would be wrong to call it a duplex: the third floor on the left and the attic above it, joined by a lovely shining stainless steel staircase. Steel tubes are, by the way, almost a statement of principles in his place, at least on the lower level, a diaphanous space that for the standards of central Amsterdam must be almost palatial, though offsetting this excess is a doggedly restrained functionalism. You, in this space, would have indulged in a glorious excess of furniture of every style and provenance, and I would have applauded you. Most likely you'd have chosen something like the enormous sofa, easily three meters long, upholstered in red, blue, and beige circles: Hendrick, in a sort of lapse, seems to have overcome his aversion to decoration for once. He's decidedly not a fan of the lavish or the varied or the superfluous, and steel tubing, straight or curved—on the armchairs with no back legs, on the sofa itself, on the large wooden table for twelve mysterious dinner guests, on the floor lamps—seems to be, in its unifying power, a force for order. A patriotic order, I'd go so far as to say. For isn't Dutch style at odds with the sense of luxury found in the eclectic, international grand hotel from which I was just yesterday cast out, as I seem to recall, with a certain sneer? Well, in a fair turnabout, here luxury and eclecticism have been expelled, and they don't seem to have been replaced by any other sentiment, since even fidelity to and respect for local tradition are curtailed by a rational modernism. This isn't a sentimental home. And, like any home with an abundance of entertainment technology—a large plasma screen presides over one of the walls—it's also not very personal. There are no photos or memories of another time; nothing old, nothing that looks inherited, preserved, borrowed, or even stolen; the enormous minimalist painting splashed with black ink was probably chosen by someone else, a professional. Still, there's a gigantic floor lamp mimicking an old silent film spotlight that might, once you give it some thought, call to mind a certain camp sensibility. But in general one has to walk over to the shelves and scrutinize the spines of the books, the CDs, the DVDs—abundant and meticulously arranged—to find any place for tastes, peculiarities, inclinations, idiosyncrasies. I got the impression that Hendrick had taken the idea of starting a new life very seriously. Not a trace of the old one remained.

I changed my mind a bit—a bit—when we reached the bed-room. When I saw the—pardon the detail—unmade bed, some shirts strewn about, a dresser drawer half-open, when I saw the spectacular tiled jacuzzi—almost a pool!—installed in front of the window, and next to it an outsized treadmill, I thought I might find there, if not exactly the outlines of a biography, at least traces of a body. The fact that Hendrick had made the attic, once a separate unit with several interior walls, as he explained, into a large open space reserved strictly for the most intimate pursuits, was somehow telling. It must be delightful to take a bath there looking out over the Prinsengracht, to drip water across the hardwood floor, to strut about naked, kiss someone, roll around in bed. For the first time I got a sense of Hendrick's new life, and for the first time I felt that the flat was full of memories. But they were, above all, my own memories; or perhaps, from a different point of view, I felt that ever since I stepped foot inside, the main memory was me.

I asked how long he'd been living there, how long the flat had belonged to him, where he lived before, and why he seemed to have kept nothing from his previous lives. Hendrick smiled and said that the lower floor he bought four years ago, but that the attic, which he acquired through a "fateful opportunity"—those were his words—he'd only had for a year and a half. Joining the two apartments had required costly renovations that took six months.

"I've really only been in this place, as it looks now, for about a year, that's why it all seems so new to you." I hadn't said that, I'd kept it to myself, but since he brought it up, I didn't hesitate to agree. We were still in the bedroom, where, as I said, I detected the first signs of life, for the moment only biological ones and—fine, yes—erotic ones, but enough to provide a base for us to recover our old familiarity. I think he started to see the same thing, that is, to see a sign in me: at that moment, with our backs to the large window and the gray of the winter morning, I must have been hazily, flatteringly back-lit.

"Everywhere in Europe," he said, "competition for floor space is brutal, but here I guarantee you it's worse."

"You didn't kill the previous owner of this attic, did you?" I asked, laughing. I noticed he changed his tone and expression.

"No," he answered, "he almost killed me."

The story that followed is long and shocking, though he didn't give me this advance warning, partly because, as I realize now that I know its unclear resolution, there was no way for him to do so; and also because, had he let me know, he would have in some sense given me a chance to escape. Instead, he suddenly embraced me; he pulled me tight to his chest, leaned his head down on mine, and before letting me go said: "I should have stayed in Madrid." I still didn't know what he was talking about, nor whether this vehement embrace, which in any case I enjoyed, came from his old or his new life, and I simply remarked that the competition for floor space probably wasn't any easier in Madrid, and that we'd have been happier as docile suburban animals rather than wild beasts intent on devouring the heart of the city. He reminded me that he actually was a suburban animal, raised in Amstelveen, a historic town that, by the time he was born, was already practically just another section of the airport, and that I, if he wasn't mistaken, came from the sunny island provinces, "way out in the Green Sea," and that this was probably what fueled our desire to "conquer" the big city.

"We wanted to conquer it even when we were pariahs. Maybe that's why we were," he said.

"As for me," I replied, "I think I still am a pariah—and not only that, but I've been conquered. Our apartment is seventy square meters."

"But I bet that's big enough, isn't it?" he asked, convinced of my response.

"Most days," I answered. He embraced me again, as though I'd admitted defeat, and I then got the feeling, so unlike what I'd felt a moment earlier, that our "new lives" were very different. The embrace caught me off guard; I was standing on the wide bathtub shelf and I wound up sitting down inside it, almost without meaning to. I took out a cigarette. Hendrick hesitated a moment, as if he didn't think we'd stay there, and looked at the staircase; then he walked to the bed and came back with an ashtray and a chair.

I understood quite well, even before entering his flat, as I waited between the lovely canal and the lovely building, that Hendrick was no longer a "pariah," if he'd ever been one. I couldn't have imagined, though, that he'd become "a sort of civic hero," as he put it, to say nothing of the way he acquired such an unusual dignity. Underneath it all there lies, he says, the need for floor space, central locations, historic grounds, and sun-filled views that won't let go of an ambitious kid from the suburbs.

When, over the years, these ambitions have been dashed, diluted, thickened, revived, and dashed again several times over; when this kid has left behind the community yards and public housing of his childhood, spent his youth in basements and squatter's flats, overcrowded apartments on the outskirts of town, bohemian houseboats, or tiny studios rented by some friend; when he's become a man, traveling the world from Ibiza to Lima, from Delhi to Madrid, sleeping on the beach or the roadside, picking up jobs and leaving them behind, wanting to stay and wanting to go … well, when that man takes one final trip and returns to the city that never belonged to him, he discovers that the desire to make it his hasn't died. To be precise: perhaps, at thirty-six, after all that globetrotting, his desire was less aggressive; it may have also been more melancholy, an attempt to identify with the city, a plea for belonging. He even reestablished contact with his family. He acted with intelligence and calm, not with resentment. Intelligence showed him the way: in his nomadic experience, he learned the laws of hospitality backward and forward, everything from what a guest needs to what a parasite demands. He knew what it took to open a bar. His calm, on the other hand, imbued him with perseverance and restrained him at the critical junctures, the times when, for example, a customer, a supplier, or a racketeer, or any part of the business of nightlife, revived his nimble reflexes to pack his bags.

All this is the foundation. Let's skip the loans, the scrapes, the lucky breaks, and the slow work of prosperity, and just focus on the achievements. In just two years Hendrick had, in effect, a new life, one solid and plentiful enough to support a mortgage for eighty square meters on the Prinsengracht. He was happy and full of energy: shortly after moving into his new home, he noticed that the unit next to his was a rental and was already after the owner in case he ever decided to sell. True, he'd already fulfilled his needs and desires: he didn't harass the owner, but he used flattery and persistence and long-term strategy, and as he lived in his eighty square meters he dreamed of what he'd do when he had one hundred and sixty. He'd never owned a home before, and he thinks all those years of uncertain housing had conditioned him not to see this one as his last. Hence it was less a case of expansionist mania than a holdover from his earlier groundlessness; and if Hendrick so prematurely desired to double the size of his home and achieve a kind of vastness, it was only to become more firmly grounded. In some sense he'd concluded he wouldn't be grounded in anyone else, as he saw happen to "the luckier ones" (he looked at me); his talent for and inclination toward transience seemed under control, but from time to time they flared up again, because killing off a life, according to him, takes at least as many years as have been spent living it.

"I married my house," he said, "and I had no intention of getting a divorce."

Meanwhile, the people who saw Hendrick's house spared him reasons for divorce, passing through but not staying; some of them, a bright young man who made ecstasy in the back of a truck, came and went suspiciously often, even daily for a few months. But none of them became that "someone else" who would threaten to uproot him, now that he'd finally found his grounding. Besides, his wariness had historical roots: in a city robbed from the sea, built up over the years at great cost atop tons and tons of clay poured into the marshes, dry land, the product of sheer ingenuity and patience, seemed more valuable than people. One could take pride in it, and in the management of scarcity: next to land, human scarcity couldn't compare.

Pride is a good ally for groundedness, and gives solitude a dignified dimension: eighty square meters. A proud solitude can withstand indignities without losing its structural integrity. The man who lived in the attic looked to be rather undignified: Hendrick had seen him in one of his bars before he realized he was his upstairs neighbor. With a laughing curiosity, he had to associate the muffled cries and the furious movements he occasionally heard through the ceiling at night with the sporadic, solitary customer who once in a while had a few beers in the bar, predictable only in the classic leather gear he wore. He asked around: others had noticed him, too, but no one knew him. Despite his look, no one had seen him in a leather bar or a sex club; but he could also have just been hard to spot in those environments, given their clientele's fondness for uniforms and willingness to dress alike. Hendrick found him attractive, but above all nearby: if he hadn't lived above him, if he had never run into him on the stairs, he'd probably never have noticed him. The sexual theater suggested by leather and zippers held no appeal for Hendrick; he liked tattoos and shaved heads, but with a different look; he liked aggressive men, but with a different manner. He started observing, when he saw him, how he interacted with others: his rigid, totem-like weight, his aloof but rather crude silence, the way he wiped beer from his mouth with the back of his hand, the way he obliged when others—generally younger, scrawnier, rather pale men—dared to elicit a response

from him. At home, when he heard noises, sometimes very loud
ones, moans and cries he couldn't quite make out, he imagined
a group scenario and smiled. At the bar he noticed that, unlike
him, his "victims" never showed up again. Of course, Hendrick's
bar wasn't really one of "those bars": he took pains to attract the
least codified clientele possible, though this just meant that it
drew a mixed crowd, and the usual tribes were always sure to find
one of their own. The city felt too small to be exclusive: everyone
ended up going everywhere.

Anthropological considerations aside, there was, as I said,
the question of proximity. If they said hello in the stairway, they
couldn't ignore each other at the bar. One day they did speak, and
Hendrick noticed right away that he readily dropped the mask
and answered him as a neighbor; they praised the Prinsengracht,
compared their floor space (he had a little more than half, forty-
five square meters) and their ownership history (he had bought
his attic two years earlier). They vaguely promised to stop by
each other's place; he said he had a flower shop, and Hendrick
burst out laughing. "I'm a man of contrasts," he added, showing a sense of humor; besides, Hendrick had occasionally heard
a piano sonata coming through the ceiling in the afternoon,
which suggested he was a man of culture. Another day, however,
when Hendrick said hello to him at the bar, he didn't drop the
mask: that night he wasn't interested in being a neighbor, and
instead wanted to test him, so to speak. In case there was any
doubt, he said: "I bet you wouldn't mind experimenting," to
which Hendrick immediately replied: "I'd rather just have fun.
I've always been a bit of a hippie." This brought about a period of
coolness. Hendrick caught the invitation and declined; nevertheless, he sometimes surprised himself thinking about it. The guy
wasn't his type; nor there was anything young or pale or scrawny
about Hendrick. Now they hardly spoke. Neither seemed to

want anything from the other. Or rather, the neighbor seemed to be happy with anyone willing to "experiment." Hendrick felt sure he was past the age of experimentation, and had been long before he arrived at the Prinsengracht; but he was also certain that, if fun was what he was after, he'd been having less and less. Sex had become a healthy routine, like a workout sequence or a vitamin supplement; not wanting to be tied down, he was amused by how many things aside from health many of his lovers projected onto it. One way or another sex had lost its mystery, if it ever had any. Had it ever, really? The answer was always no, but the interesting thing was that the question kept coming up. How long had he been wondering about these things? The last time he could remember thinking about them was when he was a complete hippie, not just a bit of one, and back then he had a theory of "seminal universalism." I asked whether I'd been a particle in that universe; considerately, he replied that what we had was personal.

In any case, a few weeks later, he was still asking the question, hands and feet tied to the bedposts of his own bed, with a dog collar around his neck and the man from the flower shop yanking on it. The answers he came up with didn't quite satisfy him—he realized he wasn't powerful enough to wish to be dominated—and he began to regret having walked onto a stage where he didn't know his role. In any case he was willing to continue, on the off chance that he'd find it, or simply because he'd entered into a sort of agreement and wasn't about to break it now—despite the fact that, viewed from the pillow, where his head lay turned to the side, the lineup of "toys" that the man was taking out of a military duffel bag wasn't very promising, and his use of them, when he began, was even less so. He made an effort to concentrate: maybe he was missing something. But the toys were being pushed deeper and deeper, and the only thing he felt

was a little discomfort, a certain incontinence, and—later—pain.
Furthermore, certain words that went along with all this motion,
and were intended to stimulate his sense of obedience, sounded
only tedious to his ears. He started to think he wouldn't be able
to cross the supposed threshold. Physically he was paralyzed, and
on the symbolic side, he was discovering he was decidedly indifferent to the pleasures of resistance, and took no pride or satisfaction in serving or enduring. Nor was he drawn to the power of
submission, the mystical desire for annihilation: such sophisticated psychological processes, reserved perhaps for loftier spirits,
never quite got going. His body was defined, complete, no longer
open to new configurations, other possibilities. Prolonging the
scene, at that point, would have entailed deferring to an extravagant courtesy, so he apologized and said they'd better quit. The
guy seemed to enjoy that request, as though he'd been waiting
for it; he drew his head near, pulled hard on the leash attached to
the dog collar, spit in his face and slapped him. "Shut up, pig!" he
shouted. Hendrick grasped then that he was tied up for real and
had devoted considerable thought to his own concerns but very
little to those of the man now staring at him with a whip in his
hand. As a last attempt, he remembered hearing that the BDSM
contract, foreseeing such emergencies, kept a security clause up
its sleeve; this clause was the safe word "stop," and it meant that
everything had to end. He said it. Several times. As a result he
was gagged: "It's too bad I won't hear you scream, but you asked
for it, worm." In short, the game wasn't getting out of his hands:
there was simply no game. Did he find it odd now that the safe
word didn't work? Too late he learned how an established code
can provide cover to an intruder who uses the game pieces to not
play. Hendrick really thought he was going to be killed.

   An eternity later—he estimates two to three hours—he was
standing in the shower trying to wash off the panic, the shards

of glass, the blood mixed with semen, the urine and spit saturating his wounds. The water didn't make him feel any better. His neck was blue, he was still bleeding between his thighs and from the countless lesions on his back. He was very frightened, he vomited, could barely stand up; he also felt a tremendous rage and anger, especially at himself. He cursed himself for walking into a situation he should have stayed away from, and for not seeing in advance how things could go sour; for not seeing his aggressor coming, when now he saw him all too clearly; for having spoiled his healthy diet with such antiquated, ridiculous, "unwholesome" mysteries. But that didn't matter now. What mattered was how much pain he was in and how afraid he felt for his own ravaged body. As much as he could, he was willing to keep it all to himself, not out of shame—the acts of a deranged man could cause him no shame—but out of a perhaps overly strict, puritanical principle of responsibility for his own mistakes. His aggressor had untied him before leaving to go back to—good lord—the apartment upstairs: "Just so you don't forget it was consensual, bitch." Nevertheless, here nothing would be "his own" or "for himself": it was, ironically, first and foremost a question of health.

He called a cab and went to a hospital, where the staff examined and treated him, of course, but also filed a report: they were required to. There, Hendrick got his first sense of how a private act, once it lands you in the hospital, always becomes a public act. In fact, according to the social worker and an on-call volunteer from a rights group, it becomes public even if it's kept confidential. The police didn't mince words: a crime had been committed. This was their conclusion, it should be noted, and not their premise: in fact, at first everyone practically lectured him for not having the "case" more carefully prepared: he knew his aggressor, he invited him into his home, he initiated consensual

sexual contact with him, and to top it off he "allowed" himself
to be untied. Under those circumstances, he'd have a hard time
proving anything! Hendrick, offended, said he'd come to the
hospital to get treated, not to provide evidence or build a "case."
They said he had a responsibility to file charges; he countered
that it was funny, given the state he was in, that they were talking to him about responsibilities. These social authorities, rather
irritated, struck back with a whole arsenal of big words. Stunned,
Hendrick heard them speak of an offense to his dignity, of a loss
of respect, and even of his status as a "human being"; not even
in the best times of seminal universalism had he heard such
nonsense. What made them think, he asked them, that a crazy
person could have offended him? Why did they assume he'd
received other harm, aside from the purely physical? For all they
knew, his pride might be too strong for him to feel humiliated.
He couldn't believe that there, in a cold hospital room, injured
and upset, he was being subjected to an interrogation about values. "You're talking like what happened was an accident. Can't
you see you've been raped, and that by talking like that you're
naturalizing the assault?" asked the social worker.

He couldn't express just then—though he would a few days
later, once things had calmed down a bit—a philosophical
thought that had accompanied him through rough times and
which in his current circumstances would be of no small service:
"Violence and misfortune have been suffered by others before us.
The same kinds. We're not the first, nor will we be the last. We
lack even that privilege." When I heard him say this, I said nothing. Still, he doubted that this depersonalization of suffering, this
loss of the self in the timeless succession of pain, would interest
those dignity specialists. The decisive twist came from the police,
who brought him down to earth. "How about we take you home
and tuck you in to the same bed where you were raped? Are you

going to say hello to your neighbor tomorrow when you run into him on the stairs? Tomorrow, and every day for the rest of your life?" That got to him. His home had been compromised, and so had, once again, his new life. For a moment he seemed to have forgotten that the asshole was his neighbor. "Do you think it's right," the officer went on, "to let the criminal do this again, to you or to someone else, and use the crime itself as his alibi?" Hendrick knew that the crime wouldn't happen to him again, though he wasn't sure that, with a stairwell separating them, he wouldn't remember. As for letting it happen to someone else, which also suggested that he wasn't the first, he didn't hesitate: he never wished harm on anyone, and tried to prevent it whenever he had the power to do so. Now he had that power. He also didn't mind the word "criminal." It was better than calling him "crazy," and it put his neighbor in the only community space— the space of the law and its defenders—that he felt his neighbor belonged, and the only one, moreover, he was willing to enter.

The defenders of the law were not at all pleased to see their field somewhat reduced, but they had to make peace with this unprecedented form of collaboration. Eventually—the trial lasted a long time—they even came to admire, if not quite to understand, his strange lucidity and eccentric disregard for any personal circumstances, something they weren't used to seeing in a docket that included serious criminal charges. The community wasn't used to it, either, but in the end, they also came around, slowly. It wasn't easy, because, as I said, the case was delicate. Hendrick was up against a shrewd criminal whose testimony would be given equal weight to his own, and who would no doubt take advantage of certain points that the community's mindset so often shares with the criminal's, such as the belief that the victim was "asking for it." As for the victim, he was astonishing: he didn't seem especially traumatized and refused to receive

psychological treatment; he declared he felt no shame; he didn't
see his life divided in two; he demanded only restitution, to the
greatest extent allowed by law, for a physical assault in which he
refused to let anyone symbolize anything: not the criminal, not
the community, and certainly not himself. Yet his idiosyncratic
take on the case proved persuasive, not least because three of the
first people to be persuaded were previous victims, prepared to
follow Hendrick's example without shame, having been freed of
fear and guilt. He couldn't help smiling when he saw that only
one of them was a pale, scrawny young man; the other two men
were the same age as him, and just as stocky. They made a tremendous contribution, of course. The defendant faced not one
but four charges; and the community, more surprised by the
day, ended up listening without shame, and one might even say
without psychology, to the individual arguments of four different
people. They would have been civic heroes even if they'd lost the
case. But they won and the criminal is still serving time.

To pay the court fees, and the restitution that the other three
victims demanded in a civil suit, the criminal had to sell his
attic and his flower shop. Hendrick didn't hear about it, but
the real estate wizard who owned the apartment next door did.
He bought the attic, intent on making a profit, and remembering Hendrick's interest in increasing his floor space, offered it
to him, not without a certain circumspection considering the
victim's possible feelings. Also, I should add, not without a certain solidarity, because there was no one in the whole city who
didn't support their new civic hero, except for some imam from
the suburbs who raised his voice against decadence and whom
everyone prudently ignored. Hendrick, as you can imagine, was
caught off guard by the offer of the attic, and at first it struck
him as ghastly: it would be like paying for his own justice. The
owner let him think it over, and he took his time; he asked to

be shown the attic once it was vacant. Free from memories, it was forty-five square meters, and he could easily imagine them without interior walls, at the top of a steel spiral staircase. By then his activism against symbols was highly developed, and this must have helped him not see more than he saw. He called an architect, who saw only space. He also thought that, if he ever had to fear his memories, a good way to keep them in check was to occupy them. His home belonged to him: so would any other home he owned.

The truth is, this man's self-assurance has never faltered. Seeing him in his flat now, in the only room that until then reminded me of him and only him, I understood how his arrangement could be considered a victory. I pointed out that the bed had no columns or bars or handles of any kind where someone could be tied up; he laughed that he always learned from his mistakes. It's strange, I thought, that he no longer slept on the lower floor, the place where he was raped, but rather in the room where the rapist had slept. In any case, if he used to have columns or bars, he no doubt had an antique bed, which led me to infer that his old flat, before the addition of the attic, must have had a different style of furniture, less modern than what he had now. He confirmed my hunch: as soon as he decided to take out another mortgage, he also decided he'd renovate the whole flat, getting rid of everything, because his old furniture, the few things he'd accumulated since returning to Amsterdam for good, didn't fit in his new plan.

"So is there another life," I asked, "after the new life?"

"Looks that way," he responded.

"Do we always have to keep changing, then?" I pressed.

Hendrick smiled but said nothing. At that moment I felt that his (now) one hundred twenty-five square meters did symbolize something after all, and that he himself, as he thought about it, trembled a little.

So there are always new lives. We always run the risk that one life will end and we'll have to start over. Now that I've found you, I hate the thought of such misfortunes. I don't want anything to happen to me. And when something like that affects a house, it passes through the walls like a ghost, and like a ghost it settles into the nooks and crannies. That was the feeling I had, as the story drew to its close yesterday, in the attic, throughout Hendrick's house, as if he'd called a ghostbuster to purge it and hadn't wholly succeeded. I even thought I recognized the ghost of the florist. At one point a cat wailed. And now, as I write this in a miniature hotel room, the feeling is back. I think I'll take your advice. I'm going to go out for a bit.


I'm back. Not five minutes after I stepped outside, it began to snow, blanketing the trees and covering the tops of cars and the blue boat covers in white. A wind picked up and I enjoyed walking against it. The flakes fell horizontally, stinging my face, thick needles that refused to touch the ground; but finally the great watery mouth of the canal swallowed them up like candied almonds. I stopped on one of the bridges; then I walked down to one of the banks, knelt on the ground, and stuck my hand in the water. It was freezing, of course, but it's what I needed, a way to come back to myself. The lives of others surround me: at one time they penetrated me, at another they remained outside, and now they wrap me like a cloak; sometimes I need to take it off. The cold, dark water was my coatrack. Besides, as I was getting up I noticed something on the ground by my shoes, a tiny thing that looked like a rusty thimble; I thought back to when

LUXOR 119

I spent all day picking things up off the ground, and I pocketed it. Don't worry: I know we have an agreement about our living space and our respective hoarder tendencies, but this is the only thing I picked up, and it could be an antique! Can you imagine how many beautiful relics must lie at the bottom of these canals? The secret, forgotten, gloriously useless things stored up in these vast, orderly lanes of water? Really, Hendrick is too perfect: always prepared for the future, courageously aware that anything—everything—can become the past, and at the same time able to talk about it, to accept it, in spite of the dangers. Just as he accepted that question from another time about the mysteries of sex, which had such deadly consequences, or just as he accepted me: I may not be deadly or stupid, but I do come from another time. I, who looks back on the past, albeit unsentimentally, and only because there I find facts, not the stupid vagueness that lies in the indemonstrable future. I, for whom sex still holds great mysteries. I, who am no stranger to the pleasures—the very risky pleasures, it's true—of symbolism. I, who in short believe that without symbolism there is no pleasure. I, who would have felt humiliated and offended, and whose life would have been broken and fallen apart if ...

As I said, Hendrick's place had started to feel like a haunted house to me, and perhaps I, after feeling like one of its few memories, began to feel like just another ghost. In any event I suggested we go out to lunch. I didn't yet dare ask him to walk me back to the hotel, so he chose a restaurant near his house, where they treated him like family. Over lunch we spoke—I did—only of you. Strangely, that's how we regained our old familiarity, at least in my view. My story, with its shipwrecks and rescues, and a long idyll in a steamy jungle of seventy square meters, was more romantic than his; to be sure, it lacked civic virtue and provided no inspiration to the community, but for that very reason it took on the quality of a fragile adventure, the charm of a tiny island in a stormy sea. I told him about our home and felt certain of the fascination of our private life. I got excited and began to tell him about the hotel. He was familiar with it, and thought it dreadful, though he admitted it was one of the few monumental structures in the city, built, along with other buildings, by a Jewish entrepreneur in the nineteenth century. I started criticizing the functionalist harmony of the furniture in his flat, and praising my hotel's lavish nonsense and Juliette Binoche's disheveled hair, and steeped in white wine I won him over with that outrageous rapture, he said, of southern blood. By the time the coffee came, the last seven years had vanished, and with them our home and his, and to my satisfaction we found ourselves, just like old times, in public with nowhere to go. We had no choice but to go back to the hotel.

We were both, I think I can say, very aroused. Awaiting us, however, was one of those stupid vague futures that choose the worst moment to, stupidly, take shape. As I walked through the lobby, the bald man at reception called my name, rather nervously, as though facing a professional ordeal. I walked over to him, with a slight, absurd fear that guests weren't allowed, as though we were in a Colegio Mayor or a hotel in Havana, and smiling delicately he told me he was afraid there had been a mistake. The reservation made in my name wasn't really in my name, or rather it was, but only because of a mix-up. The name that should have appeared on the reservation wasn't mine but another guest's, "Mr. José Hayedo, CEO of Story Press." This "regrettable misunderstanding" had come to their attention just two hours earlier, with the arrival of the man in question, a frequent guest at the hotel, who asked for his room and found it had been booked in my name, not his. Fortunately the hotel had a free room for Mr. José Hayedo, but they were nonetheless obliged to ask me to leave mine. They tried to reach me by telephone from Madrid, after some actions taken—with irritation, I imagine—by Mr. José Hayedo, but to no avail (once I met up with Hendrick, the truth is, I quite intentionally switched off my mobile). And in fact Mr. José Hayedo had left a message that he wanted to see me, at six o'clock, in the hotel's lounge. In the meantime, they had to ask me once again to leave and move to another establishment whose address was written on a piece of paper. "It's a nice hotel," he said without conviction. And he added: "We'll escort you to the room and help you with your luggage. In the meantime, I'll call a taxi and get your identification ready. Please don't forget it." And: "You don't know how deeply we regret this misunderstanding, sir." He motioned to a uniformed man who came over at once and received detailed instructions in Dutch. Hendrick, by my side, hesitated: seven years ago he would have laughed, now he didn't know how much he could allow himself to. Two minutes earlier we were at one end of time's tunnel; now we stood at this end, unsure how well we knew each other. I made things easier by putting on an appropriately serious face intended to show I regarded this setback with a certain degree of irony. That degree, in my head, was becoming increasingly dramatic. But in my attempt to neutralize it, I hit upon a rather unusual solution. I asked him to come up to my room with me, and there, in front of the watchful eye of the man in the uniform, as I pretended to search for something I might have forgotten— remember, I hadn't unpacked my suitcase—I began telling him, in Spanish, each and every one of the things I'd have done to him on top of the *toile de Jouy*. Hendrick was scandalized by my obscenities but nearly died of laughter. He told me he'd once defiled a *toile de Jouy* in this hotel, but it was green, not maroon. Green! It must have been fantastic.

I won't hide the fact that my happy remedy, which at one point dangerously ignited our libidos, lost its effect as soon as we left the room and I lugged my suitcase and mobile downstairs. It chilled completely once we got into the cab and I handed the driver the note with the address of the new hotel. The disappointment, which I'd neutralized until then, now gave way before two important witnesses: Hendrick himself, who I'd wanted to seduce with cheerful promises of ostentatious luxury, and my mobile, which contained embarrassing proof of the enthusiasm we'd shown that morning. Right away Hendrick asked me to stay at his place, but the memory of what had happened there, and of how little had happened between us, felt too recent for his proposal not to fall into the dense and growing web of riddles in which I was trapped. I said something noncommittal, but I knew I had the cab driver on my side. Meanwhile I turned my attention to other enigmas: I had four voicemails from Mercedes on my mobile, each one more frantic than the last. She'd gotten the names mixed up when making the reservations. She apologized profusely. She'd be getting an earful. In the last message she repeated for the fourth time the name and address of my new accommodations where, she said, I shouldn't "worry" that they were expecting José Hayedo, because they'd already been notified. Mr. Hayedo was perhaps the toughest knot in the web. What was he doing in Amsterdam? Why did he want to see me? The prospect of returning to the hotel I'd just been expelled from to meet with the CEO of the Story Press Group gave an ominous depth to the expression, until then merely perfunctory, "regrettable misunderstanding." Would I, in fact, come to regret it more? Had others created new problems of understanding that would affect me? I sent a message to Mercedes: "New trajectory. Facts on the ground." I still wasn't thinking about Víctor Comas.

The hotel, on the banks of the Insel, which from then on I had to consider my place, turned out to be so cramped, and such a pure example of the dreadful conditions of urban housing, that as soon as we stepped out of the cab Hendrick insisted once again on taking me back to his flat. He didn't understand whether my "company" considered me a journalist, a backpacker, or an intern, and in any event, couldn't I see that I'd be more comfortable on the Prinsengracht? "It's already late," I said by way of excuse. "Besides, it's not so bad, you'd think we'd never slept anywhere like this before." Granted, this was a little hypocritical on my part, after the unpleasant surprise I'd just been given and my unwillingness to change hotels; but that's why the Prinsengracht didn't make my fate look any better. Sorry, I was in a fatalist mood and chose to give in. This is a work trip: if I'd accepted the conditions Story Press offered, I'd also have to accept its blunders. Today I don't subscribe to that silly reasoning, but yesterday I wouldn't budge. Poor Hendrick—there's not even a bellhop here—carried my suitcase up the narrow staircase up to my second-floor room, carefully registered under my name at the front desk, no questions asked. Inside we found more cramped efficiency, presented with domestic tidiness: the lamps, the TV, even the telephone are all mounted on the wall, the bed was nicely made, and the single small table (the one I'm writing on) had a vase with dianthus flowers. The drape liner is trimmed in a diagonal stairstep pattern, and the bathroom, which is horrible, has a soft pink shower curtain. Hendrick didn't give up: "You really want to stay here?" "Well," I replied unconvincingly, "here they know where to find me." Such inspiration: "where to find me." I sought relief by opening the curtains: in the fading view of the Insel no one was drowning. I think Hendrick was a little offended when he left, though he remained hopeful I'd change my mind: he made me promise that after my interview

with José Hayedo was over I'd call him to go to dinner. I agreed.
Now he's no longer offended and I've even made, or half-made,
another promise.

Speaking of Hendrick, he just called. He's coming by to get
me. I'll go eat with him and then continue.


It hasn't stopped snowing and Hendrick looks magnificent in his
gray overcoat, now flecked with white: he looks like a large soapy
dolphin. The truth is, up until now I haven't fully appreciated
his magnificence. Last night, when he took me out to his bars,
I saw he was well-known in the community, but then, frankly,
I figured he was giving me a tour of his domain, and that the
community was more or less limited to *his* community. Today
I'm not so sure. I don't know if he chose it on purpose, but even
in the small (of course) restaurant he took me to, everyone knew
him. You know that such popular people make me uncomfortable, because I think at any moment they'll stop paying attention
to me. Today, surprisingly, I felt proud to be out with him, or
more accurately—this didn't occur to me last night—proud that
he wanted to give me that kind of publicity. I think at least one
of the people who approached him he didn't know: "I have no
idea who that guy is," he told me after saying goodbye to a young
man with a very dark complexion, probably from Suriname.
The others—an older woman in lace, a blond young man with
jagged teeth, a thickset, formal man—each had their delicate
biography; nevertheless, the restaurant staff treated him fairly
neutrally, which I assume means that, in the end, he didn't just
take me out to a place his friends owned.

When I first met Hendrick he was already someone everybody loved, one of those people who don't really need grounding

because, as I've said, the whole of humanity is grounding enough
for them, or maybe because they themselves are; and on their
way, they dredge up everything that the sea floor offers them,
an endless number of creatures and shells and a rich deposit of
mineral nutrients. But he wasn't yet a historical figure, and land
and history, and the instability of foundations, came up often in
our conversation today. He asked me if I'd noticed that the building that houses my "new hotel" is braced, like his, with those
black iron bands between each floor. I hadn't noticed, though
I did notice the ones on his house, and I said I figured it was
an architectural remedy to repair cracks or prevent them from
appearing. I was right: no building in Amsterdam was safe from
the weakness of its foundations. How lucky we were in other
countries, with our "eternal" ground of rock and stone. Did I
know that fines in Amsterdam were once paid in stones? At the
end of the fifteenth century, and very much against its will, the
city accepted the council of its protector, Emperor Maximilian
I of Austria, to reinforce its defenses and build a wall, as it was
prey to frequent incursions. The city felt a wall would ruin its
already famous commercial openness and would limit its access
to the fields and farms so closely bound to it; but even so it set to
work. The process was long and costly. Proof of stone's scarcity,
and of just how highly valued it was, can be found in certain
municipal documents of the era. One states, for example, that a
widow named Trudem or something like that, fined for insult-
ing a tax collector, was given a choice between paying in cash,
making a pilgrimage to Lille (now in the north of France, on the
Belgian border), or providing six thousand stones for the wall.
The wall was inaugurated by Maximilian in 1507; a century later,
it no longer existed. When I returned to my hotel, I admired
the braces, watching how the snow slipped down beside them.
I wanted the canals to freeze. And I wanted to see Hendrick in

his overcoat, on another unstable foundation, skating steadily across them.

I started drifting off in front of the screen and I lay down for a bit. I must have slept deeply, dreaming, for an hour and a half. Such grogginess, still. Was it those mutant lamb chops I ate, thick as a T-bone and large as pork chops? Back to yesterday afternoon. Back to my return to the frozen banks of the Amstel and to the lounge in the international hotel I'd been thrown out of in the morning. The main characters are the CEO of Story Press and one of his employees. The time, six in the evening. I arrived punctually. I hardly had to wait, sitting in a small armchair upholstered in a watery green damask, across from a matching sofa whose size I was terrified of sharing and therefore reserved for my "host." Over my head hung a gigantic gold-framed lantern, and at my side stood an end table with an impressive collection of international publications, all of them— ah, the memories!—carefully folded and ironed. On the other side, against a wall, stood a three-piece mahogany étagère that nearly reached the ceiling, whose glass cabinets displayed nothing. The intermittent and always suggestive state of emptiness one finds in hotel furniture takes on, in shared spaces, a rather bleak permanence. As for the rest, the interior aspired to evoke a British gentlemen's club, practically without gentlemen. Mr. José Hayedo didn't take long to fill this other kind of emptiness, and the first thing he did, after greeting me, was to look seriously at his watch: clearly for him, too, this was just a place to pass through. Still, I didn't need him to state his intentions to see that even in such places a passing CEO leaves significantly different traces than an employee.

He, for example, had "just over an hour to get to know me" if he wanted to get to the Amsterdam Arena on time, "the first stadium in the world with a retractable roof," to see a European

Cup match between Ajax and Inter Milan, which was why he was in town. Not even in my wildest anxieties did I expect the CEO of Story Press to devote such an extended length of time to "getting to know me," nor would I have imagined he had such a tedious schedule that he needed a visiting employee to fill the dead time. The two possibilities weren't, in the end, mutually exclusive. Clearly I provided the entertainment, that passive entertainment valued by people who can't entertain themselves without an audience, no matter how small; and clearly, too, people so in love with the sound of their own voice can draw flattering conclusions from passivity itself. Víctor Comas, though not present, was the topic at hand: would another employee, who would hardly need to know him—me, for example—agree to, let's say, stab him in the back? Or would that employee instead feel bound by some abstract notion of loyalty, or a sense of his rightful place? By saying nothing, an employee can say a great deal, and show "what he's made of," as Mr. Hayedo would no doubt put it: I'm ashamed to confess that I showed him what I'm made of, or at least gave him grounds to think so. At the same time I feel certain, and I'll put this in italics, that *I couldn't do anything else.* Hopefully this serves less as an excuse than as evidence of the trap my position led me into: as an employee, my defenses are by definition compromised.

For the second time that day, after what happened in the morning in Hendrick's flat, the absence of someone I didn't know became a palpable, influential presence. These influences had something in common, since in both cases, morning and afternoon, I felt constrained, transfixed. Yet more important was the difference, especially clear in the type of influence I could exert: though I could do nothing to change the past of the absent figures in Hendrick's flat (the rapist with the flower shop, his victims, Hendrick himself at that time of his life), I thought my behavior could intervene in the future of the absent figure in the lounge of that damn hotel. Víctor Comas had in fact already been sentenced, but I could choose whether or not to take part in seeing that sentence carried out. I think I took part.

With two cups of Earl Grey tea and some minuscule pastries, the scene took place approximately as follows:

CEO:        I hope this morning's little mix-up has been straightened out. Apparently someone (*scowl*) made a mistake with the reservations. I apologize.

EMPLOYEE:   Don't worry, sir. It's fine.

CEO:        Please, drop the sir. Call me Pepe. The important thing is that you're comfortable and able to do your job. Have you finalized the appointment with Van Booren?

EMPLOYEE:   It's confirmed for tomorrow, yes.

CEO:        I've been hearing about you for a while now. And believe it or not (*smiling*), I'm also familiar with your work. Straightforward and professional, with a touch of dryness, just how I like. You're not yet at the point where your personality gets ahead of you, unlike certain other writers. What do you think of the work of Víctor Comas?

EMPLOYEE:   (*With a telling caution.*) I'm not familiar with it in any depth, but from what I know it's excellent, and I'm not surprised he's a top name at Story Press.

CEO:            Frankly, it's starting to surprise me. I won't say it was me who suggested you for the interview with Van Boonen. But I will admit I had a hand in making sure Víctor Comas didn't get it. We have to diversify. It's a bit of a delicate matter. I've been told you're familiar with the doctor, and were waiting for your chance. I don't like people who don't get their feet wet.

EMPLOYEE:       (*After an incriminating pause.*) Well, I'm prepared, and I'm confident everything will turn out well.

CEO:            Are you a Real Madrid fan?

EMPLOYEE:       I'm afraid I don't really follow football.

CEO:            Good for you. Otherwise you'd be wiped out. Yesterday at the Bernabéu we took a beating from Arsenal. They got one by us and could have gotten seven.

EMPLOYEE:       …

CEO:            We looked like a pack of zombies. In the midfield they can't create or stop anything: poor Zidane has gone to the dogs, and of course, if he doesn't take the lead, that's it, because as far as Ronaldo's concerned … if the ball's not passed directly to him he won't budge. And the less said about Gravesen the better. Florentino sold him to us as (*air quotes*) the best footballer in Denmark, what the hell, a real attack dog. He bites, it's true, but he never even picks up the scent of the ball. What a show! In the middle of the Champions League!

EMPLOYEE:  …

CEO:  Sorry. You really don't follow football? Then you're probably bored by this. But what happened yesterday…

EMPLOYEE:  One bad day…

CEO:  This wasn't just one bad day. Or two or three. There's a guilty party here, and I could name names. And for the last five years he's been (*air quotes*) leading the club. And really, pulling political strings is something anyone can do.

EMPLOYEE:  Well, I don't know the first thing about football, but I've heard that Florentino Pérez has straightened things out financially.

CEO:  Exactly, political strings. If it hadn't been for Aznar we wouldn't have scored the Ciudad Deportiva. Look, this guy is a megalomaniac. What he tried to do is emulate Bernabéu, no less. He thought that by buying up some of the best players in the world—or let's just say some of the most expensive—we'd be all set. But if you're really a financial wizard, a big-shot impresario who's going to revolutionize the world of football, the first thing you have to do is get a good staff. Competent people you can and will delegate to. Football people. Imagine if I hadn't surrounded myself at Story Press with publishing people, true professionals. Imagine if we let someone, and I don't want to single anyone out, get too big for his britches. Imagine Comas with that Van Booten: what a clash of titans! Florentino has no inkling what the business of football is all about. He has no sense of the passion for the team, for winning. You're selling something intangible, not Beckham's briefs. If you can't get people excited you haven't done a damn thing, and the only thing Real Madrid fans care about is winning. Really, what has Florentino done? Fine, two *ligas* and one Champions in five seasons, but Del Bosque deserves credit for all that, he's demonstrated that he at least knows how to deal with all the prima donnas. And the guy throws him out because he doesn't have (*air quotes*) media presence. What does he know about media presence? They've had five coaches since then. What media presence do Queiroz, Camacho, García Remón, Luxemburgo, or López Caro have? But of course, he's made his bed, so now he has to lie in it. First they're selling Figo, now they're selling jerseys. And on top of that, that idiot Butragueño comes along and calls him

a god. (*Checks his watch.*) Speaking of Figo, I
can't wait to see him play today for Inter, to
see how he does against Ajax. I'd say he's still
got just about one more year left. No doubt
he can hold his own against that team of rook-
ies. Florentino better take note. The sad thing
is, the Dutch apparently have a lot of guys
out injured, because who I wanted to see was
Sneijder, though maybe that kid Huntelaar will
play, he's supposed to be a real phenom. In any
case, you've got to be careful with the Italians:
they're old, but they have plenty of tricks up
their sleeves.

EMPLOYEE:    (*After an incriminating pause.*) So … Real
Madrid's not doing well?

CEO:    We're not just not doing well, we're making fools
of ourselves. No one can do anything right,
no one's planning out the season. Instead of
training seriously and methodically, they're all
on summer tours in the U.S., China, Japan,
Central Europe … Lots of publicity, sure, but
at the cost of wearing out the players who, keep
in mind, are a little past their prime to be doing
all that gallivanting around. That's why Zidane,
Ronaldo, and Helguera all have injuries now
… even Raúl, despite the fact that he can play
with one leg. And the new signings … what
can I say. At first they get rid of Makelele for
not improving the lineup, and they bring us
Gravesen and Pablo García, who, with all due

respect, aren't worthy to tie his shoes. What's
unfair is that López Caro has to take the blame,
he's already got enough on his plate. He's picking up after that blowhard Luxemburgo. He was
a real piece of work. First he goes and says no
one plays with wingers anymore. Then he wants
to start with a diamond and end with a square:
basically, we have to play like Brazil, with the
"magic square." And to top it off, since he's a
modern coach, he's big on new technology …
and there you have him, with that earpiece dan-
gling off the side of his head. My blood pressure
hits the roof just thinking about it. And mind
you, I'm no die-hard traditionalist. Playing with
wingers or without them is a stupid debate.
Whether or not you have dedicated wingers,
if you don't open up the field, not only do you
make things easier for the other side's defense,
you hobble your own ability to attack. I agree
that the square doesn't have to be static, it can
open up on the wings. But in order to do that
the players have to coordinate their passing. All
they care about is what it looks like, not whether
it works. Any formation can be interesting,
but if it's not dynamic, you just end up with
eleven guys standing around, or broken lines.
In football everything's already been invented,
and even if it hasn't, you can't forget the basic
premise: there's no good team without good
players. The wingers expend so much energy
that by the second half they're out of breath and
can't regain their position. Roberto Carlos and

Salgado used to be machines, no one says they didn't, but today they're not up to it; to make matters worse, when the defense is static, no one covers for them. And what can I say about the central midfield? They put Beckham and Baptista there, where neither one is a specialist. Beckham is an expert in midfielding toward the right, Baptista got cocky scoring goals for Seville as an attacking midfielder or forward. In front of them, Zidane and Raúl. If Zidane isn't in shape, which he's not, then good luck moving the ball forward. And Raúl, sad to say, since he can be such a dangerous opportunist up high, they keep stranded far away from the goal. The point is, the forwards never get a decent ball. Ronaldo—oh, Ronaldo, regardless of what they say about him not being the same since the injury he had with Inter, is always on the edge of being offside, and as far as turning up the pressure goes, we all know that's not for him. Robinho cares more about showing the spectators what he can do than about playing for the team. The only great signing is Sergio Ramos, a fantastic player, but they're going to ruin him: he was a star as a winger for Seville, and now he plays as a center as much as a midfielder. Such a waste. Poor López Caro: with what he's inheriting, what can he do? And besides, an inside man without experience has no chance of controlling that locker room. All that has to change. In fact, I know it will. (*Doubtful.*) Can you keep a secret?

EMPLOYEE:     (*Like a dog with lowered ears.*) A professional secret?

CEO:          Florentino doesn't have a week left. If the club were a publicly traded company like the others, I'd bet my shares on it, and let me tell you, when I make a bet I know what I'm doing. In five days we'll have his resignation. But (*placing his finger to his lips*) not a word. Don't go running your mouth about this scoop. Though you look like someone who can keep his mouth shut. I can tell you things I'd never tell Víctor Comas.

EMPLOYEE:     (*Like a dog pricking up its ears.*) Well, Víctor is a professional. And I never even went to school for journalism.

CEO:          I'm not saying you can't learn from him. But stick to the good things, only the good things, and stay away from the bad ones. Focus on what he used to be like, not what he's like now. That's how you get big—not by thinking you're a superstar reporter. Let's see what you get out of Van Boolen.

EMPLOYEE:     (*Ears still pricked up.*) If I'm lucky, maybe a good portrait. In his own words.

CEO:          (*Laughing.*) So you do portraits?

EMPLOYEE:     In a way, that's the art of the interview, isn't it?

CEO:            (*Laughing.*) The art of the interview? I like it!
                I think we'll get along fine. We'll give that
                know-it-all a good scare.

EMPLOYEE:       (*Like someone trying to salvage their honor.*) It's
                not my intention to scare anyone.

CEO:            Don't worry. You will. And you already know
                the trick, which is to do it without trying. I'm
                glad to see the people who spoke highly of you
                were right. Where do you plan to interview Van
                Booven?

EMPLOYEE:       Right here, that's what we decided.

CEO:            Perfect. Good choice. And now (*looking at
                his watch*), if you'll excuse me, my time is up.
                Where are you headed? Shall we walk out
                together?

Self-pity is a feeling that suits white heterosexual males between the ages of eighteen and twenty-nine; you have to meet all these conditions for it to look sexy and fill stadiums like the boys in Coldplay. I don't satisfy the requirements, and in fact I'm sure I'm even further "past my prime" than Zidane or Ronaldo. But it's not the first time that I've been treated, at my age, like someone who's "just starting out," something which in theory is a prerogative of youth, and which—again, at my age, when one is usually on the way to the dustbin—should be a source of comfort rather than humiliation. In any case, this juvenile feeling isn't for me, and I'm not going to throw myself into its arms now the way I did yesterday—I'm embarrassed to say—as soon as I took leave of the CEO of Story Press, who can't be more than ten years older than I am. I left him as he got into a cab, when it was already dark and the cold was reaching World War Two levels, and I fell, I sunk into temptation, I felt like a wretch. Not anymore, now isn't yesterday. In emergencies my feelings quickly change masters, and though at first I demurred, obeying Hendrick left me good as new. Thanks to him I managed to leave the CEO in a silent limbo, along with Víctor Comas and—what to call him now?—Dr. Van Helsing.

Yet on the way back to my hotel, walking aimlessly as I did, not checking the map, determined to get lost and, for that matter, to die, all those absurd proper names apparently bound up with my actions seemed poised to form a basic lexicon for my life from then on. Next to them is another word which no one had actually spoken but whose possible interpretations I'd been running through since the early afternoon. I'll say it again: "expulsion." I also remembered, more tenderly, but with the same determinism, the words "a good portrait" and "the art of the interview": with these disingenuous lines I'd tried to suggest you can be pretentious without having to give anyone "a good fright," least of all third parties you have nothing to do with. But that's not true, and with this important insight I now see that everything is, indeed, linked to everything else, and that ignorance about the extent we're connected is just an excuse to drape a delicate fatalism over the scope of our possibilities, over the exercise of power, in short. This ignorance is cleverly organized to absolve us of all intentions: if we don't know whether a decision of ours can harm distant third parties, we protect our sense of morals; and if we do know, then the fact that those third parties are remote—people we haven't met, people we have no obligations to—frees us from the dark accusation that we acted on selfish motives. Thus facts are still facts, and third parties are still harmed, but the causal chain has been helpfully severed, so that it can't be traced back to any instigators or perpetrators.

Now I'm moralizing, I know. Or embracing Buddhism, who knows. Yesterday, in a predictable twist to my self-pity, I even started deliriously imagining that maybe I really could learn something from Víctor Comas after all. Given how the CEO of Story Press wanted me to know whom I'd be harming, I naturally thought of revenge. I could call Víctor Comas, even though I don't know him, I could talk to him. I doubt I could tell him anything he doesn't already know, but perhaps he'd appreciate the gesture and I'd find an outlet for my anger. Would he really appreciate it, though? Would it really be a nice gesture? The idea started to seem exceedingly foolish. Two people who don't know each other and owe each other nothing, doing each other favors. Favors? Would he think I was doing him a favor? He'd probably think I wanted to ease my conscience, calm my rage, win his forgiveness. And he wouldn't be far wrong, dammit. Now I see this differently, more clearly. I'm still trapped, but trapped somewhere else. The CEO of Story Press, to kill time before going to his football match, decided to shove me into the stadium of morals to see how I performed; he brought up Víctor Comas for the sole purpose of making me reveal whether I was playing for him or the other team. But it was a trap: Víctor Comas, who will certainly get a ball to the head, isn't on either team, he isn't even in the stadium. The one who is there, high above the scuffles, is the CEO of Story Press. If I want to play, and if I have to react, it's for or against only him.

I hadn't yet reached these conclusions when I became aware I'd wandered into a rather homely pedestrian street, where the businesses were closing and a surprisingly large crowd was dissolving into the night. I turned and walked away as though startled, and not knowing whether I was near or far from my hotel, took a cab. It would be too much to say that I came back to reality, because I'd abandoned it only in a moment's delirium; but I recovered the astonishing ability to return to a selective present, in a sense isolated from what preceded or followed it. Specifically, this happened when I decided to turn on my mobile and found a message from Hendrick. He hadn't even given me time to call him, which he made me promise I'd do; he had his reasons and I was thankful. He said he'd meet me in a café just fifty yards away from my hotel. The fact is that in my whirlwind of self-pity, I thought about not calling him: keeping to myself what I considered my worst face, the least flattering, out of both pride and convenience, and also of course so I could keep tormenting myself alone. When I saw his text, however, I changed my mind. Such things are always gratifying: when the other person takes the first step, even if it is—even if it might be—out of mistrust. I recalled that the trip's appeal always lay in getting to see him, even if it was only a perk. I thought back with unexpected excitement on that morning's encounter, the incredible story about his flat, the laughter and reminiscing over lunch, the eagerness of our journey to the hotel, even the disappointment that awaited us there, which I could now laugh about for the first time. No, Hendrick couldn't just be a happy coincidence, the hidden bonus of a work trip: he had always been, privately, a priority, and the fact that now he was openly a priority gave me a certain criminal satisfaction. I felt, frankly, like I was getting even. Not because I was taking shelter from the turmoil of professional life in the comforts of private life, not because I clung to the illusion that, no matter what happened, I'd always have another life, but because I'd altered the priorities set out for me, putting at the top what the world of Story Press insisted on relegating to the sidelines.

The cab driver had no trouble finding the café, and I got out almost in a state of grace. I decided to leave myself in Hendrick's hands, to go along with his wishes, and I was happy I took this step and spared him the burden of having to talk me into something. I think he noticed my willingness from the start, although he later told me he thought it was because I'd come away triumphant from my awkward interview. Only one small obstacle had to be overcome at the moment: Hendrick wasn't alone. I felt a slight shiver, as though I'd momentarily forgotten he had a new and different life. Seated across from him was an odd character, looking very serious in a tuxedo, a sort of older Dan Aykroyd, like in *The House of Mirth*. Even so, despite his air of a comedian pressed into a dramatic role, he wasn't at all grotesque, and actually looked quite elegant. I assumed he was a friend of his, or perhaps a supporter of his cause, but when I saw Hendrick stand up to get his coat, I realized with relief that he was eager to say goodbye. With understated courtesy he introduced us in Spanish, and the man replied in the same language, no doubt native to him.

"It's so nice to run into a fellow countryman in a foreign country."

I answered with a smile: "Are you just passing through?"

"I am," he said, with a certain gravity, "but not like you are, I'm afraid. Your friend speaks impeccable Spanish and was kind enough to keep me company while he waited."

"Are you also waiting for someone?" I asked. But even before he replied, somewhat bitterly, that he wasn't, Hendrick put his arm around me and, leaving no room for doubt, said we had to be on our way.

"You didn't even let me catch my breath," I said as we left.
"Who was that guy?"

"You heard him, a fellow countryman of yours. He latched
onto me and spent forty-five minutes telling me his life story."

"Must not have been a very interesting life," I laughed.

"Well, apparently he has an alcoholic son he's been running
away from for years. But I think you've heard enough sad stories
for one day."

Hendrick still didn't know the details of my interview with
the CEO of Story Press, so he could only be referring to the
"sad story" of his own turbulent solution to the European housing crisis. I felt a twinge of superstition, as I had that morning,
and I knew—I couldn't help it—that I would put myself in his
hands all night, but I'd refuse to step foot in his place again. He
understood this, too; and never once over dinner, in a luxurious
modern restaurant where no one said hello to him for a change,
nor in our subsequent trip to his two packed, carefree bars, did
he allude to that haunted place. I think at one point he wasn't
sure I wanted to spend the night with him at all, there or anywhere else. I didn't play hard to get: as soon as I noticed his
uncertainty I reassured him.

"This afternoon we couldn't go back to my hotel," I said. "But
now I've got a new one."

"That youth hostel?" he laughed.

"Let me remind you, we've done worse."

Then he kissed me. "All right, then, let's do worse."

We did worse in that tiny, pitiful room, and it was wonderful. True, this morning he made me promise we'd spend tonight
at his place. I said we'd see, but I think I owe it to him. Besides,
today I don't feel as if I'm at the mercy of ghosts. In fact, I have
no desire to go interview Van Booven tomorrow. What if I didn't
go? I'm considering it more and more seriously. What if I didn't

do it? What if I skip the "good portrait"? I'll wait until tonight, but I know that tomorrow the only thing I'll want—I already want—is to go home.

# A Slightly Shameful Modesty

## I

WEIGHED ON THE scales of social life, my parents, I'd say, are a bit out of balance, since my mother always contributes more. That's not to say my father's given up trying to carry his weight—far from it: last night's dinner party was an example of his efforts—but he's still helpless without her, and he's convinced that on his own his aspirations wouldn't amount to a thing. My mother takes little notice of my father's aspirations: if she were waiting for him to achieve them, she would have left years ago, and if she needed him to have any, as certain women do who like their husbands to be bold, then frankly she would have chosen someone else. My father professes to be an "even-tempered man": when he sees an opportunity, he says he has to handle it "gingerly," an expression he contrasts to "grabbing it," typical of contemptible men. When he doesn't see an opportunity, he won't go to the trouble of creating one—he's not the kind of man. He's patient, more by nature than by method, and you might even say apathetic, since he only seems to accomplish things when he's left with no other choice. He's not one to conspire with events, and even when it's clear where they're headed—so clear that even a blind man could see—he seems to think that events have conspired against him. In the end, he only "gingerly" handles opportunities he could miss out on with no risk of damage, setback, or loss. He does so to save himself, and even then he acts with the hesitation and self-doubt of someone who knows it's not their life on the line, but their job. Yet when events have clearly conspired and he has no choice but to give in, the man heaves a sigh and resigns himself to marshaling all his resources, like a miser in dire straits who has to take money from under the mattress. And what comes out from under the mattress is my mother.

Though she's perfectly capable of performing the role of wife, my mother has an unquestionably more dazzling, compelling presence: she's fiery, unique, and musical. Still, had experience not shown she possesses a certain flair for miracles, it would be quite a stretch to call her miraculous. Her menus certainly are—certainly quite a stretch, I mean. I still don't understand how a group of gentlemen doctors accustomed to staking a considerable amount of their dignity on the finest restaurants in Madrid can pass up their fish and their T-bones for the culinary stylings of the queen of the Thermomix. What happened yesterday, for example, gives me shivers: scallops with an "Oriental" sauce made of soy, ginger, and a few drops of ketchup "for balance"; pumpkin risotto with hazelnut butter; and then, without so much as a pause to catch her breath, something she enthusiastically calls a *frittata*, where the combined forces of the Thermomix, the frying pan, and the grill bring forth a spectacular gratin of eggs, bacon, cream, mushrooms, and potatoes. For dessert we had Giangrossi ice cream ... but pistachio. Fortunately, since I was asked to bring it, I also picked up an alternative tub of boring chocolate, but this, I admit, turned out to be less successful. Not even Sunan, who supposedly shares my tastes, backed me up. I've seen it happen before: by this point—dessert—the dinner guests have submitted so thoroughly to their hostess's art that they wouldn't dare take a bite of anything that wasn't green. Such is the success that crowns what should rightly be little more than a laborious failure. In another of her imaginative progressions, before dessert my mother had already trotted out her kiwi and papaya liqueurs, which are invariably humored with supreme indulgence. And then, as the ice cream "rests" in the kitchen, my presence is requested at the piano to accompany her witty renditions of—what differences does it make?—an Offenbach piece or "Making Whoopee." Usually she ends up singing both, and once the evening turns to music, the pistachio—which makes its appearance topped with a "walnut flower"—is an afterthought.

How all this seduction works is a mystery, but not a surprise. Most of the guests know what they're getting themselves into, and they not only keep coming back, but also bring along some new recruit. Yesterday's recruit, Señor Álvarez Casas, the hospital's new general manager and the focal point of an eventful evening, didn't seem especially charmed until the end, unlike the regulars, Dr. García Oviedo and Dr. Díaz Madrigal, who enjoyed themselves from the very beginning, and even enjoyed the most eventful parts. Quite possibly, in the case of the manager, there was a question of principles involved: I was warned—as was poor Sunan, as if he were capable of uttering an obscenity—that he belonged to some religious cult, I don't know whether the Opus Dei or the Neocatechumenals, which he reserved all his faults for, as if by precept. At any rate, he looked perfectly at ease in the atmosphere of sandalwood, Orientalism, and foreign travel, even after he learned this was all a product of my mother's entrepreneurial spirit. He took an interest in where her shop was located and how it was doing, and surprised her by identifying a Tibetan chest; he expressed admiration for the Chinese double medicine cabinet she showed him, with its thirty-nine little drawers, and said it was very appropriate for my father's profession; he made no comments about the food. About the music, once it began, he confessed his ignorance, but such sincerity seemed out of

place, since no one was asking him to be a cultured man, and
he didn't hesitate to discreetly join in the applause. To say he fell
under her spell would be an exaggeration, especially considering
everything that happened later. Yet after his initial reluctance, he
left convinced, I'm sure, that ours was a home where interesting
things happened, if not spontaneous acts of Christian charity. I
doubt he'll turn down a second invitation, should anyone dare
extend one, though there was some disagreement on this point.
My mother, who throughout the meal alternated between fearing
disaster and overcoming it, declared herself defeated and rejected.
By contrast, my father, who as I've said wouldn't exactly take first
place in an anxiety race, reassured her with his usual meek and
grateful air, thanking her for staying "on top of" problems that
were once again "all in her head."

With this he gave the impression, not at all unusual for him,
that he'd asked her to a make a sacrifice out of proportion with
the fruits it yielded. Or will yield, rather: it remains to be seen
what, if anything, last night's party will yield. But one always has
to stay one step ahead of my father, and that's where his reputation for calm can be mistaken for optimism: given how much
trouble he has setting out to do anything, the last thing he needs
is to worry about the results. Effort without reward is, for him, a
delusion of an evil mind, and as far as he's concerned, he lives in
an upright, orderly world, ruled by all kinds of innocent souls.

"Getting the White Pages was a brilliant idea," he said at the
end of the evening, thanking me for my contribution to keeping
that world running.

To which my mother rather sarcastically added:

"From now on, he won't be able to live without you, either."

From now on? For some time already, I'd say, my mother's
been including me in these "dinners with a purpose," because
lately I get the impression I don't miss a single one. The other

ones, the purposeless ones, of which these are merely a pale shadow, I find out about only by chance, now that I don't live at home. I wouldn't say I miss them, but I'm still glad to see, after all these years, that my parents haven't turned into that sad cell of the social organism known as the friendless couple. The feat is all my mother's doing, needless to say, but my father has never exercised his matrimonial right to a veto—even though he could perfectly well delude himself into thinking his even temper and aversion to trouble provide more than enough company on their own. He enjoys this kind of nonprofessional gathering as much as my mother does, whether it's an elaborate centennial commemoration or a last-minute masquerade in the yard. In their guests he finds surprising commonalities and reassuring differences, and doesn't know which to take more pleasure in. And even though he's not good at poker, or at holding his whisky, or at laughing or singing, he loves to hear stories of strange business deals or romance in foreign lands, and he's proud to offer his opinion on diseases and vaccines, and to see that he's respected.

These other dinner parties, in short, have that air of undiluted romanticism that the doctors catch only a whiff of, and they boast a respectable and even intimidating roster of cosmopolitan guests. They marked my childhood and adolescence, and even now, as they're starting to slow down and pass away, and I'm less prone to fascination, they still impress me with their rowdy stamina. There's the fascist adventurer Lorenzo Barberà, famous for both his daredevil piloting and his "deals"—obviously contraband—which take him from one third world country to the next; Rulfo, the set designer and source of the intimate secrets of a thousand artists, not to mention his own; the Leunens, a Flemish couple who own the Kayak Team travel agency and have lived through several shipwrecks; Azucena, the flight attendant, with her acclaimed contralto voice, who seems a bit dejected ever since she learned she was losing her sight; Mabel, the dietitian and astrologist, who kept—and keeps—a close eye on my figure, my dresses, and my boyfriends; Carlos Montalvo, the aid worker who left the classical theater to drive a truck through war-torn African regions; sometimes the children, lovers, dogs, or guests of any one of them; and always, above all, the elegant and even-keeled Señor Sawatdee, my mother's Thai business partner, and the benefactor I'll always be indebted to for introducing me to Sunan. Sunan, by the way, finds all this carousing scary and often irritating. He says they look like the cast of characters from a antiquated colonial novel, and that, given the choice, he'd take the doctors, though my mother wisely never brings the two groups together. But I remind him that it's the doctors, not them, who always make a fuss about how he must know kung fu.

Just compare any anecdote from the crass colonials with this one from the cultured doctors, delivered last night over the scallops course:

"Did you hear the latest about Adolfo?" asked Dr. Díaz, turning to us all with a cajoling smile. Then he stopped, a bit hesitant at the look of circumspection on the face of the new general manager, Señor Álvarez. "Adolfo," he explained, "is Dr. Fernández Blasco, in trauma. I imagine you've already heard about him—he's a real piece of work!" Señor Álvarez nodded. "He works because he wants to, he could live off of his family's wealth. He's got a seventy-foot boat, a Ferretti, a thing of beauty! This happened just three weeks ago, at the end of August. I heard it from María"—he looked at Señor Álvarez—"the floor three supervisor, who's good friends with his wife and was out with them."

"María is an exemplary professional," my father interrupted, likewise turning to Señor Álvarez, I suppose suspecting that the anecdote would mix the aforementioned professional in unexemplary affairs.

"They were docked in Cabrera and heard that Mister Catalonia was traveling nearby in another, smaller boat, with a ton of women, all of them gorgeous. The muscles and speedos on display had already been noticed by Adolfo's daughters and some of their little friends they brought along. But it seems the Mister must be a bit of a klutz, because he took a spill on deck, and his women thought he'd broken something. They knew there was a trauma specialist one boat over, so they asked permission to come aboard, then lowered him on the raft and brought him over. Apparently when Adolfo heard they were coming, he mysteriously shut himself in the cabin. He took his time. And guess how he came out to greet them: in one of his wife's G-strings! Ha, ha! Imagine him, with that gut, in a G-string and a sailor's cap. Ha, ha! And you know what the first thing he said to that fairy was? 'Watch it, Mister, on this boat all the bathing beauties belong to me.'"

"What a brute!" said Dr. García, still laughing. "I bet he roughed him up a bit during the examination. He must have left in more pain than he arrived in."

"I bet," Dr. Díaz agreed gleefully. "Though I heard he also gave him an anti-inflammatory. Ha, ha!"

My father smiled with clinical hypocrisy. My mother is desensitized to these kinds of jokes, but I know he still suffers. Dr. García's wife looked more resigned than desensitized, though even so she makes a good audience with her mink-colored hair. But the most important reaction, that of Señor Álvarez and the woman seated next to him, whose relationship we still hadn't ascertained, was suspiciously indulgent. They didn't object, but they didn't break out in applause, either: their silent courtesy was in its own way so cutting that Dr. Díaz and Dr. García apparently thought they'd taken the wrong approach, and spent the rest of the evening trying out other tactics. In fact, Dr. Díaz was in a sour mood for a good fifteen minutes.

I kicked Sunan under the table, but he pretended not to notice.

Maybe here I should highlight a fact I consider significant: the doctors' wives seldom join them at these gatherings. Yesterday Señora García was an exception, and one has to wonder why: most likely because her presence doesn't inhibit the off-color jokes, or because, given the occasion, the two ward heads thought at least one of them had to bring along his wife so they didn't seem like a couple of playboys. It was probably her turn, though to me she looked more honored than obliged. These dinners, I think, must have a safari-like reputation among the doctors, and even though they know they're visiting the savannah without the animals, they still feel like brave men summoned for their virtues, and not—as they really are—for a professional purpose. In their ignorance I think that they look down on my father, so guarded and unengaging, and perhaps unworthy of that live wire they can't figure out how he married; they think they have to do him a favor once in a while so he'll get somewhere in his slow career. In payment for these favors, they get to impose themselves at my mother's parties—or so they think. In fact, their invitations are subject to a convoluted calendar of "opportunities" that has been rigorously set for my father, whether he likes it or not. This time the occasion was the vacancy in his ward that will open up when the chief doctor retires in a year and a half, which my father has a reasonable expectation to fill. With the hospital's recent privatization and the new management, he feels obliged to "move"—if he heard me say this!—somewhat sooner than he would otherwise have judged appropriate. And when Dr. Díaz and Dr. García, for their own convenience, chose this setting to welcome Señor

Álvarez, inviting him themselves—"with just a few of us, at a friend's house,"—I suppose he thought he could reap the secondary benefits, more than they could reap the primary ones. They always have other, more urgent plans, and for the moment I doubt they're even aware that my father does, too. His silence will only be judged, hopefully favorably, "in due course."

But I was talking about the doctors' wives, and after what I just said, it's not hard to imagine them dispatching their husbands on the excuse that it's a "work function," or rather using the same excuse—with greater relief—to justify their own absence. On the other hand, if their husbands' histrionic admiration for my mother didn't have the not quite unintentional effect of reminding them how unlike her they are, they might feel more curious about her. But they lack even that inducement, and by now they must be too sick of those men and their careers to enter into a perverse kind of competition, on top of everything else. I remember how Dr. Díaz's wife, in one of her occasional appearances, began talking about the high rate of neck problems among the staff in radiology, where she's a nurse, something that in her opinion indicated some kind of depression. Her husband interrupted her, suggesting she not "bore us with work talk," and then just as kindly proceeded to treat us to a lecture on wines, none of which were on the table. A bit later my mother told a story about a complicated negotiation with bureaucrats in a remote Vietnamese city, which involved a bribe and the dating of some antique chests; when she finished, she betrayed Dr. Díaz's rapt attention by thanking him for not getting bored with her "work story." We don't know whether or not Dr. Díaz's wife appreciated this gesture, because some time later they ran into each other at a wedding, and according to my mother, she said my mother had her husband "wrapped around her finger."

Dr. García doesn't correct his wife, not in public at least, nor does he tell her she's boring, though he does give the impression he's dragging her along, like some cargo whose measurements meet the standard. My mother says she's been to the store a few times to buy some trinkets, and is always tempted to get something "big," but can never quite make up her mind to take the step; perhaps one day she will, and she'll amaze her family with a lacquered six-leaf folding screen. Her mindset is advanced, even if her words aren't. At my parents' home she looks curious, expectant, eager to applaud; she's too shy to make more progress, but too honest to conceal that she's open to outside influences. My father always treats her with deference, and my mother always asks her opinion, even though she knows it will be timid; she says that if she could get her to leave her husband at home, she wouldn't hesitate to invite her to a dinner with, for example, Lorenzo Barberà, who would quickly cure her of the "mystical" view she has of us, as my mother puts it. But it's nearly impossible to imagine her without her husband, since while we've seen him several times without her, we've never seen her out alone. We'll have to wait until she makes up her mind to buy the folding screen, an act that could be assumed to have a revolutionary symbolic import. Dr. García remains ignorant of these machinations, and I doubt he'd notice even if they emerged from the shadows: in my opinion he's a dull-witted man who doesn't care at all about his wife, and the appearance of a folding screen in his living room wouldn't make him think of a barricade, but just the routine privacy panels they use in the emergency room.

These antiquated marital conventions aren't irrelevant, and it's in everyone's interests to keep them in mind, so that revolution does not in fact break out. That's why last night at a certain point some alarms went off when it became hard to interpret, in the light of these relationships, the presence of the woman who accompanied—or rather followed—Señor Álvarez to dinner, giving rise to heated discussions in the kitchen and stifled tensions around the table. We knew that Señor Álvarez was married and had an indeterminate—but fairly Catholic—number of children. When my father extended the invitation, he told him that "naturally" his wife was invited as well; but then Dr. Díaz punctured a hole in that naturalness when he mentioned, with his customary carelessness, that he'd be going alone. Señor Álvarez thus faced the grim dilemma of a free man. My mother, who loathes improvisation in these doctor's dinners, scolded my father for being so "confusing" and ordered me to set two places at the table, thinking we could always remove an extra plate more discreetly than we could add a new one. I was in charge of answering the door when they arrived, and I saw there were two of them: he walked in first—lanky, balding, wearing the shoes of a priest—while she hung back—tiny, silver-haired, in pearls— somewhat clumsily closing the double door of the elevator. As soon as I introduced myself and left them in the living room in the hands of Sunan, my father, and Dr. Díaz, I went into the kitchen to whisper to my mother:

"Congratulations," I said. "He didn't come alone."

"That's a relief," she answered. "What's his wife like?"

"Pretty old, actually. She's an elegant little old lady."

"What do you mean?"

"I don't know. Are you sure he's married? That woman could be his mother."

"His mother!" gasped my mother, irritated. "How old is he?"

"I don't know. He's pretty bald but I doubt he's even fifty. And she's at least seventy."

My mother took off her apron and pointed to the oven, as though there were something I could do, and left to clear up the mystery. A minute later my father came in.

"So what do you think? Is it his wife or his mother?"

"I suppose we can't ask her," I smiled, amused. "I'd say it's his mother."

My father thought for a minute:

"Yes, I don't see him being married to such an older woman." He thought some more. "Much less do I see an older woman marrying him."

Just then Dr. Díaz walked in.

"Hey, who is that? His wife, his mom, his grandma or what? Give me a break."

"Who did he tell you he was coming with?"

"He didn't tell me anything! I hoped he'd come by himself, like I did! Now the guy goes and gets charitable and makes me look bad. Everyone brought their wife or mother except me."

My mother came back in and gave them a commanding look.

"You two, get back in the living room right now and behave yourselves. Don't leave Sunan alone in that scene."

"But who's the old lady?" insisted Dr. Díaz.

"I haven't a clue. She hasn't said a word. Our best strategy is to call her 'Señora Álvarez,' that way we definitely can't go wrong."

"It'd be better if we don't call her anything," interjected my father. "What if she's an in-law?"

"The guy could have at least had the kindness to let us know," added Dr. Díaz, annoyed. "But you know what? I'm just not going to care."

"What do you think?" I asked my mother, once they were gone.

"Who knows? She looks like his mother, of course. But with these Legionnaires of Christ you can never tell."

When I walked back into the living room, Sunan was showing the mystery couple the ukiyo-e, and Dr. Álvarez displayed a certain knowledge of the Floating World that left my father

and Dr. Díaz at a loss—apparently he recognized a sumo wres-
tler—while his companion nodded, pleased. Shortly thereafter
Dr. García and his wife arrived, and we thought we'd now have
an opportunity to clarify their relationship; but when the doctor
introduced his wife to the manager, the woman didn't wait to be
introduced and extended her hand and, all smiles, dashed our
hopes. A few minutes later she likewise dashed Señora García's
laudable attempts to engage her in conversation by continuing
to smile but failing to respond. Nevertheless, I saw her say something quietly to Sunan, as he offered her a glass of white wine,
and this time he was the one who didn't answer.

"What did she say?" I asked a little later, when we met in the
kitchen.

He looked at my mother out of the corner of his eye. "I don't
know if I can repeat it," he murmured.

"Why not?" My mother had heard him.

"Well ... she said that in this house there's nothing smooth."

"Nothing smooth?" my mother repeated. "What does that
mean?"

I laughed.

"Maybe it's all those prints in your living room?"

"How rude!" she growled, leaving with a tray. "And so
priggish!"

"What do you think?" I asked Sunan, once we were alone.
"Is she his wife or his mother?"

"I think ..." he hesitated theatrically and moved to hold me
from behind, "that you look ravishing in this dress. If you were
black, you'd look like Estelle."

"And if you were white," I answered, turning around, "you'd
look like Louis Garrel."

Sunan and I could have lingered forever in those dreamlike
comparisons, but a dreary conscience reminded us we had to play

a more responsible role. Once we sat down to dinner, Dr. Díaz's anecdote over the scallop course, about his G-stringed colleague, seemed to give that responsibility a terrible immensity, but the fact that it didn't meet with acclaim imposed some limits. Among the elements of the story—G-strings, misters, bathing beauties, sprains—it was hard to pick out anything that wouldn't just lead to a dreadful re-creation, but Señor Álvarez, perhaps since he was the new recruit, found something so fundamental that the rest of us had overlooked it: he said that he was always in awe of the sea, though he was merely an "armchair sailor," as if those present personally knew any other kind. Before my mother could wax rhapsodic about the nautical dangers confronted by certain idols of hers, Señor Álvarez declared he had a great fondness for novels, and that through them he'd embarked on "countless vicarious adventures," to which his companion nodded and smiled in agreement. Sunan, an avid reader himself, wanted to know what kind of novels these were, and between *Moby Dick*, Patrick O'Brien, *Benito Cereno*, and *The Old Man and the Sea*, they spent a good while in cultured conversation; but since the conversation now moved in a threatening direction, Dr. García seized on a reference to the memoirs of a certain slave-trading captain from the early nineteenth century to introduce the topic of new forms of slavery at the beginning of the twenty-first. Then Dr. Díaz returned from his exile and slowly transformed the apologetic humanitarianism of his colleague, whose heart went out to those "poor Chinese," into an indignant rant about sex tourism, an issue about which he had, foreseeably, various anecdotes at the ready. This was torture for Señora García, who murmured that she'd only try a little bite of the risotto. But Dr. Díaz didn't back down: on the contrary, at a certain point he began to look at Sunan strangely, that is, not as though he were one more Bangkok souvenir among the rest that filled the flat, but as a sort of active subject, and he asked him about the state of child prostitution in Thailand. Sunan replied that he had no idea, that he was an adult and had, thanks to a very talented therapist, managed to erase from his memory all his childhood traumas. Señor Álvarez showed a certain discomfort in the presence of such sarcasm. More attuned than Dr. García to the rudeness of the initial comment, and of course to Sunan's superior reaction, he adopted a pacifying tone to point out, not to anyone in particular, that every country had its "social ills." My mother, however, who must have thought she was at a different dinner party, let out a cackle.

"You're too much, Sunan!" she said, and returning to this world, channeled the chronicle of events toward Madeleine, the missing British girl.

The disappearance of Madeleine presided over the end of the risotto and all of the frittata, and one almost trembles to think that the topic was inspired by those dishes. But the fact that the girl's parents were doctors, as were most of the friends they were having dinner with when she disappeared, may have had some influence on why the topic lingered. My father, who can sometimes get quite moralistic, found plenty of blame to go around.

"I could never forgive myself for something like that," he said. "Leaving a three-year-old girl unsupervised!"

"A three-year-old girl and a pair of two-year-old twins," Señora García corrected, equally empathetic. "They left three kids unsupervised!"

"That sort of thing is why so many people assume the parents are guilty, and don't need further proof," observed Señor Álvarez.

"They say they sedated them," added Dr. García.

"Sedated them, on top of everything else!" continued my father. "I could never forgive myself!"

"Have you never sedated your daughter?" asked Sunan, teasing.

I laughed, but my father didn't. Had he actually sedated me?

"I think," said my mother, "if the public is now turning against the parents, it's because they were all too happy to expose themselves. It's one thing to do everything you can to get your daughter back, it's another to make sure there's always a camera pointed at you."

Next to Señor Álvarez, the woman, who had left her plate untouched, seemed as if she was about to say something, which sparked some anticipation. My mother gave her an encouraging look, ignoring her full plate; but when Señor Álvarez saw that she couldn't make up her mind, he stepped in:

"We live in a very complex society, and it's sometimes too much for us, don't you think? We're so hyper-informed that we run the risk of losing track of the truth."

"But does the truth exist?" asked Sunan, this time without sarcasm.

"Of course it does," asserted Señor Álvarez. "Admittedly, it shows a certain tendency to hide, so you have to peel back the layers. But it's our job to uncover it, wouldn't you agree?"

"I can't usually get past the first layer," said Sunan. "It wears me out!"

"That's because you're still very young and, if I may, a bit lazy."

Señor Álvarez formulated these accusations with a straight-forward graciousness, as though trying to connect with Sunan's language, and Sunan had no qualms about acknowledging his sins. My father, for his part, couldn't forget his own.

"However many layers it's hidden under, the truth is that this is a case of unforgivable negligence."

My mother, in her way, agreed with him:

"The parents of that poor girl have a few too many layers. They've created a whole industry around her disappearance! Is that dog and pony show really necessary? More to the point, has it really helped? She disappeared almost five months ago, and all they have so far is a bunch of dead-end leads. All those people who claim they saw her in Portugal, Malta, Belgium, Cartagena, now in Morocco ... what came of any of that?"

"The girl they saw in Morocco wasn't Madeleine, I just read about it in the paper," said Señora García. "It was a blonde girl, but she was a Berber."

"A Berber!" exclaimed my mother, as if confirming an intimate conviction. "What good was the message from David Beckham, the reward from the author of *Harry Potter*, the blessing from the Pope? Frankly I'm horrified to think that when a tragedy like this strikes, the first thing they do is get the PR machine going."

Señor Álvarez had set his fork and knife aside, and my mother, no matter how focused she is on one of her causes, never misses a detail like that. Fearing that the frittata would meet the same fate with him as it met with his uncertain partner, who kept playing with her fork without trying any of the food, she decided to use this obscurely shared action to level an accusation at both of them:

"Don't tell me you're already done!"

Señor Álvarez immediately grabbed his silverware, but his companion didn't follow suit.

"I agree," he said, clearing his throat, "that PR is a curse in the modern world, but in this case it might be justified. After all, they're only trying to combat the depersonalization and the lack of empathy that are also typical of today's world, wouldn't you say? People are so saturated with tragic news that they forget that something like this could happen to them, too, and it's good when someone reminds them."

"Look, a football star, a famous novelist, the pope himself ... I'm suspicious of empathy when it's tied to PR. It horrifies me to think that someone's pain could be used to boost someone else's image."

"But put yourself in the parents' place. If you have the resources of the modern world at your fingertips ..."

"Yes," concurred my father, "you're not putting yourself in their shoes."

"... and tell me," continued Señor Álvarez, "whether you'd reject that kind of help."

"Frankly I very much doubt that in a similar situation I'd get help from an army of celebrities."

"No," said Dr. Díaz suddenly, with a somewhat incoherent giggle. "For that you'd have to be Dr. Vázquez Romero!"

"Dr. Vázquez Romero?" Señor Álvarez was at a loss.

"The head of the geriatric psychiatry unit. You still haven't met her?" Dr. Díaz explained: "She single-handedly runs one of the most pointless wards in the hospital, tailor-made to her whims—I mean," he laughed again, "to her research."

"She's the queen of PR," added Dr. García in the same tone, "or rather, the queen of her own PR. She's got journalists eating out of her hand, but only in her department. Didn't you notice how much press the creation of that unit got?"

"And still gets. They call her a pioneer." Now Dr. Díaz was enjoying himself. "And she makes sure they keep treating her as if that lucky break were all her doing. She's terrified they'll close down her shop. You really haven't gone to see her yet?"

Señor Álvarez, unlike the rest of the guests, didn't seem to have kept up with the advancements of this particular medical star, nor did he give seem especially guilt-ridden for not having done so. Yet an awareness of his professional duties compelled him not to seem indifferent.

"No, I've hardly interacted with her," he replied.

"Well, you will, I assure you," said Dr. Díaz. "The geriatric psychiatry unit is neither economically profitable nor clinically justifiable. Scientifically, in fact, I'd say it's a result of that excessive hyper-specialization, not to say political correctness, which has no basis in science. There's nothing they treat there that can't easily be treated, and with no outside help, by our internists, neurologists, or psychiatrists. But I bet you'll have long talks with Dr. Vázquez Romero, and she'll appeal to your good feelings to convince you that's not the case."

"It's preposterous!" exclaimed Dr. García. "A hospital which doesn't even have a geriatric ward … has one for geriatric psychiatry!"

"Care for senior citizens," said Señor Álvarez, scrupulously choosing his words, as though he were the only one who remembered who was sitting next to him, "is one of the challenges of today's world."

Dr. Díaz and his colleague seemed suddenly to notice the age of the manager's dining companion, who at this point, through her very ambiguity, had become acceptably invisible to almost everyone. They backed off, as if they didn't want to look like Nazis discussing the Final Solution in front of a Jew.

"She's very close to Ruiz Gallardón, the mayor."

"And to that dancer, Duato," added Dr. García, as though naming an even more sinister crony.

"Right!" Dr. Díaz found it all very funny again. "If her daughter got kidnapped, we'd see the dancer and the mayor enlisted in the campaign … and they wouldn't be the only ones, ha ha!"

"Well, I'd hope," said my mother, happy to return to the case of the missing Madeleine, "that the dancer and the mayor would take the trouble to do their homework first."

"What do you mean?" asked Señor Álvarez, also rather relieved.

"Just that I think Beckham, Ms. *Harry Potter*, and the Pope himself …"

"Let's leave His Holiness out of this, please," interrupted Señor Álvarez, in a pleading tone that must have concealed a great weariness. It was the third time my mother had mentioned that individual with impunity.

"Of course," said my mother, backing down; and though I saw her pause to consider whether it was worth lingering on this point and redirecting the conversation, she went on: "I think it's advisable to wait a bit before getting so involved. The little girl had only been missing for a few days when all those celebrities jumped on the bandwagon to broadcast their solidarity. And now the Portuguese police are considering the parents as suspects. Would they have lent their support had they known how the case would evolve?"

"There's still no proof," said Señor Álvarez.

"Exactly! What if they're guilty after all?"

"I don't think they're guilty of anything," said my father, "except terrible negligence."

"But have you seen that picture," replied my mother, "where they're all smiles, holding up a t-shirt with the little girl's face on it? For the love of god, they've even got merchandising! How can they be smiling like that, delighted to be taking a picture?"

"I've seen interviews and statements on television where they're not smiling," added Señora García. "But it's true that they don't seem too upset, either. They struck me as very cold, but maybe it was the shock."

"That's probably how the police advised them to look," offered Señor Álvarez. "I understand that criminals can get excited at the sight of excessive displays of emotion. It's a psychological tactic."

"And the smiling, too?"

My mother was delighted to have picked up the thread again, but the doctors were again starting to get bored and seemed reluctant to leave behind the topic of Dr. Vázquez, which they evidently found amusing. This resulted in two simultaneous conversations, something a good hostess should never allow, but my mother is too used to the hubbub—from the other dinner parties, especially—to worry about its ill effects, among them the fact that it drives me crazy. A conversation's interest lies in its topic, and not so much the people discussing it, and I don't understand why some people feel that simply having to wait their turn for a few seconds—a few minutes, even—constitutes an assault on their very personality. I know my father shares my view, but last night it was Señor Álvarez, I think, who suffered most from that lack of discipline and generosity. He found himself shamefully forced to attend to both fronts, because even though Dr. Díaz and Dr. García hardly spoke to him directly, they took good care he heard everything they said about the aforementioned doctor, and especially about her dubious relations with the anti-privatization committee, while my mother continued her attack on the parents of Madeleine. Sunan, likewise trapped between the two sides, quickly gave up trying to balance them and sought freedom, as one often does when committing philosophical suicide, in the most desperate place: in this case, in the smiling, silent woman still playing with a bit of food, with whom he tried to open up—good lord—a third front in the conversation. By the fourth or fifth try he managed something like a victory, because the woman was heard to say, weakly:

"It's very noisy in here."

Señor Álvarez looked at her with a worried ambivalence, agreeing with her opinion but annoyed by her choice of expression. It came as a shock that someone who hadn't stood out for her loquacity suddenly revealed such a dangerous store of opinions. But since Señor Álvarez wasn't Dr. Díaz, he didn't tell her to be quiet; and all Dr. Díaz could do, since the woman wasn't his wife, was make a face and stifle a laugh. My mother pretended she hadn't heard, and continued a bit longer with her anti-McCann campaign, prepared to make clear her indifference to this woman who opened her mouth only to criticize her home. But I knew that soon enough she'd take it as a sign, and that we didn't have long to wait before we heard "Making Whoopee."

This saucy little tune also let her take revenge by showing off her many talents—especially that frog's voice she puts on, taking it up like a grand challenge, ever since her friend Rulfo said Stephen Sondheim would go crazy for it. I don't know whether my mother's singing tortured the woman's implacable ear, or whether she let herself be convinced that it could pass for music, but I confess that as I accompanied my mother on the piano, amid all kinds of jokes, I didn't take my eyes off her. I couldn't figure her out, and from what I saw, neither could Señor Álvarez: in fact, he didn't even seem to share my curiosity, which I assumed he would. He continued to regard her with distance and indifference, not to say violence, even though by now it was clear she was a person who required less curiosity than attention and care. He bobbed his head gracelessly, avoided looking at her, and sunk into an unnecessary concentration. For a second I even thought he was a sadist: beneath his deceptive manners, his tact, and his semi-cultured air lay a boorishness that wasn't out of place in this community of nervous, unhappy doctors, saddled with obligatory wives they found burdensome in company and in private, one suspects, an unwelcome substitute for fantasy.

Later, in the kitchen, as I helped her serve the ice cream, my mother remarked:

"She's sick!" This wasn't a clinical diagnosis, but more like the violation of a taboo. "Why didn't he let us know? You don't bring that kind of baggage to a dinner party without giving a heads-up."

When we got back to the dining room, I sensed a sort of awkward anticipation that wasn't for the ice cream. Instead of calming them down, the music had left them in a silence that seemed to demand accountability, and no one dared break it. My mother, whose recitals are usually followed by a rowdy enthusiasm, frowned at this widespread unease. Judging by the look she gave my father, she must have hoped he would save her from the wreckage. Sunan, with the best of intentions, but unsure of what he was invoking, began to hum "Making Whoopee." Dr. Díaz swirled his glass in an act of bravery.

"This liqueur is superb!"

My mother smiled, somewhat composed, and started talking about papayas with an unhealthy erudition. When she served the ice cream, the woman looked up and said:

"It's green."

"Don't worry," replied my mother, prepared for the worst. "It's delicious, it's pistachio. Come on, try some, you've hardly eaten a thing all night."

This was much further than anyone had dared go. I saw a look of terror on my father's face, and a new look of displeasure on Señor Álvarez's face, as if he'd once again been asked for explanations he wasn't willing to give. The woman continued to stare vacantly at my mother, in a now characteristic expression that could make sense only in another world. But this time her stare came with a gentle tremble that grew as she seemed to become aware of her confusion. Suddenly, with startling force she shoved her plate away, as though warding off a demon, and without getting up, pushed her chair back.

"Is everything all right, Señora Álvarez?" asked Señora García shyly, seeing that Señor Álvarez continued not to intervene. "Are you feeling ill?"

The woman remained a few feet away from the table, as though looking for some protection she couldn't find. She didn't answer, but Señor Álvarez spoke.

"Señora Álvarez?" he said, not even looking at her. "I'm glad I finally have the chance to clear up a misunderstanding that should not be allowed to go on any longer. You seem to think that I have some sort of relationship to this woman, when the truth is I've never met her."

"What?" said my mother. "But didn't you arrive together?"

"Well, no … I ran into her in the elevator and we rode up together. Then I saw her follow me into your home … I assumed she was one of your guests."

"What? She's not with you?"

Señor Álvarez felt liberated.

"Certainly not. In fact, I wondered why nobody had introduced me."

"We were wondering why you hadn't introduced her to us!" said my mother, practically breathing a sigh of relief. "We didn't know whether she was your …"

"But then who is she?" My father interrupted her, focusing on what was perhaps the central question.

We all turned to the woman as if she could solve the mystery, though at that point we should have known that she was an even greater mystery to herself. It was a reflex action whose pointlessness was immediately apparent, so with a sudden commotion that everyone was thankful for, measures began to be taken. The woman no longer had that vacant expression: now she seemed genuinely terrified.

"She clearly just wandered in. Does she have Alzheimer's? Korsakov syndrome?" whispered Dr. Díaz, standing up and looking toward Dr. García.

"We'll have to give her a mini-mental state exam."

"And check the backs of her eyes."

"Get a Valium," said my father, sitting up and looking at my mother. She went to the medicine cabinet, and Señora García exclaimed:

"She's a missing person!"

In this way, in the space of a few seconds, the woman who up until then had been the object of a forced and irritated curiosity, not even about herself but about the more interesting story of Señor Álvarez, acquired an infectious autonomy and became a case of serious concern, medically and socially. As such she had to be placed in quarantine. The doctors began by taking her by the arm and leading her not to a bed, as they intended (my mother wouldn't let them), but to an armchair in the living room—despite objections from Sunan, who reminded everyone that the prints on the wall seemed to upset her. Once she'd been cast into that hostile environment, Dr. García proceeded to interrogate her rigorously but wholly unsuccessfully, while Señor Álvarez shrugged with vague culpability. Señora García was excited by the chance to witness a criminal arrest.

"Can you tell us your name? Do you know what year it is? Who is the king of Spain?"

Clearly, the woman had landed abruptly in a reality she'd been oblivious to, and the shock was brutal. No wonder: how could anyone endure such a dinner party except in a state of unconsciousness? My father made her take a Valium, which she accepted as though familiar with the procedure: she kept her mouth open for a moment, apparently expecting more. This remedy might be considered cheap and desperate, but presumably my father knew of no better way to try to return her to the limbo she'd stepped out of. At least there, in that limbo, her lack of identity caused her no apparent discomfort, and more significantly, caused only minor discomfort to everyone else. Until then her identity had been secondary, at best, as the "companion" of a man we didn't hesitate to make the focus of our speculations. I found it strange, as I said, to see her suddenly attract the attention—somewhere between savage and dogmatic—of the same people who had so quickly thrown up their hands at her hazy but untroubling status. If she lacked an identity, it was because no one had given one to her. Once we saw that our assumptions rested on a false premise, though, a real void opened up, disastrous and unbearable. We had to urgently mobilize all available forces to fill it.

Yet even while those forces could now act freely, unconstrained by courtesy—which in the case of Dr. Díaz and Dr. García meant a showy professionalism, while my father simply looked apologetic—they likewise ran the risk of failing. The fact was, the question of this woman's identity could no longer be answered by clarifying her relationship to Señor Álvarez—and these doctors, who hardly ever left the circle of their expertise, may not have been especially qualified to answer it any other way. An expedition outside that circle required an inordinate (because unusual) effort, and wouldn't necessarily lead to any answers, or even to a sense of what to ask. What could they want to know about an intruder, a stranger? For the moment they were content to treat her as a patient, rather than as a missing person, but even so the search focused on finding a proper name, an address, or at the very least a document issued by the State. It was I who realized, when my mother asked, that I hadn't seen her carrying a purse when she walked in. Such a source of information would now be invaluable, but search as we might (Señora García lingered mysteriously in my parents' bedroom), no purse was forthcoming, and my mother reproached me for missing such an important detail.

"A woman without a purse! How could you not notice something like that?"

"Never mind that now," said Señor Álvarez. "This woman walked in very confidently. Are you sure you've never seen her?"

I don't know if Señor Álvarez had sensed at some point that someone had secretly accused him of being a sadist, but he now seemed to return the compliment. "Think back," he insisted.

Dr. García carried on with his inquisition:

"Is your name Carmen? Elisa? Cristina?"

The woman, totally devastated, seemed to be making an effort, not to help but to find a way back to her dream world, since my father's Valium was taking its time. But harried by the enemy, she finally succumbed.

"My son ... Where is my son?" she whispered, slowly turning her head from one side to the other.

"She has a son!" announced Señora García.

"My ... Dr. Gandía."

At last, a name.

"Gandía ... Gandía ... Sound familiar to any of you?"

The doctors looked at one another at length, but they gave no response, to the disappointment of Señor Álvarez, who seemed to expect a more effective response from the profession. He insisted, with even more reason, that it was "odd" that no one knew the aforementioned doctor, especially since we could now deduce that the woman knew one by that name; since no one reacted, he suggested calling the Board Association. Here my mother almost jumped up in indignation, but my father, in his most soothing tone, restrained her by telling Señor Álvarez that calling at this hour would be of no use. Instead, it occurred to me to look up the name Gandía in the White Pages, the only directory on hand just then. The proposal met with skepticism, but Sunan sat down beside me and together we came up with a strategy. We counted twenty-eight Gandías, a number we felt wasn't unmanageable, and we decided to start with the ones with the nearest addresses. Neither the Gandía on Andrés Mellado nor the one on Galileo, though both very eager to help, turned out to be doctors, but the one on Santa Engracia was, and he even had a mother who more or less fit the description of our guest— though she didn't live with him and he didn't have any reason to assume she was "missing." Asked whether she suffered from blackouts, he replied with a promising "I wouldn't be surprised" and, plainly alarmed, he said he'd try to locate her and would call us back. The thought that we'd found a possible savior with the third Gandía made us feel clever, and helped create a sense of relief; when the man called back to say he couldn't get ahold of his mother, and that even though she might have just gone to the movies with her friends, he was uneasy, we felt a sense of triumph. The man was invited to come and personally make sure his mother hadn't "done anything odd," and as we waited for him, my own mother began to serve everyone malt whisky. Everyone downed it practically as if they were just coming out of a long period of probationary abstinence. Even the poor woman, now visibly affected by the Valium, gave the impression that she harbored a certain hope.

Hardly twenty minutes later Dr. Gandía appeared, a handsome man of about forty with a fondness for UV rays, who turned out to be a dentist and showed a certain awe for the experts who introduced themselves to him. He disappointed us all when he didn't recognize the woman he'd gone to such trouble for as his mother. Nor, needless to say, did she recognize him. A few minutes later a call from his wife informed us that his mother was safe and sound in her own home, and hadn't taken kindly to the suspicion that she could be out doing "something odd" when she had, after all, simply gone to the movies with her friends. Dr. Gandía then accepted a whisky, and rather than return to his own concerns, eagerly joined in everyone else's, adopting an air of competence and solidarity. Since she wasn't his mother, he was sorry the woman wasn't at least his patient.

"What a sad situation," he said.

Meanwhile, Sunan and I, somewhat discouraged, returned to our exploration of the White Pages. We had no luck: the next twenty-five Gandías either weren't at home or weren't doctors, or didn't have a mother prone to getting lost. The woman looked more and more alone, even if sleepy (or "calm," as my father made a point of noting); the questions about her identity had been abandoned in view of the minimal credibility of her testimony; and her state of technical abandonment had only confirmed that the diagnosis of "ill," as vague as it seemed, was on the contrary sufficient and precise. The doctors had done their job, and in due time, the hospitals would do theirs. Meanwhile, said the dentist, with a clarity that his status as an outsider conferred on him, everything that could be done had already been done, so all they could do now was treat her as a missing person and call the police.

Señora García had said as much all along, and when the officers arrived—an athletic pair, a young man and young woman, powered by the hypnotic sound of their walkie-talkies—she took charge of the situation, offering an ordered account of all the causes, misunderstandings, and symptoms observed over the course of the evening. My mother, no doubt tired of surprise guests, remained deliberately in the background. In her view everything had gone terribly wrong, and I could see she judged herself harshly, convinced she hadn't risen to the occasion. She was probably thinking about the sorry story she'd have to tell her more worldly friends, among whom the matter would have been resolved differently. (Not too differently, I'd say: the woman might have been ushered out with less confusion or delay, but her destination would have been the same.) I think she let herself be comforted when Señor Álvarez, seeing that Sunan insisted on going along to the police station, so the woman wouldn't spend all night alone waiting for someone to pick her up, congratulated her on having "such an altruistic son-in-law" joining the family.

"Sunan is great," said my mother. "But they don't want to get married."

"Coming to this house is always an adventure," added Dr. Díaz.

This was, with little moral variation, the conclusion reached by all the guests, even Dr. Gandía, who now seemed eager to go home. Shortly after the woman left, offering no resistance, escorted by the officers and followed by Sunan, the party broke up, perhaps because everyone realized that, had they stayed longer, they would have celebrated. Satisfied with this small feeling of decency, they opted to go home knowing they'd done a good deed. Dr. Díaz and Dr. García left with the added bonus of having shown in practice, with their abilities, the uselessness of the geriatric psychiatry ward. As he made to leave, Señor Álvarez stated that he didn't regret what had happened, because life puts us to the test when we least expect it, and you should never waste a chance to help others. My father smiled, at last.

Sunan returned early this morning. The missing persons report for Irene Ramil was filed around six and shortly thereafter a shaken, disheveled man showed up, apparently the same age as the woman, who claimed to be her husband. He explained he'd fallen asleep very early, around eight o'clock, and hadn't woken up until dawn, at which point he noticed his wife's absence. He knew right away what had happened.

"They live three blocks away from your parents and don't have any children," Sunan told me, rolling a joint. "She didn't seem to recognize him—but then, really, he also seemed a bit lost. I'm curious who this Dr. Gandía is."

## II

Really, instead of aiming for simplification and general validity, rules should exist to handle the tricky cases: that's when we need them and when they'd really be useful. In business, for example, people often quote a rule that goes, "don't make friends with your clients," and failure to follow it is supposed to lead to great misfortune. This truism, with its fatalist overtones, doesn't reveal any hidden conflicts, as a good rule should, because it doesn't take a genius to sense when a friendship is forced or doesn't grow out of affection. You don't need much help, unless you're really gullible, to recognize when someone's trying to curry favor with you, secretly hoping for discounts, handouts, or credit, and you'd have to be pretty unprofessional—to take the opposite scenario—to hope to find, in a business transaction, a closeness or attachment that's not bound by self-interest.

So if rules are redundant in general, how could they not be redundant in particular? Where's the rule that tells us what to do, for example, when someone who was once a friend becomes a client? Do we refuse to enter into a new kind of relationship? And what if, more precisely, someone who was a friend and became client disappears as a client only to reappear as a friend? What if, on top of that, the friend had no chance of ever becoming a client again?

I reflected on these convoluted relationships, under the effects of some rather desperate circumstances, after I got an email from Javier with the schedule of the "autumnal events" of the Valle Medio del Lozoya Hiking Association. The message had obviously been sent to his entire contact list, and this fact, along with the more than three years it had been since I last saw him, left little doubt about whether I'd slipped in or been included on purpose. But in an optimistic interpretation of this lapse of time,

I also remembered that at least two years had gone by between when we stopped hanging out as friends and when he showed up again as a client. More awkward was the fact that when he disappeared as a client, he also disappeared as a friend. Could his email be seen not only as an accident, but as further proof of a tendency to reappear? Of course not.

Still, the desperate circumstances I was in gave me an idea, and I wrote him a few lines, barely mentioning my life but showing great interest in his—now focused, apparently, on forest activities and organizations. I assumed I'd received his email by mistake, and I invited him with exaggerated, melodramatic humor to rectify the error. Two days went by which I spent, more dramatically than melodramatically—as it were—packing my bags and getting my furniture ready for a move, with no idea what I'd do next. I broke my lease, I hired some movers to take my things to a storage facility, and for the time being I moved into an extended-stay hotel. My Mexican friend was still showing no signs of life, in an alarmingly literal way. I didn't know anyone who knew him—that really is a rule—so I had no other way of getting in touch. Once the extended-stay hotel began to feel like it was being watched, I got an answer from Javier.

His response wasn't long or effusive, and he hid a little behind the distance, mysteriously reporting that his life had taken a "strange turn," and that he'd spent the last six months "in a sort of town, a community," eighty miles outside Madrid. He said he'd been living in "seclusion," though this word didn't suggest any great spiritual profundity. He'd lost his job and stopped working on his doctorate, and everything had gone "pretty bad," and now he and his girlfriend, Rebeca, were "waiting," though for what he didn't say. She was the one who accidentally forwarded the first email to his whole contact list, he said—the hikers are always asking them to "spread the word"—and when she got my message, she encouraged him to reply, since he was now "basically an invalid." After that came a smiley emoticon, but he concluded by saying, "Enough about my boring life."

A less self-interested reader would have declined to ask for details and left this little psychological feast for another time. Probably in other circumstances I would have held back, sticking to the letter of the message, which didn't invite further questions, and offered an excuse for not asking any. But instead I stuck to its spirit. In his invalid status and his "boring life," I saw a rather childish display of gloominess, and beneath that I saw a masked, restless, inexpressible plea for help—a normal plea, in other words. I saw that his girlfriend Rebeca, with less agitation, was also pleading, and I saw, in those eighty kilometers that led to their community, a providential escape route.

I wasn't unaware of my friend's talent for understatement: when he said he didn't want to be a bother, he might well mean he'd rather not be bothered. Even so, without giving it much thought, I typed out a few more lines, much less funny that the first ones, expressing regret for the distance and accusing myself of opportunism, because my life, too, I admitted, had taken "a strange turn," and I could use "a refuge," someplace I could disappear for a time. I'd just disconnected my mobile number, but I already had a new one, and I gave it to him in case he wanted to call me.

I realize I'd taken a step on some very slippery terrain—the terrain where you find people you remember but don't know if you know. I doubted whether the times before our "strange turns" (though what times were those, really?) justified an appeal to hospitality. Javier and I had met, when we were in school, in a shared flat: we moved in at the same time and had the two worst rooms, which our other two roommates had assigned to us, asserting their privilege as long-standing tenants to take the best ones for themselves and treat us as if they were the owners. That made us allies, but it also turned out we came from the same ancient provincial city. And even though, somewhat surprisingly, we'd never met, we inevitably discovered we had friends and acquaintances in common. We spontaneously formed a united front against the preexisting tenants, stealing their candy and roast chickens; and less spontaneously, since he was studying sciences and I was doing humanities, we made a point of coordinating study schedules and including each other in parties, hangovers, and trips to McDonald's or to the Chinese joint.

We got along: he was from a good family, a traditional one—that is, the kind that leads a double life. He was always falling for bar waitresses, and he managed to sleep with them with a regularity that made me jealous—all the while keeping a vague girlfriend he spoke to on the phone. My father ran a frame shop, and had a group of more or less artistic contacts, which in me had given rise to certain aspirations and a flair for striped t-shirts—something which often worked, if not on waitresses, then on their less pretty friends. My secondary status wasn't a source of humiliation, and besides, it wasn't set in stone, either: I remember how Virginie Lausson fell spectacularly for me, and for a few weeks Javier had to make do with Katia Ruiz. We lent each other money, we smoked each other's cigarettes, we drank from the same cup; we waited for each other to make plans, we traded oddities of comparative literature and gross anatomy, and I don't think we felt alone for even a moment.

The situation changed in our third year, when his parents found him more luxurious housing with some cousins who had just moved, and I stayed in the old apartment with his old nightstands and a replacement who turned out to be just as fussy as the previous tenants. I thought about moving, but I didn't do anything more than think about it—inertia was already becoming a character trait of mine. Barely leaving my room, I became a loner and focused on school, and soon began to show a lot of promise. Something similar must have happened to him—his upstanding cousins must have rubbed off on him. We saw each other less and less in the city, but more and more on vacations, in the town where we were born and where we never used to see each other at all: that's where, in the chill of an ancient city building, we rung in the arrival of the third millennium. That was one occasion, but to recall another I have to fast-forward about two years, to the Strokes' first concert at La Riviera. We didn't go there together, but we left together, and it turned out to be a perfect night: we took just the right combination of drugs to get high as kites, then ended up practically curled up in the corner of an after-hours bar, far away from everyone else. It was clear we had run into each other at a critical time, but it became just as clear, since we didn't see each other afterward, that we wouldn't follow through all the way. We didn't have another real encounter until the day when he showed up, introduced by a regular, at the place I was living. By then I was a supplier, and he was now a customer.

We were both surprised, and also—why deny it—embarrassed, but a remnant of our old familiarity and a sober assessment of what we stood to gain helped us overcome the awkwardness. He didn't come back right away, but eventually he did, and for a few years I could count on him to stop by two or three times a month, between Thursday and Saturday, looking for "just a gram"—he always used in moderation—and forty-five minutes of "sampling" and chatting. He decided our arrangement was optimal from a safety standpoint, first because I wouldn't cheat him, which he wasn't far wrong about, and second because at my place he wouldn't risk being exposed to some "sketchy scene." About this he was less right, but fortune spared him the exposure,

as far as I remember. Aside from the ease of business, moreover,
I offered a certain social dignity, which back then was important
for him: I didn't sell on the street and I looked presentable, and
artists and musicians were always coming and going from my
place, something he liked. He said I had a "select clientele" and
was happy not to look more closely.

As for him, he was on the right path: he'd graduated with
honors, was enthusiastic about his residency, and found time
on the side to do research—his "calling," he said. Sometimes
he felt like the next Ramón y Cajal. He probably didn't understand what had happened to me, since I also did well at school,
and here I was, peddling drugs. He was polite enough to ignore
this fact, and when I confessed one day that I was wasting my
talents, he laughed and said that doing that took a lot of courage. Besides, wasn't I publishing reviews—of books, concerts,
albums—in several magazines? Wasn't I the webmaster for the
Harmony site? Didn't I have a free pass everywhere? Yes, I did
have all that, back when I still tried to conceal my activities, but
what I mostly had was a case of *mal du siècle*, and some goth
accessories to match. He prudently ignored this, and it didn't
occur to him that at such a young age you could feel like you'd
lived a hundred years without ever knowing where you were
going. I won't deny it sometimes did me good to feel embarrassed about being such an arts and letters type: I now think of
this business with a slightly shameful modesty, though a modesty free of remorse; back then I saw it as a sacrifice conceived
in apathy but fiercely carried out. That's why it was nice to have
someone like him, who could remind me of other times and
other possibilities—times and possibilities that he believed still
hadn't been sacrificed—and who was himself an example of how
to balance competence and recreation. As far as balance goes, he
used to say that the best antidote to drug use was laziness, since

he'd soon get tired of looking for a fix if he didn't have one so
easily within reach. But there must have been reasons other than
laziness, because even though I remained available, he told me
one day he was going to stop coming by as often. He said he
wanted a "break," but in fact he never came back.

I started to feel that the business had taken over my identity,
since for many people I couldn't "be" anything else. But it wasn't
the first time, nor would it be the last, that I'd gotten used to—
maybe even taken a liking to—being invisible.

I sent him the email asking for "a refuge" at night, and the
next morning he called me. Or rather he didn't call me, Rebeca
did, on his behalf. She said that Javier didn't have a mobile phone
"at the moment"—a white lie—but they had talked and would
both be "delighted, of course" to have me come. "We've got
plenty of room, so you can stay with us as long as you want,
starting tonight, if you'd like." It was all very strange, really: the
intermediary voice, the generosity of the gesture, the quick reply.
We seemed to be—all of us—in a state of emergency, though
not the kind decreed by the government. Was Javier really doing
that badly? Rebeca told me that if I didn't have a car, I'd have
some trouble getting to the community, since all they had was a
small van running between four or five nearby towns and a bus
to Madrid on weekends. If I didn't want to wait until Saturday,
she said, she could come get me any night I wanted—"today,
even"—since she drove down to Madrid every day for work,
and although she left late—we wouldn't be able to meet before
nine—she thought this would be the most convenient option,
if that sounded good to me. I told her, offering no justification,
that it sounded great, and that as far as I was concerned I could
be ready that very night. With a tactlessness I later regretted, I
forgot to add that I was looking forward to seeing Javier; but then
before she hung up she asked me, with a similarly questionable

tact, though obviously on Javier's instructions, if I could bring "some product." I didn't tell her that several days earlier I flushed all the "product" I had left down the toilet.

I was a little worried, wondering how I'd pay for my lodging now that the issue had, after a fashion, been brought up. My travel bags, suspiciously bulging, might give the wrong idea— rather than an imprecise idea—of my intentions. A few hours later, as I loaded them into the trunk of Rebeca's car, making room among a bunch of very full grocery bags, I noticed she hadn't said anything about them, and we were barely halfway when I began to guess why. Everything began in an extremely confusing fashion, with smiles and kisses on the cheek in the parking lot of a small clinic off Arturo Soria, on a cold, rainy night between two utter strangers. I had enough time to realize how exceedingly attractive she was—in that, Javier must not have changed—and she too seemed to remember, beneath her tangled hair, her umbrella, and her visible fatigue. But minutes later we were in the car, not knowing what to say, inconceivably listening to an awful show on talk radio about the queen of Spain's recent statements on homosexuality and abortion. I asked whether she worked long hours, and she said, "it's insane," explaining that she spent the day stepping in for people wherever she was needed. I gathered that, like Javier, she was a doctor, and that if things had taken a "strange turn" for her, at least it wasn't for lack of activity.

The rain grew worse. At one point it poured so hard we had to pull over. In a flooded town just off the highway we stopped at a bar that struck me as full of refugees, and that's where I learned what the price of my lodging would be. Hearing her speak, though, with her cautious hope, someone else might consider "price" to be an ungracious term for what she presented to me as a noble mission. In all honesty, she said, Javier needed "company," "a friend": he spent the whole day alone, not doing a thing, refusing to take any medication. She apologized for speaking "so directly," but she had no choice: she had to prepare me to find him "wallowing in anxiety." She couldn't rely on the thirty-four residents of the community, and even though there could be up to eighty on weekends, the extra people didn't seem to do anyone any good. Certainly not her: she needed to find "something else" for him, someone like me who could remind him of "the things he'd lost," at least until they could move away. Earlier—in a sort of prehistory—they both lived in a "nice, very large apartment with a patio," near the Plaza de España, but "when things went sour" all those virtues suddenly took a backseat to paying rent, which "ate up everything." They had to move out. Javier had a seasonal contract in a state-run hospital and was absolutely certain that once it ended he'd get an intern position; but he had "bad luck," and the new management closed down the unit he applied for, and with this as an excuse, decided to downsize him.

Winding up on the street must have been a tough blow for someone like him, since up till then he had his pick of jobs. Yet apparently he took it well at first, and quickly landed a temporary position in a private practice. The two of them were very close: they'd never been closer; they knew how important it was to "roll with the punches," to keep working while they waited, and "not just wait around." But this relationship between the "punches" and his stoic, honorable spirit didn't last, and two or three months later everything that didn't happen when he was laid off happened now that he had a job: a "minor conflict" about the air conditioning—it was hard to imagine what it could have been—led to an "outburst of rage," and Javier, not thinking of the consequences, fired himself. "I'm tired of being prudent," he said when he got home, and he stayed that way for a long time: furious, with no prudence and no severance.

At this point Rebeca's story took on a more clinical tone, as if until then it had been too personal, even though it was clearly not her first time telling it: she seemed used to airing certain intimate details, probably after keeping them unproductively locked up for a time. Nor was her transition to a clinical tone (Javier had "presented symptoms of depression") tentative: she must have decided long ago she had a case to treat, and perhaps it was easier to have a patient at home than a boyfriend adrift. Their reasons for moving to the community were mainly financial—now they paid four hundred euros in rent, less than a third of what they paid near the Plaza de España—but also naively therapeutic: she thought that "out there in nature" he'd find sufficient "peace" and "distance" to be able "think and find calm." It was clear it hadn't occurred to her that "nature" might also show him its worst face. As for me, no fan of abrupt changes, I felt that such a clean break with city life, where one could remember one's failure but also envision overcoming it, closed off more paths than it opened up. This idea had been "both of theirs," and they were determined to stick it out, farther and farther away from the murky abyss of desperation where they conceived it; and now it was just "a pity" that he wasn't "doing a little more on his end." Rebeca was really angry about his refusal to take medication, which not only hindered her clinical handling of the case, but seemed to have shattered her hopes, too.

In my opinion, the ideas these two had about nature were very confused. First, they called a work setback a "storm," and second, they sought "peace" in a small mountain community. And the one most affected by the catastrophe insisted on not taking medication and letting "nature" run its course, without any scary artificial chemicals. Obviously I didn't say any of this at the time.

I couldn't help thinking now, however, that the allusions to medication, which came up over and over, incriminated me. Rebeca may have had some sort of alternative therapy in mind, and I figured it would be best to disabuse her of that notion as soon as possible. I told her I hadn't been able to get the "product" she asked for.

"Don't you do that anymore?" she asked in reply. Seeing me hesitate, she drew her own conclusions. "Probably better that way. I'd rather not think what it'd be like to have him up there high all day."

So probably the idea, this one at least, wasn't hers.

She didn't ask about my ideas. Nor about my motives. I hadn't stopped looking at her and thinking that, gorgeous as she was, with everything she could be doing in a sunnier setting, it was a shame she devoted so much time to a wreck of a boyfriend and an uncooperative nature. She hadn't taken off her parka, and her figure was still baggy, but I was almost certain she had big breasts. I've never understood couples that spend time all their time with each other. I surprised myself wondering if I could squeeze in through a crack.

In a certain sense I was happy to see that the situation, so dependent on its own internal logic, wasn't suddenly going to focus on me. They were unlikely to pay me much attention. What's more, I'd discovered a way to take my mind off my worries, through an unexpected and not entirely altruistic interest in Javier's. My desperate optimism was put to certain tests over the following days, as I'll explain, but I'd say I voluntarily stuck to it, on the whole.

Javier, hollow-eyed and reticent, welcomed me quietly and without enthusiasm. He'd hardly had the time—or the spirit— to prepare himself for an occasion that threatened his routine and which he'd probably agreed to under pressure. Even so, he gave me a warm hug and looked at me as though we'd both just been caught in some criminal activity, calling to mind what I'd consider a happy memory of the last time we saw each other. He didn't seem too disappointed when I broke the news that I didn't have any product. As Rebeca unloaded the grocery bags, he showed me around the house and took me up to what would be my room, which I noticed had been swept, mopped, and dusted. Inside there was only a desk and a computer, an office chair, a small recliner, a freshly made cot, a bookshelf with some boxes, and several more boxes on the floor. He told me he used it as an "office," though it looked more like a storeroom. There was no dresser, so I'd have to use his, in his bedroom, or make room on the bookshelf, which is what I opted to do: this reinforced the sense that the arrangement was temporary, a feeling we felt it advisable to cultivate from the start.

The house was on one side of what had originally been an old manor, practically torn down and renovated a few years before by the owner, a builder who also happened to be the mayor of the community. It was three stories tall: the ground floor had a living and dining room, separated from the kitchen by a countertop, a bathroom, and place for firewood under the stairs; the second floor, where I'd be staying, had a smallish but not cramped bedroom with a large window and a bathroom on the landing; the upper floor had a sizeable attic bedroom, with a Japanese bed, where Javier told me I could put the desk with the computer, if they were in my way. The strange thing, I thought, was that he didn't mind leaving them there. He explained that, because of some quirk of the telephone network, the right half of the town had ADSL, but the left half didn't, and "we" were on the left; in any event, if he wanted to check his email or get online, he had friends on the right-hand side he could call on. "This is like a commune," he smiled. "We all share everything." I felt, if not quite comfortable, then at least relieved, as though I'd reached safe harbor after an uncertain journey. For the moment I didn't worry whether the harbor might turn out to be a stormy, hostile place; compared to what I'd left behind, it was a safe place, and that was what mattered.

When we came back down we found Rebeca cooking. She had taken off the parka and finally I saw her, looking impressive in skinny jeans and a brown turtleneck sweater; I wasn't wrong about her chest.

"Did you get the interdental brushes?" asked Javier.

"They didn't have any at the supermarket."

"Well, you'll have to go to a pharmacy," he grumbled, "and in a pharmacy they're much more expensive."

Rebeca didn't answer. She turned to me, smiling, but said mostly to him:

"I'm making you a meatball stew, so you'll have food for a few days. In the freezer there are still three pieces of lasagna and chicken curry for two."

Afterward we had cheese, paté, and German bread for dinner, somewhat guiltily, at least on my end. I was beginning to get an idea of how the responsibilities were divided in that house, and I didn't really like finding myself so easily assigned to the side that had none. I decided right then that I'd take charge of the kitchen the very next day, and I told Javier so as soon as Rebeca, after eating dinner and washing up, had gone to sleep. "Don't worry about her," he said, and I asked him if he meant that he was taking care of her.

"I can see," he replied, "that she's brought you up to speed," adding that he didn't want to talk about the situation just then. Maybe I'd like to bring him up to speed on my problems? I realized I was taking on the role of "friend" too literally and too soon, and I decided to back off a little. Pretending I was so familiar with the situation from the start wasn't a good idea. Among "friends" there's supposed to be no need to beat around the bush, but I'd assumed, prematurely—to make up for how much time had passed—that our friendship still existed, while Javier, with the shrewdness of a loner, seemed to think we still had to regain it.

So with the best of intentions, I openly told him about my situation. I explained my motives, the ominous disappearance of my contact, my suspicions that he'd been arrested, and the precautions I'd taken to pack up my operations and get out of town while I waited for things to clear up. It wasn't the first time this had happened, and actually I was confident everything would calm down and return to normal.

"The worst part is moving," I ended. "But by now I've gotten used to living like a monk, without many possessions."

"And what do you do with the money?"

I don't know what he would have said if I'd told him I had twenty thousand euros hidden in the lining of one of my travel bags.

"Well, I certainly don't buy a lot of furniture."

We were sitting on the large white sofa covered in blankets, but its impeccable minimalist design was clearly visible. All the furniture I'd seen up till now, with the exception of my cot, was expensive and elegant; so were the pressure cooker, the dinnerware, and the glasses, which still had a bit of wine. They stood in sad contrast to porcelain tiles and the Provençal details on the doors and the kitchen cabinets, all in the most exaggerated rustic style. The contrast gave the sense of an extended transience that felt threatening when looked at as fate. Javier, however, seemed to have adapted to living among expensive things on a cheap floor. In response to my story, all he did was give a quick sketch of his own. He acknowledged that it had been "quite a blow" to

lose his job, right after (and because) he'd applied for a position
in a ward where he thought he had a future—the chief doctor
had all but guaranteed he'd get it, promising as well all kinds of
facilities for his "research on mitochondrial dysfunction"—and
the experience had "cured him once and for all of making plans."
He was normally "cautious and sensible," but he'd seen how he
could "snap" and still hadn't gotten over "the shame" that this
caused him. He couldn't make sense of what he did. He worried
a little about what he was doing now—indefinitely prolonging
his retreat to lick his wounds, out there in the country—but not
one bit about what he'd do later on. He was confident that time,
"through its own dynamic," would sort things out.

"Please don't get on my case."

That night we didn't talk much more. I got the impression
we were both just doing the minimum. I did find it a little
strange when he suddenly suggested we watch a movie on his
enormous plasma screen TV. A friend from the right-hand side
named Juanma downloaded movies on eMule and passed them
along. Just then he had *Wanted*, with Angelina Jolie. In any case,
I was still taking in his suggestion, so incongruous for a night
of reconnecting with a friend, when I saw him put the disk in
the player and press play on the remote. Since he'd accepted the
idea that he'd have to consider me part of his routines, I suppose he wanted to signal that I'd have to consider him part of
mine, too—and that I'd better adapt quickly. Ten minutes were
enough for me to see that the recording, made in a theater, was
out of focus, jerky, and barely audible, and that he didn't care.
Thinking I'd asked too much of myself for one night, I opted to
let him surrender alone to that sacrifice of quality, and wishing
him a good night, I went up to go to bed.

Before I started undressing, I heard steps on the landing and a quiet knock on my door, which I hadn't closed all the way. It was Rebeca, in gray silk pajamas with white polka dots.

"Did everything go okay?"

I wanted to reassure her and said yes. She was just about to ask for details, but then she thought better of it. I was about to say she was right about what she told me on the trip up, and I also shied away.

"Don't forget to go to the garden tomorrow. See if there's any cabbage left."

The weeks I spent with them passed by in a flurry of rules, open and reiterated in Rebeca's case, silent and convoluted in Javier's, and there was a moment when I tried to set some myself, though I had the help of some accomplices. I hadn't gone there to save a friend, really, but since I was there and the beautiful Rebeca had asked me to, I wasn't going to not lend a hand—and anyway, it would be better than spending my time looking out on the landscape where my own path had led me. It's too soon to talk about that, though. Maybe it's best to tell first about the conditions that made it possible for that contagious atmosphere to grow.

But I can't help mentioning here that later that same night I had an erotic dream about Rebeca. We were doing it standing up, clothed, she in her polka-dot pajamas, in a packed metro car at rush hour—a digital clock somewhere read 19:20—but we were pressed together so close that no one noticed. I guess it was a way for me to tell myself that out there, "in nature," none of that would happen. In the morning I made the bed quickly to cover up the sheets.

When I came downstairs the first person I saw wasn't Javier but Jacinta. She was emptying a bag of potatoes into a basket on the kitchen counter. Javier, wearing a robe, was putting firewood into the hearth. He introduced me and even allowed himself a little joke: "Don't get on her bad side," he said, "she's in the firefighter reserves." She had good-looking dark features, slightly curly hair, a broad face and large lips and teeth like some French women have. She was around thirty years old, and was wrapped in an electric-blue down coat that came down to her knees: once again the cold got in the way of bodily appreciation. She seemed broad-shouldered. Later I found out that, sure enough, in the summer months she worked as a firefighter in a mountain pass while the rest of the year she lived—rather frugally—off her unemployment and her savings. She radiated strength and clarity: the way she insisted that Javier get dressed to go to the garden made me wonder whether she was another source of help Rebeca had arranged, or whether she lent a hand of her own accord.

"Are you coming?" she asked me.

She didn't seem sure; she wasn't aware of the conditions of my stay. With mouthful of muffin, I said I was.

Outside more novelties awaited me. The first, a rather complicated apparatus that in my ignorance I confused with a lawn-mower, was a "rototiller." It's used, I was told, to "till the soil," that is, to prepare it for the sowing after the summer months. They also called it a mechanical mule, an expression I felt I understood better. The second was a wheelbarrow filled with manure. It was the season when they clean the barns, removing the accumulated manure and taking it to the garden so it can decompose and fertilize the ground. A neighbor who had "animals" gave them as much as they could want. I looked at the wheelbarrow with a certain apprehension.

"Out of the way," said Javier, very much in control of the situation. "I've got it. I don't want you to stink on your first day."

On the way to the garden, I proceeded with my immersion in rural life. They explained to me that the owner of some property, who lived in the main town, three kilometers away, lent the residents of the community a fenced-off corner they could use to grow vegetables. Jacinta shared one of those plots with Javier and had initiated him in the secrets of horticulture. "We're living in the Stone Age here," he remarked, as though in a good mood; but I got the impression—as I had with Rebeca a day earlier, in our conversation in the bar—that this happy phrase belonged to a pretty well-worn repertoire that he latched onto, like a very valuable but by now somewhat scraggly hostage. I asked Jacinta if this "Stone Age man" took well to his new chores, and she answered, not rudely, that he was still an apprentice. To which, without thinking, I quickly added that maybe our friend wasn't cut out for this kind of life.

The rest of this Stone Age town, which I had the chance to visit as we headed to the garden, seemed defined by spontaneity and a lack of planning. Aside from two or three genuine stone constructions, old haylofts or stables, most of the buildings followed the rudimentary principles of do-it-yourself building, without designs or blueprints, and were built pragmatically out of cement, and not always painted. Some of the structures that were painted, bravely fleeing from all that functionalism, made a show of oranges or yellows on their façades, like in a Mediterranean village. There were other, more carefully planned buildings, though these seemed to be the product of a somewhat poor imagination, almost from another time, which gave them the air of a barracks house or an old boarding school. The church and the grand residence of Javier's landlord—without a doubt the most ambitious constructions—shared porches and arcades of different styles, and an outer layer of little stones made according to the recent guidelines, which recommend these kinds of mosaics inspired in the almonds of a *turrón*. Not far from the community, visible from all sides, stood a high-tension tower.

In that bitter cold, and under an unbroken layer of clouds, it was fun to watch how Javier submitted to the farm duties, or at least appeared to. I say this because I saw nothing in him comparable to the ease with which Jacinta managed the rototiller, or to her expression of sadness when she said, grabbing a couple of cabbages, that they would be "some of the last." I myself, after some instruction, gathered a few strands of saffron, delighted by that generous, bright-eyed woman who identified so strongly with what she was doing. Javier, on the other hand, as he unloaded and piled up manure, never quite lost that look of having been assigned to do occupational therapy. Jacinta supervised and guided his movements, sometimes by shouting over the noise of the machine, and at one point he turned to me and whispered, and in a tone that wasn't bitter, only testy: "That woman is one bitch of a sergeant." I didn't like that at all, and in any case, it appealed to a united front that was mostly imaginary. Jacinta tried to teach me to push the rototiller, a task at which I spent exactly five useless minutes; she asked me if I'd be staying long, pessimistically calculating how much she could expect from me. She said that, in this season, "at least until January," and at this altitude—we were at a thousand meters—there wasn't much to do in a mountain garden.

"If we were lower down, right now we'd have escarole, chard, spinach, romaine lettuce ... practically the garden of Eden."

I liked that image, it had a gentler irony than Javier's Stone Age.

We must have spent over an hour there. Eventually I saw Javier look at his watch and tell Jacinta that "we" were leaving. We left her there, and went home with an empty wheelbarrow, a large cabbage, and my strands of saffron.

Despite that blatant desertion, Javier spent the way home talking to me about all the things he'd learned, which he wanted to show he was familiar with. We stopped for coffee at the only bar in town, where I met two little old men, retired cowherds who sat watching TV, and a young Colombian woman, Roxanne, who had emigrated because she was in love with Juanma, "a man with a complicated history." She gave us a DVD with six new movies. Outside it was still bitterly cold, but since we'd already started making the social rounds, we sat down on a low stone ledge surrounding a white house that looked out over the only place in town that everyone had to pass by, which they called, maybe because of a small fountain and two benches that were right there, "the plaza."

This ledge, more than the bar, was the favorite meeting point for the residents of the community, most of whom I eventually got to meet. That day Javier played host, rather proud to exhibit proof of his past, and I met a representative demographic sample. In particular, I remember the single active cowherd, who came by leading his herd of enormous cows on his way toward some pastures he rented outside the town. Javier explained that the rent was cheap, and the man lived off of the sale of calves and what he made from the community funds. Subsidies, seasonal work, an occasional disability pension, and above all unemployment benefits seemed to make up the economic life of the community, just as retreat—not necessarily dishonorable retreat—from the minefield of the city seemed to be a key factor in its moral life. True, Ana, the high school teacher, came and went to Madrid every day, just as Rebeca did, and Yolanda, who that morning stopped by for a moment to "take a break," looking incongruously stressed, had the strange job of transcribing the Channel 2 news for a Japanese news agency. But in general the dependence on the city and its institutions was conveniently covered up by solitude and distance, which fostered a fragile but acute sense of safety. The brief, unpleasant bursts of memories became, more than enemies, allies of forgetting. In the entire town, only the cowherd was a vestige of continuity; everything else rested on a desire for a break.

Back at the house, determined not to go back on the previous night's resolutions, I started to make lunch, over Javier's objections, since he saw no reason to stray from the menu prescribed by Rebeca. The truth is, I didn't quite know what to do with that cabbage, much less with the saffron, so we reached a compromise: I'd cook the cabbage with some of the potatoes Jacinta had brought, and he'd heat up the meatballs in the microwave; the stew we'd leave for dinner. After lunch we sat on the sofa and Javier proposed, once again, that we watch a movie from the DVDs that Roxanne had given him. There were six to choose from. I decided on *Hancock*, because it starred my beloved Charlize Theron, and even though this time the quality was a bit better, after fifteen minutes I was out cold.

I awoke to find the TV off and a blanket covering me. Javier, somewhat distracted with a day-old newspaper, looked up. Outside it was dark and raining again. He made me a cup of tea, took out some cookies, brought over an armchair and sat down in front of me. From the looks of it, he was ready to open up and have the conversation we broke off the night before. Now, seized by a sudden motivation, he seemed to want to get through it as quickly as possible, as though my presence required it. Needless to say, I required nothing from him; in fact, at no time that day had I seen him do anything that needed justifying. But I realize that both he and Rebeca—in her therapeutic plans—had conferred on me the role of the outsider who comes to stir up their little world of silent understandings and shared oddities. In front of an outsider, a mysterious intimacy doubles its mysteries, and its secret rules seem even more secret; and logically, perhaps, it seeks, when it finds it's being observed, a way to expose itself—and to decipher itself—to the eyes of the uninitiated.

I realize, in other words, how the mechanism works, and exposure was no doubt on Javier's mind. The scene took on a form similar to a first visit to a therapist: that is, on the one hand, he made a deliberate effort to explain the case in an orderly fashion, and on the other hand, he used all the resources at his disposal to prevent any possibility of invasion, real or imaginary.

Javier began by attacking me, in fact, saying he doubted that "someone in the shadow economy" like me, whose morals are equally "shadowy," could understand what it meant for him, an upstanding person with nothing to hide, to be "expelled" from a career that he not only poured all his hopes into but moreover single-mindedly pursued, never straying from the "path," and never questioning any of the steps along the way. Living on the margins of society, I seem to remember him saying, I couldn't grasp the rewards that honest, hardworking people aspired to, nor could I gauge the magnitude of his loss. He admitted that his disappointment, despite opening his eyes, or perhaps because it opened them, had exaggerated results, such as "this forced exile" whose only advantage was that it hid him from those who knew him, who he himself had turned his back on.

I did feel, actually, that I was on the outside, right where he put me, and from that viewpoint everything he was saying seemed like a lot of foolish suffering. But I held my tongue and adopted a conciliatory tone. I pointed out that there was no need to feel he'd been "expelled" at the start of his career, especially for something that was only a minor setback. I also appealed to the respect he still felt for "those who knew him," to reassure him that no one would think he had any less promise, and that people still had high expectations for him.

From the outside, there's no way to sound inspired when you try to occupy the inside. I don't know if that was when he took out the bottle of wine, but that was when he asked me to please not add to his guilt, which he called "one of his most crushing problems." The others, as they made their appearance, included "lethargy and a lack of strength," "apathy about everything," a sense of being "completely beat," and a "dread" of getting up in the morning and going to bed at night. This last part struck me as less abstract—at least it explained the movies—and he must have noticed my reaction, because he hastened to point out that his case wasn't "severe." Yet how could I see it as anything else, shadowy outsider that I was, practically a visitor from another planet? The fact is, to me this whole tragedy of professional loss struck me as shallow, even in its overblown state, and I couldn't empathize, which may have been just as well for him. Still, the element of paralyzing resentment wasn't entirely unfamiliar to me, since I'd had to deal with it—mixed with fits of rage, in fact—in some of my clients. Javier insisted he had to "let time do its work" and that there was no need to "medicalize" his condition. As a neurologist, he knew what he was talking about.

"I suppose Rebeca told you I'm depressed. But believe me, the only precise definition of depression is what antidepressants treat. Currently one doesn't exist without the other, to the point that if someone doesn't respond to antidepressant treatment they're not considered to be suffering from depression. So," he smiled, "as long as I'm not medicated, I'm not depressed."

This clever deconstruction reduced Rebeca's opinion to the level of clinical vulgarity. Javier didn't seem aware of how much he'd turned against the person who, so far as I knew, was the only one looking out for him. I began to think that he didn't have the slightest idea what his real symptoms were. That night, when Rebeca came home, once again laden with bags, we were on the second bottle of wine and I saw her react with joy, as if she'd caught us on a guys' night out. And practically the first thing she said was:

"I brought you the interdental brushes."

The case was much more "severe" than I thought!

Also that night, when I went up to go to bed, Rebeca came down discreetly to the landing to ask me how things had gone. I didn't know what to tell her. I looked at her pajamas.

I've lingered on certain details about what happened on my first day not to give a sense of what the other ones were like, but to show how different they were. It didn't take me long to realize to that the first day was like a recently polished show window of the best Javier and Rebeca had to offer; from then on, everything went back to the way it was—I imagine—before I arrived, dustier and less accommodating. I understand why Rebeca might think the situation, stagnating as it was, required a jolt; and at the same time I understood that my good timing and goodwill weren't up to the task I'd been given.

Over the course of the following days, we abandoned our garden chores. Jacinta said earlier that this season didn't require much persistence, providing a reasonable excuse, and the bad weather—it continued to rain and hail—added another. Javier, who had taken to heart the principle of occupational therapy, began to mop the floors and clean the windowpanes. Our visit to the bar every morning lasted a bit longer, until Javier decided there was no need for such a diverse social circle: he had his plaza ledge, and that let him fulfill his daily prescription of an hour outdoors. This leisure activity—let's call it that—he scrupulously respected during the entire time I was there, and since I came to see in such habits the outlines of a penitentiary routine, I concluded that this must be the hour the inmates go out to the prison yard.

For a while I thought, as I watched those regular encounters outdoors—where people exchanged provisions, old newspapers, brief reports from a world that moved to a different rhythm— that most of the people there shared the same routine: like prisoners, they lived in an unchanging world, with a past full of reasons to forget and a future too remote to think about. The present had managed to shrink to fluctuations in the weather, updates on the locals, speculations on outsiders, the reliable passing of cows through town, maybe an upset stomach or a mysterious spot on the skin. (Javier, as a doctor, had to attend to these particulars.) Nature was more often a source of complaint than a sign of another life, which I imagine it is for real prisoners, and it didn't inspire any hope. No one seemed to think of it as something that continues and renews itself independently of the jolts and uncertainties of human life.

After coming back from the yard—practically on a stopwatch, as though there were a penalty for returning late to the cell—I would make lunch: slowly I managed to free Rebeca from this burden, though not from shopping for food, since the community didn't have any stores, just a truck that came by with bread every day at noon. Javier would barely have a bite to eat: he wasn't hungry, everything tasted bad to him, he was bonier by the day. Another missed opportunity. Nonetheless, the afternoon movies remained, in their varying states of deterioration, and he'd watch them absorbed while I fell asleep. I think I only made it through one of them all the way to the end, *Cloverfield*, and that one I'd seen in the theaters. When I woke up, I wouldn't find him there, waiting for me to share a friendly but slightly unhinged chat and a bottle of wine; usually he'd already gone up to his loft, where he'd moved the computer, and he'd spend time in the dark, with only the light of the screen, classifying and reclassifying documents with material from his thesis. Or, distressingly often, he'd lie down on his bed, retreating into his body, as if that were all he had left … and as if he felt he was losing it too, since he had nothing else.

My efforts to draw him out of his apathy were occasionally met with politeness—that is, with a trace of shame—but as the days went by, he stopped bothering to put on a nice face, and he'd ask me to leave him alone, sometimes weakly, sometimes with open hostility. Rather than inducing some kind of catharsis, my presence seemed to make clear that none was possible, and I felt more and more like a witness inflicted upon him, like a jailer not stipulated in the terms of his punishment. I tried to help him in his obsessive, idle pursuits at the computer, I tried to read *David Copperfield* aloud to him, since I'd brought it along. I brought up pleasant memories and adventures, I encouraged him to leave the house or at least open it up to visitors. None of these suggestions worked. He wanted neither companionship, nor company, nor entertainment. I couldn't talk to him about what had happened over the course of the day, because over the course of the day nothing happened. And there was nothing else I could offer: were I more morally rigorous, I might have provoked a confrontation; I could have goaded him into a fight. But my character tends more toward distraction. In this sense I should say that I began to resent Javier, because not only could I not distract him, but the whole situation made it difficult for me to distract myself. I can't say I envied his sordid devotion to silence, his grandiose contempt for any plans of attack, his submission to not knowing what to do; but he at least must have found something there, a sort of extreme existence. I get along better on the middle levels of existence, and for that I need something to do.

Rebeca could have been a good distraction, but as soon as Javier refused to come down from his room to eat with us, a decision he made within less than a week, he perversely lay the groundwork for giving our meetings a conspiratorial air. Both of us were aware of the danger—myself much more so, I think—and we kept those times as light as possible, and if the conversation happened to flow, something we'd both been missing, one or the other of us would cut it off as though an alarm had sounded. Rebeca took the dinner upstairs, and when he finally came down, she didn't come with him. We'd again be alone, like the rest of the day, with some horrible movie, like *Quantum of Solace*, with background coughing and a close-up on the heads of the audience.

After ten or twelve days of this strict regimen, I felt I had to get out of there, and I went to Madrid with Rebeca. She clearly saw what I had in mind, and practically begged me to come back that night and meet her in the clinic parking lot. I'd stopped dreaming about her and no longer looked at her pajamas, among other reasons because I hardly ever saw her wearing them. I didn't really know whose view of the situation she shared now, mine or Javier's. I spent the morning going to banks, I opened and closed some accounts; I didn't dare go by the Mexican's place, after checking my secret email account in a cybercafé and seeing I had no messages, and calling him from a phone booth and getting no answer. I also called a friend I occasionally fool around with, and she invited me to her place for lunch. We fooled around, ate, fooled around some more. I spent the last hours of the day in a movie theater, as though to recover (though, strangely, I no longer remember what movie I saw). At nine I was in the clinic parking lot.

Rebeca was happy to see that I hadn't run away, and I didn't want to explain why I'd come back. I've already said that her attitude was starting to seem suspicious, because the truth is, she was the one running away the most, understandable though this was. Her exhausting workday—she had jobs in two clinics—was longer on Saturdays, but most Sundays she also left early in the morning, for her parents' house, and didn't come back until nighttime. She told me that Javier, who of course didn't go with her, couldn't force her to "give up this last remnant of family life." However, Sunday mornings were livelier than usual, and with the community bustling—so to speak—with weekenders and a few visitors, Rebeca's absence became less noticeable. Javier would occupy his spot on the wall with an almost ceremonial dignity, as if even a prisoner had a duty to follow the rhythms of the calendar. On one of those very Sunday mornings, just a few days after my attempt to escape, something happened that cleared up the problem of whose view Rebeca shared, or at least pushed her to take sides.

I remember we were all there that day. The parishioners had just left the church, and the priest, always interested in "the youth," had come over to say hello to us. The mayor of the community, a rotund, paternal man who spoke in a low voice, discussed some church renovations with him. Juanma and Roxanne, with a loaf of bread under her arm, were enthusiastically recommending *The Dark Knight*. Yolanda gave me a little wooden horse. Jacinta wore a short skirt and some eye-catching flower-print leotards. Suddenly Javier got up, and very violently said to me:

"Come on. We have to leave."

I saw him looking out the corner of his eye at one of the houses that faced the plaza, a large one in good shape, with gratings over the windows in the Andalusian style, the one that earlier I said reminded me, on a smaller scale, of a barracks house. A woman of about fifty, who had a city air and didn't look like she belonged with the other prisoners—no doubt she was a visitor—had just stepped out from the large wooden doorway, followed

by a girl who may have been her daughter. They were both looking at and discussing the façade.

"Don't look!" cried Javier, his head down, very upset. "Don't
look!"

"But what's the matter?"

"That woman. Don't look at her. I don't want her to see me.
I don't want her to see me here."

Not stopping to say goodbye to the others, he hurried back
to the house. I followed him. He tried to explain himself, almost
against his will, as though he thought that keeping it to himself
would be worse. He told me, again, that he lost his job at the
hospital because he applied for a position, theoretically a sure
thing, in a unit that was later shut down. The woman he saw
leaving the house was the head of that unit, Dr. Vázquez Romero,
who would have been his boss. Closing the unit hadn't been her
fault, but "a management decision," although it was clear that
at least at first, in a promisingly irrational way, he blamed her.

"But if they shut down the unit," I said, "they must have let
her go too, right?"

He didn't answer.

"And she couldn't do anything to transfer you?"

I got the impression that she tried to do something but didn't
succeed. Javier seemed to find himself in the awkward position of
having to be grateful to someone directly involved in his misfortune. He didn't hate her, clearly; she was just one of those people
he'd told me he was hiding from, who he was afraid would see
him now, in the current state of his "career." She was one of the
people he respected. What came next was a full-blown panic
attack, which we both had to get through with nothing to calm
him down. No matter how much I asked and searched, I couldn't
find a single sedative anywhere in the house; only Javier's well-
established fear of witnesses prevented me from going to try to

get one in the plaza. He was sweaty, cold, and short of breath, and I made him lie on the floor and place his legs against the wall. With an unsuspected authority, explicable only by my desperation, I guided his breathing for at least forty-five minutes. That day there was no lunch and no movie. In the mid-afternoon, when I went up to the loft, where I'd taken him once the crisis was over, I found him awake, curled up in a ball, with the light off. Somehow or other he detected my expression of reproach, which I couldn't mask, and said to me:

"I'm sorry, I'm really sorry. It must be hard for you. It's like the smell of shit. It's comforting when it's your own, but disgusting when you come across someone else's."

Maybe I should have been offended, but what impressed me about that graphic insight was mainly the self-absorption and time wasted on coming up with it. This wasn't the product of a single day, nor of chance, even if the unexpected reappearance of the doctor may have had a devastating effect: to give her such symbolic weight, he needed to have grounds where panic had already been fertilized, and for a long time. For so long, in fact, that I wondered whether in the years we spent together, intimately or intermittently, in one kind of relationship or another, Javier had always been so blind to instability, and so prone to suffering its social effects. One never knows, I suppose, whether instability will manifest itself as a latent, unidentified illness, or instead as a condition of life; whether social setbacks will upend our world, leaving nothing but wreckage, or whether they'll build another in its place. I looked for signs in the past, and the only conclusion I reached was that we lived for a while under a sort of protection, and that this protection had, for one reason or another, lasted longer for him than for me. In any case, instability has a retroactive power, and now that I saw beyond a doubt that I didn't know Javier at all, I began to wonder if I'd ever known him.

Yet seeing him as a stranger, when Rebeca came back at the very end of the afternoon, helped me raise the question from what we might call a medical point of view. I'm not a doctor, but I do know something about drugs, that is, medications, and I've seen enough to have an idea about their subjective effects. It's clear that drugs don't radically alter anyone, much less "possess" anyone: they're not some omnipotent being that slips into unprepared minds to subdue or destroy them at will. No one under the effects of drugs does anything they hadn't conceived in a previous state of their own "nature." On the other hand, it's true that after overcoming the initial resistance, drugs have the ability to awaken hidden faculties, buried memories, talents held in check; and all this in a space that seems to run parallel to that of the will, a space that allows the will to observe without getting involved, and—very frequently—to breathe a sigh of relief that it doesn't have to put up resistance. The will usually blesses those actions, attitudes, and thoughts which for once don't require it to do any work, and which pass unheroically over barriers that took years to erect and have a solidity and height worthy of a better cause. Javier's will, now limited to carrying out the consequences of an everyday setback literally as a sentence—so literally, in fact, that he viewed himself as a criminal, not a victim of depression—must have been more than a little tired from such an effort. And while I was no longer sure, as I said, what he was like before, I believed he couldn't help but wish for a different kind of working order. A break would do him good, at any rate, so I told Rebeca we shouldn't waste another minute, we had to give him antidepressants.

Rebeca, to her credit, showed some reluctance at first, since what needed to be done would clearly have to be done behind the victim's back—and this was a violation of her professional ethics, as well as the loyalty she believed she still owed him as her boyfriend. I told her that, whatever the situation, "that thing" couldn't be her boyfriend, and that this might be a way of getting him back, if she wanted to. Besides, there was no reason he had to find out, and if he ever did, he'd probably thank her. She responded that Javier was a neurologist and well aware of the effects of antidepressants, which he couldn't help but notice; I countered that the neurologist hadn't been very competent at detecting his own symptoms, and that the only way to combat his stubborn refusal to submit to medical treatment was by subjecting him to that very treatment. We had to trust, I went on, that if he ever found out, it would be because of a sudden improvement, a sign that the medicine was taking effect, something he couldn't then refuse to acknowledge.

Rebeca also worried that, since Javier at this point was little more than a "body in pain" that occupied all her attention, he'd quickly notice anything unusual, even before they saw signs of "positive developments." Decreased lethargy, increased appetite, an occasional rush of well-being might attract his suspicion, as could certain possible side effects of the medication, from nausea or vertigo to dry mouth.

"If he finds out," she said, alarmed, "we're lost. He'll turn against us and stop taking it."

But in that case, couldn't we just deny everything? If he suffered from adverse effects, couldn't we argue that these were symptoms of his sickness, not of a medication? And if they were positive . . . well, then, hadn't he said we had to "let time run its course"? So we'd agree with him and say that time was running its course.

Rebeca didn't seem convinced, but she also knew she'd run out of ideas. Or rather, for some time now she probably had only one left, which wasn't how to help him or be loyal, but whether or not to leave him. Seeing the doubt in that pretty face made me once again regret being doomed to only seeing this facet of her private life. She wanted to think it over, and I understood why.

The next day Javier, ashamed, wanted to act decently and even suggested we go out for a walk. We'd been outside for barely twenty minutes, in a nearby meadow, in the company of cows, when it started to hail and we had to go back. That day there was no meeting at the wall, either. Jacinta came by to see us and brought a bottle of blueberry liquor; she was very concerned with checking up on Javier—when he ran off from the plaza, it was noticeable—but he received her mop in hand and indicated he was in the middle of something very important. I spent a lot of time upstairs in my room, reading.

That night Rebeca came home with a load of groceries, as planned, and a box of Venlafaxine. She said it was a fast-acting antidepressant, which could take effect in two weeks, and that we should give the contents of one capsule every day to the "patient," as he could now be called, according to his theory, since he was in treatment. To cover up the taste, we needed to spread it out over meals, and I'd have to make sure I didn't arouse his suspicions—or if I did, dispel them. "Don't worry," I told her. "Ever since I took over the cooking, he says that everything tastes weird." Rebeca had brought a bunch of exotic spices to broaden the range of unfamiliar flavors, and right away we began to cook a nice array of camouflage soups, from cream of leek with roquefort to a hearty stew of blood sausage. The pressure cooker couldn't keep up, the four burners on the cooktop irradiated optimism, and while we tasted and conspired, we forgot to eat dinner. Great care was taken so that our movements and glances didn't meet—we were both afraid of anything indecent—but the task kept us busy, its goal guided us and told us what to talk about. Despite the institutional amounts of food, that kitchen no longer seemed like it belonged in a prison. For the first time I saw Rebeca happy, and I was happy, too.

When Javier came down at midnight, asking why we hadn't brought him dinner, I decided it was time for a test. I went to the bathroom for a moment, washed and dried my hands, poured half a capsule in one palm, left, and with the deftness of a dealer passing off a tab, I sprinkled the Venlafaxine into a bowl which Rebeca had just filled with a Chinese soup of mushrooms and kelp. Neither one of them noticed. Javier ate exactly half, his usual portion, and said it was good. I winked at Rebeca; her expression of terror and understanding, which only I could understand, felt like victory.

That night I stayed up with Javier to watch *The Dark Knight*, an advance copy with an echo. I found it not only kitschy but interminable, too. But my attention was elsewhere: according to Rebeca, we'd have to wait at least two weeks, but I was used to more immediate drugs, so I couldn't let go of the hope that I'd see results within a few minutes.

I didn't lose hope over the following days, when I embraced a new kind of patience, with even more reasons for optimism, we might say. But the fact is that I found little reward for my careful observation. I may have been watching him too closely, but my impression was that Javier's state got worse rather than better. Now he noticeably neglected his hygiene: he didn't shower, he didn't shave, he didn't comb his hair, he spent all day in his pajamas, in hiking socks, wrapped in his Calvin Klein bathrobe and in a checkered blanket; he did, however, spend a half hour after every meal picking his teeth with the interdental brushes. On his daily walk, a ritual he still mechanically observed but which left him exhausted, because of the demands it placed on his social capacities, he put on some jeans and a parka over his

pajamas. I didn't hesitate to tell him he really shouldn't identify
so closely with Stone Age man. He didn't react aggressively, but
said that he "forgot," that I "couldn't even imagine" how "difficult" these basic tasks were for him. Enforcing them, even doing
them along with him, soon became one of my duties. The look in
his eyes became more and more catatonic; sometimes he'd break
his silence uttering three or four surprising words, meaningless to
me, something like "I have no intention of telling her," or "Take
it or leave it," and when I asked him what he was talking about,
he'd say that he couldn't help it, that it was his way of reining
in an obsessive thought or overpowering memory. Maybe such
containment strategies could be viewed as a promising sign, but
they certainly didn't amount to conclusive evidence of improvement, and they were dramatically displayed. His appetite didn't
improve, either: he had more and more trouble finishing even
half of what I served him, which forced me to increase the dose
of Venlafaxine, and therefore the risk of being discovered.

The next Sunday, in a gesture of solidarity, Rebeca spent all
day with us, which of course for me was a relief, especially since
at noon, from the ledge in the plaza, we again saw that damn
doctor walking into her barracks house, this time in the company
of a man her age. Once again, it seemed as though a rabid dog
had burst into the middle of a summer camp. Terrified, Javier
ran away, dragging Rebeca along. She was curious about the doctor's presence and wanted to go say hello. When we got back to
the house, we were spared the panic attack—was the treatment
starting to work?—but not the gloomy, tedious afternoon, which
Rebeca tried to enliven by inviting four or five neighbors over
for tea. Javier, of course, didn't come down from his room, and
we, instead of getting our mind off of him, spent every stupid
bit of energy in not losing our cool. We were terrible hosts, and

the gathering quickly and clumsily dissolved. Rebeca took Javier his dinner in tears.

All my displays of concern and care, all my efforts to embrace modesty and accept that Javier's world was impenetrable, that no one could even imagine—as he said—what was going on inside him without oversimplifying, turned his problems into something almost sacred. In spite of our subterfuge—which, by the way, concealed nothing more than hope and faith, aside from exhaustion—we were still forced to treat his pain as a mystery. Yet while not knowing what to do, and not being able to do anything, didn't bother Javier, who saw helplessness as a natural part of his condition, Rebeca and I, who couldn't accept such a justification, found ourselves in a frustrating, toxic darkness. We groped our way forward, unsure of the walls around us and the ground beneath our feet, and unsure, most of all, whether we, too, would be contaminated.

Our Sunday afternoon tea must have made a sorry impression on the neighbors, because one morning a few days later, when the sky was clear for once, Jacinta showed up with an empty basket and a backpack full of sandwiches, inviting us to spend the day outside. Javier of course declined, but the desire we both had to be rid of each other made it easy for me to say yes, almost enthusiastically; my only qualm was that this would deprive him of his lunchtime dose of Venlafaxine. Jacinta was mostly thinking of him and, upbeat, tried to persuade him to come along. Still, she didn't seem too disappointed that she only got the "guest," as she called me—after all, she could have gotten two no's instead of one. Nor did it take her long to figure out, if she didn't already know, that the guest's situation was also desperate.

As we set out, she put the basket over my arm.

"You take it," she said. "I brought it just in case, but don't get your hopes up. Even though it's rained a lot, it's a little late for mushrooms, and the old grandpas around here get up earlier than anyone else. By the time the rest of us arrive, they've already made off with the haul. They never forget exactly where to look, year after year, and once they pick some, they cover the roots with leaves so the rest of us won't find them."

What delightful conversation! I'd never gone foraging for mushrooms, not even as a kid, and I've never been especially in touch with nature, but I like hearing about it. During those days, I'd have listened to anyone talk about anything! But Jacinta, with her interest in teaching outsiders, wasn't just anyone, and she made me feel profusely educated. The harvest wasn't so meager, after all, or at least I didn't think so: in the forest, among trees which I learned were "old-growth oaks," we found some porcini hidden under the leaves; later, in a small "secret" clearing that took us more than an hour to get to, up steep trails which the "old grandpas" weren't up to climbing, we found some king oysters and button mushrooms. I put all these treasures in the basket, because the wicker let them continue releasing spores: plastic bags were forbidden, and while few people paid any attention to this rule, she was "inflexible"—she laughed—in her "ecological mindfulness."

"I can't allow this all to get spoiled. I need it for myself."

Her tone wasn't patronizing, though, nor did she harbor any resentment toward me as a representative of the urban world, which she seemed very familiar with. Neither of us was too explicit about our motives or our lives. I could see she was making an effort to come across as someone free, and she was convincing. If she'd ever run away from something, she didn't do so to lock herself up; if she'd left something behind, she didn't leave it to look back on it. She said she didn't like people who "come to the country in search of healing," but she also didn't waste time resenting them; instead, she did what she could to help "the sick" recover quickly and leave.

"The country has its own sicknesses," she added, "and they should be plenty for us. This isn't a sanatorium or a refuge."

She said everyone had to know where they belonged, and I asked if she knew many people who really did. Softening her tone, she said she didn't, but admired people who had things figured out. For example, there was a doctor from the city who had recently and suddenly inherited a house in town from a distant relative, and since she knew perfectly well she wasn't missing out on anything here, she was getting ready to sell it, and for a good price. Others, she said, would have opted for the country idyll, but that woman didn't have any illusions. I confirmed that if that doctor was, as I imagined, the famous Vázquez Romero I'd heard about, then from what I knew she was very healthy.

"See?" she laughed. "Only the crazies come here."

"Like me," I admitted.

"I was crazy, too. But not anymore."

We ate in another one of her secret places, one with a well-chosen view that looked out over both the community and the town proper, which from up here seemed free from confusion or illness. The cold itself brought out gorgeous colors in the land and the trees, and at our feet the stream ran musically. The sky had once again clouded over, and for fifteen minutes it snowed, an event that we welcomed with a truly soothing silence, after the silences I'd recently been subjected to. I was happy and covered in bruises: I'd fallen on my rear three times, and each time Jacinta reacted with a laugh. She liked how I relied on her, and when I hungrily attacked the sandwiches, I had the feeling I was eating out of her hand.

When we got back it wasn't entirely dark, but the street lamps in the plaza were already lighting up, a romantic gesture worthy of José Luis Garci. Jacinta told me I could keep the mushrooms, but that I shouldn't wash them with water because that would ruin their "texture"; you had to clean them with a brush. I must have given her such an idiotic look that she invited me over to her place for a moment; she thought that if she didn't do it herself, I'd never figure it out. When I got there, I asked her if we were on the right-hand side of town, so I could check my email, if she had a computer.

"Of course I do," she said, "what do you think I am?"

The house was modest and clean, and although there was no lack of rustic motifs—bells and wagon wheels hung on the wall—it wasn't the work of a dilettante, nor the frugal adaptation of Javier's house. The computer was in the living room, and as she lit a fire in the hearth, I signed in with my encrypted account. I had a message from the Mexican from several days earlier: "Don't worry, *wey*, we're on the road." So that was it. Every sign, misread; every precaution, simple paranoia; my whole flight … I felt a sudden anger at the Mexican and his lack of professionalism, but I also felt an unquestionably greater sense of relief. Actually, a deep and immediate joy. When I looked up, Jacinta was coming over to me with a beer. Our eyes met. I got up and we didn't turn our eyes away.

"I just got some news," I said, "and I think you'll soon be rid of one crazy, at least."

"News?" she smiled. "I thought I was the one who got rid of crazies here."

We did it on the rug, in front of the fire in the hearth.

When I got back to the house, it was already very late and Rebeca was back. I had my cargo of dirt-free mushrooms—we'd lingered, naked, using the brush—and with the recent, liberating news and the lingering aroma of that strange measure of rural love, I was euphoric. Surprisingly, Javier was in a similar state.

He was still wearing the robe and hadn't showered, but he was walking around almost joyfully with a newspaper in his hand. He smiled at me as if he knew what I'd been doing, and I wondered how on earth he hadn't succumbed to Jacinta's charms—one more reason, I thought, his sullen resistance wasn't doing him any good. While I proudly handed the mushrooms to Rebeca, he said:

"Listen to this." In a pompous, sarcastic voice: "I was barefoot, Narciso saw an injured woman and I stepped in pools of blood as I ran away."

"What happened?"

"Our dear leader in the Madrid government, Esperanza Aguirre! She just escaped unscathed from an attack on a hotel in Bombay!"

"An attack on her? In Bombay?"

"Of course not! Do you think people in India care about her? If only!" Javier read on: "'We were pushed by the hotel staff through a door behind the front desk, but since we were the last ones out and the gunfire was getting more intense, we dived behind the desk. Later they came to look for us. I was wearing an open shoe, which came off and got stuck on my ankle, and then I went barefoot.' Like Cinderella!"

"It must be horrible to get caught in the middle of a terrorist attack," said Rebeca.

"Not for our Esperanza! She's got nine lives!" laughed Javier. "Remember a few years back, when she escaped a helicopter accident that Rajoy was also in? There's no getting rid of her. What a missed opportunity!"

"How can you say such things, Javier?" Rebeca interrupted him, with an unexpected harshness. "How can you joke like that about a person's life?"

"A person? But how do you go from Esperanza Aguirre to 'a person'? That's some leap. Are you crazy? What does one thing have to do with the other?"

That was the first time I saw Javier react in a way that wasn't a panic attack, on the very day he didn't take his medication. But Rebeca couldn't see it that way.

"You don't know what you're talking about! You've spent so long playing with the lives of others that now you don't even see the damage you're doing."

*But Rebeca,* I thought, *at least he's saying something!*

"What's your problem?" asked Javier, throwing the newspaper down on the kitchen counter. "All I said was, she's someone you can't kill! It's not like I was planning to kill her myself! Besides, need I remind you, if it hadn't been for Esperanza's ER privatization, I'd still have a job."

"And now who's the one making leaps?" Rebeca was furious. "Do you really think it's Esperanza's fault they didn't renew *your* contract?"

There was no way—there never had been—to avoid this *casus belli.* Javier's job at the hospital, his unrenewed contract, the specter of the doctor, and now Esperanza Aguirre ... His drama seemed to need to expand its cast of characters, in order to hold onto its rationale ... or whatever lay behind it, if there was anything. In any case, neither one of them, who looked plenty aware they'd stirred up something beneath the surface, wanted to go any further, even though it was increasingly clear—it was clear now, for instance—that they were being swallowed by the depths. That night, the first time we'd eaten together in a long while, the silence of that devastation dominated everything. The mushrooms, so clean, and free of Venlafaxine, might as well have tasted like mud.

Rebeca deliberately broke the routine by going up to bed first, and Javier, resentful, had to move his own routine up. He was putting in a DVD when I told him I had something to say. I didn't give much of an explanation, only that things were getting sorted out and that there was no longer any reason for me to stay. In the morning I'd go to Madrid with Rebeca and would start making arrangements.

"It will only take a few days," I said. "I'm leaving, and you should, too."

"You can't stand me, can you?" he answered, almost in the same tone he spoke to Rebeca in.

"No, and you can't stand me, either. But that's beside the point. You should pack your bags, go back to work, and get out of here." And then I had a brilliant idea, or so I thought. "Besides, you won't have a choice. Now I know what Dr. Vázquez is doing with that house. Jacinta told me. She just inherited it from a distant aunt and she's coming to live here. I assume you won't want to have her as a neighbor."

I know this lie was cruel, but it had a point. Like them, I couldn't go on. I had to make use of what I had at hand, and of the only forces that I'd seen guiding Javier's actions: panic and resentment. I watched without regret as my lie began to take effect, much faster than any drug. Even so, I got up, saying I felt like making a drink to celebrate "our" return to the city. I remembered seeing a nice cocktail shaker in the cupboard and a well-stocked bar, a memory of more social times. I got some ice, mixed orange juice and tequila and a dash of the still unopened blueberry liquor that Jacinta had given us. I took out two equally forgotten glasses, and into his, just in case, I threw a whole capsule of Venlafaxine.

That night I made up my mind to watch a whole movie with him. When I saw him go to put in *Prince Caspian*, I told him no way. He switched it—I swear he wasn't ready—for *Eagle Eye*. It was terrible, but I made it to the end.

In the morning Rebeca came down to find me awake and already dressed, sitting at the kitchen counter with a freshly made pot of coffee. On the way I tried to convince her I was never the answer, and that they were wasting their time—I said—drawing out a painful "exile" that wasn't doing anything for them. I reminded her, too, that in spite of its clumsiness, Javier's reaction the night before was an indication that his apathy was beginning to crack, and that no matter what she shouldn't stop giving him the Venlafaxine. But she hardly said anything in reply. I imagine she wanted to make me feel like I'd kept my part of the bargain. Since I didn't want to tell her about my lie, I couldn't tell her we'd soon find out. It started to snow.

I thought to call my old landlord, in case he still hadn't rented out my apartment. I'd just found out it wasn't "hot," so I wanted to move back in. I was in luck: it was still free. The man was happy, perhaps because he'd been thinking about lowering the rent. I went to see him, and we negotiated. He told me that even though he preferred "someone quiet" like me, who he knew wouldn't give him any trouble, he'd also noticed I was a bit "unpredictable," so he had to insist on a security deposit. I paid it in cash, along with the first month's rent, and walked out with the keys. In the afternoon Rebeca called me: it hadn't stopped snowing, and the highway was closed, so we couldn't get back that night. She was going to stay at her parents' house. She worried about Javier, "alone up there," but I thought he deserved it. I called the storage facility and scheduled the move for two days later. At night I stopped by a few places where I thought people might have figured I'd disappeared. I still didn't give anyone my mobile number. Some of my clients missed me.

Like the Mexican, I said I'd been "traveling," but unlike him, I apologized. I slept peacefully in a good hotel.

By the next day it had stopped snowing and the highways were clear. I thought about taking a cab and being through with it as soon as possible, but that struck me as a bit insensitive. I spent the day outside, enjoying the cold and the leftover dirty snow, and I saw that the same things I'd left behind when I moved out would be waiting for me when I came back. I wondered whether the experience that was now drawing to a close had any significance or consequence for me, and I told myself there's no reason experiences have to mean anything or even, perhaps, be worth anything.

Though maybe they did mean something for someone. Javier surprised me again that night. Incredibly, he'd prepared a "farewell" dinner, and didn't even resort to frozen meals or the microwave—so happy was he, I imagined, to be free from the witness to his misfortune. I figured fear had worked its first effects: several fears, in fact, because the way he looked at and doted on Rebeca, shyly, like someone on a first date, suggested he'd considered the possibility he might lose her. Rebeca, incidentally, didn't give in right away. Now that she'd recovered some of her authority, she no doubt thought it was worth holding onto. She didn't surrender to his flattery, nor did she pretend nothing had happened. In any case, there were signs of some kind of understanding: the Esperanza Aguirre affair, which she only briefly alluded to, was in the past.

After dinner, I went out to say goodbye to Jacinta. The quiet, snowy town, in the light of the street lamps, or in spite of them, at last looked like a place one could come back to. As though remembering where I was headed, I slipped and fell. Jacinta opened the door wrapped in a blanket, with tousled hair and sleepy eyes. How did it not occur to me that she had her own schedule? I stayed on the doorstep.

"Sorry to wake you. I just wanted to say goodbye. I'm leaving tomorrow."

"It's about time," she said, and kissed me.

There was no movie to finish out the evening, thank God. Javier really had made up his mind to break the rules. Almost with excitement, he asked me to make him a couple of drinks. I did so gladly and added the Venlafaxine.

"You know?" he said. "I've been thinking."

"Wow, that's a first."

"Don't be an ass. What you said about Dr. Vázquez Romero …" He stopped for a moment. I could have screamed. "It's funny how we both ended up here, in this horrible place. Imagine . . . her, with her prestigious career, such an authority, an innovator in her field, a fighting woman … ending up here!"

"What do you mean, 'ending up'? I imagine if she's moving here, it's because she wants to."

He gave me a look of incomprehension, and I realized this thought hadn't even crossed his mind.

"Maybe," he said without conviction. "But up here by myself these last two days, I imagined what this place would be like as a colony of great doctors. I saw myself sitting there on the ledge each morning, watching them walk by one by one: Dr. Vázquez Romero, my old section boss, my old mentor, my thesis adviser … heads down, barely acknowledging each other, all looking extraordinarily sad. As if there were a sort of coup in the medical ranks and they all got deported here. I'd see them and wave to them from afar, and sit down among them, privileged to share their fate. You think that's weird, don't you?"

I thought it was extremely weird. I'd hoped my lie would inspire a bit of panic, because I'd seen that panic, in Javier's delicate state, could spur him to action. I didn't expect to find another driving force, a sort of pride—could it be called anything else?—that perhaps, with everything else that lay dormant within him, was what most wanted to awaken. If I'd only known earlier! How hard it was to know Javier, to know anyone! And still, thinking about others, no matter how crazy it is, is the only thing that saves us from ignorance and suffering. Will this story have a Christian ending after all? Well … for Javier, the only others he thought about were the people he admired in his career, and I don't know if that's very edifying. But sometimes you have to find a key to let someone reveal themselves, and all it took for him to stop feeling lonely was to imagine that fate had dealt one of those people a blow.

"Something must have happened to her," he insisted.

Knowing what had really "happened" to Dr. Vázquez Romero would have done him little good. It was better for him to hold on to that illusion of a shared fate, with that imaginary bond that gave him a feeling of privilege, and raised him to the level of the misfortunes of the great. He hated his weakness precisely because he thought it cornered him, and him alone, in a world where everyone else was strong. He'd been punishing himself harshly for this weakness, but perhaps now he'd begun to accept it. It was all an invention, but maybe it worked.

As for me, the strangest thing was moving back into my own apartment. It's a terribly contradictory experience. To offset the strangeness, I rearranged all the furniture.

# Winter Landscape

## I

IT WAS THE first time the family wasn't coming to Savonnières
for the summer. Mme. Boulat's health wouldn't allow it. My
mother's wouldn't, either, I might add. To a certain extent I was
glad, even though I saw that the news saddened her. "Madame
isn't doing well," she said, in a tone I'm all too familiar with,
which usually follows terrible premonitions or tragedies confirmed. In this case, I suspect she felt the tragedy was hers, too—
something which, as I noticed early on, my mother didn't mind
so much. She always worried about what would become of her
once "Madame" was no longer around, and now she seemed to
accept a bargain with fate whereby neither of them would be;
in her way she found this outlook reassuring. Together, more or
less, they would take leave of this world that no longer belonged
to them. When she was told to wrap up the small winter landscape by Sisley—"very carefully, please"—because the two middle
children, Corinne and Olivier, would be coming to pick it up,
she felt a general sense of things being dismantled, and a more
concrete sense that the end was indeed drawing near. She didn't
even ask why Mme. Boulat wanted to take the painting: her worries turned immediately to me. I'd come to spend a couple weeks
with her, to help her get the house ready for the Boulats' arrival,
as a matter of fact; and I found her, once again, archaeologically

combing over my prospects for a future in which she was "no longer around." She thinks I'm "far too old" to be living off of fellowships, and the truth is that I too had entered, as I always do when waiting to hear about an extension, one of those periods when I stop mistaking the transient for the eternal. I suppose out of a sort of resentment, or just so she'd stop pestering me, I didn't mention that I'd finished the screenplay and had made some plans.

When I heard that Olivier and Corinne were coming to pick up the painting, I told her I'd go back to Paris with them that same day. They arrived on a Sunday, around twelve; my mother had made their favorite dish, duck breast à l'orange, and we ate, dozed for an hour in the living room, and left. As if to reassure everyone that it wouldn't be a good summer to spend in Savonnières anyway, it started to rain as soon as we got into the car.

CORINNE:    (*Waving back at my mother, who is saying goodbye from the gate.*) Is your mom doing well? She looked fine to me.

ME:         Around you two, she puts on a good face, as always. On me, as always, she unloads her worries.

OLIVIER:    Early July and just look at this weather.

ME:         What about your mom? Is it really serious?

CORINNE:    Our mother is quite the actress. Until the operation, no one will know for sure if it's cancer, and the doctor says the chances are very slim. But she's putting her affairs in order …

ME: That's why she wanted the Sisley?

CORINNE: Yes, she actually said she wanted to see it one last time!

ME: I wrapped it up myself. (*Noise from the trunk.*) I hope it makes it all right.

CORINNE: (*To Olivier.*) Hear that? Drive slowly.

OLIVIER: (*To Corinne.*) But didn't you tell me to hurry?

ME: We're taking the A10, right?

CORINNE: I have to see Pascale. We made plans. (*To me.*) Do you remember Pascale?

ME: I don't think so.

CORINNE: Sure you do. When was it, Olivier? Three years ago? She stayed with us for a few days.

ME: Three years ago I think I spent the whole summer in Turkey.

CORINNE: Really? I was certain you two knew each other. At any rate, I haven't seen her in a while, either … (*Pause.*) Do you ever get the feeling you're seeing someone for the last time? And that you could have done something to stop it?

OLIVIER:      Done something to stop what?

CORINNE:     Stop it from being the last time you saw them.

OLIVIER:      How can you know whether it will be the last time? What do you want, to see the future?

CORINNE:     No, not to see the future. Just some insight, some prescience.

OLIVIER:      That's what seeing the future means.

ME:          (*Interrupting maybe.*) Is your mom really doing so bad that she has to spend the summer in Paris?

CORINNE:     She's having surgery.

ME:          And that's going to take all summer?

OLIVIER:      Are you worried about leaving your mom alone?

ME:          A little. In any case, I'll probably go back for a few days, maybe around the middle of August.

OLIVIER:      Honestly, this summer none of us were going to go. I don't have time off and don't know when I will, Corinne declines to respond, Jean-Baptiste and his wife have already left for Spain,

their kids are with her mother, and the young-
est of the family has solemnly declared that,
now that he's back from his Interrail trip, he's
going to stay in Paris and go out every night. I
think Mom's convalescence is going to be my
responsibility.

CORINNE:     I don't think she likes the idea of being stuck
             in Savonnières alone. (*Looking at me.*) Alone
             with your mom, I mean.

OLIVIER:     I don't think so, either. (*Laughing.*) She's prob-
             ably afraid it would turn out like *The Maids*.

ME:          (*Laughing too.*) I can't imagine either of them
             trading places.

OLIVIER:     Neither can I! Ah... and the secret to life lies in
             trading places ...

ME:          For as long as you can ...

OLIVIER:     If you were there, it'd be different. You could
             direct the scenes.

ME:          Please.

OLIVIER:     Mom said so, right?

CORINNE:     "Since Paul won't be there, either ..."

ME:          I don't get it. What about her attachment to the house?

OLIVIER:      What's a house but the people in it?

ME:           You don't need people to—

OLIVIER:      If only you were there! She really dotes on you,
              doesn't she, Corinne?

CORINNE:      (*Slightly uncomfortable, as though pressured.*) Yes.

OLIVIER:      (*To me.*) When Dad died, she said from then on
              she'd have to be a father to us, just like she was
              for you.

ME:           She was a father to me?

OLIVIER:      You know what she's like. She doesn't need to
              be asked. She just steps in and takes charge, and
              that's that.

CORINNE:      Or thinks she's taking charge ...

OLIVIER:      Yes ... or thinks she's taking charge ... and that's
              that! The important thing is the "that's that."
              Maybe she's not cut out for trading places, but
              for *re*placing ...

CORINNE:      Or for thinking she's replacing ...

OLIVIER:      Really, Corinne, don't be so sour. (*To me.*) I hope
              you're going to go see her before the operation.

| ME: | Of course. And if you need me at the hospital, or afterward, I'll be in town. |
| OLIVIER: | She can't wait to see you. |
| CORINNE: | (*Irritated, but trying to contain herself.*) Olivier! (*She turns on the radio. Michael Jackson's "Billie Jean" is playing.*) |
| OLIVIER: | No, not Michael Jackson! That's all we've been hearing for two weeks! |
| CORINNE: | Fine. (*She changes the station. Many of them are in fact playing Michael Jackson. She doesn't seem to find anything she likes and switches the radio off.*) One more tragic death … |
| OLIVIER: | One more? Who else died? |
| CORINNE: | Sorry … it's just that thinking I have to see Pascale is setting me on edge. |
| OLIVIER: | Why? Is she about to die? |
| CORINNE: | It's what I was saying before. How could you know? |
| OLIVIER: | Sis, you're out of your mind. (*My cell phone rings. It's Emina. She wants to know when I'm getting in and whether I'm going straight to her place. I tell her we only just left and that I want to stop by my apartment to drop off my*) |

|        |                                                                                                                                                                                      |
|--------|--------------------------------------------------------------------------------------------------------------------------------------------------------------------------------------|
|        | *things. She asks if I've made a copy of the screen-play. I tell her I have. She tells me not to forget to bring it—"Emir" is eager to see it. We hang up.)* |
| ME:    | That was Emina.                                                                                                                                                                       |
| OLIVIER: | That delightful Bosnian you introduced me to at Marcel's party?                                                                                                                     |
| ME:    | That's right. But she's Albanian, not Bosnian.                                                                                                                                        |
| OLIVIER: | How are thing going with her? She was a delight!                                                                                                                                     |
| ME:    | It's all really intense. She's really intense. Too intense. (*To Corinne.*) I'm supposed to see her when I get in, and just thinking about it sets me on edge, too.                |
| OLIVIER: | (*Laughing.*) Is she also about to die?                                                                                                                                             |
| CORINNE: | (*Angry.*) Olivier!                                                                                                                                                                  |
| OLIVIER: | (*Goading.*) Ah, the secret to life lies in predicting when your friends are going to die …                                                                                       |
| CORINNE: | (*Angry.*) You're an ass.                                                                                                                                                            |
| ME:    | (*To Corinne.*) Why are you on edge, exactly?                                                                                                                                        |
| OLIVIER: | (*To me.*) What about you? Is the Bosnian too demanding?                                                                                                                            |
| CORINNE: | I worry that I don't know my friends well, that                                                                                                                                      |

I don't know what's going on inside their heads. It's unnerving when I haven't seen them in a while. I can take pleasant surprises from them, I'm happy when they've done something that I never would have imagined, I don't mind finding out that they're suddenly a different person ... as long as it's a change for the better. But when it's for the worse ...

ME:          Right, you think maybe you could have done something. It's true.

CORINNE:     That's happened to friends of mine who ... well, who weren't such close friends, and I didn't really mind. One day someone would say to me: "Did you hear Julie got a divorce?" or "Did you know Michèle joined a cult?" But they were people I'd never been close to, so it wasn't something I expected or didn't expect. It didn't bother me.

OLIVIER:     You weren't close to the one who joined the cult? I don't buy that.

CORINNE:     (*Ignoring him.*) But recently this has happened to close friends of mine, friends who I'm supposed to know well. Serge, my ex, for instance: he seemed so happy with his wife ...

ME:          Wow, Serge ... I liked that guy. Do you still see him?

CORINNE:     Well, as you know, it was a friendly breakup. I'd become infatuated with that graphic designer who turned out to be a disaster. But Serge was considerate to a fault, he never had a big ego—that's what I loved about him: it's extraordinary to find a man without an ego, most of you are so—

OLIVIER:     Whoa there—don't lump me into the same category.

ME:          Me neither!

CORINNE:     Fine. Anyway, Serge let me go …with a smile. He said he understood. That smile really bothered me. There was a smugness to it, a phony worldliness, it was like the smile of a man who willingly lets an impulsive woman go because he knows she'll come back. Then I found out I was wrong, because he certainly didn't wait for me. When my affair with that moron fizzled out and I tried to go back to him, he was already with that Jewish girl from Avenue de Villiers. I was crushed. I even thought he was going out with her to get back at me. But no, not at all. Before I knew it he was converting to Judaism and getting married.

ME:          Maybe he was just taking his revenge to an extreme. Although Serge didn't seem the type …

CORINNE:     No, not at all. I admit, that's what I tried to tell myself, but no. In this at least I can say I know Serge well. Resentment has no place in him. He simply met his Jewish girl and fell in love, without expecting to. The fact that he didn't expect to made him all the more convinced. He believed in the miracle of love, or that's what he said.

OLIVIER:    He was always one for schmaltz.

CORINNE:    I did what I could to hide my disappointment. He could tell, of course, but didn't say anything. He literally didn't have time, he didn't have space in his lovesick soul to think about me. To have two women in love with you at the same time! Something so many men (*pointedly*) would kill for …

OLIVIER:    Ahem!

CORINNE:    … didn't even cross his mind. There was only one woman for him, and it wasn't me.

ME:    Were you okay with that?

CORINNE:    What choice did I have? We never stopped seeing each other, alone of course, and eventually I started to think of him as a good friend.

OLIVIER:    Right. And you say he's not the kind of man who wants to have two women in love with him? Sounds like he is, seeing you so often.

CORINNE:      But he only ever talked about her!

OLIVIER:      To make you jealous, obviously.

CORINNE:      What do you know? (*Turning to me.*) So anyway, three weeks ago he told me he'd left her and didn't love her anymore.

ME:           Just like that?

CORINNE:      That's the sad part! For me it came totally out of the blue. I didn't know how to react. In my mind his life was picture-perfect! And I was so wrong! Suddenly I find out that for a long time his relationship had been a living hell, and I had no idea. And I thought I knew him so well …

ME:           I don't know. Some people are really impulsive. Maybe his life hadn't been a living hell for that long. Maybe it had only been a couple of days. It could have been an argument, a sudden flare-up, you know: we get in a fight, we yell, I smash a vase, slam a door, and two days later I'm back.

OLIVIER:      "Smash a vase"? When have you ever smashed a vase?

ME:           Never.

OLIVIER:      Well … I'll grant you there are hells that last days, hours—minutes, even. Mini-hells.

| | |
|---|---|
| ME: | (*To Corinne.*) When you last saw him, did he call you or did you call him? |
| CORINNE: | I called him, and I didn't notice anything in his voice. Then I saw him and he was devastated. Serge! Who seemed indestructible! |
| OLIVIER: | Yes, he survived even you! Can't you see you're still pathologically jealous? You can't stand it that he took your breakup in stride, and now, with the other woman, he's fallen apart. |
| CORINNE: | What difference does that make? That's not what I mean. What bothers me is that I wasn't able to tell. Since the last time I saw him, he hasn't called and his cell phone is always off. I called his work one day and they told me he was on leave. I don't know where he is or how to reach him. It drives me crazy to think what might have happened to him. What if he's dead? What if …? |
| OLIVIER: | Don't be so melodramatic. |
| CORINNE: | Why not? That's what happened to Marion. |
| OLIVIER: | Marion? What happened to her? |
| CORINNE: | Didn't you know? She killed herself. Last week they found her dead inside her home, covered in ants. |

OLIVIER:      Corinne!

CORINNE:      It's true! She took lord knows how many boxes
              of roofies. She'd been dead for several days and
              was being devoured by ants.

OLIVIER:      But what neighborhood did she live in, that she
              had ants?

ME:           That's horrible!

CORINNE:      And I had dinner with her at Germain's just ten
              days earlier. She was the same as always: cheer-
              ful, upbeat, full of plans. She'd gotten a fantastic
              offer from some university somewhere and was
              considering leaving the Diderot for a few years.

ME:           I wonder why people who commit suicide make
              plans.

CORINNE:      Marion wouldn't have been Marion without a
              plan. She didn't always follow through, of
              course. A while back she got into rock climb-
              ing. She signed up for a group, practiced in a
              rock gym …

OLIVIER:      What's that?

CORINNE:      One of those places with climbing walls …

OLIVIER:      Oh, right. So ridiculous.

CORINNE: And she spent a few months preparing for an expedition to Montblanc. But then she never

went. Overnight her passion for mountaineering vanished.

OLIVIER: I feel bad for her. I didn't really like her, but … I mean, what can you do?

CORINNE: That's exactly the response you'd expect from an insensitive ass. Besides, you don't like anybody.

OLIVIER: I like Paul. And loads of other people.

CORINNE: Sure, but when someone commits suicide your only reaction is to say, "What can you do?" You're a cliché.

OLIVIER: What do you want me to do? Go out and stop the world's suicides?

CORINNE: (*Irritated.*) See? That's what I mean. People like you don't think for a second about others, about how they feel, what they might be going through, whether they're happy or unhappy. It wouldn't bother you to be having dinner one night with a friend you've known your whole life and then to hear two days later she'd been found dead in her home—after all, "what can you do?" It wouldn't even cross your mind that there was something you could have done, or said, even unintentionally, to make her change

her mind, something to give her hope, and ...
and ... I don't know (*she starts to sob*), ease her
suffering. And now, when we get there, I have
to see Pascale ... and who knows if tomorrow
she'll get a divorce, or sink into depression, or
lose hope ... or shoot herself or get hit by a
bus ...

OLIVIER:      (*Conciliatory.*) Come now ... Don't be like that.
              That's not what I meant. It's just that I seem
              to believe more in the inevitable than you do.

CORINNE:      (*Calmer, but still crying.*) All I want is for every-
              one to be happy.

OLIVIER:      (*Conciliatory.*) But that's not always possible,
              Corinne.

ME:           I remember a story Goethe told in his auto-
              biography. It was about a shoemaker in
              Dresden. He said the shoemaker was a person
              who considered himself happy and demanded
              that everyone else be happy, too. And how
              those kinds of people always make us some-
              how uneasy.

CORINNE:      (*Drying her tears.*) I don't consider myself happy.

OLIVIER:      Goethe, Goethe! Leave Goethe out of this. The
              secret to life is in Balzac. "Ah, to know, young
              man! Is that not to take intuitive delight? Is it
              not to uncover the very substance of the matter,

to grasp its very essence? ... Thought is the key to every treasure: it offers the joys of the miser with none of his worries."

CORINNE: Olivier, Olivier ...

OLIVIER: But that's what your problem is. You think too much, you want to know everything, you want to seize the very essence of things, see things before they happen ... to know all the signs, find all the clues. You'd like that, of course, since it would put an end to your worries. But don't you realize that you aspire, like a witch, to have the key to the world's secrets?

CORINNE: On top of everything else you call me a witch.

OLIVIER: (*Laughing.*) Because that's what you are. A little witch's apprentice. Come on, stop getting ahead of yourself and wallowing in morbid thoughts. If you want, I'll go with you to see Pascale. Maybe that way ...

CORINNE: Some insight I can expect from you.

OLIVIER: As much as you would from a platypus.

CORINNE: Will you really go with me?

ME: Besides, can you imagine what life would be like if we didn't wear masks, if we couldn't guard, conceal, cover up our feelings? If we had to walk around emotionally naked?

OLIVIER:        What a nightmare. That must be what hell's like.

ME:             Hypocrisy is one of civilization's great
                achievements.

CORINNE:        Such cynics.

OLIVIER:        I may be a cynic, but you're not exactly an
                idealist.

ME:             She wants everyone to be happy! Such pressure!

CORINNE:        What's so bad about that? I really don't get you
                two.

ME:             I don't like being expected to be happy. It over-
                whelms me and forces me to feel guilty if I'm
                not. If I'm going to be happy, I'd rather it not
                be because others demand it.

CORINNE:        But what would become of us if we didn't at
                least have someone wishing for, looking out for
                our happiness? (*To me.*) You, for example, who
                have always been spoiled, what would you do?
                The big man who doesn't need anyone! You'd
                be surprised how many people are concerned
                about your happiness. (*As though she regretted
                what she said, after a pause.*) Anyway.

OLIVIER:        (*Looking at Corinne.*) Anyway … and indeed.

CORINNE:      Quiet. (*Long silence.*)

ME:           What's going on between you two? What's with
              the silence?

              (*Olivier starts to whistle mischievously.*)

CORINNE:      Be quiet.

OLIVIER:      You brought it up.

ME:           Brought what up?

OLIVIER:      Look, Corinne, I'm going to tell him.

CORINNE:      Don't even think about it.

OLIVIER:      (*To me.*) Our mother is planning to give you the
              Sisley. Since she, too, is a drama queen who
              thinks she's in possession of the world's secrets,
              she's decided, as she puts it, to settle her estate.
              She says we're getting our share—"and then
              some," she always adds—and that in any case
              we'd sell the painting. She doesn't care if we sell
              the others, but this one she wants to end up in
              the hands of someone who can appreciate it.
              Her words.

CORINNE:      You've got a big mouth. (*To me.*) Sorry, Paul,
              but it hasn't been decided yet.

OLIVIER:      It's beyond decided.

ME:               I don't know what to say. I can't even imagine…

OLIVIER:          It's the only good painting that's always been
                  in Savonnières. A winter landscape in a summer
                  home, oddly enough. She considers it part of
                  the house and associates it with you and your
                  mother. And you, "such a bright, hard-working
                  boy," have always surprised her: (*laughing*) you
                  refute her theory of social determinism. We,
                  on the other hand, who according to her have
                  never done a thing on our own, confirm it.

ME:               I refute it? Please, I'm living from fellowship to
                  fellowship.

OLIVIER:          She's convinced you're on your way to becom-
                  ing a great intellectual, a great artist … and
                  maybe even a great minister.

ME:               Please …

CORINNE:          (*To Olivier.*) I don't know why you had to tell
                  him. I think it's perverse. It hasn't been decided
                  at all. It's just an idea she's got in her head now
                  that she's worried about her illness.

OLIVIER:          (*To me.*) As you can see, Corinne, who wants
                  everyone to be happy, is against it. And of
                  course so is Jean-Baptiste. But there's nothing
                  they can do.

CORINNE:          Why do you have to get his hopes up?

ME:               (*Somewhat offended.*) Keep me out of this.
                  My hopes aren't up. And I don't want to be the
                  object of your condescension.

OLIVIER:          There's that social determinism. What conde-
                  scension? This is what she wants to do, and
                  that's all there is to it.

CORINNE:          She always talks like we've never accomplished
                  anything on our own. As if she had done some-
                  thing to deserve that painting! That painting,
                  along with everything else, she inherited from
                  her father, and he inherited it from his. Had she
                  purchased it with what she calls "the fruits of
                  her labor," then fine, I'd understand if she felt
                  she had the right to do with it as she pleases.
                  But she didn't. The Sisley is an heirloom, and
                  heirlooms belong in the family.

OLIVIER:          (*Very sarcastic.*) Hear, hear!

CORINNE:          Am I right or am I wrong?

OLIVIER:          You're a relic. Balzac would have made a nice
                  caricature out of you. In fact I think he did.

CORINNE:          I'd like to know what "labor" she's done.

OLIVIER:          And I'd like to know what "labor" we've done.

Look at me, unable to keep anything together. Since the crisis began, I keep downsizing the company month by month and have become the bane of the union. Meanwhile our mother says, "Your father would never have let this happen."

CORINNE:     That's what I mean. What does she know? She lives in a made-up world.

OLIVIER:     She knows perfectly well that as soon as she's not around, the first thing we'll do is sell the paintings. Starting with the Sisley.

ME:          All right, that's enough. I didn't ask for anything, and I don't feel comfortable listening to you discuss these things in front of me. I feel like I'm implicated.

OLIVIER:     But you are implicated. (*Laughing.*) That's what you get for copying the Sisley so many times when you were little. "Such talent, such technique! Mme. Joubert, your son is a prodigy!"

CORINNE:     Nonsense.

OLIVIER:     Seriously, Paul, the Sisley is for you. It's not, whatever Corinne says, some recent whim, some hospital delirium. Our mother has been saying this for a long time, and you shouldn't take it as condescension, but as a token of affection and even gratitude. So accept it, especially

since, the way things are going, we might have
to sell it before she dies. Lock it down.

CORINNE: It's not a sure thing, Paul. I'm sorry but it's not.

ME: I don't know, it doesn't seem like something that
belongs to me.

OLIVIER: It does belong to you. Your whole life you've
been an example for us in our mother's eyes.
She's such a pain!

ME: But a very patient one, all things considered.
Mine is the opposite. She's convinced I'm hur-
tling headlong into the future, empty-handed.

OLIVIER: (*Laughing.*) You've got the Sisley, for a start.

ME: No, I haven't got anything.

OLIVIER: But I'll bank on your future profits. Don't even
think of selling it while our mother's alive, of
course. And if you think of doing so after she's
died, she's liable to come back from the grave
to haunt you. I'd rather be free of that burden.
Sentimental memories are a never-ending curse.

CORINNE: For me feelings aren't a burden.

OLIVIER: Why would they be, if you could sell them?
Besides, if Mom came back from the grave you'd
be thrilled to say you talked to a ghost ... once
you're sitting on your pile of money, of course.

ME:                 (*Uncomfortable.*) Drop it, will you?

CORINNE:       See, Olivier? You've upset the boy.
OLIVIER:        How are your fellowships going, Paul?

ME:                 (*Confused.*) Not bad, given the times.

OLIVIER:        Is there a freeze on payments in that sector as
                    well?

ME:                 Eventually there will be.

CORINNE:       But you've got one, right?

ME:                 I applied for a one-year extension on the one I
                    have now. I'll be lucky if I get six months. But
                    I'll be happy with whatever I get. I've already
                    finished the project I was supposed to do. Any
                    extension will be a bonus.

OLIVIER:        You're a regular con man.

ME:                 No, I'm just an anxiety-ridden grant recipient.
                    Extensions are the worst kind of pathos. I'm
                    thirty-three, I don't have much time left. The
                    age limit for most grants is thirty-five. At that
                    age you're officially no longer young.

OLIVIER:        A pretty generous definition.

ME:                 I don't disagree. But I can't even imagine what comes next.

OLIVIER:        Shall I tell you?

ME:             Spare me that agony, please.

CORINNE:        So what's the project you say you just finished
                about?

ME:             (*Hesitant.*) Well ... it's silly. It's a screenplay.

CORINNE:        A screenplay for a movie?

ME:             Yes.

CORINNE:        And do you plan to direct it?

ME:             No.

CORINNE:        What do you mean? Everyone wants to direct
                their own screenplay.

ME:             In our country, yes, given the national obsession
                with auteurs. But that's not the case almost any-
                where else. It's just one more point of national
                pride, that is, one more French vice.

CORINNE:        To me it seems perfectly natural to want to
                direct what you write, and not leave it in the
                hands someone else, when who knows what
                they'll do with it.

ME:                Well, at the moment what I'd most like to be is a professional screenwriter. I don't care what someone else does with my work.

OLIVIER:           I doubt that. In any case, there's always television ... although I've heard that those screenwriters are twenty years old.

ME:                Ugh, television.

CORINNE:           I don't get you. Earlier you were criticizing us for not feeling attached to the house in Savonnières, and now you want us to believe you're not attached to what you write?

OLIVIER:           Paul is preparing for professional alienation. He's thinking realistically about his future.

ME:                This is a screenplay, not a novel. Screenplays are by nature malleable, adaptable, just a guideline. And anyway, perhaps the reason I think I have to leave it in someone else's hands is that I do feel attached. Without distance, it could turn out terribly as a film. And I have hardly any technical background: I wouldn't know how to tell one lens from another, or how to set up a shot / reverse shot ...

CORINNE:           You don't need a technical background. Agnès Jaoui says she still doesn't know a thing, and she's made three fantastic films.

OLIVIER:      Well ... the last one is pretty weak.

ME:           Sure, but she's an actress ... She has a deep
              knowledge of acting. One thing makes up for
              the other. I wouldn't know what to say to an
              actor ... I wouldn't know what to say to any-
              one. I'm still afraid of people. I'm incapable of
              managing a team. They'd eat me alive.

OLIVIER:      It's not as hard as you think. You have to imag-
              ine that they're sheep and you're the only
              human being, the shepherd. You'll also need a
              sheepdog, which is easy because they're a pro-
              lific breed, though you have to know how to
              train them. The secret to life is in dealing with
              sheepdogs.

ME:           Dogs always growl at me.

OLIVIER:      They never stop growling. You have to grant
              them that pleasure. The important thing is not
              to let them bite you.

ME:           I don't think God has given me the gift of that
              kind of learning.

OLIVIER:      Nonsense! Direct your film and hire me to bark
              and bare my teeth.

CORINNE:      Do you really not care who directs your screen-
              play? Or is there someone in particular you'd
              like to do it?

ME:                 That's the problem. I don't have anyone in mind,
                    but my girlfriend does.

OLIVIER:            The Bosnian beauty?

ME:                 She's Albanian, Olivier.

OLIVIER:            What difference does it make?

ME:                 Well, it's a bit complicated. Emina is involved
                    in the film world, on the production side. On
                    the other hand, she considers herself a key
                    player in the Balkan community in Paris. She
                    says she knows Kusturica and wants to show
                    him my screenplay.

OLIVIER:            Does it have gypsies?

ME:                 Not a single one.

CORINNE:            Does Kusturica direct other people's screenplays?

ME:                 Not really, no, though some of them he's written
                    in collaboration.

OLIVIER:            If I were you I wouldn't let myself be tempted.
                    Kusturica is pure Orientalism, an exporter of
                    Balkan stereotypes, and of course, like so many
                    others, a French invention. The next Fellini, ha!
                    This need we have to create *auteurs* is nothing
                    but sheer self-congratulation, a pathetic attempt

to reaffirm our traditions, to believe we're still the light of the world. *Auteurs* are over, they belong to another time. I applaud your decision to leave the screenplay in someone else's hands ... but please, not in Kusturica's.

CORINNE: Are you finished?

OLIVIER: Now that you mention it, no, I'm not. I hate picturesque families, first loves, back alley thugs, street processions, soccer players, exuberant women and ugly men. Kusturica was the son of a Tito regime bureaucrat, not a circus troupe. All those childhood impressions are just phony memories to please the West, and perhaps, fool that he is, to please himself. And even if they weren't, who can work with dignity nowadays with something so old and worn out as childhood memories?

CORINNE: (*To me.*) Poor Paul! I don't think you should let the opportunity pass you by, if it presents itself.

OLIVIER: If you do, I swear you won't get the Sisley.

ME: The funny thing is, I pretty much agree with you, Olivier. And that stirs one of my deepest fears: to be the protégé of someone who deep down you despise. It's happened to me once or twice. Not with the fellowships: fortunately, in that world things are all very impersonal and bureaucratic; you never get to know

anyone, you don't know who's backing you
or why, really. You work for the prestige of a
ghostly entity. But at university I had a professor I really couldn't stand, the typical gentleman
scholar, priggish, stupid, long-winded. Anyway,
he doted on me, he made me out to be the
model of his ideal student. And don't think I
took advantage of the fact or sucked up to him.

OLIVIER:      Everyone's sucking up one way or another.

ME:           Believe me, I didn't, I was revolted by him,
              it was something visceral. The more I disagreed
              with him, the more he praised my independent
              spirit. He left no way out. All my friends knew
              I couldn't stand him and found the situation
              very entertaining. But it really bothered me. I
              know one person dropped him some hints, but
              he took no notice. In fact he went after the guy.

OLIVIER:      He must have been infatuated with you.

ME:           Even that would have been manageable! No, it
              was a question of sheer vanity. He wanted me
              to be his disciple, so he could say as much and
              brag about me. Pardon my lack of modesty, but
              I was a very hardworking student, even a bril-
              liant one.

OLIVIER:      Corinne, tell him to stop going on about how
              smart he is. That's what we have Mom for.

ME:              Well, it's true. He wanted to go around saying
                 I was his creation, that I owed it all to him. It
                 was really awkward for me.

OLIVIER:         That means you never really stood up to him.

ME:              It's true, I didn't. But it was humiliating to
                 accept his praise.

CORINNE:         It's never humiliating to be praised. That's what
                 we live off of.

OLIVIER:         Yes, it's worse not to be praised even by those
                 who love us.

CORINNE:         No one's ever made me their protégée, inten-
                 tionally or otherwise.

OLIVIER:         Lucky you. Paul's story reminds me a bit of my
                 own story with Dad. Sorry, by the way, Paul,
                 but perhaps that's what you get for not having
                 had a father ... that is, (*laughing*) not having
                 a father who wasn't our mother. Maybe you're
                 unconsciously looking for paternal figures in
                 order to enjoy the conflicts that you've missed
                 out on.

ME:              Spare me the psychoanalytic readings, for love
                 of God.

OLIVIER:         In any case, I did become the protégé of someone I hated, and that was my father. Of course, he wasn't proud of me and didn't have me play the role of being his creation. That was for Jean-Baptiste, but Jean-Baptiste turned out to be a dud, which is to say, very dumb, and he had to resign himself to having me. He never forgave me for not being Jean-Baptiste.

CORINNE:    Jean-Baptiste isn't that dumb, he just wasn't cut out for ...

OLIVIER:    Neither was I. And I had to learn and adapt.

ME:         That means you let yourself become his protégé.

OLIVIER:    Of course, just as you let yourself become the professor's. Though I have a hunch that in my case it was more humiliating. (*Silence.*)

ME:         In my case it was more awkward than humiliating. Fortunately, when I chose a different thesis adviser, he stopped talking to me. That was really awkward, too ... Running into him in the halls at school and seeing him turn away.

OLIVIER:    (*Rather seriously.*) I hope now you're not going to become Kusturica's protégé.

ME:         (*Laughing.*) No, I won't ... though I sense a fight with Emina.

CORINNE:    Why don't I know Emina?

OLIVIER: Because you don't go to Marcel's parties. Ever wonder why you don't have any friends in common with Paul?

ME: I feel bad for saying this, but Emina is pretty temperamental. She's convinced she can help me—someone else looking out for me!—and above all, she's got a mind to do so.

OLIVIER: That wasn't my impression. She seemed sweet, laid-back, and mysterious.

ME: Well, I can assure you she's got a lot of personality.

OLIVIER: Typical dynamic woman?

CORINNE: What's wrong with being dynamic? And why is that typical? Olivier, how can you be so sexist?

OLIVIER: Sexist, me? I adore women!

CORINNE: You're utterly sexist. Women aren't there to be adored.

ME: Emina had to make her own way, she hasn't had it easy.

OLIVIER: Is she here illegally?

ME: She's been here for a long time. She says her

papers are in order.

CORINNE:    But you don't believe her.

ME:         It's not that. But her ... dynamism—sorry,
            Corinne—always seems to get the better of her.
            I'm not even sure she knows Kusturica. She says
            she does, but ...

OLIVIER:    That would be an advantage for you.

ME:         It's even occurred to me that she doesn't know
            him and is hoping to use my screenplay as a
            pretext for meeting him.

OLIVIER:    That leaves you without the advantage.

ME:         In any event, I'm afraid of complications. There's
            no way Kusturica will be interested, I'm not
            worried about that. But if he ended up taking
            a look at it and making some suggestions, I'm
            lost. Emina will want me to follow his advice.

CORINNE:    Well, if in the end he likes it ...

OLIVIER:    Not a chance! There aren't any gypsies.

ME:         If he likes it I'll put a gun to my head.

CORINNE:    So what's the screenplay about?

ME:         (*Flustered, as though caught off guard.*) Ha, it's silly.

CORINNE: Come on, tell us about it.

ME: (*Blushing.*) I'm embarrassed.
OLIVIER: (*Deviously.*) It's not about us, is it?

ME: Well, actually …

OLIVIER: I feared as much! Such sad inspiration, Paul!

CORINNE: But what about us? What's the story?

ME: Well … there's no story, really. Let's just say it's a series of coming-of-age memories.

OLIVIER: Like Kusturica?

ME: No, not like that, please. I've tried to reconstruct some events.

OLIVIER: I can't believe it. That's what you pour your talent into? First: you're too young to look back; looking back is for old people. Second: half of all memories are made up.

ME: Third: only in memory can I reconstruct how the terms of our relationship were set.

CORINNE: So it really is about us?

OLIVIER: "Terms?" I don't "remember" any terms.

ME:                It's a figure of speech. It's about how we decided
                   to remain friends at an age that could have sepa-
                   rated us.

OLIVIER:           The defeat of social determinism? That's what
                   it's about? You don't believe in that ...

CORINNE:           Am I really in it? What am I like?

ME:                Like a beautiful young woman, fun, wily,
                   charming ... Like you were before you started
                   worrying about who was going to die. Like you
                   were that summer that Uncle Gérard spent with
                   us.

OLIVIER:           Uncle Gérard? That lout?

CORINNE:           Uncle Gérard came on to me.

OLIVIER:           What a scene! The delightful young woman, the
                   lecherous uncle ... what's left? Swimming in the
                   river, riding bikes, country siestas, first kisses,
                   first wanks? Paul! You don't deserve the Sisley!

ME:                (*Laughing, but insecure.*) Well, yes, there's a little
                   of all that.

OLIVIER:           What a tremendous disappointment! Such
                   vulgarity!

ME:                Hey, hold on ...

CORINNE:   You have to portray me better. Why didn't you talk to me? I have memories, too. Your description of me is flattering, but ...

ME:        But what? I was trying to give you the gist. What do you want me to say? That your character has depth? It's a good thing we're almost there, because a little more of this and you'd have to wheel me out of here on a dolly.

OLIVIER:   And do you copy the Sisley in it?

ME:        (*Irritated.*) Actually, yes, the character who's supposed to represent me does copy the Sisley over and over.

OLIVIER:   You really should direct it ... now that you'll have the original. What a luxurious prop!

ME:        Didn't you just take it back?

OLIVIER:   And if Kusturica directs it, will you lend it to him?

CORINNE:   No, Paul, don't ever do that.

ME:        (*Nervous.*) I'm not explaining it well. The way I just told it, the story sounds full of clichés.

CORINNE:   In that case the only way for it not to sound

like that is for you to direct it yourself. Besides, I wouldn't feel comfortable leaving my life in the hands of strangers.

ME:            Listen, I've had to deal with some pretty big issues. Every coming-of-age is to a certain extent similar: biologically and socially, the varieties of human experience are limited, and that's why there are so many clichés. I made an effort to leave in what's true, stripping them of added sentimentalism, of the mythologizing tendencies of memory, of their status as accepted truth that doesn't need to be rethought. And that's what I'm trying to do: present adolescence in a way that lets it be rethought. It's unfair of you, Olivier, to write it off from the start as a fantasia of adolescence, because I didn't take inspiration in fantasy. I took inspiration in reality—earlier I said memory, but no, it was in reality—I put my ideas, my experiences, my perspective to the test, and I've read what the great authors say, Goethe, Tolstoy, Turgenev, Dostoevski, Vallès, even Bernhard and Salinger ... It's not vulgar!

OLIVIER:       (*Laughing.*) It still sounds to me like material for Kusturica. Who still believes in the ages of man anymore?

ME:            (*Angry.*) What's the matter with you? Do you have to keep rubbing Kusturica in my face? Do you have to imagine it all as something grotesque? I hate the grotesque as much as you do.

Why don't you imagine it as something by Gus Van Sant?

OLIVIER: Because I only like Gus Van Sant's commercial films.

ME: Now who's vulgar?

CORINNE: I love Gus Van Sant. With those marvelous boys...

ME: The boys aren't marvelous. He's the one who makes them marvelous.

CORINNE: Weren't Keanu Reeves and River Phoenix marvelous in *My Own Private Idaho*?

OLIVIER: That was one of his commercial films. Go see *Paranoid Park*.

CORINNE: I have, it's fantastic.

ME: It doesn't matter. My screenplay isn't for Gus Van Sant, either. It was just an example of the fact that there are other ways to approach the topic, and not only the ones that Olivier, in his stubbornness and nastiness, has in mind.

OLIVIER: I see I've offended you.

ME: No, not at all.

(*Silence.*)

CORINNE:    Forget about it, Paul. Olivier has always been a sad man.

OLIVIER:    Does the sadness come through in my character?

ME:    I'm taking you out of the screenplay.

OLIVIER:    Please do. I don't want to appear in a Gus Van Sant movie—and, by the way, I wouldn't be surprised if he were another French invention. I'm going to look into that.

ME:    You're my best character.

CORINNE:    Better than me?

ME:    You didn't stand up to Uncle Gérard when he told you not to hang around with me.

CORINNE:    I didn't pay him any mind, either.

ME:    And you also didn't suffer for it. It didn't mean anything to you. I suffered and so did Olivier.

OLIVIER:    Memories! I get the impression that you're making all of this up. (*Turning to me.*) But of course, if my character is the best one, I have nothing to say.

ME:            Thanks.

OLIVIER:       But promise me you'll think it over.

CORINNE:       Can I read the screenplay?

ME:            No.

CORINNE:       Is everyone else but me going to read it?

ME:            Everyone else isn't going to read it.

CORINNE:       What do you mean? I bet you'll show it to Olivier.

OLIVIER:       No way! I'm not reading anything.

CORINNE:       And your girlfriend, and Kusturica …

OLIVIER:       Not Kusturica!

CORINNE:       And the people that gave you the fellowship …

ME:            I do have to give it to them, there's no way around that. I have to have something to show for the money they gave me … (*laughing*) what I learned in the courses. But not yet. I'll say I haven't finished. That I need *the* extension.

OLIVIER:       Aren't you tired of going to class?

ME:            Tired doesn't even describe it. But sometimes

there are good professors ... and getting to
live in Berlin, Rome, or New York ... isn't that
worth it?

OLIVIER:        And what will you do if you get the extension?

ME:             I have two choices: pretend to work for six more
                months, or pretend to work for another year.
OLIVIER:        You could use the time to come up with a better
                source of inspiration. What about a more con-
                temporary story? Or for that matter, one that
                takes place on the moon?

CORINNE:        Then you'll have time to introduce me to Emina.

ME:             (*Sighing.*) If I make it through, yes, of course.
                You guys would get along.

OLIVIER:        (*To me.*) Where should I drop you off? Is the
                Bastille okay?

ME:             Perfect.

OLIVIER:        (*To Corinne.*) What about you? Where are you
                meeting Pascale?

CORINNE:        I'm not sure. I have to call her. Are you really
                coming with me?

OLIVIER:        Call her, then.

CORINNE:        (*Looks in her bag for her phone and dials a num-*

*ber.*) Pascale? ... Yes, yes, we're almost there ... How are you doing? ... Oh? You're really doing all right? ... Really? I'm glad ... I'm excited to see you ... By the way, my brother's coming along, he's excited to see you, too ... No, not my little brother ... That's right, Olivier ... Where do you want to meet?

OLIVER:      Somewhere close to Mom's house.

CORINNE:   Why?

OLIVIER:    We have to drop off the painting. You don't want to leave it in the trunk, do you?

CORINNE:   (*Into the phone.*) Listen, we have stop by my mom's house first ... Yes, to drop off something we brought back from Savonnières ... Does somewhere nearby work for you? ... Le Vigny? ... Olivier, is Le Vigny all right?

OLIVIER:    Yes, sounds good.

CORINNE:   (*Into the phone.*) Great ... Sure ... In an hour... See you soon. (*To us.*) Oof, she sounded odd ...

ME:          When you get a chance ... I'll get out here. (*The car stops. I get out. I take my bags out of the trunk. Corinne gets out and gives me a hug.*)

CORINNE:   Promise you'll introduce me to Emina?

ME:              (*Giving her a kiss goodbye on the cheeks.*) Promise.
                 (*Sticking my head in through the open door.*)
                 Goodbye, Olivier.

OLIVIER:         Good luck! I'll let you know just how tragic
                 Pascale is.

[Translated from the French by María Teresa Gallego Urrutia]

# II

The worst imaginable nightmare for most parents is to discover that one of their children has been murdered. For Lionel Dahmer, the discovery that Jeffrey Dahmer, his son, had murdered so many other people's children is what has turned his life into an unimaginable nightmare. Arrested at his Milwaukee apartment in 1991 and sentenced to 947 years in prison, Jeffrey Dahmer had taken the lives of seventeen men, dismembered many of them (storing body parts in the basement of his grandmother's house and in his own refrigerator) and, toward the end of his bloody career, even begun to cannibalize his victims. It is to these seventeen men and their families Lionel Dahmer has dedicated *A Father's Story*—a hauntingly self-reflective and, at times, even clinical autobiography of a father who couldn't see the monster he helped create. Some have charged that in writing this book, Dahmer has exploited his son's crimes for profit.[1]

This introduction to *Interview* magazine's advance publication, in March 1994, of excerpts from Lionel Dahmer's memoir, *A Father's Story: One Man's Anguish at Confronting Evil in His Son*,[2] raises clearly—and efficiently, for the present purposes—the issues I wish to address in the following pages, along with some others. It pares the case down to what I consider its essential features: Lionel Dahmer's status as father to a high-profile murderer, and the link between this status and the fear and "nightmare" all parents share; his relationship to the victims' families; and the equivocal nature of his decision to publicize his guilt. As a private confession and public statement, these three facets define the book, I think, and it is on them that I wish to focus. As for the "bloody career" of the "monster"—such elegant language is

typical of how Jeffrey Dahmer is described—I'm afraid the reader
can't expect very much. It is not my intention to get into the
crimes of the "Butcher of Milwaukee" any more than is necessary.
Nor is this his father's intention in writing his memoir, so far
removed from familiar kinds of sensationalism. "I can't imagine,"
declared his publisher, Paul Bresnick, "that those with prurient
interests would find satisfaction in this book ... There's virtually
no discussion of the crimes themselves. This is a father's story.
[Lionel] was just an average guy with an average family. All our
children have problems at one time or another."[3]

   This appeal to "all our children" and to the "average family"
will give me plenty to say in these pages, but let us briefly consider for a moment the question of the "crimes themselves" and
their displacement for the sake of, we suppose, a nobler purpose.
Clearly, the publisher of *A Father's Story* sought to defend the
book against the accusations of sensationalism and opportunistic
moneymaking, which, as Thomas H. Cook states in his prologue,
had cropped up even before it was published.[4] One of the last
taboos in media culture seems to be "explicit violence" (whatever
"explicit" means in this context), especially in the chronicling of
real events, since decency and a fear of fueling a morbid fascination have to contend with the author's need—or obsession—
with not straying from the facts. In any event, it is impossible to
ignore that even though the book does not discuss the "crimes
themselves," whoever picks it up does so out of an interest in
those very crimes. They may not be looking for "explicit violence," but this may be because they are already familiar with it.
Unlike so many celebrities nowadays who are famous for who
they are, Jeffrey Dahmer is famous for what he did, and knowing
about his crimes, being interested in them, either vaguely or with
"unhealthy" detail, is a precondition for reading the book—and
perhaps for reading this very essay.

As for me, without being defensive about it, I think I detect in my own interest in crimes and criminals a sort of false bottom that could be called irrational. Personal experience has provided me no encounters with murderers or violent psychopaths, so I suppose I run the risk of sounding like an amateur. Nor am I unaware that there is something childish about a predilection for evil figures, from the bogeyman to the serial killer, which not even the most diligent readings—historical, sociological, anthropological, constructivist, or biological—manage to redeem. By placing them within a context (which is, in a way, what Jeffrey Dahmer's father also does), I have acquired tools, concepts, a vocabulary, and some background in how "evil" is seen and described in our society. But that still tells me little about why, at age forty-eight, I'm glued to the television each time *Silence of the Lambs* or *Copycat* comes on. I am drawn equally to true account of serial killers and to their fictional representations—or distortions, as is so often the case—and this fact also warrants reflection, because of the confusion it can invite, and because of how easy it is to slip into the realm of mythology, at once macabre and alluring. "Our fascination and revulsion for the 'monstrous' among us," says Joyce Carol Oates, author of a novel inspired by the Dahmer case, *Zombie*—"has to do with our uneasy sense that such persons are forms of ourselves, derailed and gone horribly wrong."[5] Indeed, as we shall see, Lionel Dahmer went so far as to state he was "a man whose son was perhaps the deeper, darker shadow of himself."[6]

However, I'm wary about such identifications. For aren't these "forms" and "shadows" in which we recognize ourselves—distorted, magnified, outside of any rules or restraints—equally mythological? Are we not applying, to a real phenomenon, the same tools we apply to deciphering a myth? Must we conclude that we can only make room for serial killers in the real world—where they already exist—by viewing them as a chimera, a minotaur, a creature of Dr. Frankenstein? A relaxed, accepting attitude toward the unconscious—what am I saying, "accepting"? downright submissive—may ultimately be a clause stipulated by rationality itself, in one of its paradoxes. Even so, I'd rather not get lost in paradoxes. I'd like to be less fascinated, less confused, more perceptive.

The other irrational factor leading me to a book like this, which I want to examine a bit more closely, has to do with the "worst nightmare" that afflicts "most parents," as the opening line of the passage quoted above puts it. We could even extend that fear: it is not only the fear that your child could be killed—fear that they could die is enough. And it could even include, as Thomas H. Cook points out in his prologue, another fear which, "to one degree or another, *all* parents share, the terrible sense that your child has slipped beyond your grasp, that your little girl or boy is spinning in the void, swirling in the maelstrom, lost, lost, lost."[7] This emphatic, melodramatic language, no doubt a bit opportunistic—since the symbolic death of a child gone astray, presumably down the wrong path, is not the same as their physical death—illustrates quite well the common ground that Lionel Dahmer, overtly or subtly, at this and other levels, searches for in his memoirs. Every book creates, in one way or another, its own audience, and the audience of *A Father's Story* is an audience of anxious parents: not only those who really have lost a child—murdered, dead, "beyond their grasp"—but also the numerically much larger group of parents who are afraid of losing them.

A significant double reduction takes place here. On the one hand, this gesture excludes everyone who is not a parent from the audience of this "legitimate claim on our attention,"[8] suggesting that nothing contained in the book could be valuable or even intelligible outside the scope of parenthood—or even, I'm afraid, that anyone outside the scope of parenthood occupies an unnatural position, cut off from life's greatest, most solemn, most fundamental mysteries. Parenthood ensures membership not only in society, but in the essence of life; childlessness becomes a socially parasitic and metaphysically disabling condition. On the other hand, this fear that "to a greater or less degree, all parents share" is not presented as part of a contemporary description of anxiety disorder, but rather as an intrinsic, universal feature of parenthood. I should reiterate that the fear of loss is not at all the same as the pain of real loss. Grief for a child has been documented since time immemorial. (As has, incidentally, the subsiding of grief: "A sane one may endure / an even dearer loss: a blood brother, / a son; and yet, by heaven, having grieved / and passed through mourning, he will let it go. / The Fates have given patient hearts to men," says Phoebus Apollo in the *Iliad*.[9]) But the unreal fear, the morbid anticipation of their death, is a historical contribution from societies anxious about safety, and particularly from individuals within them who have internalized parenthood as a duty to be vigilant, or simply as one more source of failure and guilt. Consider, for example, the impression that reading Lionel Dahmer's book left on Anne Lamott, author of self-help bestsellers like *Operating Instructions: A Journal of My Son's First Year* or *Bird by Bird: Some Instructions on Writing and Life*:

> My nearly 17-year-old son, Sam, and I had a fight last Saturday that was so ugly and insane that it left me wondering if anyone in the history of time had ever been a worse parent, or raised such a horrible child. I believed the answer was no, because I had not yet read anything that would dispute this, except perhaps for Lionel Dahmer's great memoir of the mistakes he made in raising his son Jeffrey.[10]

This is a hardly unforeseeable way to read the book: as a negative parenting manual, an illustration of the "mistakes" a parent can make in their educational duties, like a dark mirror reflecting, in spite of everything, *our* worries. The memoirs of the father of a necrophile, cannibal, serial killer who confessed to the murder of seventeen people can inspire and provide a lesson to us when our teenage son refuses to wash the car as we asked, and goes so far as to talk back to us. "I slapped him across the face, for the first time in our lives," writes Anne Lamott, "and I knew that I was a truly doomed human being, and that neither of us could ever forgive me." An anxious parent never misses a chance to find reasons for guilt, and can well learn from Lionel Dahmer how to find them in the seemingly most banal situations. He encourages, and teaches by example, the cultivation of fear.

No doubt Lamott's allusion is partly tongue-in-cheek, and one would not want to think that the way she casually skips from a typical adolescent to a serial killer is socially representative. What I suspect is representative is the connection through fear—fear of a child murdered, a child dead, a child gone astray. Strangely, however, hardly anyone ever suggests that such widely shared anxieties might stem from a misguided way of thinking— a neurosis or a delirium, if not mere pettiness. Behind a parent's fear of loss, does no one see a fear of dispossession, of losing what is legitimately theirs? Or a fear of destitution, of being deprived of the power that they likewise believe they are legitimately entitled to wield over their children? Or a fear of seeing their own expectations dashed? Or perhaps a fear of rejection, because they know that, without their child, the entire institution of the family would proclaim their inadequacy as a figure of authority, as a protector, as a nurturer? And couldn't fear of a child's death conceal the more primal fear of one's own death?

I'm ashamed, alarmed, and angry to acknowledge that I, too, am an anxious parent. If I were a different kind, I wonder whether I'd still be interested in a book like this. Either way, the book and its predetermined audience seem to collude to convince me, in their assumptions, that being an anxious parent is natural. After all, what Lionel Dahmer berates himself for throughout his confession, so filled with retrospective clues and signs of his son's criminal behavior, is not being anxious enough: not being able to foresee, prevent, *fear* everything that eventually happened.

This preliminary exposition of the tangled motives that led me to read *A Father's Story* and guarantee my membership in its target audience has a necessary testimonial value. It also puts me in the ideal position to take up the question of strategy, which is where we are ultimately headed. I'm not sure whether I've chosen the right term. A strategy implies a specific objective and a mechanism set in motion to achieve it, along with some often very astute calculations. Aside from the fact that Lionel Dahmer's objective is vague and wavering, he cannot easily be accused, on the face of it, of being calculating, because in a case like his—the father of a convicted serial killer who offers a public testimony of his experience—the cold, exhaustive measurement that a good strategy requires would take superhuman strength. This is not to say that Lionel Dahmer is not after anything: in fact, he is after many things—some obvious, some less so, some even subliminal—but nothing that seems to be in the service of any larger purpose than a bid for publicity, in the broadest sense of the word. His is a frank and open account, the product of a painful self-examination, confident but risky, persuasive but uncertain of whether he will ultimately be damned or absolved: it is the search for a moral space where such a verdict is possible, regardless of the results. Not knowing what will happen, whether he will be punished or pardoned, is precisely what gives value to his act, what makes it possible see it as his duty, and perhaps as his redemption.

Since absolution of guilt is certainly not the point—the point is practically the exact opposite—calculation would seem to be counterproductive for his strategy, or perhaps simply impossible. Even though Lionel Dahmer introduces himself in the first chapter as a man of science, a chemist by training, who "thinks analytically"[11] (he repeats this over and over), he reminds us at the same time that his analysis, in the case of his son, is all retrospective—that is, formulated after the crimes were made public. He is therefore obliged to combine his "analytic" perspective with that of a man blind to the facts. This combination is one of extreme pathos, and therefore strategically effective, but it is patently forced in every other sense. The chronological order he imposes on the account, beginning with "Jeff's" gestation and ending with his confinement in prison, is useful but unwieldy, and he constantly alters it with detours and digressions about all the "omens" he failed to interpret in his son's actions, gestures, and looks, which now torment and haunt him: "When we went fishing, and he [at age four] seemed captivated by the gutted fish, staring at the brightly colored entrails, was that a child's natural curiosity, or a harbinger of the horror that was later to be found in Apartment 213 [of the Oxford Apartments in Milwaukee, where he committed most of his crimes]?"[12] In some cases these are not even omens, but merely different moments of awareness that he superimposes on one another: when Jeffrey comes home on leave in the summer of 1979, after six months in the army, Lionel is happy to see a smiling, handsome, athletic, hardworking, chatty young man who does not smell of alcohol. But he immediately adds something he could not have guessed at the time: "Not far away, at the top of a hill, the dismembered body of Jeff's first victim lay in a storm drain."[13] A discussion about a box that Jeffrey refuses to open, and which he would later claim contained pornographic magazines, is explained with a revelation from the police investigation carried out years later: what Jeffrey really guarded so jealously in the box was the head of one of his victims. On Thanksgiving Day in 1990 (by then there had been six), the family gathered in Jeffrey's grandmother's house and his father films the occasion on video:

> Now, when I look at that video, I see much more than I could possibly have seen before. In the chair, Jeff sits with one leg over the other, a single foot dangling in midair. At each mention of his apartment, his foot twitches slightly. With each mention that I or someone else in the family may drop by to pay him a visit, it twitches. With each mention of what he is doing now, of how his job is going, of what he does in his spare time—it twitches. Something in his distant, half-dead gaze says, "If you only knew …"[14]

The psychologist—the fortune teller, practically—that Lionel Dahmer became after he learned about his son's crimes is the best author he can imagine for his book, and he finds an ideal rhetorical tool in digression and speculation, in retrospective premonition. Consequently, the narrative is arranged according to what he knew later, rather than what he knew at the time, and the result is not unlike free association.

The nearly three years that passed between Jeffrey's arrest (July 22, 1991) and the publication of the book (March 1994) gave his father time to acquire new tools for reflection. On the other hand, in the media he became, he says, "rather than the father of the accused, an agent in my son's crimes, perhaps their ultimate cause."[15] He therefore had the means and the motive to take charge of his public image and to publish, by himself, his own version.

In this strategy, the publicity that condemns him can also save him, and Lionel Dahmer does not hesitate to point to himself as the "ultimate cause" of his son's crimes. Yet from this position of guilt—albeit carefully shielded, on higher ground—he feels around for possible support. As noted above, he cannot be said to have written his book in a state of shock, although this does not make him any less confused about where to look for possible allies. He apparently feels obliged to look first of all among the victims—already present, with their seventeen first and last names, in the dedication—and among their families, to whom he intends, as he states, to give part of the proceeds from the book. This initial gesture, emphatic and incriminating, also serves to silence suspicions about his motives, which cropped up with a certain virulence as soon as word got out of the book's publication. Paul Bresnick, his publisher and defender, hastened to state that the author felt compelled to "embark on this journey to try and understand" and that in no way had he been driven to "make money," even though he admitted he was "trying to defray some of the (legal) expenses [he'd] incurred." But this rationale did not please everyone. Jeannetta Robinson, director of a support center in Milwaukee for those affected by the crimes, was unequivocal: "The murderer gets a chance to murder people and his daddy gets to make money"; David Weinberger, the father of one of the victims, was equally categorical: "I'm not going to read it ... I'm going to give it to my lawyer."[16] The very month the book was published, it was reported that "two of the families have sued Lionel for failing to get written consent before using their names in his book, and another claim is pending by the parents of Steven Hicks [Jeffrey's first victim], who allege the Dahmers' negligence contributed to the death of their son."[17]

Among the victims' families, evidence of goodwill is scant. Only the sister of one victim, Theresa Smith, named in the acknowledgments, approved of Lionel Dahmer's decision: "If anyone has a right to write a book," she stated, "it's them [Jeffrey's parents] and the families [of the victims]. If that was my brother and my brother killed their son, I would not abandon my brother."[18] It should be remembered that, at the time of publication, Jeffrey Dahmer was still alive, serving his sentence in a maximum security prison in Portage, Wisconsin; there was no way to know that later that same year, on November 28, 1994, he would be killed by another inmate. Lionel Dahmer wrote and published the book while his son was still alive, knowing he would read it (which he did immediately and which seems to have led him to complain: "Dad, why couldn't you have put in more of the good stuff?"),[19] and the words of Theresa Smith support his choice as a way of meeting his paternal obligations under the most adverse circumstances. They also hint at an interesting possibility: the families' right to do the same, to take part in the economy of publicity. In any event, as far as I know, Theresa Smith never wrote a book.

In a long interview on CNN's *Larry King Live* in June 2004, Lionel Dahmer and his second wife, Shari, Jeffrey's stepmother since he was eighteen years old, speak of "a very close friend, of the sister of one of the victims," perhaps the very same Theresa Smith. Lionel says it was Shari who "engendered that relationship" and that they even arranged for her to speak to Jeffrey in prison; when he was killed, she attended the funeral and approached them to say she had forgiven him. According to Shari, "she and we are sounding boards … And it's helpful …to share our thoughts and feelings with someone who's on the other side. They—she must know how we feel, and of course, we want to know how she feels. And that's healing."[20]

In his book, Lionel Dahmer also mentions a Mrs. Hughes, the mother of Tony Hughes, another victim, who had "approached us, assuring us that she bore us no ill will, that she did not blame us for what Jeff had done."[21] Still, it seems they didn't see any other gestures of solidarity from the families. Lionel recounts how, when the judge allowed the family members to speak before issuing a sentence, "[t]hey were emotional, as they had a right to be, but they remained carefully controlled," and how Mrs. Hughes in particular "was very dignified."[22] Only one, Rita Isabel, the sister of Errol Lindsey, "lost control. Shouting obscenities, she actually stepped from behind the podium and rushed at Jeff … and after that, the judge refused to allow any more statements."[23]

"Control," of course, even as a double-edged sword, is one of the most contentious virtues in the book, and Lionel Dahmer obviously holds it in high regard. No judge was present to stop what happened later with the victims' families—on the contrary. On top of their pain and anger, they felt an understandable desire for retribution, and did not hesitate to use all the forms of pressure permitted by the legal system and the media's arena of public morality. Lionel Dahmer's promise to donate part of the proceeds from his book was called in five months after publication, in August 1994, by Thomas Jacobson, the lawyer for eight of the families. According to him, they had yet to see a cent, and they had no hope of ever seeing anything: "[Lionel Dahmer] wants people to believe he is atoning for his son's misdeeds," he declared. "In fact he's pocketing the money."[24]

Thomas Jacobson plays a peculiar role in this challenge to Lionel Dahmer's morality, given the price he put on the victims' deaths and the resources he deployed to force payment. In 1992, once the criminal trial had ended, a Wisconsin civil court granted eight of the victims' families $80 million in damages to be paid from the present and future property of the convicted killer. In February 1994, before Lionel Dahmer's book came out, Thomas Jacobson met with Jeffrey in prison and suggested he sell the rights to his life for a film version for one million dollars, as a way of paying off part of his debt. Jeffrey refused and the lawyer then hatched another plan: to auction off his belongings, which had been confiscated by the police in the apartment where he was arrested and committed most of his crimes. If a New York auction house had brought in $220,000 for Jack Ruby's pistol or $8,800 for Lee Harvey Oswald's toe tag, who knew what they could get for the freezer where Jeffrey kept his victims' heads and other body parts, for his saws, knives, and drills, for his gargoyle figurines? Jacobson estimated the value of the entire lot at a million dollars, but an unexpected campaign for the public image of the city of Milwaukee forced him to make do with a little less than half. A group of citizens, horrified at the prospect of the auction and the negative publicity it would bring to the city, founded an organization, Milwaukee Civic Pride, which raised $407,225 in order to acquire the property and discourage the collection of such gruesome paraphernalia. Jacobson consulted the families, and they voted five to one to accept the organization's proposal. They split the money, and the objects from Jeffrey Dahmer's apartment were destroyed in 1996.[25]

The families' right to the spoils, as insane as it was, did not fall outside of what the law, in its strange provisions, allowed. Milwaukee Civic Pride wanted to make clear, however, that there were questions of decency that could not be ignored. A delicate limit had been reached when the victims' relatives tried to satisfy their desire for reparation by selling the very instruments used to murder their sons or brothers. In fact, "delicate limit" may be an understatement, if some of the news circulating on the internet is true. The following passage must be regarded with caution, coming as it does from one of the countless webpages about serial killers that contain a maniac's collection of stories but show a woeful indifference to documenting sources, perhaps because their interest lies solely in what they add to the legend. This one specifically belongs to the joking variety and is entitled "The Wacky World of Murder: Mocking the Insane since 1996." Its author, someone with the username bundy23, who attributes the page's creation to the existence of "enough sick people on the net to have a site like this be popular," tells the following story:

> On a U.S. talk show (Donahue I think) they had the families of some of Jeff's victims. Well, at this point they were suing for millions. And they wanted Dahmer's stuff auctioned … and when Donahue asked them what they would prefer, the money or there [sic] children back, almost immediately nearly every one of them said "THE MONEY!" It was the most vile thing I think I've ever seen on TV.[26]

Nonetheless, it is to these families, who had already avoided sitting next to him in his son's trial,[27] that Lionel Dahmer dedicates his book and promises "something positive."[28] This gesture is no doubt part of the atonement that Jacobson, the attorney, so emphatically dismissed, and it builds on the reconciliation efforts of Reverend Gene Champion, who during the days of the trial, approached Lionel and his wife "trying to bridge the gap between us and the victims' families."[29] This was a truly significant attempt, insofar as it shows Lionel's desire for personal growth: he admits in his memoirs that from the start his wife, Shari, felt "the pain of the victims and their families much more than I was able to," because he was "a strangely disassociated man, limited in my ability to respond with feeling to another's feelings, often confused by my own lack of responsiveness."[30] Attending his son's trial, he describes feeling "no connection at all to the unspeakable things that were described … [It was] as if I were being forced to watch a horror film I did not want to watch, from which I could learn nothing, and from which I only wanted to escape,"[31] and as if each piece of evidence brought out were "a mere trial exhibit, not a human act at all, and certainly not part of a larger story that was also mine."[32]

This "larger story," which progressively takes over the book and gives it the form of a revelation, also unmistakably points, as we shall see, to the story of the audience described above (average anxious parents). Yet this story cannot be—and is indeed far from being—the story of the victims' families. Lionel Dahmer does attempt, after a fashion, to put himself in the victim's role, to convince us he is no stranger to victimhood. For example, he views his mother, who died with senile dementia in December 1992, as "another innocent victim,"[33] and he tells about how when the police informed him that Jeffrey was involved in a homicide case, the first thing he thought (one of the countless mistakes he catalogues) was that he was about to get "the worst news a parent could ever receive, that someone has killed his child."[34] Later he adds that "his shyness, his passivity, his low self-esteem, all of these things made him fit the role of victim far better than any other I might have imagined in a murder scenario."[35] His memoirs start precisely with speculation about what would have happened had the police told him "the same horrible things they had to tell so many other fathers and mothers in July 1991." Then "he would have done what they did": seek punishment for the murderer and, above all, mourn his son, think of him "warmly," visit his grave "from time to time,"

speak of him "with loss and affection," and be "the custodian of
his memory."[36] But of course all these consolations are denied
to him, because "my son was still alive. I couldn't bury him. I
couldn't remember him fondly. He was not a figure of the past.
He was still with me, as he still is."[37]

It may be worse, we infer, to be the parent of a murderer than
the parent of a victim ... and this unique status, this forsaken-
ness, this dark, lonely path he must walk without the guidance
or the dignity that the tradition of mourning provides, does not
exactly bring Lionel Dahmer closer to the side of the victims'
families. His attempts to find something in common are clumsy
and forced, doomed to failure from the start, for practically all he
manages to do is make his experience as the parent of a murderer
seem more grueling, more selfless, more morally courageous,
and therefore superior. On this path Lionel Dahmer will find
no solidarity, and he will continue to be the same "disassociated
man" who attended his son's trial as though nothing it brought
to light had anything to do with him.

In fact, he continues to be that man until he finds a connection that lets him acquire a certain community social consciousness. The key to a community was always there, unrecognizable
at first for the man who had been "disassociated" since the days
following Jeffrey's arrest. Because of his fateful loss of anonym-
ity, after July 22, 1991, any letter addressed to "the Dahmers,"
even without an address, was promptly delivered to the family's
house. Most of what they received were "letters of support, letters of advice,"[38] which he refused to read, though his wife Shari
"read all of these letters ... and it was hard for me to understand
why."[39] Shari understood that these letters offered condolence
and solidarity, a generous chance to *associate* with others that
could not be disregarded: parents who wrote them to talk about
"some child they no longer saw or talked to, of a boy or girl who

had slipped beyond their grasp, fallen into drugs, bad company or simple isolation, and never returned again."[40] Cases of symbolic death, in short, which later on Lionel Dahmer would not hesitate to recognize with an astonishing metaphor: the letters came from "people who identified with us as parents whose lives had finally been consumed in the fire of parenthood."[41]

Is this not at last an opening, a way to approach the place of the victim? A place to burn, a sacrificial altar where it need not be your own child, the one you can't abandon, but the common child of "parenthood" who is consumed on the pyre? The final words of the book point unambiguously to this very conclusion: "Fatherhood remains, at last, a grave enigma, and when I contemplate that my other son may one day be a father, I can only say to him, as I must to any father after me, 'Take care, take care, take care.'"[42]

Watching Lionel Dahmer read passages from his memoirs on an NBC program,[43] and talk in an interview in front of the house in Bath, Ohio, where his son lived with him and committed his first murder, gives a sense of the scale of this "fire" and this "enigma." One cannot burn in private: the atonement would not be exemplary and the fire would not illuminate. "I really want to tell parents about what I think they should look for in rearing their children," he told Larry King even in 2004, ten years after writing the book. "I have no other motivation, except to try to help people."[44] There is no place for a mere act of private purification: trotting out one's guilt on television, publishing it in every corner of the media world, answering for a murderous child, is the only way one can prompt a true catharsis, one that is not just a projection of shared anxieties but offers a preventative—and therefore potentially useful—model of parenthood. If on the way one is accused, vilified, sued, humiliated, called a fame seeker or a money grubber, this is not so much a danger as it is a demand of publicity. No suffering is redeemed without suffering, especially unjust suffering. How else could it be a Calvary? Wasn't Christ crucified among thieves?

But what is Lionel Dahmer guilty of? What does any parent have to "take care" of after him? On what common ground can we cultivate our anxiety? For now I will just say that his focus is psychological, to a certain extent psychogenetic, and fits wholly within the kind of therapeutic culture that endorses and promotes public atonement. In any case, before getting into it, I'd like to consider other factors that could well be the title of a chapter on the "causes" of a killer son but which Lionel Dahmer puts in a secondary, dubious, or practically irrelevant place. His faith in psychology as a site of intervention leads him to overlook, or treat with a certain dismissiveness, two factors that are less susceptible to intervention but are all the same among the most commonly cited by experts: first, the social naturalization of violence and the failure of the institutions charged with regulating it; and second, congenital brain damage, on which biologically oriented theories and research are based.

Jeffrey Dahmer's "profile" doesn't tally with certain features generally established for North American serial killers. Above all he lacks the history of child abuse or maltreatment, of which there is absolutely no indication. True, in the United States there is a widespread notion that children of divorce, like Jeffrey, are by definition the product of a broken or dysfunctional home, but this seems to be a purely ideological argument from the far right. According to the available information, the "dysfunction" of the Dahmer family is limited to a father absorbed by his work, and often away from home, and a mother described by her husband as emotionally unstable with some sort of psychiatric diagnosis for her "state of anxiety."[45] Even if the breakdown of the marriage before and during the divorce manifested itself in fights and tension (Jeffrey himself believed he started drinking as a "way of handling the home life"[46]), none of this suggests that their son was not raised in "an actual home where he was loved, hugged, and indulged despite his parents' divorce and his own alcoholism."[47]

We can therefore discard brutality in his immediate environment. On the other hand, there are aspects of Jeffrey Dahmer's upbringing that specialists commonly point to as factors that may not cause, but do help consolidate, the lack of empathy and the victim dehumanization typical of the modern serial killer. These factors have to do with the way we become familiar with violence in the media. According to the anthropologist Elliott Leyton, "television coverage of the Vietnam War ... brought real bloodletting and killing into every American living-room, and rendered death sacred no more." According to him, this familiarity fosters, through repetition, a certain naturalization of the pain of others that can translate into insensitivity, and it encourages, through the romance of fiction, the adoption of violence as an immediate, easy, and valid response to any kind of dissatisfaction. "Whether in the media or at the level of the street," says Leyton, "the glowing mythology often surrounding violence creates a situation in which the most trivial provocation can result in a savage explosion."[48] "Serial killers today were raised," he says, "in a civilization which legitimizes violence as a response to frustration."[49] Detective Robert K. Ressler, a pioneer in criminal profiles, and creator of the term "serial killer," seems to be of the same opinion: according to him, "These psychological pushes toward interpersonal violence are exacerbated in all of our young people by the way that violence is often portrayed as an accepted part of life, by our new media and fictional representations alike. In the 'entertainment' products shown on MTV, on broadcast channels, or cable television, on a big-theater movie screen, we see constant intermixings of sex and violence that serve to legitimize interpersonal, sexually based violence. Often there are news reports of young men using guns to eliminate their enemies—presented without comment that this an unacceptable way of solving a difficult situation."[50]

Even if partly right, this reading, which holds that representations of violence suppress morality and that the young mind has some deficit in its ability to discriminate, sounds at times like a paternalistic sermon, and it may indeed appeal to the father of a serial killer, especially one with a conservative mindset. Nevertheless, Lionel Dahmer devotes barely two lines to this possibility, on the second-to-last page of his book: "Could Jeff," he wonders, "have been influenced by the level of violence in our society that surrounded him or by the constant violence that his peer group watched in movies and television?"[51] Incidentally, the only thing he mentions about his son's cultural consumption is a love of pornography and occultism. To hear about the role that movies like *The Return of the Jedi* or *The Exorcist* played in his fantasies, as well as in the staging of his crimes, we have to turn to Ressler's book. One gets the impression that, for Lionel Dahmer, "society" is a very distant backdrop, almost invisible from the stage where he faces the public, exploring the causes behind his criminal son's actions; and one gets the impression, too, that this backdrop, however far behind and far away it is from his point of view, lends him a certain protection, holding him back from the void. This relationship is somewhat strange, as though society and its institutions were there only to inculcate values, but not really to uphold them: upholding them seems to be the exclusive responsibility of the individual, while society, in its role as a mere framework of inspiration, becomes a passive entity, and nothing can be demanded of it. It does not occur to Lionel Dahmer that society might create antisocial individuals, much less that antisocial individuals, as Elliott Leyton contends, could be taking revenge, in their grotesque, pathetic way, on society. Lionel Dahmer believes in institutions: not only does he not question them, he respects them unconditionally. Family, the university, work, and the army appear in the book as sources of genuine civic and moral values: his son's failure in these environments is not their fault but always his own. Lionel Dahmer never criticizes the police (eight officers are mentioned in the Acknowledgements), nor even the media, though one might think he had plenty of reason to do so. One of the most striking omissions in the book, with regard to Jeffrey's "criminal career," is an event commonly cited not only by reporters but by the victims' families: the lack of police diligence in the death of the fourteen-year-old Laotian boy Konerak Sinthasomphone on May 27, 1991. Two young African American women called the police when they found the boy naked, drugged, and bleeding: he had just run away from the apartment where Jeffrey Dahmer had sawed a hole in his skull in his attempt to create a zombie sex slave. Jeffrey arrived before the police did and tried to take him back, but the young women stopped him. When the police arrived—and with them the firefighters and a paramedic unit— the women pointed out that the boy was just a child, showed signs of having been beaten, and was trying to escape from the very man set on taking him back. The three officers ignored their protests and even threatened to arrest them. Sinthasomphone could barely speak, and what he said he said in Laotian.[52] As Jeffrey Dahmer himself recounts:

> I went [out of the apartment] for a quick beer across the street
> before the bar closed; and I was walking back and saw him

sitting on the sidewalk, and somebody had called the police. I had to think quickly, and told 'em that he was a friend that had gotten drunk, and they believed me. Halfway up a dark alley, at two in the morning, with the police coming one way and fire trucks coming the other. Couldn't go anywhere. They ask me for ID, I show 'em ID; they try to talk to him, he answers in his native tongue ... they checked him out and figured he was real drunk. They told me to take him back; he was not wanting to go back; and one officer grabbed him on one arm, the other officer grabbed him on the other, and they walked him up to the apartment ... They laid him on the sofa, looked around ... They didn't go into my bedroom. If they had, they would've seen the body of [a previous victim], still lying in there. They saw the two pictures that I'd taken earlier, lying on the dining room table. One of 'em said to the other, "See, he's telling the truth." And they left.[53]

Dahmer killed the boy that very night. Before he was captured, he would kill four more times. The officers were temporarily suspended and then allowed to return to work; the victim's family sued the police and the city of Milwaukee for failing in their duty to protect, and for intentional discrimination against the rights of racial minorities and homosexuals.

Lionel Dahmer does not mention this horrific episode, which could have made him doubt the preventative efficacy of the police force, though as noted above, he does not seem to think prevention is a public responsibility. In any case, another parent might have concluded that more competence—or less prejudice—would have saved, at that point, five lives. But Lionel Dahmer's parenthood is steadfastly reduced to a private sphere that, free from any other influences, paradoxically explains and encompasses everything. The obliviousness of some police officers remains outside his world, irrelevant because it adds nothing to its magnitude. Perhaps this, and not a polite distaste for sensationalism, is the reason he gives so little space to Jeffrey's crimes: in that enormous universe subsumed into family life and personal psychology, the crimes seem practically unreal. They are almost never presented in the language of facts, but in the language of enigmas and obscurities of "the mind."

Lionel Dahmer does not regret his somewhat blind faith in institutions, but he does see his own obliviousness as a decisive factor in his guilt: he believes that a hyper-attentive and psychologically attuned parent could have foreseen, and maybe stopped, several things from happening. As we have seen, all his attempts to socialize his son, to keep him away from alcohol and put him on the path of a life of study and work, ended in failure. He also tried to take him to therapy sessions (including Alcoholics Anonymous), though Jeffrey quickly abandoned them. In a decision that showed more consistence than desperation, he enlisted him in the army in January 1979. He did not see him for six months. When Jeff came back on a two-week leave, he was unrecognizable—sober, active, cooperative, proud of his military experience—which led his father to conceive all kinds of hopes. Then he was sent to Germany, where he spent two years, and from his calls it seemed that "the 'new' Jeff was alive and well, and still at work building a decent future for himself."[54] Years later, after Jeffrey died, his roommate in Germany, Billy Capshaw, had his story as a patient diagnosed with post-traumatic stress disorder appear on the website of Dr. Eugene Waterman. Among the information the therapist provides is the following:

At first, Dahmer seemed like a likeable person and had a certain amount of charisma, but within a few days Billy became

frightened as Dahmer began his process of completely controlling Billy by various means. He physically beat him.
When Billy complained to those in authority, he was told
that he was a "pussy" and was not taken seriously ... Both
Billy and Dahmer were medics, and when Dahmer injured
Billy, he went with Billy to the doctor and convinced them
that he was taking care of him. He also convinced them that
he was not the one who had injured him, even though Billy
said otherwise ... Billy thinks that Dahmer drugged him. He
remembers waking up and being tied with ropes and unable
to get loose. On several occasions he was choked unconscious.
Dahmer had anal intercourse with him while he was tied
up. Billy felt ashamed and guilty about this, and for years he
didn't tell anyone.[55]

Billy Capshaw, incidentally, was one of the first "retrospective"
witnesses to make statements to the press, barely one month after
Jeffrey Dahmer was arrested. At first he was not as explicit, but
he said that "when he'd drink, he'd get real violent with me ...
You could tell in his face that he wasn't joking. It was for real."[56]
Jeffrey was given a general discharge from the army one year
before his three years were up; "the reason, we later found out,
was alcoholism."[57]

Of course, Lionel Dahmer knew nothing of Billy Capshaw,
but it is nonetheless darkly ironic for his system of values that the
institution that was supposed to give Jeffrey "a decent future,"
provided him a way to carry out his criminal activities with
impunity. The father still thought, at that time, that "alcoholism" was his only flaw, the one that explained everything, and
he would cling to that explanation for a long time.

A small disagreement with the legal system would end up suggesting to Lionel Dahmer that the passive nature of institutions

might not always work in his favor. In September 1988, Jeffrey, who by then had killed four young men and been arrested twice (in 1982 and 1986) for indecent exposure, took home to his apartment a thirteen-year-old Laotian boy—a cousin of Konerak Sinthasomphone!—photographed him naked, drugged him, and abused him, but the boy managed to escape and reported him. Jeffrey was arrested, tried, and sentenced to one year at a work program and five years' probation. That was when the father found out about his previous arrests, and even then, with alcoholism in mind, he continued to think that "all those grotesque and repugnant behaviors could be thought of as a phase through which he would one day pass."[58] So he insisted that his son be enrolled in prison "in some sort kind of highly structured treatment program."[59] Jeffrey's lawyer, Gerald Boyle, who would later defend him in the trial for the murders, replied that this was a question that would have to be raised after his client was released, not while he remained in prison. He added, however, that his client's attitude was "very positive," and his desire was to get "back to the community," and that he as an attorney had the duty to obtain for him everything the law allowed, especially "consideration by the Court for his early release."[60] Dissatisfied with such a prospect, Lionel wrote directly to the judge. "I have tremendous reservations about Jeff's chances when he hits the street," he wrote, and insisted again that Jeffrey should be subjected to a 'rigorous program' for alcoholism."[61]

Even then, Lionel had faith in psychological intervention, and over the years it would grow stronger and come to pervade all the accusations he leveled at himself in the book. But his efforts were in vain: Jeff was released from prison in 1990, having served ten months of his sentence, with no treatment whatsoever; he regained his position at the chocolate factory he had worked at since 1983 and soon moved to Oxford Apartments, no. 213, "duly approved by Jeff's probation officer,"[62] where he killed again that May. He also seems to have met consistently with his probation officer, Donna Chester (the last time was seven days before he was arrested), and her impressions, "recorded in an 81-page document released by the Wisconsin Department of Corrections[,] give no indication that Mr. Dahmer set off alarms during their chats."[63] When Lionel visited him in his new apartment, he was surprised to see that his son had bought a freezer, but Jeffrey explained he had done so to save money ("When there's a sale, I can stock up on things") and he thought this was "a sensible idea."[64]

Everyone, in short, was fooled, an ability—and source of pride—that is incidentally not at all unusual in serial killers. (Edmund Kemper had a head in the trunk of his car when he went to see the psychiatrists tasked with deciding whether to clear his criminal record … and indeed they recommended clearing it.[65]) Lionel Dahmer recreates at length the lies Jeffrey told to cover up criminal acts or intents, and he acknowledges he was unable to "see" these other impulses, "even more dangerous and destructive" than alcoholism.[66] His requests for "treatment" indicate, in any case, that he "saw" something else, and though he is careful not to point an accusing finger, the actions of the police, attorneys, judges, prison authorities—all the institutions charged with "seeing" and keeping watch—speak for themselves. Yet there is something unequal in how this blindness is shared, since only on one side—his—does it lead to fear and suffering. Perhaps Lionel Dahmer's reluctance to criticize institutions is not just a result of his conservative inclinations: after all, institutional blindness abounds in his self-portrait, as a father who was powerless, alone, who couldn't have known and didn't know how to know, and who had no one to help him.

This recurrent "not knowing" also involves questions of another sort, other places where guilt could lie, such as congenital disorders, about which Lionel Dahmer is ambiguous and cautious, never conclusive. In the last pages of his book he sums up his position:

> Although, as a scientist, I must accept genetics as a powerful contributing force in the formation of a human being, I also understand that only half of my son's genetic make-up came from me, and even more, that genetic mutations can occur at any time in any living organism, their influence on later development entirely unpredictable. I don't know, and will never know, how much drugs contributed to Jeff's crimes, either his own alcoholism, or the medications my wife took while he still lay in her womb.[67]

Before turning to the issue of medication and the mysterious presence of Joyce Dahmer in the book, it is worth recalling that the trial, in which Jeffrey pled "guilty but insane," centered entirely on the question of whether the accused was conscious, cognitively and morally, of his criminal acts, or whether he suffered some mental disorder, in which case he could be confined in a psychiatric hospital instead of prison. The defense's strategy "was to try to convince the jury that Dahmer's acts were so bizarre that only someone who was legally insane could have done them. Thus, Boyle purposefully emphasized every unusual and gruesome aspect of the murders." Forty-five expert witnesses, among them criminologists like Robert K. Ressler and a good number of psychiatrists, declared that Jeffrey "did not understand the nature of his crimes due to the influences of his sexual and mental disorders."[68] Even a court expert, the forensic psychiatrist

George Palermo, testified that "he had a serious personality disorder that required medical treatment." The prosecution also had forensic psychiatrists on its side, and apparently they proceeded to use the same strategy as the defense, insisting on the most grotesque aspects of the crimes to persuade the jury to reach the opposite conclusion: Dr. Park Elliott Dietz, for example, "acknowledged that Dahmer seemed to be a case of paraphilia as well as a person with a strong dependence on alcohol. However, he also claimed that Dahmer knew right from wrong and could have stopped himself at any time. Specifically, Dietz pointed to the fact that Dahmer always used condoms when he had sex with a corpse to show that his acts were not impulsive."[69]

This emphasis on psychological bizarreness is clearly based on a notion of psychiatry as a science of the soul; no one, it seems, thought to consult the sciences of the body, perhaps because at that time they were still more precarious, from a legal standpoint, than they are now. Lionel Dahmer himself writes about an interview he gave to the ABC program *Inside Edition*, after his son had been given fifteen consecutive life sentences. In the interview he suggested his madness "might well have been caused by the prescribed medications Joyce had taken during the pregnancy," adding that at the trial "no one at any time addressed the issue of possible genetic changes during conception and the early stages of the pregnancy." Reflecting on these statements in the book, however, he makes one of his typical retrospective corrections: "Clearly, at that time, any deeper consideration of the relationship I had with Jeff, either emotionally or biologically, still remained beyond my grasp."[70]

The very possibility of genetic changes both attracts and repels Lionel Dahmer. On the one hand, it allows him to maintain his faith in science and the predictability that he dedicated his life to, while relieving himself of guilt in the process. On the other hand, perhaps because the guilt then reverts to his ex-wife, Jeffrey's mother, he finds it unchivalrous, so to speak, if not immoral—and in a way of course it lowers the intensity of the parental identification he takes up in his Calvary. For this reason, throughout the book the figure of Joyce Dahmer, née Flint, is blurry, incomplete, half absent, even if she is always linked—with the necessary discretion, so as not to show undue spite—to abandonment, illness, and disorders. In his discussion of the "permanent state of tension and bad feeling"[71] that presided over her mother's house (where they were living) during the first months of Jeffrey's life, Lionel reveals that Joyce was the daughter of an alcoholic with a domineering, explosive personality, and that he didn't know what to do "about her past" other than try to make her forget "whatever fear or cruelty that she'd experienced as a child."[72] In addition to these facts, which Lionel never connects to Jeffrey's alcoholism, even though they could support a genetic argument, Joyce had a difficult pregnancy, with frequent nausea, hypersensitivity to sounds and smells, irritability and a series of episodes of "stiffness" in her legs and jaw. Doctors suggested a problem with her "mental state"[73] and gave her injections of barbiturates and morphine. In the final months of the pregnancy, Joyce was taking up to twenty-six pills per day. Even so, the medications didn't alleviate her irritable reactions or her sense of "helplessness and isolation": according to Lionel, "this first troubled experience laid the foundation for a longer, and even more troubled, marriage. In some sense, our relationship never recovered from the damage done to it at this early stage."[74]

The situation did not improve much with the birth of Jeffrey. Joyce was reluctant to breastfeed him and stopped doing so after a few days. The fights intensified with her mother-in-law and with her husband. Moving out to live on their own provided some relief, but two years later Lionel was spending all day at work, at the chemistry lab where he "understood the laws that governed things,"[75] and she, alone at home with the child, repeatedly dreamed she was being chased by "a large black bear." The fights were frequent and, "at times, physical": Joyce went so far as to threaten him with a kitchen knife.[76] After this episode, with the exception of an important incident I will discuss below, Joyce Dahmer practically disappears from the book for nearly fifty pages, which cover fourteen years. We do not see her again until the end of 1976, in the house in Bath, diagnosed with "an anxiety state," under psychiatric care, even frequently hospitalized.[77] Group therapy, in which she vented her anger at her father, seemed to help, and there she made some friends; she made decorative objects out of leaded glass and macramé; she saw a UFO and published her experience in the *Beacon Journal*. Her relationship, however, far from stabilizing, deteriorated: when they fought—as Lionel would eventually learn, thanks to his other son, Dave—Jeffrey would go outside, gather branches from the ground, and start lashing the trees. In August 1977, Joyce's father died, and in the presence of the body, she felt that "our marriage was certainly dead, too."[78] Then Lionel discovered she had had an affair. In the divorce they fought over custody of the children, who were sent to live with their mother; very soon thereafter, Jeffrey turned eighteen, and Joyce moved away with Dave, now eleven, without telling him where. That's how Lionel found him one day: living alone at home, with a broken refrigerator and hardly any food, holding a makeshift séance with some friends. It took Lionel over a month to locate his other son.

The fact is, by "running away" with one son, and consequently "abandoning" the other (now legally an adult), Joyce Dahmer, once again Flint, takes leave of the reader. From this moment on, allusions to her are minimal, and almost always implicit—part of the complex picture that Lionel develops of his own personality as it relates to their failed marriage. (I should note that he accepts his share of responsibility for the failure, as an absent husband and father, and as a man lacking emotional education.) From him, therefore, we do not learn what happened to Joyce when Jeffrey was arrested and sentenced, whether they ever spoke or met, what she felt or how she reacted. Other sources inform us that she did not attend the trial,[79] that she nonetheless never lost contact with her son, and that, in the words of Boyle, the attorney, "she had to live with the idea that she was the mother of a monster, and it just drove her crazy ... It was clear she bore no responsibility. She was a great mother; [Jeffrey] Dahmer told me that over and over again."[80] It is also clear that Joyce Flint, who avoided statements and interviews, chose not to become a public figure, unlike her ex-husband. She had a job as a social worker in a center for AIDS victims in Fresno, California, and died of cancer on November 27, 2000.

The "clues" strewn throughout Lionel Dahmer's memoirs seem to open the door for the image of the *bad mother* so beloved of biographers, journalists, and fans of serial killers. A front-page headline in the *Chippewa Herald Telegram*, in the small town of Chippewa Falls, Wisconsin, where Joyce moved with her son Dave after the divorce, published on July 25, 1991 (three days after Jeffrey's arrest) reads: "Mother of Accused Mass Murderer Lived Here."[81] As we have seen, Lionel himself admitted to having spoken on television, two months after Jeffrey's arrest, about the medication that Joyce took during the pregnancy, but it seems that on that program he also said his ex-wife had "a history of mental illness, [which] he feels had a negative impact on their son."[82] The biographer Brian Masters, for his part, worries that Joyce weaned Jeffrey too soon, since some children "may feel the abrupt change in their tactile world as a form of rejection or distance" that is "incorporated, absorbed into their view of their own place in the world, and gradually presumed natural and deserved, or just 'right'": he concludes by saying that "it's notable how often, as an adult, [Jeffrey Dahmer] has said that he's never handled disappointment well."[83]

Beyond the pregnancy and breastfeeding, the determining role played by Jeffrey's mother, and her influence on his psyche, have inspired plots worthy of a conspiracy thriller. Akira Mizuta Lippit, a professor at the University of Southern California, notes in an article that "[a]ccording to Dahmer's probation officer, Donna Chester, Joyce called Jeffrey after a five-year absence and told him she knew he was gay and that it was not a problem for her."[84] The call took place in March 1991, which leads Lippit to imagine Joyce as the Queen of Diamonds in *The Manchurian Candidate* and to cobble together the following conclusion: "Whether by accident or by design, that phone call from Joyce precipitated Dahmer's final rampage in which he murdered seven times between March and July before being apprehended."[85] I really cannot say which is more outlandish: imagining the mother as the "intentional" trigger of her son's final crimes, or ascribing to her, as to a demiurge, control over the "accidental."

The best antidote to the figure of the bad mother is perhaps found in Lionel Dahmer's own memoirs. I do not mean his attempt to claim a monopoly on the guilt, but rather a circumstance that does not fit with the terse, smooth simplification of myths. In October 1966, says Lionel,

Joyce was pregnant again, a pregnancy that exhibited the same problems as her first. Noise was bothering her again, and she was often nervous, sleepless, and irritable. She took two to three Equanil a day [meprobamate, a common anxiolytic in the 1960s] ... But they did not seem to help very much, and so the dosage was increased to three to five tablets a day.

Even this increase did not ameliorate her general condition, however. The nervousness continued, and as it did, Joyce became more withdrawn until, by the time of David's birth, in December of 1966, we hardly had any social life at all.[86]

That is, the same medicated mother with a "history of mental illness," who gave birth to a serial killer, gave birth six years later, in comparable clinical circumstances, to a son whose path in life, as far as anyone knows, has not been marked either by psychopathy or criminality. This fact does not refute the biological hypothesis, for we know that the combinations of genetic inheritance are not uniform but multiple, and that, largely for this reason, children turn out different from each other. But it is nonetheless striking that neither Lionel Dahmer nor the countless commentators on the case ever point out this divergence, even though it is crucial, or at the very least noteworthy, in any discussion of hereditary features or the "genetic mutations" that may have occurred during pregnancy. One factor might be David's express desire to remain anonymous even in the book written by his father (he changed his name once his brother's crimes came to light), or simply his father's desire to protect him. But the effect of his absence is, significantly, to narrow the private circle that Lionel draws around himself and Jeffrey, outside of which there seems to be no basis for contrast.

Undoubtedly, it is not outside the circle that this father has decided to mount *his* case: as we have seen, his biological allusions are timid, tentative, and undeveloped, altogether very toned down with respect to his first public statements in September 1991. We cannot expect them to include a (decisive) comparison between the different fates of his two sons. To push the case that direction, toward the point where Jeffrey could be tied to someone else more than him, might perhaps have put Lionel

Dahmer on the path of a broader kind of argumentation, one
that was biosocial and not merely—meagerly—biological. This
might have led him to consider the complex interaction between
nature and nurture that the majority of today's biocriminologi-
cal research takes into account.[87] Yet moving in such a direction
would no doubt have meant running the risk of relativizing his
extremely particular relationship to Jeffrey; instead, he prefers to
see him only as a pathological version—or, as he would say, "a
deeper, darker shadow"—of his own psychology, his own personality, a version irreducible to both biological and sociological
language. Lionel Dahmer complains that at the trial no one mentioned genetics when determining whether his son was mentally
competent; even he, however, feels more at home in psychiatric
language—the language of "the mind" or the soul—and this is
what he uses to present his exploration and his explanations.

In 1995, the psychologist Judith Rich Harris published an
article in an academic journal[88] that, in her words, posed "a challenge—really a slap in the face—to traditional psychology."[89]
In it, she postulated, radically, that "parental behaviors have no
effect on the psychological characteristics their children will have
as adults."[90] Harris attributes 40-50% of adult-age personality
traits to inheritance, and the remaining half to environmental
circumstances, for which she proposes an explanation where parents, surprisingly, play no part. According to her, what children
learn at home usually stays at home; they discover very early on
that what they learn "in the context of their home may not, in
fact, work in the world outside the home,"[91] and outside the
home is where they are socialized, becoming members of a group
and identifying with it. That is, "identification with a group, not
participation in dyadic relationships [between only two people,
such as a father and son or mother and son], is responsible for
environmental modifications of personality characteristics."[92] If

this theory is correct, Lionel Dahmer's environmental influence on his child—by his intervention or his absence—was minimal, and his exploration might have been more worthwhile if, instead of emphasizing the particulars of his personal relationship, he had focused more on the "group" (friends, school, neighborhood) to which Jeffrey belonged—or rather, as can be gathered from the book's account of his childhood, to which he never belonged.

According to Harris, there is a likely correlation between adult-age psychopathy and the rejection experienced by a child or adolescent when they join a group of youths their age and acquire, within it, the assimilation and differentiation strategies that turn them into socialized adults. She pays special attention to the changes of home and school, which "jeopardize a kid's standing in the peer group and interfere with socialization because it's difficult to adapt to group norms when the norms keep changing."[93] Lionel Dahmer does not discount the influence of their various work-related moves throughout Jeffrey's childhood, and he even notes that in 1966, shortly after they had moved to Akron, a teacher voiced concern about the boy's shyness and isolation. "My son, it seemed to me, was not very good at adapting to new circumstances, but this was a flaw that could hardly be seen as fatal."[94] He then goes on to elaborate on his own psychogenetic profile ("as a child I'd been horribly shy, just as he was"[95]), and he seems to trust, as usual, time and the intensity of parental care to rectify the anomaly. In his analysis, and in his steadfast focus on prevention, there is hardly any space to consider any "group" other than the one made up of him and his son. Neither Jeffrey's brother David, nor his schoolmates, nor the social rules that govern the world outside of the home enter into it.

To return to biology, today several studies of the relationship between psychopathy and certain congenital forms of dysfunction in the activity of the frontal cortex suggest that "psychopaths suffer from difficulties connecting the cognitive and emotional areas of the brain." Seeing and recognizing the suffering of others is not, for them, tied to the ability to imagine that same suffering within themselves. Psychopaths *know* that the other person suffers, but their brains, because of a deficit in neuronal activity, prevent them from empathically associating that suffering with the suffering they would feel if they were in the other's place. "As the legal profession becomes more enlightened about how the brain functions, a defense based on the frontal lobe may become another legal strategy like the mental alienation defense," claim some researchers today, even concluding that "criminal behavior should be treated as a clinical illness."[96] In 1992, however, Judge Gram's final words of guidance to the jury deliberating on Jeffrey Dahmer's mental state were that "an abnormality manifested only by repeated criminal or otherwise antisocial conduct [did] not constitute a mental disease."[97] Lionel Dahmer could not agree with this judicial opinion, but he also could not have written the book he wrote had he subscribed to the frontal lobe theory.

The biological discussion has a curious corollary in the Dahmer case. When Jeffrey was killed in November 1994, his body, after the autopsy had been carried out, was cremated according to his wishes, and his ashes were divided equally between his father and his mother. Only his brain was preserved, while his father and mother fought over whether or not it should be donated to science. Significantly, it was Lionel who opposed preservation, and a judge agreed with him in December 1995, after a year of fighting, and Jeffrey's brain was cremated.[98] A columnist in *The Independent* wrote an open letter to Joyce attacking her scientific interest: "You must have asked yourself many times whether you, as the mother of this monster, had any responsibility for his acts. It is understandable that in our modern secular age you might seek absolution from science rather than religion," but it is nonetheless "nonsense to think that physiology of the brain can reveal the mind."[99] It's odd. The columnist wrote to Joyce. If he had read Lionel Dahmer's memoirs, perhaps he would have congratulated the author for following his advice and separating the path of science from the path of atonement.

Lionel Dahmer's path to atonement began, presumably, with a psychological report. As noted above, he attended his son's trial shocked, detached, and almost numb to the horrors described there. Earlier he had requested that his lawyer and the police not tell him "the details of the case,"[100] and in his first television appearance, he declared that "[w]hen I disassociate myself from this thing ... I'm OK."[101] Later, when he saw himself on video, he was struck by the desperate avoidance his words reveal: "It is hard to find," he says, "a father racked by grief and care."[102] Yet in the following months, when Lionel reviewed the testimony brought by the psychiatrists at the trial, he no longer saw "technical evidence only": suddenly, "once I began to explore my own connections to Jeff, the disturbing implications of the psychiatric testimony emerged."[103]

A Father's Story is no doubt a product of this post-trial exploration, facilitated in large part by the reading of the psychiatric report. The report is mentioned in the first chapters of the book, in relation to the age at which Jeffrey had his first sexual fantasies,[104] and this prompts Lionel to recall when he had his own, and to tell us about a busty comic book heroine who captivated him at age ten. Associations with Jeffrey's secrets are a constant in his memoirs, especially in the final chapters, although they make a decisive appearance in the early ones, about his son's childhood. The story of the four-year-old's curiosity about the entrails of the fish, mentioned above, and another about a game involving the bones of a rodent, at the same age, remind his father of his own childhood fascination with fire, which one day almost led him to burn down a neighbor's garage. Lionel calls it an "obsession," which automatically turns Jeffrey's interest in the gutted fish and the rodent bones into an "obsession" as well. "In me, of course, an early obsession with fire had led to nothing more unusual than chemistry, and a lifelong work in scientific research."[105] Work and the laboratory will always serve to bring order to Lionel's life, for in them, aside from the "great relief from the chaos I had at home," he found "a wonderful comfort and assurance in knowing the properties of things, how they could be manipulated in predictable patterns."[106]

Lionel Dahmer succeeded in sublimating and disciplining his obsessions into a job that provided him both a refuge from life's inevitable woes and also, paradoxically, an ideal vision of a fixed, knowable reality—a reality which, compared to the chaos outside, seems almost like a utopia. His repeated displays of respect for institutional values, throughout the memoir, thus turn out to have a strange false bottom, since institutions themselves (work, in this case) make it possible to realize one's fantasies. No doubt Jeffrey discovered the same thing in his years in the army, by confining and abusing Billy Capshaw with impunity. But of course, unlike his father, he did not know the sophisticated compensations of regulating mechanisms.

In Jeffrey's adult life, and specifically in his criminal acts, Lionel Dahmer does not need to transpose so much. He is no longer concerned with comparing objects of obsession but with recognizing himself in concrete "tendencies." Soon, with the invaluable guidance of the psychiatric report, he had no trouble finding "areas of my son's mind, tendencies and perversities which I had held within myself all my life ... odd thoughts and fantasies, impulses that were abnormal and, to some extent, bordered on violence." Obviously, Jeffrey had "exponentially multiplied those tendencies,"[107] but their origin and substance are not unfamiliar to the father. From age eight to twenty, he tells us, he had the repeated sensation—even if it never lasted more than a minute—that he had killed someone, normally after a dream on a day he had been attacked by some bully. As a child Lionel was the typical "four-eyes" who everyone makes fun of in high school, and who girls ignore except "as an object of curiosity."[108] He felt physically and intellectually inferior (his parents were both teachers, and he felt he did not live up to their expectations), and as a teenager, reacting to this feeling of inadequacy—and with openly vindictive intent—he used his scientific knowledge to gain the respect of others: he electrified a sofa, for instance, so that anyone who sat down would receive a shock, and he even built a bomb. "The bomb made me formidable, and in doing so, it also made me 'visible.' With the bomb I was no longer a faceless nonentity."[109] Of course, later on he left bombs behind, but in subsequent efforts—body-building, the pursuit of university degrees, work: everything he wanted to, and couldn't, initiate his child into—he now found strategies for overcoming his inferiority complex and cementing his social adaptation: once again, institutions become sources of sublimation. Looking back, he wonders whether those childhood transgressions might not be "early expressions of something dangerous in me, something that might have finally attached itself to my sexuality, and in doing that, turn me into the man my son became."[110]

Jeffrey's shyness, his withdrawal, and his lack of friends were always a big worry for his father, so affected by his own past as a "four-eyes." But his identification goes one step further. The 1978 murder of Steven Hicks, Jeffrey's first victim, whom he picked up on the highway and killed at the house in Bath because, as the trial revealed, the boy had tried to leave, prompts his father to reflect on his "extreme fear of abandonment."[111] Jeffrey admitted that this was the cause of most of his crimes, as it had been for another homosexual necrophile serial killer, Dennis Nilsen, who avowedly "killed for company."[112] Once again Lionel realizes he, too, is familiar with this fear, which for him began in childhood when was sent to live with an aunt and uncle while his mother underwent an operation and had to be interned. At that time he cried incessantly and began to stutter, which caused humiliation at school. A fear of abandonment and the ensuing retentive desire, with their disfiguring effects, would shape his whole life: "I relentlessly clung to a first marriage that was deeply wounded. I had clung to routines and habits of thought. To guide my behavior, I had clung to highly defined personal roles."[113]

This defensive need for control also reveals its perverse side, and in this regard Lionel thinks it advisable to devote a couple of pages—the only ones in the whole book—to certain details of his son's crimes, concretely how he went from leaving the men that aroused him unconscious (with violence or drugs) to lobotomizing them, killing them, and eating them. The total passivity of the victim, deprived of consciousness and will, in a progression from stupor to death and cannibalism, was indispensable for Jeffrey to carry out his fantasies, since he had "developed such a psychotic need for control, that the mere presence of life itself had come to threaten him."[114] A dead body, after all, is a lover who not only will never leave you, but will always be subject to your control; and not even this necrophile reasoning seems foreign to Lionel Dahmer. He recalls with a certain intensity that, at age twelve or thirteen, he wanted to hypnotize a neighbor and more or less succeeded: he then had the euphoric feeling that the girl was his, and now he notices that such a "need for control, itself, had been, at least in part, a sexual need."[115] Lionel does not venture to say whether the need for control is inherent in the male sex, but in his typical argumentative indifference, he is also unable to find a biological or cultural basis for it. The hypnotized girl, like Jeffrey's victims, belonged to the realm of secrets. Even after he makes her public, she still seems to be a question of heredity, a personal matter between father and son.

This double gesture is characteristic of Lionel Dahmer's tortuous rhetoric: on the one hand he seems to point to a certain, let us say, human community (in the way he lays out the frustrations and transgressions that define a personality and identifies them as risk factors for psychopathology). On the other hand, he is stubbornly limited to personal idiosyncrasy and private life. It is not lost on the reader, least of all the reader who is an anxious parent, that none of these features is unique to this individual case: not the childhood marked by feelings of inadequacy, nor the pranks that indicate a fixation or desire in need of discipline, nor the early male identification with power in sexual relationships that has to be worked through, nor the blind subjection to routines in adult life. This is even more true of the familiar fear of solitude and abandonment. And if we venture into the terrain of the "return of the repressed," since the book has more than paved the way, then it is easy to go not just from the particular to the general, but from the particular to the universal.

Just as familiar as this psychological background, if not more so, is the chapter on family relationships. Lionel Dahmer blames himself for his distant relationship with his son, full of misunderstandings and perceived on both sides as intrusive. The probation officer wrote in one of her reports that Jeffrey felt uncomfortable with his family, among other things because "his

father [was] controlling."[116] Although the father never sees himself like this, we need think only of all his attempts to straighten
him out—from leaving him in a mall for an entire day to look
for work, to signing him up for therapy sessions—to get a sense
of what Jeffrey meant. On the other hand, when a serial killer
is asked by his father to reveal what's inside a box, or to explain
why he bought a freezer, it is hardly surprising that he would
feel subjected to intolerable surveillance. Nevertheless, as I said,
even if the book implies he was a controlling father, Lionel never
presents himself that way—on the contrary. To Larry King he
explained he felt "guilty that I didn't spend more time with Jeff,
rather than on my—with my wife. The common knowledge is
spend the time, make the relationship with your wife right, and
everything will fall into place with your children. But it didn't
happen that way."[117] Lionel accuses himself of being more a husband than a father, and of thinking that his nominal presence
would ensure family order, with no need for deep involvement
or constant intervention. He finds his mold in the category of
the absent father.

Richard Tithecott recalls that "the dysfunctional family unit
is largely figured as a place lacking the father," and if we parents
or future parents harbor a fear of "fathering a monster," it will
always be, "[a]ccording to common wisdom … because of our
absence, not our active participation. While Lionel Dahmer feels
guilty for not spending enough time with his son, masculinity's
involvement in the 'creation' of Jeffrey is represented negatively,
as a 'good' force not implemented."[118] Ultimately, by confessing
to being an absent father, Lionel Dahmer seems to reconcile
himself to the "common wisdom"—twice over, in fact, since by
doing so he yields the burden of "presence" to the figure of the
(bad) mother. Immune to cultural stereotypes, however, he insists
on explaining his harmful absence through his hyper-devotion to

work, as noted above, and to his "almost wholly analytical" personality, also noted above. At one point this trait prompts him to state: "now, when I glimpse Jeff's picture in a book or on television, I wonder just how close I came to that state of deadness and emotional flatness into which my son at last descended."[119] Even when Boyle, the attorney, informs him that the police had found remains of bodies in Jeffrey's apartment, he asks: "What does a father do with such information?" and he immediately answers: "I did what I had always done. I collapsed into a strange silence that was neither angry nor sullen nor sorrowful, just a silence, a numbness, a terrible, inexpressible emptiness."[120]

The inability to show emotion seems to end up suppressing emotions themselves, and in that situation father and son are once again alike. Between two emotionally flat individuals who lack common interests, nothing more than a perfunctory, accommodating relationship is possible, a sort of token minimum. In Jeffrey's adolescence, "our conversations were reduced to question-and-answer sessions."[121] After age twenty-one, "we spoke, but we did not converse. I made suggestions. He accepted them. He gave excuses. I accepted them."[122] The first time he visits him in prison, they have "a conversation that was utterly typical of us in its featurelessness, in the clipped phrases we used, the whole array of quick evasions by which we slipped into triviality."[123] They stare at each other "blankly"; they talk about the rose bushes that Jeffrey planted in his grandmother's garden, they talk about the cat; finally, after each saying "I don't know what to say,"[124] Jeffrey admits that this time he "screwed up," and his father responds that maybe he can "get better" if he puts himself into the hands of mental health "professionals."[125] This episode, presented as a dialogue—practically the only time such a device is used in the book—strikingly and illustratively sums up a lost, unsalvageable relationship, propped up solely by forms, between two people who seem to be playing roles they're forced into, because for a long time they truly have had nothing to say to each other.

Emotion, of course, enjoys a great prestige in the culture of therapy, and Lionel Dahmer attributes a good part of his troubles to its absence or avoidance. But if this dialogue in prison serves to demonstrate anything, I'm afraid it demonstrates something very different from what he says. When Lionel asks himself, "What does a father do with such information?" talking about the cat and the rosebushes in grandmother's yard does not seem like such a crazy answer. What else can they talk about? The biceps that Jeffrey kept in the freezer to eat? Going back to Jeffrey's introverted, lonely times in high school, Lionel himself acknowledges as much: "How could a teenage boy admit, even to himself, that the landscape of his developing inner life had become a slaughterhouse? A morgue?"[126] Does he really mean to say that if Jeffrey's budding inner life had not turned to criminal fantasies, but, say, to punk or the study of minor eighteenth-century German poets, their communication would have been any different? And if instead of thoughts of necrophilia he had merely had thoughts of homosexuality, does Lionel really think—so suspiciously elusive on the topic of homosexuality, which he mentions only in passing—that his son would have been able to share them? That they would have had a relationship of honesty and mutual trust, open to discussing any topic, no matter how awkward, as modern parenting guides recommend? This is, frankly, another parental fantasy: I think that many parents (for once, not necessarily anxious ones), as well as many children, would find those "question-and-answer sessions," that humble exchange of monosyllables, that feigned interest in everyday family life which avoids, politely, arguments and conflicts, very familiar. They reveal, if not a sheer lack of interest, then a typical phase in the relationship between parents and children when both sides try, clumsily but effectively, to deal with the sad, unavoidable awareness that they no longer belong to the same world. And for that your child does not have to be a serial killer.

Consciously most of the time, unconsciously some of the time, Lionel Dahmer paints a picture of relationships and personalities that is merely the shadowy copy of a family dynamic that readers (anxious parent readers) can easily recognize in their own lives. If the picture is necessarily a bit removed from the community and stays rooted in the personal realm, where not all experiences are interchangeable, this does not imply a contradiction. Insistence on the self—the self with a child—in its private pettiness or immensity, detached from biosocial influence or determination, is required by the sort of Puritanical introspection that Lionel Dahmer performs, both for its public credibility and for its therapeutic usefulness. Yet none of this suggests that his is an isolated case. The unexceptional nature of Lionel Dahmer's personal history and self-portrait has led some observers to joke about his self-incrimination as the origin of his son's behavior. According to Frank Rich, if his theories were "credible," the United States "would have more serial killers than lawyers,"[127] and according to Joyce Carol Oates, "Lionel Dahmer's 'confession' and his stringent self-censure are so disproportionate to his son's pathology as to seem bleakly and unintentionally comic, like blaming oneself for having slammed a door and precipitating an earthquake."[128]

But such jokes only put the father of the butcher of Milwaukee right where he has always wanted to be: the place where he seeks common ground. They reaffirm his unspoken status as a *normal* father, putting him in a category he does not dare utter. The family photos illustrating each chapter of the book show a Jeffrey who continually calls to mind a smiling, healthy baby

... until we see him in the last one, almost without warning, in prison. The normal was only a mask, and what Lionel Dahmer's books urges us to do is distrust it, decipher its secrets, look past appearances. This is a terrible, painful task that we have to take up alone, because social institutions—at least until the creation of a Psychiatric State—have no obligation to help us, and all the work of detection and prevention falls on our shoulders. Lionel Dahmer not only describes the constitution of the normal, but also defines our responsibility within it, once we have identified with its patterns. Because, dear parents, if anyone ever does slam a door and precipitate an earthquake, that someone will be like you or like me.

While writing these pages, I spent some nights on the sofa, on account of a snoring issue. One of those nights my daughter Paula, who is now twelve years old, woke up with a stomach-ache. Worried when she didn't find me in the bedroom, she woke up her mother: "Mom, Dad's not here." Her mother told her to check the sofa, where she indeed found me. I made room for her, she lay down beside me, and I pulled the blanket over her and gave her a stomach rub I know makes her feel better. In that confined space we fell asleep. At seven in the morning, getting ready for work, her mother woke us up: "What are you doing here? There's no room for two! Come on, back to bed." We got up, stumbled down the hall like sleepwalkers, one after the other, and went to back to sleep for the short time we had left, each in our own bed.

# Notes

For citations found on the Internet, I give the address of the web page only if the source did not originally appear in print; if it did, I give the original source directly (though, unavoidably, without page numbers). All sources were consulted between April 13 and May 15, 2009. (They were consulted again between May 11 and June 11, 2016, for the translation.)

1. Mark Marvel, "Confessions of a Serial Killer's Father (Lionel Dahmer, Father of Jeffrey Dahmer)," *Interview*, March 1994, 56-57.
2. Lionel Dahmer, *A Father's Story: One Man's Anguish at Confronting the Evil in His Son* (New York: William Morrow, 1994).
3. Quoted in Amanda Vaill, "Have These People No Class – Are You Kidding? Capitalizing on Celebrities," *Cosmopolitan*, March 1, 1996.
4. Thomas H. Cook is the author of several mystery novels. Although his name does not appear on the cover or in the credits, he wrote the prologue, and one suspects he worked as an adviser to Lionel Dahmer in writing the book.
5. Joyce Carol Oates, "I Had No Other Thrill or Happiness, " *The New York Review of Books*, March 24, 1994.

6.  Dahmer, 185.
7.  Ibid., 14.
8.  Ibid., 12. The words come from Thomas H. Cook's prologue.
9.  Homer, *The Iliad*, translated by Robert Fitzgerald, (New York: Farrar, Strauss and Giroux, 1974), Book 24, vv. 53-57, pp. 562-63. The "patient hearts" given to men by the Fates are not the only antidote for the grief of a lost child handed down by a tradition which otherwise certainly emphasizes pain more than palliatives. Though not the subject of this essay, I can't resist citing a recent example, the words of a father at his six-year-old son's grave, at the opening of the film *A Christmas Tale* (*Un conte de Noël*, 2008): "My son is dead. I looked inside myself and saw I felt no grief. Suffering is a painted canvas. Tears do not make me touch the world any better. My son detached himself from me as a leaf detaches itself from a tree, and I have lost nothing. Joseph is now my founder. This loss is my foundation. Joseph has made me his son. And I feel an immense joy." According to the director of this wonderful film, Arnaud Desplechin, the text is a mix of passages from Ralph Waldo Emerson's diaries about the death of his son (http://reverse-shot.org/interviews/entry/576/arnaud-desplechin).
10. Anne Lamott, "My Son, the Stranger," *Salon*, May 22, 2006 (http://www.salon.com/mwtfeature/2006/05/22/lamott_fight_son).
11. Dahmer, 27 (and elsewhere).
12. Ibid., 54.
13. Ibid., 109.
14. Ibid., 146-147.
15. Ibid., 203-204.
16. Statements by Bresnick, Robinson and Weinberger in "Dahmer's Dad's Book Stirs Pain," *The Chicago Sun Times*, March 2, 1994.

17. Paula Chin, "Sins of the Son," *People*, March 28, 1994.
18. "Dahmer's Dad's Book Stirs Pain."
19. Chin.
20. *CNN Larry King Live*, "Interview with Father and Stepmother of Serial Killer Jeffrey Dahmer," June 17, 2004 (http://www.cnn.com/TRANSCRIPTS/0406/17/lkl.00.html).
21. Dahmer, 232.
22. Ibid.
23. Ibid., 233.
24. David Grogan, "Cashing In," *People*, August 8, 1994.
25. On Thomas Jacobson, his initiatives and the story of the auction, see Grogan, "Auction of Dahmer Items Is Apparently Off," *The New York Times*, May 29, 1996, and "Serial Killer's Possessions to Be Destroyed," *The New York Times*, June 15, 1996.
26. http://www.wackymurder.com/dahmer.htm. (This site is now defunct. For the translation its contents were retrieved from the Internet Archive's Wayback Machine at http://web.archive.org.)
27. Dahmer, 209.
28. Ibid., 5.
29. Ibid., 232.
30. Ibid., 205.
31. Ibid., 211.
32. Ibid., 212.
33. Ibid., 250.
34. Ibid., 148.
35. Ibid., 159.
36. Ibid., 25.
37. Ibid., 25-26.
38. Ibid., 194.

39. Ibid., 195.
40. Ibid.
41. Ibid., 194.
42. Ibid., 255.
43. http://www.nbcnews.com/video/nbc-news/17387771.
44. *CNN Larry King Live.*
45. Dahmer, 87.
46. Robert K. Ressler and Tom Shachtman, *I Have Lived in the Monster: Inside the Minds of the World's Most Notorious Serial Killers* (New York: St. Martin's, 1998), 147.
47. Frank Rich, "Journal: Loving Jeffrey Dahmer," *The New York Times*, March 17, 1994, 23.
48. Elliott Leyton, *Hunting Humans* (New York: Carrol and Graf, 2003), 2nd ed., 350.
49. Ibid., 45. *Hunting Humans*, 32.
50. Ressler and Shachtman, *I Have Lived*, 243.
51. Dahmer, 254.
52. The Estate of Konerak Sinthasomphone v. the City of Milwaukee (http://www.law.umkc.edu/faculty/projects/ftrials/conlaw/Sinthasomphone.html.).
53. Ressler and Shachtman, *I Have Lived*, 132-33.
54. Dahmer, 110.
55. http://www.survivingjeffreydahmer.org.
56. James Barron and Mary B. W. Tabor, "17 Killed and a Life Is Searched for Clues," *The New York Times*, August 4, 1991.
57. Dahmer, 111.
58. Ibid., 139.
59. Ibid., 141.
60. Ibid., 142.
61. Ibid., 143.
62. Ibid., 144.

63. Barron and Tabor.
64. Dahmer, 144.
65. Robert K. Ressler and Tom Shachtman, *Whoever Fights Monsters: My Twenty Years Tracking Serial Killers for the FBI* (New York: St. Martin's, 1993), 254.
66. Dahmer, 141.
67. Ibid., 254.
68. Ellsworth Lapham Fersch, ed., *Thinking about the Insanity Defense: Answers to Frequently Asked Questions with Case Examples* (Lincoln, NE: iUniverse, 2005), 145.
69. Ibid., 146.
70. Dahmer, 234.
71. Ibid., 39.
72. Ibid., 40.
73. Ibid., 34.
74. Ibid., 36.
75. Ibid., 44.
76. Ibid., 45.
77. Ibid., 87.
78. Ibid., 90.
79. "Mom Says Dahmer Lusts for Victims," *The Chicago Sun-Times,* October 19, 1993.
80. Tom Held, "Dahmer's Mother Spent Her Life Comforting Others," *The Milwaukee Journal Sentinel,* November 30, 2000.
81. Quoted in Richard Tithecott, *Of Men and Monsters: Jeffrey Dahmer and the Construction of the Serial Killer* (Madison: University of Wisconsin Press, 1997), 44.
82. Minette McGhee: "Dahmer's Parents Express Shock, Sorrow, Shame," *The Chicago Sun-Times*, September 11, 1991.
83. Brian Masters, *The Shrine of Jeffrey Dahmer* (London: Hodder & Stoughton, 1993), 33.

84. Akira Mizuta Lippit, "The Infinite Series: Fathers, Cannibals, Chemists …" *Criticism*, June 22, 1996, note 29.
85. Ibid.
86. Dahmer, 61.
87. See Nicole Rafter, *The Criminal Brain* (New York: New York University Press, 2008). Chapter 9 of this book (199-236) offers an excellent overview of current trends in biocriminology.
88. Judith Rich Harris, "Where Is the Child's Environment? A Group Socialization Theory of Development," *Psychological Review* 102, no. 3 (1995), 458-489.
89. Judith Rich Harris, *The Nurture Assumption: Why Our Children Turn Out the Way They Do* (New York: Free Press, 1998), xv.
90. Harris, "Where Is the Child's Environment?", 458.
91. Ibid., 462.
92. Ibid., 476.
93. Harris, *The Nurture Assumption*, 305.
94. Dahmer, 63.
95. Ibid., 64.
96. Miguel Ángel Alcázar-Córcoles, Antonio Verdejo-García, J. C. Bouso-Saiz: "La neuropsicología forense ante el reto de la relación entre cognición y emoción en la psicopatía," *Revista de Neurología* 47, no. 11 (2008), 608 and 610.
97. Masters, *The Shrine*, 271.
98. "Body of Wisconsin Serial Killer Is Cremated," *The New York Times*, September 18, 1995, and "Judge Orders Cremation of Jeffrey Dahmer's Brain," *The Washington Post*, December 13, 1995.
99. Tom Wilkie, "Dear Joyce Flint," *The Independent*, September 19, 1995.
100. Dahmer, 188.

101. Ibid., 200.
102. Ibid., 201.
103. Ibid., 219.
104. Ibid., 75-76.
105. Ibid., 54.
106. Ibid., 61.
107. Ibid., 224.
108. Ibid., 224.
109. Ibid., 227.
110. Ibid., 228.
111. Ibid., 216.
112. *Killing for Company* (London: Jonathan Cape, 1985) is the title of a book by Brian Masters about Dennis Nilsen, drawn from the killer's own statements.
113. Dahmer, 218.
114. Ibid., 220.
115. Ibid., 223.
116. Barron and Tabor.
117. *CNN Larry King Live.*
118. Tithecott, 45-46.
119. Dahmer, 92.
120. Ibid., 162.
121. Ibid., 82.
122. Ibid., 128.
123. Ibid., 180.
124. Ibid., 181.
125. Ibid., 182.
126. Ibid., 83
127. Rich.
128. Oates.

# Acknowledgments

I think it's clear that this book is dedicated to my daughter Paula.

In this book I wanted to date the story's action, and in order to spare readers the laborious task of working it out for themselves, I don't think it's a bad idea to offer some help. "Ten Minutes Later" takes place one morning in April 2008. The first section of "Luxor" is dated December 7, 1990; the second, February 22-23, 2006. In "A Slightly Shameful Modesty," the doctors' dinner party is held in late September 2007; what follows is set a little over a year later, in November 2008. The dialogue in "Winter Landscape" is from July 12, 2009 (and by the way, if anyone's still wondering, they end up giving Paul the Sisley). The essay that follows . . . well, what's the time of an essay? When does it occur? I can say I wrote it between May and June of 2009.

I continue to make my friends' heads spin. The setting for the cruise section of "Luxor" I owe in large part to Teresa, who offered me her graphic memory, and her enormous talent for reproducing it; the part about football in the second section was written almost in its entirety by my good friend Pep Lluís.

Heartfelt thanks for their contributions in technical or empirical knowledge also go to Manu (in a broad sense), Queque, Mari Ángeles, Marta, Dr. Caude, Adrián, Paco M., Ígor,

Diego, Breixo, and of course José Carlos, nicknamed Sinelcual
("Withoutwhom"). To Pedro González Candela, for his years of
experience and kindness. To Pepe, for his imagination, generous
as always. To Paco S., Miguel Ángel, José Andrés, Ignacio, and
Arcadi for their observations and inordinate patience. To Toni,
because he's been inspiring me since I was eight. To Menchu,
because I got a feeling. And to Maite, for signing the translation
and for her always lively friendship.

I'd like to remember, on a separate line, my friend Casavella,
whom I miss very much.

*M., October 2009*

Born in Palma de Mallorca in 1960, LUIS MAGRINYÀ is the author of five works of fiction, including *Intrusos y huéspedes* (2005) and the Herralde Prize-winning *Los dos Luises* (2000), as well as one book of usage and style, *Estilo rico, estilo pobre* (2015). He edits a world classics series at Alba Editorial, has worked as a lexicographer, and has translated Jane Austen, Henry James, and C. S. Lewis. In 2011 *Double Room* won the Otras Voces, Otros Ámbitos Prize and the City of Barcelona Prize. He lives in Madrid.

ALLEN YOUNG is a freelance translator based in Minneapolis.